UNDER
THE
HICKORY
TREE

A NOVEL

JO CHINN

The
Book
Guild

First published in Great Britain in 2025 by
The Book Guild Ltd
Unit E2 Airfield Business Park,
Harrison Road, Market Harborough,
Leicestershire. LE16 7UL
Tel: 0116 2792299
www.bookguild.co.uk
Email: info@bookguild.co.uk
X: @bookguild

The manufacturer's authorised representative in the
EU for product safety is Authorised Rep Compliance Ltd,
71 Lower Baggot Street, Dublin D02 P593 Ireland (www.arccompliance.com)

This work is entirely fictitious and bears no
resemblance to any persons living or dead.

Typeset in 11pt Garamond Pro

Printed and bound in Great Britain by CMP UK

ISBN 978 1835742 310

British Library Cataloguing in Publication Data.
A catalogue record for this book is available from the British Library.

To my sister Denise,
for teaching me to read and write before I started school.
This book is for you.

BRYN EVANS FAMILY TREE

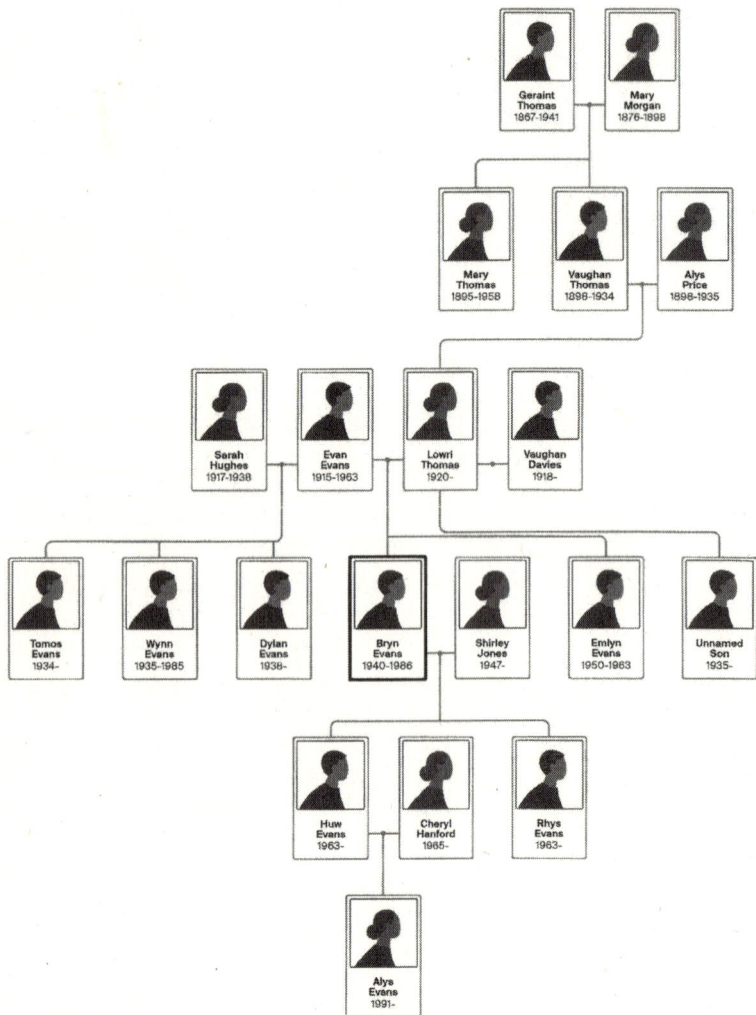

Geraint Thomas 1867-1941 — Mary Morgan 1876-1898

Mary Thomas 1895-1958 — Vaughan Thomas 1898-1934 — Alys Price 1898-1935

Sarah Hughes 1917-1938 — Evan Evans 1915-1963 — Lowri Thomas 1920- — Vaughan Davies 1918-

Tomos Evans 1934- | Wynn Evans 1935-1985 | Dylan Evans 1938- | Bryn Evans 1940-1986 | Shirley Jones 1947- | Emlyn Evans 1950-1963 | Unnamed Son 1935-

Huw Evans 1963- | Cheryl Hanford 1965- | Rhys Evans 1963-

Alys Evans 1991-

GWENNA GARLAND FAMILY TREE

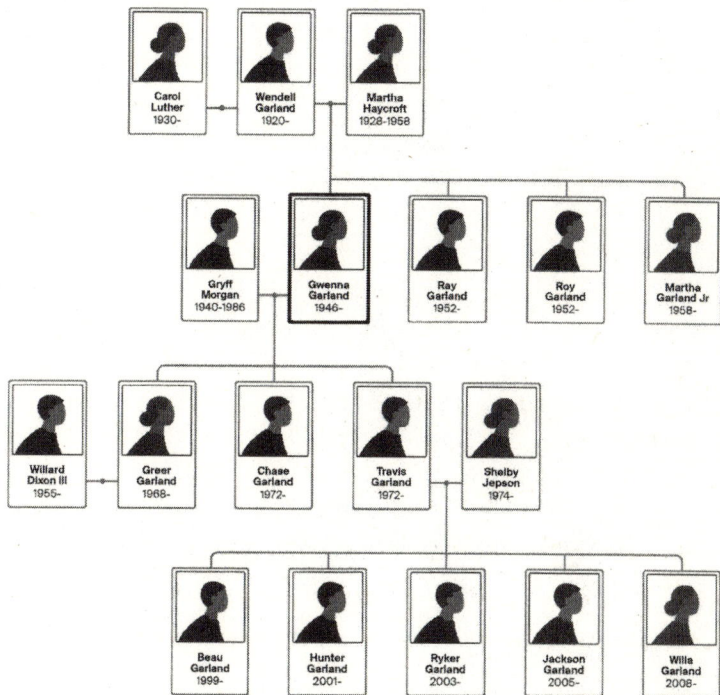

Carol Luther 1930–
Wendell Garland 1920–
Martha Haycroft 1928-1958

Gryff Morgan 1940-1986
Gwenna Garland 1946–
Ray Garland 1952–
Roy Garland 1952–
Martha Garland Jr 1958–

Willard Dixon III 1955–
Greer Garland 1968–
Chase Garland 1972–
Travis Garland 1972–
Shelby Jepson 1974–

Beau Garland 1999–
Hunter Garland 2001–
Ryker Garland 2003–
Jackson Garland 2005–
Willa Garland 2008–

SHIRLEY JONES FAMILY TREE

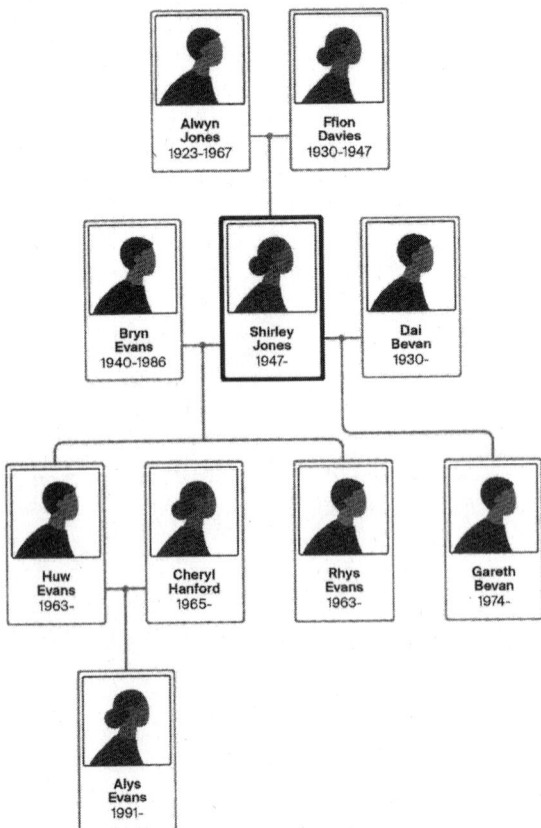

Alwyn
Jones
1923-1967

Ffion
Davies
1930-1947

Bryn
Evans
1940-1986

Shirley
Jones
1947-

Dai
Bevan
1930-

Huw
Evans
1963-

Cheryl
Hanford
1965-

Rhys
Evans
1963-

Gareth
Bevan
1974-

Alys
Evans
1991-

PROLOGUE

LOWRI
1934

ABERYSTWYTH, WEST WALES

n later life, the smell of freshly baked bread had the power to transport Lowri, in a heartbeat, back in time to the bakery in Aberystwyth, where she was born.

Young Lowri loved nothing more than to sneak into her father's bakery at four in the morning as he stoked the huge bread ovens. Snuggled into a warm corner on top of a pile of coarse sacks, her long raven hair dusty-white with flour, she watched Vaughan Thomas work his magic, transforming simple ingredients into heavenly crusty loaves, her eyelids heavy with sleep. Lowri was convinced that her dadi's glorious Welsh baritone, singing *Cwm Rhondda* as he worked, was the secret to his wonderful bread.

Once the bread of heaven was baked, Vaughan turned his hand to bara brith and crempogau, said by many to be the most delicious fruit bread and pancakes in the whole of Mid Wales. Only precious floury Lowri knew his secret recipe, passed down through generations of bakers.

The passage of her childhood was marked by the regular swell of her mother's belly and, by the time she was thirteen, Lowri was the eldest of nine children, including three sets of twins. Among the care-worn mothers of Aberystwyth, Alys Thomas was famed and pitied for producing babies in matching pairs. Combing for nits, administering gripe water, and replacing and washing endless soiled tailclouts became second nature to Lowri as she did all she could to ease the burden from her exhausted mam's thin, sagging shoulders.

At the end of each day, when all the younger children were topped and tailed in the same wrought iron bed, grateful Alys would brush her eldest daughter's hair with a hundred strokes of her ivory-handled horsehair brush until her cascading ebony locks shone like polished glass. In the bosom of her ever-growing family, Lowri couldn't imagine a time when she would ever be happier. A week shy of her fourteenth birthday, she began to cough up blood and everything changed.

'Now then, my precious—' Her dadi's voice was strained as the St John Cymru ambulance truck waited outside the bakery to take her on the seventy-mile drive to Swansea, where her grandfather had a disused attic above his confectioner's shop. 'I know it's a long way, but I'll visit as soon as I can. Once a month, after church on Sunday, regular as clockwork. I promise.' He slipped the ornate watch from his wrist and pressed it into Lowri's deathly white hand. 'Keep this safe for me, my lovely. A treasure for my treasure.' The white cotton muslin covering his nose and mouth muffled his words as he took both her delicate hands in his mighty gloved one. 'Aunty Mary will look after you and you'll be home in no time.'

Mustering every ounce of courage she possessed, Lowri nodded and clutched her dadi's watch close to her heart as her stretcher was loaded into the back of the truck, any hope of replying stifled by the painful lump in her throat. She understood the reason she had to be quarantined away from her brothers and sisters, but she'd never met Tad-cu Thomas or Aunty Mary and had no idea what to expect. But if her dadi trusted them, then everything would be fine – she was sure of it. Gulping back her tears, she whimpered as the truck doors slammed shut with resounding finality, determined to keep up a brave front for her dadi. Once alone in the smothering darkness, having been unable to hug or kiss him goodbye, the floodgates opened and Lowri wept until her tears ran dry.

At the top of three flights of steep wooden stairs, Lowri's attic eyrie contained few furnishings – a small metal framed bed with a hard sheep's-wool mattress, musty yellowing sheets and a faded grey blanket; a battered washstand and an old three-legged milking stool. Laths of wood and horsehair poked through gaps in the walls where lumps of plaster had fallen away and the exposed roof tiles above the bed rattled whenever there was a gust of wind. Aunty Mary appeared in the doorway as Lowri took in her wretched surroundings. Her hair was scraped back into a severe bun, her mouth and nose were covered with muslin, and her gloved hands clutched an enormous black leather-bound Bible to her chest.

'You are going to be here a long time, child.' Her brisk tone dashed Lowri's hopes for an aunty as kindly as her beloved father. 'I think you may find this of some comfort to you.' She deposited the Bible on the stool beside Lowri's bed with a hefty thump. Lowri sat shivering on the bed, mute with fatigue from the four-hour journey, while Aunty Mary looked her up and down with flinty eyes before retreating and closing the door. Moments later, she returned with a large pair of dressmaker's scissors. Lowri submitted in silence as her precious raven hair tumbled to the floor.

When Mary left, Lowri closed her eyes and wrapped her thin arms around herself for warmth and solace. Shivering in her bleak new world, devoid of the few comforts of home or the heart-warming babble of her brothers and sisters, she'd never felt so alone.

As days turned into weeks, Lowri passed long hours watching from the grimy attic window as the trawlers landed their catches at the Swansea fish wharf, dominated by the tall landmark chimney of the ice factory. Rows of rusty-ochre metal cranes stood like sentries along the wharves, providing vantage points for the giant white gulls awaiting the next catch. Their raucous screeches reached her ears when the wind blew in the right direction. She inched open the stiff window and filled her inflamed lungs with fresh sea air, longing to feel the salty tang of a whipping breeze against her skin. Her body ached at the thought of never being allowed to leave her lonely attic quarantine.

As night fell, the scruffy sheds and warehouses were swallowed up by the darkness and, in their place, the distant tungsten lights of the wharf cast an enticing glow, as mysterious and alluring as she imagined a Bedouin camp might look under the night sky in the Sahara. She'd had to leave her favourite book, *One Thousand and One Nights*, for her brothers and sisters, so she turned her attention to Aunty Mary's Bible to pass the time. The sepia-tinged pages were almost translucent with age as she let the book fall open randomly, landing on the Book of Job.

'Agree with God and be at peace.' The unfamiliar sound of her own voice in the draughty cell surprised her. If agreeing with God was what she needed to do to make her miserable existence bearable, then that was what she would do. She turned to the start of the book and began to read.

There was a man in the land of Uz, whose name was Job. This man was blameless and upright.

Lowri wound her precious watch every day without fail, keeping count of the days until her father's first visit, but as time passed with no sign of him, her anxiety grew. He'd promised her he'd come, and he never broke a promise. Something must have happened, but when she pleaded for news of her family or for pen and paper to write a letter home, she was met with stony indifference from Aunty Mary. 'He's got more important things to do than travel seventy miles to see you.' Mary's glare was harsh as she deposited the tray of meagre rations in her doorway. Confused and heartbroken, Lowri turned to Job for comfort.

As the nights drew in and the wind that rattled the roof tiles grew cooler, Lowri received an unexpected visitor. Clad in a white protective coat and gloves, the lower half of his face was shrouded in a muslin mask. Only his waxy dark eyebrows and grotesquely magnified eyes behind thick lenses were visible. The black leather case he carried unfolded to reveal an array of frighteningly unfamiliar implements, although Lowri did recognise the stethoscope, which he used to listen to her naked back and chest, and the thermometer, which he put under her tongue. Lowri shrank from him as his bony fingers prodded at her budding breasts.

When the examination ended, he folded up his leather case and departed with an enigmatic grunt. The tonic in the green glass vial he left on her washstand, which Aunty Mary administered with relish three times daily, could not have been more revolting.

Two weeks passed before the physician returned. 'It will be necessary to examine you more thoroughly on this occasion.' His facemask of protective muslin muffled his stilted manner. 'Now, remove all of your clothes.'

Lowri complied with all his instructions, flinching as he laid his gloved hands upon her shivering naked body. It took less than ten minutes for him to finish with her, but it felt like an eternity.

As he left, he deposited a fresh bottle of the vile tonic on the washstand. She lay on her unyielding mattress, staring with unseeing eyes at the roof tiles until the daylight disappeared.

'Agree with God, and be at peace,' Lowri repeated to herself to suppress her uncontrollable tremors.

A grim-faced stranger delivered Lowri's son in the middle of a pelting Atlantic rainstorm. The wiry woman wore a heavily bloodstained apron, which smelled pungently of fish. The roof tiles rattled and lifted threateningly as an icy wind whistled through the cracked plaster, while rain drummed deafeningly on the thin glass window. Aunty Mary swaddled the black-haired, red-faced bundle in a towel and swiftly took the bawling infant from the room. Through the haze of pain and exhaustion, Lowri heard the bang of the street door and her son's wailing fading away as she slipped into unconsciousness.

The following morning, the sky over Swansea Fish Wharf was bright blue, and the sunlight sparkled on the harbour as if a storm had never happened and a baby hadn't vanished. If it wasn't for her flat belly and the wracking pain in every fibre of her body, Lowri could almost have believed it was all a terrible nightmare.

Aunty Mary brought Lowri's paltry breakfast on a tray, as usual. 'All you need to know, Lowri, is that your baby died,' she said with brutal finality. 'Blessed be the Lord.'

Wordlessly, Lowri pushed away the tray, reached for the Bible, and opened it to the Book of Job.

Naked came I out of my mother's womb, and naked shall I return thither. The Lord gave, and the Lord hath taken away; Blessed be the name of the Lord.

1938

ABERAVON, SOUTH WALES

'Now then, boys, meet your new mam.' Evan cradled newborn Dylan in his arms as his young sons Tomos and Wynn hid behind his legs in the kitchen of the tiny cottage in Aberavon, where Evan worked in the colliery.

'I'm sorry, Lowri—' his soft hazel eyes swam with sadness. 'It's been hard for them since Sarah died – and me too. I'm sure they will get used to you soon enough and this little one will never know any different.' He jiggled Dylan, who began to bawl lustily.

Lowri reached out instinctively. 'Here, pass him to me, Evan.' Her heart ached with pity for this family of motherless boys and their distracted, grief-stricken father.

Dylan's round baby-blue eyes focused on her face, and a chubby smile spread across his hot flushed cheeks when she took hold of him. The warmth of her smile concealed her inner turmoil, as his weight in her arms brought back memories of the infant brothers and sisters she'd cradled. They'd all perished along with her parents as the white plague swept through the bakery, despite her months of quarantine.

Evan's face was wan as he returned her smile. 'There, see, he likes you already. You cannot believe how grateful I am that you've been sent to save us, Lowri. I don't think we could have managed much longer.' His voice cracked as he ground the heels of his palms into his eyes. 'It's only been three weeks.'

Lowri returned her soothing gaze to Dylan's beaming face. 'It is the Lord's will,' she said. 'He has brought me to you in your time of need.'

Lowri's ten-year indenture to raise Evan's children was brokered by Tad-cu Thomas through the South Wales Methodist Welfare Society and she was the last person to be told. But she readily accepted her new circumstances. To her mind, she was born to care for children and could think of nothing more important or meaningful to do with her life. Newly widowed Evan Evans couldn't pay Lowri a wage, but he agreed to provide board and lodging in return for childcare. He would sleep in the front parlour on the sofa.

With few personal possessions, it didn't take long for Lowri to settle seamlessly into the family home, taking up the baton of motherhood laid down in childbirth by poor Sarah. Every night, Lowri prayed for Sarah's soul and her own lost baby and thanked the Lord for guiding her path to a man as kind and honourable as Evan.

As Evan predicted, the boys quickly took to her.

1939

Lowri was in the kitchen baking bara brith when Evan burst in, breathless and sweating.

'It's war, Lowri!' He strode across the tiny kitchen and took her by the shoulders.

Lowri dusted the flour from her hands onto her apron and raised her eyes to his worried face. 'Can it be true, Evan? Will you have to go?' She glanced at eleven-month-old Dylan sleeping quietly in a basket by the stove, and Tomos and Wynn on the rag rug, playing with a wooden horse carved by Evan one evening in front of the fire. 'Don't worry about the boys though, Evan – I'll take good care of them.'

Evan embraced her to his warm chest. 'They've announced full conscription, Lowri. I have to go. They say it won't be for long, though. But there's something important I must do first.'

Lowri felt an inexplicable twist in her belly as his racing heartbeat pounded against her cheek. 'What's that, Evan?'

He dropped to one knee on the rough slate floor. 'I should have asked you months ago.' He took both of her floury hands in his. 'Lowri Thomas – my angel of salvation, will you marry me?'

Lowri broke into peals of delighted laughter. She didn't even have to think about it. 'Of course I will, you daft fool!' She threw her arms around his neck, her heart skipping a beat as their lips met for their first electrifying kiss. His strong arms enveloped her in his musky embrace. Giddy with desire, she pulled away and gazed into those kind hazel eyes.

Evan gently unpinned her glossy ebony hair from its messy bun and ran his fingers through the cascading tresses. 'I never imagined I would ever be happy again, Lowri,' he murmured. 'God undeniably answered my prayers the day you came into my life.'

Lowri's face flushed with pleasure. 'And mine too.' She rested her cheek against his chest, the coarse cloth of his wool jacket prickling her soft skin.

'Right, let's go!' He grabbed her hand, pretending to drag her to the door.

'Not so fast, Evan! Where are you taking me?'

'To the church, of course! There's no time to waste.'

'What about the babbis?' she protested with a giggle. 'And the banns? You can't expect me to get married in my pinny!' She swatted him with a tea towel as he swept her off her feet with ease.

In all her days, Lowri had never known such joy.

***

Evan slipped his arm around his new wife's slender waist and pulled her close for their wedding photograph under the canopy of the ancient yew tree in the churchyard at

Aberavon Methodist Church. Wreathed in radiant smiles, the bride cradled Dylan on her hip, while toddlers Wyn and Tomos scattered rice. She'd never looked more luminous. A light seemed to shine from within her; he could scarcely believe she was his.

As the camera shutter clicked, not even the dour faces of Aunty Mary and Tad-cu Thomas could cast a shadow on Evan's perfect day – after all, he had Tad-cu Thomas to thank for bringing Lowri into this life. They exuded an air more suited to a funeral in their heavy black coats and hats, having travelled by omnibus from Swansea to act as witnesses. They were the only relatives that either Lowri or Evan could muster.

Evan was struck by an idea as the photographer packed away his tripod. He tapped the man on the shoulder. 'I'm about to leave for war,' he said. 'It would be marvellous if I had a portrait of my beautiful new wife to take with me. Could you possibly?'

'That's all anyone wants these days', the photographer grumbled. 'It'll be tricky outdoors – the light's all wrong for portraits.'

Despite his reservations, the photographer captured an astonishing image of Lowri that would later sustain Evan through the darkest moments of wartime despair. Her glossy ebony hair framed the flawless alabaster skin of her cheeks in sleek waves; her pale dove-grey eyes held an expression of serenity and a touch of a smile curled the edges of her full, bow-shaped lips.

He truly was the luckiest man on earth.

***

Lowri cradled her week-old son Bryn on the Swansea Victoria railway station platform as the LMS locomotive taking Evan off to war pulled away in a cacophony of slamming doors, shunting piston drives and clouds of hissing steam. Six-year-old Tomos, Wyn, five, and two-year-old Dylan clung to her skirt as their father's smiling face receded into the distance, leaning from the carriage window along with all the other bravely smiling faces going off to join the Royal Welch Fusiliers.

Lowri turned away as the last of the soot flakes from the smokestack fluttered from the sky like black snow, the void in her heart left by Evan's departure already filling with dread. Her thoughts turned to bygone separations from the father and first-born baby son she'd never seen again. She gathered the boys around her and made her way along the eerily silent platform with all the other ashen-faced wives and mothers towards the bus station for the crowded ride back to Aberavon.

Holding baby Bryn close to her heart on the omnibus, she kissed him protectively on his silky black hair and vowed never to let him go.

PART ONE

BRYN, SHIRLEY and GWENNA

1963-1972

ONE

8TH MARCH 1963

ABERAVON, SOUTH WALES

B ryn Evans had longed to follow in his father's footsteps as a coal miner since he was in his mother's womb – or so it seemed. 'It's in your blood, mab', his father Evan used to say, his rich Welsh baritone brimming with pride. But now, with his father's untimely death at the hands of the very job he cherished, the once-treasured dream felt like a curse, casting a shadow over his every thought.

Disgorged from the clattering mine shaft cage into the stillness of the midwinter dawn, Bryn turned his coal dust-smothered face towards the gently fading stars. It was a welcome relief to be safely back above ground. He inflated his lungs with a much-needed breath of crisp cold air. The pithead gantry loomed above him, dark and menacing against the rust-streaked sky, a dragon's skeleton of tarnished steel and soot. A deep rumble vibrated through the soles of his boots as the blackened brick chimneys of the engine room belched smoky, acrid clouds into the icy atmosphere. He'd beaten the beast once more, but it was a battle he had to win every time. As he stowed away his helmet and collected his numbered token from the tally board, he knew his luck wouldn't last forever. The job would kill him, just as surely as it had killed his father. A shudder coursed down his spine like somebody was already walking on his grave.

Deep in contemplation, Bryn picked his miserable way through inky puddles and upturned coal carts, heading home towards the village of Aberavon, slumbering at the base of a vast grey slagheap. His hobnailed boots scraped unnoticed on the paving as he trudged uphill, burdened by the weight of his thoughts. His father's Royal Welch Fusiliers uniform was still in its trunk in the loft and it was preying on his mind. Tad had been clear that he wanted to wear it to meet his maker and, with the funeral being tomorrow, Bryn knew he couldn't put it off any longer. His father was gone and no amount of playing for time would bring him back. He could do the dreaded task as soon as he got home to get it over and done with, but that would disturb his mam and brothers, who would all still be in their beds, and he didn't want that. Besides, he was weary to his bones; he'd be in a better frame of mind once he'd had a couple of hours' sleep – if he was lucky enough to get any.

Bryn stopped to remove his boots on the back step of his family home and slipped quietly in through the unlatched door. An enticing fug hung in the air. His empty belly growled as he scooped a wedge of bara brith from the stovetop into his greedy mouth. He peeled off his filthy pit rags and dropped them into the washing pail by the stove. Stripped to his shapeless vest and pants, Bryn's alabaster torso contrasted starkly with his ebony hands, neck and face as he leaned over the kitchen sink to scrub away the grime. On the wooden draining board, a bar of crusty, yellow coal tar soap rested on the upturned lid of an old snap-tin. Bryn turned it over in the palm of his hand, his eyes brimming. This was the soap that Tad used. On the back of the kitchen door, his tad's cap hung on its usual peg and his boots stood by the stove, warming for him.

Bryn's freshly scrubbed skin glowed bright pink as he climbed the narrow wooden staircase, carefully stepping over the creaky third and seventh steps to avoid disturbing his little brother Emlyn, who would be sleeping soundly in their shared bed. He adored the cheeky, inquisitive mab but would never dream of telling him so. As he looked down on his brother's untroubled sleeping face, his jaw tightened at the thought of the sweet boy toiling in the filthy guts of the pit, ending up like their father, coughing his lungs up into a bucket of blood. He would give anything for there to be some other job for Emlyn in Aberavon when he left school. Anything would be better than coal mining.

Emlyn barely stirred as Bryn climbed in beside him and pulled the candlewick counterpane under his chin. His teeth chattered quietly as he acclimatised to the gratifying warmth of his brother's body on the threadbare sheets. He prayed for sleep to come quickly, yet his restless mind wouldn't settle; something was wrong, but he couldn't put his finger on it. In the oppressive silence, his ears picked up the faint creak of ancient floor joists and the distant tick of the kitchen clock before the answer came to him; the reverberating rumble of his father's snore was missing. As the new day broke, the fragile dam of Bryn's self-restraint finally crumbled, flooding his pillow with a torrent of silent bitter tears.

When he woke just before noon, the cottage was quiet, the weak winter sun streaming low through the tiny casement window. He slumped back on the still-damp pillow to collect his thoughts. Tomos, Wynn and Dylan were working their last shift at the colliery before the funeral, and Emlyn was in class at the village school. That just left his mam, who was probably sitting with his tad's casket at the chapel, waiting for the regimental uniform.

Tad's uniform! Bryn scrambled out of bed, hurriedly pulling on his trousers and slipping the braces over his shoulders. He unhooked the loft ladder from the bracket on the landing and used it to push open the loft hatch. He reached into the darkness and located a battered pit helmet with its torch still attached that his tad always left there. It would fall to Tomos to keep the family's wheels turning now. He wasn't entirely sure Tomos was ready.

Bryn was surprised by the loft space's soft dry warmth as he climbed into the dark void. Donning the pit helmet, he twisted the stiff torch switch and swept the beam around the clutter of torn cardboard boxes and battered suitcases. The wooden trunk etched with his father's eight-digit service number was tucked far into the eaves. His heart sank. Reaching it would be a beggar of a job.

Bryn cursed mildly under his breath as he began to inch towards the trunk, kneeling along two joists, wary not to put his foot through the ceiling below. Armies of spiders scuttled and clouds of dust motes swirled like gun smoke in the beam of his headlamp as he shoved boxes to one side to create a route to the trunk. As he coughed to clear the dust from his throat, he thought he heard scratching coming from behind him. The hairs on the nape of his neck sprang up. *Please, God, don't let it be a rat!* Bryn hated the filthy vermin; they plagued the mine shafts and spread disease among the miners. He turned slowly to look behind, dreading the glint of beady red eyes. The headlamp beam landed on a mop of thick black curly hair, crowning a grinning face poking up through the loft hatch.

Bryn blew his cheeks out with relief. 'Emlyn, you little bastard!' he cried. 'You scared the crap out of me!'

Emlyn chuckled. 'Did you think I was a rat, you big softhead?' His shoulders shook as he climbed the loft ladder and reached for another headlamp.

Emlyn's laughter was contagious and Bryn couldn't help but join in. 'You are a rat, *pen-coc*.' He found it impossible to stay angry with Gremlin for even a minute. 'Why aren't you at school, Grem?'

'What are you looking for? Can I help?' Emlyn's voice brimmed with curiosity.

Bryn shook his head with amused exasperation. It was typical of his little brother to dodge questions he didn't want to answer. He'd been just the same at that age. He smiled to himself at the cheek he used to give his three older brothers and the thick ear he'd earn in return for his troubles. There would be no thick ears for Emlyn, though. Bryn would never lay a finger on his little brother in anger. *Never.*

'No, you can't,' Bryn said. 'There's barely enough room up here for one, let alone two. Anyway, cloth-ears, you didn't answer my question. What about school?'

Emlyn's face twisted tearfully as he clambered fully through the hatch and perched on a joist, his head cranked awkwardly under the roof's pitch. 'I'm off today and tomorrow for Tad—' His voice trembled. Bryn's exasperation evaporated and he reached for Emlyn's hand in the dim light. How could he have been so thoughtless? Of course, Emlyn was off school until after the funeral. He was still a nipper and needed time to deal with the loss of his tad. Even more importantly, he needed his brothers, now more than ever. Bryn vowed silently to guide Emlyn safely into manhood as their tad would have done – although he could never measure up to his father.

'Now then, *cariad*,' he murmured. 'Stay and help if you wish, but keep out of the way.'

Emlyn nodded with a tight smile.

Bryn turned his attention back to his father's old trunk, which was almost within touching distance now. Another slide forward on his knees and a long reach should do it. Grunting with exertion, he grasped the rope handles on either side of the trunk and hauled strongly. The trunk didn't budge. It was a lot heavier than he'd expected. He'd need to get nearer. The headspace closed in, and sticky strands plucked at his hair and face as he crawled further into the musty space. Spluttering the cobwebs from his lips, he heard Emlyn's anxious voice call out: 'Everything all right, Bryn?'

'Stay there, Emlyn!' Bryn commanded more fiercely than he'd intended. 'The last thing I need is you falling through the ceiling.' He took a deep breath and, with all his might, gave the trunk another hefty tug. This time, it shifted with a jolt, becoming unstuck from its resting place. He hauled the trunk across two joists and dragged it slowly towards himself. He could see a metal hasp holding the lid closed but, luckily, there was no sign of a padlock.

His spine tingled as he lay his hands on the trunk lid. As far as he knew, this chest had been closed for almost two decades. The moment the lid was raised, he'd be breathing in the same air last breathed by his tad twenty years ago. He squared his shoulders, preparing for the magical moment, and inhaled deeply as the hinged lid opened smoothly, revealing the immaculate battledress uniform of his father's regiment, the Royal Welch Fusiliers. The stink of camphor that greeted him was a small price to pay to keep the moths away from this stunning regalia.

'What is it, Bryn?' Emlyn called from his perch on the joist near the hatch. 'Can I see?'

Bryn lifted the magnificently white plumed cap into the beam of his headlamp to show his brother. 'This is Tad's cap from when he was in the Fusiliers, Grem.' His voice was loaded with admiration. 'Look how beautiful it is!' Undoubtedly, his father would look magnificent on his journey to heaven and everyone would know he was a patriot who served his country with honour. Thank God he was one of the lucky ones who came home.

Placing the plumed cap carefully to one side, Bryn's searching hand discovered a small velvety pouch tucked under the tunic. Reaching across the joists, he passed the pouch to Emlyn, keen for him to share the thrill of discovering their tad's past. 'Here, mab, take a look – medals, I think.' Emlyn's wide eyes glowed in the beam of Bryn's lamp as he took the pouch reverentially from Bryn's outstretched hand.

With Emlyn occupied examining the medal pouch, Bryn plunged his hand back into the trunk beneath the uniform, his fingers closing around a rigid shape wrapped in a woollen scarf. Extracting it from the chest, he unwrapped the scarf, exposing a layer of oilcloth tied with coarse string. His fingers trembled with excitement as he untied the knot and unfolded the oilcloth. His sharp intake of breath drew Emlyn's attention once again.

'What've you found, Bryn?'

The Webley Mark IV service revolver had become dull with age but appeared in good condition to Bryn. The dark metal gleamed dimly in the light of his headlamp as he lifted it from the cloth and weighed it in his hand.

'It's Tad's war gun!' Bryn found it hard to imagine that his tad had ever handled such a terrible thing. He might have even used this gun to kill someone, although it would only have been an enemy soldier. Even so, it was still a disturbing thought.

'A gun!' exclaimed Emlyn. 'Lemme see! Can I hold it? I've never seen a gun before in real life!'

Bryn's shoulders stiffened. 'Not likely, mab! Tad shouldn't have kept this, Em. We could get into trouble, see?' His brow creased as he tried to fathom why on earth his tad had kept his service weapon. It made no sense.

'What are we going to do with it, Bryn? Are we to keep it? Shall we tell Mam?'

He needed to think and Emlyn was being a nuisance. 'Quiet, mab,' he snapped. 'Give me a chance—I don't want to worry Mam right now; she has enough on her plate.'

'Shall we give it to the constable then, Bryn? He'll know what to do with it.'

Bryn exhaled slowly. Emlyn was right, for once – he should hand it over to the police immediately. But if he did that, they might confiscate the whole uniform and he couldn't risk letting that happen. 'No, mab,' he replied.

'If we do that, they might not let Tad wear his uniform to heaven.'

Emlyn's bottom lip trembled. 'So, what are we to do, Bryn?'

His little brother's persistence was beginning to irritate him, especially as he had no answers for the boy. 'If you don't shut up, I may just have to shoot you!' He pulled his meanest 'tough guy' face and pointed the revolver at Emlyn.

Emlyn obligingly put up his hands, as they always did in the Westerns on a Saturday morning at the Roxy. 'Stick 'em up,' he drawled in his best cowboy voice. Bryn grinned despite his exasperation. Emlyn was such a scallywag. Playing along, Bryn cocked the hammer, *as they always did in the Westerns on a Saturday morning at the Roxy.*

The force of the recoil as the gun went off threw Bryn backwards into a stack of boxes, knocking off his headlamp. An almighty crack rent the air.

Gasping with shock, Bryn struggled to haul himself upright in the dark. The stench of cordite filled his lungs, his ears ringing with the deafening report.

'Emlyn!' His throat tightened with terror. 'Emlyn!'

Emlyn's lamp lay askew beside the open hatch. Bryn scrambled towards the light, dreading the sight of the injured boy, fallen through to the floor. *Lord, don't let it be bad!*

His hand sank into a soft warm pile. For a fraction of a second, he didn't understand. Then the world lurched on its axis and everything changed.

It was Emlyn's lifeless body.

Bryn's life, as he knew it, was over.

TWO

The front parlour of the terraced miner's cottage wasn't quite what Detective Inspector Vaughan Davies expected when he stepped into the room straight from the street. Far from being the usual museum of worthless family heirlooms and best china, the floor was strewn with underclothes and boots, and the unmistakable aroma of stale sheets lingered in the air.

Lowri beckoned him through with an apologetic smile. 'You'd best come into the kitchen if you don't mind,' she said. 'It's Bryn. He can't sleep upstairs in that bedroom anymore. He used to share it with Emlyn.' Her pale complexion was as translucent as Nantgarw porcelain and the profound sadness that sat in the creases around her dove-grey eyes moved him deeply. She looked like a raised voice might shatter her into tiny pieces. The urge to put a comforting arm around her took him entirely by surprise.

'In fact,' she continued, pouring boiling water from a

stovetop kettle into an earthenware teapot, 'he can't sleep at all, won't eat anything, won't see anyone – not even Shirley, poor geneth.'

'I'm sorry to hear that, Mrs Evans,' he murmured. 'I've spoken to his fiancée already. She seems like a lovely girl. Worried sick about young Bryn though.'

Lowri sighed. 'We all are, Inspector Davies. He refuses to go anywhere near the colliery and he's pushing away anyone who wants to help him. I can't even clean that room.'

She drew a kitchen chair from under the well-scrubbed wooden table for Vaughan and perched herself on the edge of the big iron stove, distractedly stirring the pot of tea.

'Hopefully, I have some news that might help, Mrs Evans.'

'How so, Detective Inspector?'

In the homely surroundings of her kitchen, the formality of his rank seemed out of keeping and, before he knew it, he found himself saying, 'Please call me Vaughan, Mrs Evans. Yes, actually, I have some excellent news for you.'

An ethereal beauty lit her pale face when she smiled. 'Vaughan – that's a lovely name. My father was called Vaughan. Please call me Lowri.'

Warmth flooded to Vaughan's face, at the tenderness with which she said his name. He rummaged needlessly in his briefcase as his pulse quickened.

'The good news, Vaughan?' Lowri's expectant eyes searched his face.

Vaughan cleared his throat and adopted his most official demeanour. 'I am pleased to inform you that there will be no prosecution in this case,' he declared. 'There is no evidence of any criminal act on the part of your son – Bryn Evans –

13

and you and your family have already suffered more than enough. It was impossible to determine why the revolver was loaded. I imagine it will remain something we will never get to the bottom of.' Frustratingly, the only person who knew the answer to that mystery was Evan, who'd taken the secret to his grave.

Lowri bowed her head and clasped her hands. 'Thank the Lord. It's the first piece of good news in months.'

Vaughan pressed his business card into Lowri's hand, as she showed him to the street door. 'If you need anything, Lowri, anything at all, please don't hesitate to call.'

Standing in the backyard, wearing only his vest and trousers, Bryn had overheard every word of his mam's conversation with the detective. The man was a bloody fool! An innocent boy was dead and there was no doubt about the culprit! He had to go to prison – he *needed* to go to prison. How else would he pay for his mindless stupidity? He clasped his hands over his unshaven face in dismay and doubled over, crippled by the weight of his guilt and shame. He let out a long anguished groan. The thought of living without his due punishment was unbearable. How would he ever find meaning in life again?

He crept out of the backyard, his hollow features twisted with despair and disappeared into the darkness.

***

Shirley sat on the edge of her single bed in her tad's gloomy colliery house, pouting into a handheld vanity mirror as she applied a coat of lipstick directly from the tube. She gazed at the grimy casement windowpanes with a sigh and wiped the red stain off her teeth with her thumb. Cleaning the windows to let in extra light was pointless – they'd be smothered in filthy gangue dust again in just a few days. It had only been three weeks since the funeral but she could barely remember any of it – other than gripping Bryn's mam's hand in the front pew as the Aberavon male voice choir sang *Suo Gân*, an aching chasm in her chest where her heart had once been. The rest of the service was a blur. Bryn had slipped away immediately after the funeral and she'd heard nothing from him since – even though she'd gone to his mam's house over and over again to check on him.

This morning, Shirley was in a much more determined mood. She urgently needed to speak to Bryn and wouldn't take 'no' for an answer. Things had reached the point where they couldn't wait any longer. She was sure that people were starting to notice.

A shower of gravel rattling on her window startled her. It was Bryn, standing in her backyard dressed in nothing more than a faded vest and trousers, his hollow face dark and unshaven. His haunted expression tugged at Shirley's heart and she hurtled down the stairs, desperate to comfort him.

She flung open the back door and threw her arms around his neck, sobbing with relief. 'Oh Bryn, bach, I've missed you so badly.'

His arms hung limp at his sides. 'I'm sorry, Shirley. It's been...' His unfinished words hung hopelessly in the air, his face a picture of defeat.

A chill ran down her spine. He was a shadow of his former self and it scared her. *What if he was never the same again?* She quickly dismissed the thought. Now, more than ever, she needed him to be strong for what she was about to tell him. 'I know, Bryn, I know,' she said, her voice quivering as she held him close. 'But it's going to be okay eventually, I promise. I love you and I want to help you.'

'Sorry, Shirley, let me finish.' Bryn grasped her shoulders and prised himself from her embrace. 'I've come to say goodbye.'

His words hit her like a coal truck. 'Goodbye?!' she gasped.

'Yes, I'm leaving and—'

Her stomach lurched with fear. This couldn't be happening. 'But what about the investigation?'

He gave a bitter laugh. 'Let me finish, please, Shirley – this is hard enough as it is. The investigation is over. I'm a free man.'

Shirley's heart leapt with relief. 'That's great news, Bryn! We can—'

'Shirley, please!' he snapped. 'Listen to me!' He took a deep breath and released it slowly. 'I have to go away, Shirley, because there's no life for me here anymore. Everyone in the village either despises me or pities me. I honestly don't know which is worse.' His shoulders sagged. 'Some of my old mates even cross the road to avoid me. I'm telling you, Shirley, I feel like a leper in my own village and I can't bear it. And the pit will be closing any day soon – so I'll be out of a job, too.'

'That's not true, cariad.' Shirley took hold of his calloused hand. 'Everyone in the village cares for you deeply. Me and your mam, more than anyone.'

He pulled his hand away and gnawed at his knuckles. 'I can't even bear to face my own mam anymore for all the pain I've caused her – and Tomos, Wynn and Dylan haven't spoken to me since the funeral. They all hate me and who can blame them?'

'Bryn, you've got that all wrong. They're just dealing with their own grief. It was an accident – a tragic, tragic accident.'

'No, Shirley, you're the one that's wrong.' He wiped the back of his hand over his eyes. 'They all hate me, but nobody hates me more than I hate myself.'

His words ripped through her like a chainsaw. There simply couldn't have been a worse time to bring up the subject weighing so heavily on her mind, but it was now or never. She steeled herself with a deep breath. 'Look, Bryn, I've got something to tell you, something important.' But as she looked into his unfocused eyes, she could tell he was lost in his own world, utterly blind to her anxiety.

'Everything reminds me of Tad and poor Emlyn,' he wept. 'I'm really sorry, Shirley, but I've decided. I'm taking the redundancy and I'm going overseas.' He wiped his eyes on the front of his vest. 'I'll send for you when I can. There's nothing here for me now.'

The ground shifted beneath Shirley's feet and she grabbed his arm to steady herself. 'No, Bryn, you don't understand – wait!'

Bryn wrenched his arm away from her grasp. Coming to see her had been a mistake but it was too late to worry about that now. He braced himself for a scene. Before his eyes, the colour drained from Shirley's pinched face and she crumpled to the ground in a faint. 'Shirley!' he cried, catching her before she hit the ground. He lowered her onto the kitchen step and stroked the long dark fringe from her fluttering eyelids.

Remorse twisted in his gut like an adder. Poor Shirley, she didn't deserve any of this but he couldn't help how he felt. She was taking the news far worse than he'd expected. She was as light as a sparrow as he swept her up in his arms and carried her through the tiny galley kitchen to the low-ceilinged living room, where he laid her on her tad's battered old settee.

'What's all this then?' A hoarse voice from an old wing-backed chair beside the fire caught Bryn entirely by surprise.

'Mr Jones!' He span round to face Shirley's father. 'I didn't see you there! It's Shirley – she's fainted, but I can't deal with this right now. I'm so very sorry.'

'Be gettin' away with yourself then, lad.' Alwyn's jaundiced skeletal hands rested like eagle claws on the chair's armrests. 'You've had a lot on your plate lately. Leave her with me, lad – I can take care of her. She'll be fine in a bit, no doubt.'

'Thank you, Mr Jones.' Bryn backed towards the door, despising his own spinelessness but desperate to be anywhere else but there. 'Would you please tell Shirley I'll send for her when I'm settled?

THREE

Bryn stepped off the train at Liverpool Lime Street station, stretching his stiff legs on the platform as he got his bearings. Oblong shafts of weak sunlight filtered through the polluted glass panes of the great steel cathedral arching overhead as his fellow travellers from Cardiff jostled past, surging towards the ticket inspector's gate. After nearly seven hours in an old third-class carriage on the overnight train, travelling on the cheapest one-way ticket he could get to eke out his meagre redundancy money, his aching joints weren't thanking him.

Carriage doors slammed, whistles blew and steam hissed as the station went about its business. Bryn remained rooted to the spot, his senses overloaded. In every direction, young women's shapely thighs were exposed in eye-popping short skirts, while the men his own age strutted about exuding purpose and confidence, sporting sharp suits with long slim lapels, half their faces concealed by floppy fringes.

Hopelessly out of place in his shabby workingman's attire, Bryn's confidence deflated like a punctured rugby ball. The urge to turn around and get back on the train was almost irresistible. His big idea to go overseas was beginning to seem a bit half-baked, especially if he couldn't handle a city such as Liverpool. The problem was he'd never been further from home than Cardiff before. What did he know of the world outside Aberavon? Without a plan in mind, where would he even start?

His grumbling belly and the enticing aroma of hot coffee coming from nearby reminded him he was famished. He rattled his trouser pocket and pulled out a handful of coins – half a crown, a couple of shillings, two or three sixpences, and a thruppenny bit – easily enough for a bite to eat while he thought about what to do next. He hauled his bergen onto his shoulders with a grunt and headed towards the Di Mateo café on the concourse, its windows steamy and inviting.

'You look proper starvin',' said the wiry lad pouring stewed tea from an enormous steel pot as Bryn approached the counter clutching his fistful of coins. 'Well, you've come to the right place for some sound scran.' He cocked the teapot questioningly at Bryn. 'You havin' a brew? I'm Joe, by the way.'

Bryn grinned to himself at Joe's scouse accent. He could just about work out what the lad was saying – well, most of it. He ordered a full English and found himself a spot in a leatherette booth by the window, where he could observe the comings and goings of the station. Bryn's steaming plate of food arrived quickly and he fell on it hungrily. As he ate, Joe slid into his booth without waiting for an invitation.

'Mm, good,' Bryn mumbled between mouthfuls of fried egg, sausage, bacon and black pudding.

'Me ol' fella's done y' proud with that little lot.' Joe nodded towards Bryn's plate. 'Should keep you goin' a while.'

Bryn wedged in one last bite of toast and sat back replete. 'So, it's your tad who does the cooking, is it?'

A proud smile lit Joe's face. 'He was a chef in Italy before the war. Now he owns this place. Done all right for a POW.' He reached to clear away Bryn's empty plate and dirty cutlery. 'You're not from these parts, yourself?'

Bryn grinned. 'How could you tell?'

'It's your baggy kecks, fella. You stand out a mile.' Joe beamed a gap-toothed grin at him. 'So, where youse off to?' He glanced at Bryn's bergen on the next seat. 'The bizzies after yer?'

Joe seemed a decent enough lad but Bryn was in no mood to confide his sorry life story to a stranger. 'No, I'm not in trouble with the law or anything like that,' he said, hoping he'd guessed correctly what 'bizzies' were. 'I'm looking for a fresh start – going overseas.'

'I could do with a few adventures meself, see a bit of the world, like,' said Joe, brushing toast crumbs from the table. 'But it's just me and me ol' fella, so it looks like I'll be going nowhere fast.' He sighed, despondently. 'I envy you.'

Bryn swallowed the last of his tea in one gulp. Joe wouldn't envy him if he knew the truth. He'd call him a coward who'd killed his own brother – a yellow-belly who'd made things worse for his poor widowed mam by running away. He rested his elbows on the table and sank his face into his hands. What on earth was he thinking? He was a selfish bastard and should go home to face the music like a man. But if he did that, he wouldn't get the punishment he deserved for taking poor Em's life. They were all better off without him.

Joe's voice interrupted his thoughts. 'D'you know where yer goin'?'

Bryn laughed bitterly. 'I've got no real plan. Wherever the wind takes me, I s'pose.' He didn't have any idea where he wanted to go and that was part of the problem. But what did it matter anyway?

'Whatever you do, look for a ship with a red ensign flag,' Joe said. 'That's the British Merchant Navy. You'll be safe with them. Don't go jumpin' on no old rust bucket if you wanna make it alive to the other side!'

Bryn slumped back on the bench seat, blowing his cheeks out despondently as he considered his next move. He didn't know the first thing about ships and the sea, but was he really going to let his fear of the unknown derail his quest for redemption? Was he a coward for leaving or would it be cowardly to stay? He groaned inwardly. He had to make a choice and he had to make it now.

'The dock's not even a mile from here,' said Joe, fizzing with enthusiasm. He grabbed a paper serviette, licked the end of the pencil he kept behind one ear and scrawled a rudimentary map on it. He shoved it across the table to Bryn. 'There you go, lad. Sorted.'

Joe's enthusiasm was contagious and Bryn's resolve stiffened. He drew the serviette towards him and examined the map. The docks were only a couple of streets away and he'd come this far for good reason. His whole life lay ahead of him, weighed down by the guilt of killing his brother. If he was ever to live with himself for what he'd done, he needed to test himself to see if he was worthy of his family's forgiveness. There was no turning back.

He pocketed the serviette map. 'That's jolly good of you, Joe, thanks for your advice. What do I owe you?'

'Nah, you're all right, fella, that one's on me.' Joe grinned his gap-toothed smile again. 'I wish I was goin' with yer, mate. I hope it works out for yer. Good luck, fella.'

The pair shook hands like old pals. 'I'll write,' Bryn joked with a smile.

'Nah, you won't,' Joe replied with a laugh. 'Now do one, fella, before I change me mind about yer brekkie.'

Outside the station, Bryn was engulfed by the city's bustling energy. Black cabs hooted and jostled with green and cream open-platform double-decker buses as he struggled to orientate himself in the morning rush-hour crowds. Clutching his serviette map, he set off toward the docks on foot with a spring in his step, feeling decidedly more upbeat about the challenge ahead thanks to his complimentary breakfast and encounter with Joe.

As he approached the docks, a brackish smell of seaweed and dead fish filled the air. Huge white gulls wheeled low overhead in chaotic screeching clouds, their enormous webbed feet dangling comically, their strong yellow beaks threatening to rip the food from an unwary hand. He took a deep breath of the briny sea air and his veins tingled with exhilaration. He hadn't appreciated how big and noisy the port of Liverpool was until that moment. From where he stood, the dock heads stretched as far as his eye could see in either direction, the skyline pierced with angular derricks towering above the corrugated cargo shed rooftops like a flock of giant grey herons.

With no idea where to begin, he randomly headed north along the dockside in his search for a ship bearing the British Merchant Navy red ensign, just as Joe had advised. The granite docks swarmed with flat-capped stevedores, as nimble as mountain goats and numerous as rats, clambering mountains of lumber or balancing on the swinging pallets of textiles that were being craned from the massive cargo sheds before landing with resounding booms in vast half-filled holds. The slippery cobbles teemed with slithering ropes, as thick as Bryn's arm and slick with green seaweed, writhing like mighty sea serpents capable of breaking a man's leg at the slightest wrong step. Elsewhere, haphazard piles of rusting chains sprang into life without warning like furious rattlesnakes, ready to trip and ensnare the unwary. He was gambling with his life with every step as he picked his way through the hazardous obstacle course. It was a noisy stinking hostile environment, yet he'd never felt more alive.

Bryn estimated he must have covered more than three miles – the underground distance from the mineshaft to the coalface at Aberavon – and was beginning to lose hope when he finally saw her – the *Buenos Aires Star* – moored alongside at Canada Dock. Her red ensign fluttered brightly in the cold early afternoon sun. She looked less than ten years old and her deep navy-blue hull gleamed with the high-gloss finish of a grand piano. Craning his neck, he could just about make out the enormous white funnel, topped with a navy stripe and a navy star in a white circle. Her beauty took his breath away and his spirits soared.

As he stood at the foot of the gangplank, the idea of sailing to Buenos Aires sent shivers down his spine. His heart pounded. He could almost taste the sweetness of the pineapples that grew on every tree in South America. But was he doing the right thing? The nagging voice in the back of his mind would not keep quiet. This was his last chance to change his mind before committing to a decision that would change his life forever. He took a deep breath, pushed aside his doubts and stepped forward, shouldering his bergen for the last time. 'Wish me luck!' he said aloud to nobody in particular as he strode bravely up the gangplank into his new life.

ABERAVON, SOUTH WALES

Shirley Jones had never known her mother.

She'd never felt the tender caress of her mother's loving kiss or the warmth of her protective embrace. No mother had ever plaited her hair for her first day at school nor wiped the tears from her infant cheeks as she cleaned her scraped and bloodied knee. No mother would ever smile proudly as she walked down the aisle with her handsome new husband nor dangle her first grandchild adoringly on her knee. Mothers were for other people, not for Shirley.

Shirley's most treasured possession was a photograph of Ffion on her wedding day in a simple mother-of-pearl frame. She'd studied every grain of that picture and knew that if it were ever lost in a house fire, she'd simply have to close her eyes to resurrect it in perfect detail.

In the photograph, her mother was a young slim girl with fashionably curled raven hair peeping from under her pillbox hat, a nervous gap-toothed smile flitting across her face. Ffion clutched a modest bunch of irises and gypsophila, standing beside her strapping new husband, Alwyn, in his best and only suit. There was no silky white fabric for a traditional wedding dress in 1946, so she wore a neat fitted skirt-suit, which she'd sewn herself from the bell-bottom legs of her brother's Royal Navy uniform trousers.

Shirley knew this much about her mam from her Aunty Ruth, who'd been pressed into service the day Shirley was born – the day Ffion died aged just seventeen.

Raising two boys of her own, Ruth seemed to everyone like the perfect answer to the tragedy of the motherless baby girl, but Ruth had never been close to her brother Alwyn and resented the imposition. Shirley grew up fighting – fighting for space, fighting for care, fighting for love, fighting to be heard, until fighting was all she knew.

Now, as she regarded her ghostly complexion in her small handheld vanity mirror in her room in Aberavon, she faced the biggest fight of her life.

New life stirred in her belly and she was on her own. Shirley was determined to be the mother she never had. Her child would experience love, joy and happiness, never have to go without and never live on pancake suppers.

A trickle of blood, bright red against the whiteness of her skin, ran from her lower lip, bitten through with the fierceness of her determination.

But first, she had to tell her father.

Alwyn's hoarse roar took Shirley by surprise.

'Oh, my word, Shirley! A babi! I suspected as much when you fainted last week. That's wonderful news.' He pulled her into his shrunken embrace.

'Is it?' gasped Shirley. How could being an unmarried mam at seventeen possibly be good news?

'Oh yes, Shirley, my angel. It is, absolutely!'

Unexpected tears tumbled down her cheeks, leaving black snail trails in their wake. 'But what... I don't...'

'Listen to me, Shirley.' He cupped her streaky face in his withered hands and wiped away the tears with his thumbs. 'There's a lot I've wanted to tell you but you were too young.' His rheumy eyes brimmed and flitted uncontrollably with miners' nystagmus. 'Now you're about to be a mam yourself, it's time. Come and sit with me.' He patted the cushion beside him.

Faded sepia photographs of long-dead relatives looked down from the walls of Alwyn's parlour as Shirley snuggled into her father's embrace, his once-burly arm across her shoulders now as light as gossamer.

'Your mam was the girl of my dreams,' he began. In a faltering voice, Alwyn painted a picture of his bride, a shy sweet-natured girl who wanted nothing more dearly than to be married with children. Three, she'd wanted: a girl and two boys; she'd even picked the names: Shirley, Huw and Rhys.

The skin on Shirley's arms turned to gooseflesh. *Huw and Rhys?* This was the first she'd heard of them – two unborn brothers who never got a chance to live because of her. She swallowed hard. So, it wasn't only her mother's life she'd ended.

'Shirley? Shirley, *bach*?' Alwyn's mottled hand patted her arm. 'You all right, love?'

'Sorry tad, carry on.' Shirley ran a knuckle along the underside of her lashes. 'I'm fine, honestly.'

Alwyn pinched the bridge of his nose and took a shuddering breath. 'It was the worst day of my life. She was gone, my beautiful young bride, and there you were – the most precious, fragile thing in the world. I was terrified I'd break you.' He cast his flickering eyes at the threadbare rug beneath their feet. 'I did what I thought was best for you, Shirley. You needed a mam.'

Shirley raised both of Alwyn's papery hands to her lips. 'I can see that now, Tad,' she said. 'I've been so selfish. I thought I was the only one who lost her.'

Alwyn turned to face her. 'Don't blame yourself, love. I was the selfish one. Seeing you growing up at Aunty Ruth's, the image of your mam…' He paused, his eyes and nose streaming. 'I just couldn't bear it, so I stayed away.' His head dropped, his shoulders shook and he gasped for air. 'You were all I had and I gave you away!'

Shirley wrapped her arms around her father's skeletal frame, rocking him until his grief subsided. Poor Tad was getting weaker every day; if she lost him, she'd be an orphan – a pregnant, unmarried, seventeen-year-old, homeless, penniless orphan whose mother died in childbirth – *at seventeen!* She slowed her breathing, trying to suppress her rising terror of history repeating itself. Now was not the time for self-pity.

'So, you see, my lovely, your babi is my second chance to be a good father – to you and to her.' A weak smile stretched his purple lips as he placed his hand delicately on Shirley's tummy.

Warmth rushed to her face at the tenderness of his touch. 'How do you know it's going to be a girl?'

'She has to be – so that her name can be Ffion.'

FOUR

Under the watchful gaze of two copper birds perched on the twin clock towers dominating the Liverpool waterfront, Bryn followed the swarthy deckhand, who he'd met at the top of the gangplank, onto the *Buenos Aires Star* bridge. Dry-mouthed and with trembling hands, he wracked his brain for something impressive to say, to persuade the captain to take him on as a passage worker and give him a free crossing in return for his labour. He squared his burly shoulders and clenched his hands to fend off the shakes, hoping his apprenticeship as a colliery mechanic would stand him in good stead.

The captain of the *Buenos Aires Star* looked him up and down with a practised eye. 'I could do with a strapping young man like you on my crew,' he said. 'Work on board ship takes a lot of brawn and you definitely fit the bill in that respect. What skills do you have?'

Bryn's hands trembled as he gave the captain his apprenticeship certificate. 'I'm a qualified mechanic, Sir, but I can turn my hand to anything that needs doing. Anything at all.'

The captain inspected Bryn's paperwork before handing it back. 'That's the sort of attitude I'm looking for,' he said. 'You can start on general-purpose deckhand duties and we'll see how we go from there.'

Bryn's heart pounded with excitement. He'd done it! A free passage to South America! He could hardly believe his luck.

'One last thing before I hand you over to the purser, young man,' the captain added, his voice becoming cold and stern. 'The last time I hired a Welshman, he made me regret it. You'd better be more reliable than him.' His steely eyes searched Bryn's face. 'You look like a decent lad, though. Don't make me regret it again.'

Bryn followed the purser along the gangway, his stomach churning with nervous energy, the captain's parting words playing on his mind. What did he mean by his cryptic warning? The more Bryn thought about it, the more peculiar it seemed.

His unease grew as he sat in the purser's office for what seemed like an eternity, filling out paperwork and registering his passport details. Finally, after half an hour, a deckhand arrived to escort him below. The dormitory passage was a black hole at the bottom of a deck ladder so steep he had to toss his bergen down ahead. Climbing down into the darkness was like descending into limbo. Following behind the deckhand, he tried to dismiss the unnerving feeling as he made his way inside the windowless belly of the ship, his eyes struggling to adjust to the stygian gloom. The air was thick and heavy, its ripeness almost suffocating. In the oppressive atmosphere, he couldn't shake off the unease in the pit of his stomach.

'Purser says to tell you this one's yours, Scaff,' the deckhand said to a wiry seaman with sinews as thick as cables in his leathery forearms and hair scraped back into a greasy ponytail. 'You gotta show 'im the ropes.'

Scaff rolled his eyes. 'Great! Jus' what I don't need. Go an' tell that purser I'm not a soddin' babysitter, will ya?' he yelled after the deckhand, who was already halfway back up the ladder.

'Get stuffed! Go and tell 'im y'self!'

Bryn stuck out his hand, determined to get off on the right foot with his new crewmate. 'Pleased to meet you, Scaff. I'm Bryn Evans.'

Scaff snorted loudly, ignoring the outstretched hand. 'Not another bleedin' Welshman! Will they never bleedin' learn?'

Bryn shook his head in confusion, refusing to let Scaff's rudeness discourage him. What was it with this other Welshman? And why was everyone so pissed off with him?

Scaff's voice dropped to an ominous growl. 'Your predecessor in that very same bunk was a right useless Taff.' He tossed a crusty grey boiler suit to Bryn. 'We lost 'im in Buenos Aires. Knife fight on the dock. 'E was carted off to the slammer by the local Ol' Bill, and we never saw 'im again.' Scaff eyed Bryn with a deranged glare. ''E was a drunk and 'e cheated at cards, so 'e got what 'e deserved.'

31

A chill ran down Bryn's spine. The other Welshman sounded like a dreadful wrong'un, but Scaff was just as disturbing. 'You'll get no quarrel from me, Scaff. I'm not looking for any trouble,' said Bryn, resisting the urge to look over his shoulder as if something sinister was lurking in the shadows.

'Right then, Taffy boy, keep yer 'ead down an' you'll be fine. Now dump yer kit and get up on deck – we've got work to do.'

The light was already draining from the sky as the *Buenos Aires Star* set sail, leaving behind the bleak industrial reaches of the river Mersey and venturing out into the Irish Sea for the start of the journey across the Atlantic to Buenos Aires. Two days had passed since Bryn's hostile induction but, against the odds, Scaff was turning out to be a good, if surly, teacher.

On deck, having completed his undocking duties, Bryn leaned on the handrail and watched as the industrial shoreline slid away, taking with it his old life. A lump formed in his throat as the cold breeze ruffled his thick curly hair. His eyes and nose tingled at the thought of the vast distance he was about to put between himself and his loved ones. It was his decision, a self-imposed penance for destroying their lives the moment he'd pulled that trigger, but it was tearing him apart. His mam used to be so proud of him but he'd let her down in the worst possible way. Guilt ate at his innards like a tapeworm.

He swallowed hard. 'Goodbye Mam,' he whispered. 'One day, I'll return and make you proud of me again.' He closed his eyes, fighting the prickling sensation behind his eyelids.

He took a deep breath, kissed his fingertips three times and blew the kisses into the air: one for Mam, one for Shirley – and one for Emlyn. He turned away with a haunting sense of emptiness, as if a part of him was being left behind. He wasn't sure he would ever be whole again.

That night, the ship rolled gently as it passed from the Irish Sea into the Atlantic, but it was enough to keep Bryn awake. As he tossed restlessly in his narrow bunk, he felt an uncomfortable digging sensation in his back. Poking at the mattress, his fingers made out the shape of a firm flat object with corners, which had been roughly sewn into the lining. He ripped apart the clumsy stitches, slid his hand gingerly into the musty stuffing and extracted a slim black folio. Holding it up to the nightlight, he instantly recognised the familiar cover of a British passport. He flipped it open to the photograph and looked at the unremarkable features of the bunk's former resident, the shaven-headed, good-for-nothing Welshman, Gryff Morgan.

So, this was the Welsh troublemaker everyone was moaning about. He scrutinised Gryff's expressionless face in a futile attempt to read his character. There was something oddly familiar about his features but he couldn't put his finger on it. He tossed the passport into his locker. He'd hand it to the purser in the morning, he thought sleepily as he finally drifted off.

Two weeks later, Scaff lay on his bunk, listening to Bryn snoring in the neighbouring berth. He didn't much care for passage workers. They were a useless bunch of half-wits who were just in it for a free ride and who made everyone else's life a misery in the meantime. In the weeks since they

33

left Liverpool, he hadn't expected the new Taff to be any different from any of the other idiots he'd come across in the past but, against the odds, the geezer was turning out all right. For a start, he was a lot tougher than Scaff had imagined and had taken on all the filthiest tasks that nobody else wanted to do. There was this one time after a force ten had put the heads out of action when it was Taffy boy who went in with a plunger, bucket and mop, and cleaned up the sick and shit without adding to the stinking mess himself. He had to admit it – the boy had guts of steel.

There was something funny about him, though, and Scaff couldn't figure out what it was. Nobody in their right mind volunteered for all that crap. It was almost like he had some kind of downer on himself. Whatever the reason, Scaff didn't give a toss if it saved him doing the filthiest jobs himself.

Yet the thing that impressed Scaff most about the new boy wasn't just his willingness to shovel shit; it turned out he was pretty nifty with a spanner, too. That boy could fix anything and by Christ could he climb! The way he went up the rigging, even in high seas, it was like watching a lizard climb a wall. Scaff'd never seen nothin' like it. It was why he'd started calling him Gecko.

'You ain't as useless as I thought you'd be, Gecko,' Scaff said to Bryn one evening in the ship's mess over dinner of boiled cabbage and meatballs. Bryn had worked miracles to repair a vital broken refrigeration unit that afternoon, potentially saving the Blue Star Line thousands of pounds in spoiled cargo.

Bryn snorted derisively. 'Well, that's mighty generous of you, Scaff.'

A backhanded compliment was better than no compliment at all, Bryn supposed, grinning inwardly at Scaff's praise. Scaff was a tough man to impress but it seemed that he'd done it. He could scarcely believe the foul jobs he'd done just to win over the cynical old cockney docker although, for the life of him, he couldn't recall why he'd wanted to.

He scooped a forkful of the repellent slop into his mouth, so tired that he barely noticed how foul it was. Deckhand work was physically exhausting but he still struggled to stay asleep at night. Most nights he jolted awake, his heart pounding like a jackhammer, his body drenched in sweat, on the brink of pulling the trigger one more time. Reliving the torment every night was hellish enough, but there were times when the merest waft of diesel and grease could put him right back in the attic, choking on cordite and screaming his brother's name. Even sudden loud bangs from the engine room could trigger a flashback, leaving him a quivering wreck.

In the endless darkness of his sleepless nights, tempting visions of his lifeless body on the ocean floor passed through his mind's eye. But that would be the easy way out, which he didn't deserve. Life at sea was like being in prison or, at least, how he imagined prison to be. Every day was an endurance test in the confined space, with dreadful food, filthy jobs and no chance of going anyplace else. The stench of unwashed bodies, unsavoury galley aromas and human flatulence only intensified the sensation of being detained at Her Majesty's pleasure. It was a living nightmare with no escape. It was no more than he deserved.

After several weeks, life aboard ship began to subtly change as the *Buenos Aires Star* sailed closer to the equator.

Warm gentle breezes caressed the freighter and the seas became almost tepid. Alongside the ship's bow, schools of sleek grey dolphins raced, revelling in the rollercoaster of turbulence created by the hull. Bryn was captivated by their graceful movements as they swooped and crossed the prow with daredevil timing. The clarity of the sky lent an unparalleled intensity to the vast empty seascape, and the equatorial sunrises and sunsets were truly breathtaking. In these tranquil hours on watch, Bryn was suffused with a deep sense of peace for the first time in months. He almost wished he could stay there forever.

FIVE

BUENOS AIRES, ARGENTINA

Dense fog engulfed the *Buenos Aires Star* as she proceeded cautiously along the Rio de la Plata towards the port of Buenos Aires, having covered more than seven-and-a-half-thousand nautical miles since leaving the port of Liverpool almost six weeks earlier. It was 0500 hours and every deckhand was on watch, stationed around the upper deck, straining to see more than a few feet into the eerie gloom. An experienced Argentine maritime pilot had boarded in the fog an hour earlier and was guiding them through the shallow Punta Indio channel, but the atmosphere on deck was tense.

Amidships, Bryn and Scaff huddled together, their necks wrapped in mufflers, their thin overalls offering little protection from the cold moist air. Bryn slapped his arms to generate some warmth and distract himself from his growing unease. Gradually, he began to detect the faint sound of another ship's engine in the distance. Was it the fog playing tricks with his senses or merely an echo of their own engines? But as the minutes passed, the outline of another freighter emerged slowly from the fog in the outbound channel.

Bryn rubbed the knot of tension in his chest and turned to Scaff with a worried frown. 'That freighter's getting a bit bloody close, don't you think?'

Scaff seemed utterly unfazed. 'Don't worry, mate. There'll be a local pilot on that ship, too. They can do this stuff in their sleep. It'll be fine. I've been on this route fifteen years, never 'ad a problem.'

Bryn's heart pounded as the massive freighter loomed closer and closer, its prow bearing down on them like an unstoppable iceberg. He turned to Scaff again in rising panic and grabbed him by the collar of his overalls, his voice tight with urgency. 'For God's sake, man! Look! We're going to be crushed!'

Scaff's eyes widened as he prised Bryn's fists from his collar. 'D'you know what, mate? You're right!' He turned towards the ship's bridge, waving his signal lamp frantically. 'About-ship! About-ship! About-ship!'

Bryn's legs buckled as the *Buenos Aires Star* steered sharply to port. The slippery deck heeled steeply and the two men slid sideways, desperately snatching out for a handhold. The terrifying sound of metal groaning and creaking filled the air.

'*Jesus H. Christ!*' yelled Scaff as the prow of the other freighter slid by, mere feet from their new position. 'That was soddin' close!'

Bryn's reply was drowned out by an ear-splitting crack as the hull hit a sandbar with a violent judder and jolted sharply to starboard. Thrown off his feet, Bryn landed with a bone-shaking crunch that knocked the breath out of him. He careered along the sloping deck, frantic to save himself from hurtling into the ocean, and screamed in agony as he latched onto a cleat, shooting a bolt of pain through his shoulder. With an explosive boom that reverberated through the air like an earthquake, the Star's prow smashed into the hull of the other freighter sending a blinding shower of sparks and metal shrapnel hurtling in all directions. A volcanic shockwave rippled through the deck and Bryn almost expected to be enveloped in lava as he hung desperately by one screaming arm, his ears ringing from the screech of tearing metal and the aftershock of the impact. When both ships finally came to a shuddering halt, Bryn hauled himself unsteadily to his feet, panting with shock and pain, his heart thumping like a piston, as an eerie silence momentarily descended. He looked around for Scaff, but Scaff was nowhere to be seen.

'Scaff! Scaff!' Bryn clutched his arm against his body, hoping against hope that Scaff would appear unharmed.

Shouting crewmen ran in all directions, their panicked cries adding to the breaking chaos and confusion, but none of them were Scaff. It could only mean one thing.

'Man overboard!' Bryn's voice strained to be heard above the mayhem. 'Man overboard! Man overboard!' In a matter of seconds, a dozen or more deckhands raced to his side, their faces pale with fear. A few men scrambled to lob buoyancy aids and life jackets over the side while others began to pan their search lamps from the spot where Scaff had been standing moments before. But it was no use – in the dense fog, the surface of the sea was invisible just thirty feet below.

'Scaff! *Scaff!*'

Time was running out. If Scaff had been knocked unconscious, it might be too late already. 'Lower me down in that tender!' Bryn dashed across the sloping deck towards a small wooden rowing boat suspended from a launching winch. Half-a-dozen men sprang into action, deftly lowering Bryn and two other deckhands in the ship's dinghy into the murky gap between the two collided ships.

They'd only just reached sea level when a voice muffled by the thick fog reached them from above. 'What can you see?'

Bryn's teeth chattered uncontrollably from the dank chill seeping into his bones. 'Nothing yet, give us a chance!' He clenched his jaw and wrapped his arms tightly around himself, wincing from the pain of his wrenched shoulder. The ghostly silence at sea level was broken only by the sound of his own ragged breathing and the rhythmic plash of the oars as his two shipmates rowed carefully in the fog, picking their way through the collision debris. He strained his ears for cries of help but there were none. It was looking bleak for Scaff but he would search for as long as it took to find his crewmate – dead or alive.

The fog was even more oppressive down at sea level than on deck. Bryn could scarcely see his hands in front of his face. His hopes soared several times when he thought that a buoyancy aid was Scaff, only to be dashed when it turned out to be a false alarm. Finally, he spotted a life jacket floating awkwardly in the gentle swell. He reached out with a long-handled boathook, his pulse throbbing so powerfully he feared he would burst an artery at any moment. He caught hold of the jacket and pulled it towards him, praying with all his might that it would be Scaff.

Scaff was slumped to one side, eyes closed and mouth gaping slackly. Bryn's stomach knotted with fear. *Please, God, let him be alive!*

'We got him!' he yelled at the top of his voice towards the ship. 'Quick, lads, haul him in.' The weight of Scaff's waterlogged clothes and boots almost dragged Bryn and his crewmates overboard as they wrestled Scaff into the small unstable tender. He was unresponsive, with a massive gash above one eye where the shocking whiteness of his skull showed through. Bryn tried to find a pulse but his cold wet hands made it impossible. Cursing under his breath, he hauled Scaff's inert body onto its side, grimly noting the gush of water that poured from his throat. He rubbed Scaff's back and scanned his deathly white face for signs of life. 'Come on, mate,' he muttered. 'You can make it.'

As the tender scudded back to the ship, Bryn saw that a stretcher had been readied and lowered to the waterline. With his adrenaline ebbing away, his shoulder burned as he clambered up the boom nets slung over the ship's side. Strong hands reached out and grabbed him by his life jacket, dragging him over the guardrail. He landed on the deck with a heavy thud, intensely grateful as the same hands wrapped him in a thick warm coat.

Through salty stinging eyes, Bryn watched Scaff being carried away on the stretcher. 'Is he alive?'

One of the stretcher-bearers gave a flippant laugh. 'Yeh – more's the pity!'

Bryn's shoulders slumped as the tension flooded from his body. Scaff was alive. He could breathe again. Trembling from head to foot, Bryn was supported into the sickbay, where Scaff was already lying on an examination table, his eyes closed and his body covered with a thick layer of blankets. The medical purser was working busily on the deep gash in Scaff's temple, cleaning it with an orangey-coloured antiseptic wash. The wound looked even worse under the bright lights of the sickbay. As the purser began stitching the edges together, layer by layer, Bryn had to look away.

The medic looked up as Bryn sat down. 'Take your time, Doc,' Bryn rasped, taking the weight off his injured shoulder with his other hand. 'I'm not going anywhere.'

As Bryn spoke, Scaff's salt-encrusted eyes cracked open, forming red-rimmed slits in his pallid face.

'Gecko,' he groaned. 'The doc says you saved my life. I owe ya.'

The following morning, Bryn stood on the prow of the freighter, his arm cradled in a sling as he gazed at the endless expanse of flawless azure sky that stretched before him. His shoulder throbbed like hell but he'd been lucky not to tear anything. According to the doc, he just needed to rest it for a week or two, and that was precisely what he planned to do, as there would be no return trip for him once they reached Buenos Aires.

In the bright clear sunshine, with a warm breeze in his hair, it was almost impossible to believe that the fog of forty-eight hours earlier had ever happened, were it not for the small flotilla of tugboats that surrounded him, expertly manoeuvring the giant wounded freighter into Buenos Aires harbour. A glimmer of optimism flickered inside him as he reflected on his journey. Whatever challenges lay ahead, he was ready to face them. If he could save a man's life at sea, he could do anything.

Slicking back his hair with a spit-dampened palm, Bryn squared his shoulders and took a deep breath before rapping on the glossy varnished door. He'd been summoned to the captain's stateroom and was unsure what to expect.

'Enter,' boomed the captain's voice.

Bryn was amazed by the captain's luxurious quarters as he opened the hatch door and stepped over the raised threshold. The room was spacious, with large windows facing fore and aft, and portholes along both sides. The floor was covered with real carpet and an imposing, deeply burnished wooden desk stood in the centre of the room. On one side, elegant furniture was grouped around a generous coffee table.

Sitting in a comfortable-looking chair in his spotless white uniform, the captain gestured to Bryn to sit in another. Conscious of his grimy clothes, Bryn perched on the edge of the plush cushion.

The captain cleared his throat noisily. 'I would like to offer you my personal thanks for saving the life of Able Seaman Paul Holding on Monday.'

Bryn frowned. The captain must be mistaken. He'd never heard of anyone by that name. But as he debated whether it would be rude to contradict his boss, the penny suddenly dropped. The captain was talking about Scaff! Bryn chuckled to himself as it dawned on him why everyone called him Scaff.

'I've never yet lost a life on board any ship under my command,' the captain continued. 'It's a source of great pride and valuable professional reputation for me.'

Bryn shrugged modestly. 'Anyone would have done the same thing.'

The captain's steel grey eyes narrowed. 'I'm not sure I agree with you, young man. The collision was the dominant issue and a man overboard could easily have been missed. Your vigilance saved Paul's life and protected my reputation. In recognition of my gratitude, I am awarding you the sum of fifty pounds, which you can collect from the purser when you leave. I've also written a personal testimonial that you may use as a reference for any further passages you wish to apply for.' The captain strode across to his impressive desk, where a sheaf of notepaper lay on the blotter. Taking the top sheet, he folded it in three, slid it into an envelope, wrote Bryn's name on it and handed it to him with a flourish.

'You are a good man, Bryn. You've taken to seafaring well and made good use of your engineering skills on this ship over the last six weeks. I can always use a good fitter. You are most welcome to stay on if you wish.'

Bryn shook his head, his mind racing as he traced his finger over the embossed company logo on the thick envelope. He couldn't believe his luck but he had no intention of returning to Liverpool. He expressed his gratitude and politely declined the offer.

The captain proffered his hand. 'I wish you well in the future, young man. You are dismissed, with thanks.'

Bryn returned to his bunk dazed by the unexpected turn of affairs, clutching the envelope tightly. The testimonial inside was written on luxurious headed Blue Star paper, and the handwriting was elegant and precise.

To whom it may concern,
I would like to highly commend to you the bearer of this testimonial, for his vigilance and courage in saving the life of

a man overboard, an Able Seaman of the Merchant Navy, on the MV *Buenos Aires Star*.

He has also proved himself to be an excellent mechanic and a reliable man of impeccable character, with a strong work ethic. He has my personal endorsement, as well as the gratitude of the Blue Star Line.

Sincerely,

Marcus Cruikshank, Captain

Bryn refolded the letter, brimming with pride at the captain's words. As an unexpected bonus, Captain Cruikshank had accidentally included an extra sheet of the top-quality headed notepaper, which Bryn could use to write to Shirley when he settled somewhere. He smiled to himself, imagining how impressed she'd be by the fancy stationery and news of his heroics. What would she think of him now, after six weeks at sea? With any luck, she would understand he needed to prove to himself he was a good man before he could come home and be worthy of his family once more. Saving Scaff's life was a great first step along that journey.

SIX

Later that afternoon, as the *Buenos Aires Star* was being towed into the harbour, Bryn remained on deck watching the final act of the salvage operation conducted by the small tugboats. It was astonishing that boats so small could tow something as enormous as a refrigerated freighter, but it was thanks to the swift work of the engineers who had sealed the bulkheads below the waterline that the vessel could be salvaged at all.

As the dockside grew closer, deeply tanned stevedores in white canvas hats came into view, swarming the long diagonal jetties that poked out into the vast River Plate like fingers on a giant hand, stacked high with containers and pallets of unimaginable treasures. Overhead, unfamiliar birds with strange cries wheeled in escalating circles, while the warm breeze brought mouthwatering aromas of cooked meats and sweet fragrances, and the clamour of countless foreign tongues competing to be heard. It was an intoxicating mixture and, after six weeks at sea, Bryn could hardly wait to get ashore.

The ship boomed slightly, reverberating through the soles of his boots, as it was nudged alongside by the tugs. It was time for Bryn to disembark but first he had to pay a visit to the sickbay.

Scaff was sitting up in bed with his head wrapped in a heavy bandage covering one eye. The left side of his face was black and purple, and swollen like a ripe Victoria plum. He grinned broadly as Bryn walked in – then seemed to regret it immediately.

He touched his hand tenderly to his face. 'Blimey, this don't 'alf 'urt.'

Bryn winced in sympathy as he sat on the edge of Scaff's bed. 'I've come to say farewell, *Paul, me old china.*' He grinned, hoping for a reaction to his cheeky mocking. 'Buenos Aires is where I'm getting off. Thanks to rescuing you, I've got some cash in my pocket and I'm ready to spend, spend, spend!'

Scaff gave him a killer glare with his one good eye. 'Not so fast, mate – and knock it off with the "Paul" malarkey. Only me old mum ever called me that, an' she's been dead ten years. Anyhow, I've been 'avin' a think.'

Bryn wasn't sure he liked the sound of what was coming. 'Oh, yes? What about?'

'Well, it's like this, see? That was a close shave for me back there.' Scaff's voice quivered. 'It could've been curtains if it wasn't for you. I think I've used up me nine lives over the past fifteen years, so I've decided – I'm jackin' it in.'

'You're *what?*' Bryn wasn't sure what he'd been expecting Scaff to say, but it certainly wasn't that.

'I'm coming with you, lovely boyo!' Scaff's face broke into a half-grin.

Bryn gaped as he took in the news. He'd won Scaff's begrudging respect over the past six weeks and saved his life, too, but that didn't mean he wanted him as his travel companion.

'Don't look so 'appy about it.' Scaff scowled, sounding miffed.

Bryn collected himself hastily. 'But what will you do?' he asked. 'Don't you have family back in London?'

'Ah,' said Scaff, with a canny expression on the uninjured half of his face, 'that's the good bit, see? I've been doing this same route for fifteen years. I've got a girl here.'

'You?' spluttered Bryn. 'With a girl?' He found it hard to imagine any woman would find Scaff lovable and he was certainly no oil painting.

'Yup,' Scaff said proudly. 'And – *Yo hablo Español también.*'

Bryn's jaw dropped even further. 'You speak Spanish? I don't believe it!'

'And you thought I was just a thick cockney.' Scaff rubbed his hands together gleefully. 'So, it's a deal. I'm coming with you – or, more like, you're comin' with me. I can show you around. You can stay at my place till you get sorted. Rosa will teach you a bit of the lingo, too, if you be'ave y'self. Go and get yer kit. Meet you in ten minutes at the top of the gangplank. I've already been discharged.'

Bryn hurried back to his berth, his thoughts in turmoil at the sudden development. He pulled out the bergen stashed below his bunk and threw everything from his locker into it. There was no time for neat packing. He'd sort it out later.

Fifteen minutes later, Bryn found himself walking beside Scaff along the Avenida de los Inmigrantes, the bright sunshine warming his skin while Scaff talked nineteen to the dozen about his brilliant plans for the two of them. As they headed towards the Plaza General San Martín, Bryn couldn't help reaching for a handhold every few steps.

Scaff chuckled at Bryn's unsteadiness. 'It won't take long to get rid of them sea legs.'

Bryn leant against the trunk of a vast tree smothered in fragrant purple flowers, just like the rhododendrons that grew wildly out of control in the Brecon Beacons. 'I certainly hope not,' he replied. 'I'm all over the flipping place!'

The stunning city, which soared elegantly into the intense blue sky, was a complete surprise to Bryn. As he and Scaff made their way through the city streets, they crossed beautiful plazas bursting with exotic carmine-red flowers. The blooms' long seductive stamens filled the warm air with their heady aroma, reminding Bryn uncomfortably of Shirley and the cheap sweet scent she liked to dab behind her ears. He pushed the thought away resolutely as he turned his attention back to what Scaff was saying – something about it being the national flower. He seemed strangely well-informed for a deckhand.

Further along their route, they passed an imposing red-brick clock tower standing in formal grounds that were laid out like the Palace of Versailles, which Bryn vaguely remembered from the history lessons of his schooldays. Benches were positioned invitingly under the shade of mature trees, offering shelter from the intense sun and beckoning Bryn, who was charmed by the unfamiliar birdsong that filled his ears. Classical boulevards stretched to the left and right, packed with bookshops, opera houses and theatres, and elegant architecture redolent of Paris or Madrid. Everywhere he looked, there was a sight that took his breath away. Bryn could scarcely believe his eyes. Buenos Aires must be the most beautiful city on earth, he decided. Why would anyone ever want to leave?

Scaff laughed at Bryn's wide-eyed amazement. 'Wait till you see this place at night,' he said. 'That's when things really heat up!'

They'd been walking for twenty minutes when Scaff eventually turned off the main road into a cool shady side street lined with lofty lime trees, their canopies meeting across the thoroughfare like tango dancers reaching for their partners. The three-storey terraced buildings were painted in rich hues of salmon, mustard, pink or sky blue, with white-framed doors and windows. Each building had an ornate metal trellis balcony on the first floor. To unworldly Bryn, it was the most elegant and beautiful street he'd ever seen.

''Ere we go, Gecko,' said Scaff as they approached a building painted a dark forest green. ''Ome sweet 'ome.' They climbed three stone steps and a metallic bell tinkled as Scaff pushed open a glass door. Enveloped by the musty smell of old leather and paper, and surrounded by shelf after shelf of books, Bryn realised with astonishment that it was a bookshop! *A bookshop?* Scaff lived in *a bookshop?*

Glancing around in amazement, Bryn noticed a petite woman behind the counter who appeared to be in her mid-twenties, with shiny black hair swept up into a chic chignon. Her dark eyes were fashionably winged with heavy eyeliner.

Her face lit up at the sight of Scaff and she rushed around the counter to greet him with a fierce embrace.

'Pablo, *amorcito*, it's so good to see you! But what did you do to your head?' She touched the bandage gently. Bryn was astonished – she spoke perfect English! He'd seriously underestimated this wonderful city and its people.

'Just a scratch, Rosa, *querida*.' Scaff's cockney accent melted away as he transformed into Pablo. He gestured towards Bryn. '*Eso es mi amigo Gecko*.'

Rosa smiled warmly at Bryn. 'Pleased to meet you. But why are you a lizard, *amigo*?'

Returning her smile, Bryn held out his hand 'Bryn,' he said. 'My name's Bryn.'

She took his hand and shook it firmly. '*Tanto gusto*, Bryn. But I shall call you "El Gecko". I like it!' Her dark eyes glittered with humour and mischief. 'Do you speak any Spanish?'

'Not a word.'

'Then you are in luck, for I am a good teacher! The best!' Her melodic laughter filled the air. 'I will help you. Repeat after me: *"Me llamo El Gecko"*.'

Repeating the words perfectly, Bryn was rewarded with another dazzling smile. '*Muy bien!*' Rosa declared, triumphantly. 'You have a good accent. Now you know how to introduce yourself.'

Scaff took Bryn by the arm. 'Come on, Gecko. There'll be plenty of time for Spanish lessons later. Let me show you where you'll be sleeping.'

Bryn followed Scaff (or was it Paul or even Pablo, now?) between the high mahogany shelves of books to the back of the store, where Scaff pushed open an old wooden door and descended a few steps into a shady cobbled courtyard. An ornamental water fountain bubbled invitingly in the centre. Across the courtyard was another door leading into a cool stone-built single-storey cabana. Creepers with stems as thick as a man's arm swarmed up the walls and across the roof, almost completely concealing it.

'This was Rosa's parents' house before the war,' Scaff explained. 'When the surrounding buildings were put up, it became almost completely enclosed, so they used it for storage. There's no running water or power, and it's just two rooms, but it's clean and dry. You can use it till you find something better.'

Bryn looked around the bare stone interior, sparsely furnished with a low single bed, a bedside table on which a glass gas lamp stood, and one wooden chair. 'It's perfect,' he said. He was beginning to see that he simply wouldn't have coped alone in this foreign city without speaking the language or even understanding the money. His impulsiveness could get him into a lot of bother. Thank goodness for Scaff's generosity – and what incredible luck to have found himself in the company of such hospitable people.

'I'll be in the basement apartment below the bookshop with Rosa if you need anything. I'll come and get you in two hours,' said Scaff. 'Get some shut-eye now if you can – we stay up late in this town!'

Bryn tossed his bergen onto the low bed in the back room. He'd need something clean and presentable to wear later, so he decided to rinse a shirt in the fountain and leave it to dry in the sun. As he tipped the contents of the bergen onto the bed, he noticed Gryff Morgan's passport among his underclothes.

Oh, blast! he thought, annoyed with himself for his forgetfulness. He should have given it to the captain when he saw him. But it was no big deal – maybe Scaff could take him to the British Embassy tomorrow. He would hand it in there.

He tossed the passport into the small bedside table drawer and threw himself on the bed. Within minutes, he was in the deepest, most restful sleep he'd had in months.

SEVEN

When Bryn awoke, long shadows filled the room. Someone had been in while he slept. The gas lamp now burned dully, throwing out a low warm light that barely reached the corners of the room. A pair of blue denim trousers with a thick leather belt lay neatly draped across the chair seat and a pair of slightly scuffed brown leather boots stood below. A red shirt with a long pointed collar hung on the back of the chair. On the side table, a towel and a small piece of soap had been thoughtfully placed, and there was a gaudy ceramic pitcher of water with a matching bowl on the floor.

Bryn rubbed his face vigorously and ran his fingers through his wild wavy hair as he swung his bare feet out of bed onto the rough stone floor, trying to figure out how Rosa had all this spare gear and how he would ever repay her kindness.

Five minutes later, his unruly mane tamed and wearing his new clothes, Bryn emerged from the cool of the stone cabana and was greeted by a symphony of cicadas chirruping their night music. The juicy mouthwatering aroma of jacaranda filled the warm evening air as a black witch moth the size of an outspread hand flitted silently, adding to the magical atmosphere. The lush moonlit garden was barely recognisable in its evening attire. He'd stepped into a different world. He stood for a few heartbeats in awed silence, barely breathing, bewitched by the enchanting moment.

From across the courtyard, Scaff was heading his way – transformed in a brightly patterned short-sleeved shirt, the open neck revealing a chunky crucifix on a thick gold chain, pale canvas wide-legged trousers and open-toed leather sandals. His habitually greasy ponytail was gone and, in its place, his hair fell in shiny dark-golden waves to his collarbones. The bulky turban bandage had been replaced with a more discreet dressing and the uninjured half of his face radiated happiness.

Scaff laughed and gestured at Bryn's outfit. 'Hey, *gringo*! Look at you! You scrub up all right!'

'I'm sorry, do I know you?' Bryn cast an admiring eye over Scaff's new look.

'Meet my Argentinian alter ego, Pablo,' Scaff said with upturned palms and half a smile. 'I can be a different man when I'm 'ere,' he said. 'A better man. I leave Scaff behind on board.'

'Well, it's certainly an incredible transformation. Just don't expect me to start calling you Pablo any time soon.' Bryn's eyes wrinkled with mirth. 'Anyway, where did all this gear come from?' He looked down at his own clothes. 'And what do I owe you?'

Scaff gave Bryn his familiar killer glare. 'Look 'ere, Gecks, don't go offending me on the first night.' He slapped his pal on the shoulder. 'You saved my life, remember? Look, Rosa 'ad some spare stuff lying around, all right? It's no big deal.'

'Well, if you say so, Scaff.' Bryn returned the backslap. 'You're the boss!'

'Right, let's get going – we're 'aving a night on the tiles!'

'Where are you taking me?'

'You'll have to wait and see! You're gonna love it!'

Leading the way, Scaff took Bryn to a dark corner of the courtyard, ducking underneath the low-hanging branches of the jacaranda tree, where a door concealed with vines led to a dark passage between the back of two tall buildings. He put an index finger against his lips. 'Keep the noise down – we don't wanna disturb the neighbours.'

Bryn could barely see his hand in front of his face as he followed Scaff blindly along the long passage, thick with glossy overgrown foliage, eventually emerging into the open air behind a garbage dumpster on a different street. Scaff peered out cautiously before sliding out of the shadows into the well-lit avenue and merging into the festive crowd. Caught up by the clandestine mood, Bryn followed Scaff's example, looking about furtively as if he were a character in a spy novel.

The brightly dressed street crowd, mostly couples of all ages holding hands, seemed to be converging towards a small plaza, lured by the sound of lively trumpets, accordions and violins. On all sides of the plaza, bars and cafés nestled among trees laden with purple blooms, their intoxicating scent filling the air. Festoon lanterns perched like colourful parakeets among the branches. The infectious macarena rhythm beckoned to Bryn, threatening to commandeer his feet and take him for a wild ride. He was swept along in the exuberant crowd, his senses turning cartwheels.

'What's going on?' he asked, raising his voice to be heard above the clamour.

'It's tango night,' Scaff yelled into his ear. 'But every night is tango night in Buenos Aires!'

Scaff found them a table at a café, just feet away from where dozens of couples danced energetically with syncopated footwork that took Bryn's breath away. Some couples were intimately entwined, joined at the thigh, their hips swinging provocatively in perfect time to the playful upbeat music; others danced more vivaciously in an open embrace. Many couples wore figure-hugging costumes in shimmering satins and silks, while others happily joined in wearing denims and casual shirts. The kaleidoscope of colour and motion took Bryn's breath away.

'*Oiga, camarero!*' Scaff clicked his fingers at a passing waiter bearing a small tray. '*Dos cervezas, por favor.*'

'This is incredible,' said Bryn as their beers arrived. 'I'd love to be able to move like that. Just look at how much everyone's enjoying themselves.'

'I was just the same as you, my first time in Buenos Aires. Fifteen years ago, it must be.' Scaff had a distant look in his eye. 'This is how I met Rosa. She taught me to dance the *Chacarera* and we never looked back.' He turned his face away briefly, eyes glistening. 'Those couples you see there,' he cleared his throat and nodded towards the gyrating crowd. 'They're not all "proper" couples. People come and dance with other people. Complete strangers. That's how it works.'

Bryn took a mouthful of his chilled beer, lost in thought. He'd completely underestimated his friend's sensitive side; he could see that now. On board the ship, Scaff was the toughest of tough nuts, but now, seeing him in this different light, he seemed to be a changed man. It must be love. Taking another sip of his beer, Bryn sighed wistfully. Had he ever looked at Shirley with the same adoration that Scaff looked at Rosa? He doubted it.

Bryn wiped the foam from his lips with the back of his hand. 'I can't believe you can tango, Scaff. You really are a dark horse, mate.'

Scaff pursed his mouth in an enigmatic smile, gently supporting the swollen side of his face in his palm. 'Darker than you think, Gecks me ol' china, darker than you think.'

With conversation all but drowned out by the music, they sat companionably for a while, Bryn drumming his fingers to the beat as he tried to make sense of Scaff's enigmatic words, and Scaff tapping his feet and swinging his shoulders, clearly itching to join the sweating dancers. After a few minutes, Bryn leaned across to Scaff and yelled in his ear: 'So how does it work with you and Rosa?' It was a mystery to him how a woman as incredible as Rosa found Scaff so adorable, even as his alter ego, Pablo. 'You being at sea most of the time must make it difficult for you both.'

Leaning back on his chair, Scaff scratched his stubble. 'It's complicated. Let's leave it at that, shall we?' He swallowed the last of his beer. 'Let's go! The night is young and you ain't seen nothing yet!'

Bryn downed his drink and rapped the empty glass on the table. 'Lead on, maestro!' With his new best mate beside him, he plunged eagerly into the lively crowd, keen to experience everything that Buenos Aires had to offer.

Hours later, as the night sky slowly gave way to dawn and the first streaks of orange were gently erasing the stars, Bryn stumbled back to the cabana, his eardrums buzzing and his belly full of beer and tequila. His bed lurched as he tried to board it. 'What a night!' he muttered as he flopped onto the thin mattress before spewing into the gaudy bowl.

***

Rosa and Scaff were sitting in the courtyard, having a simple breakfast of fruit and pastries under the shade of the jacaranda tree, when Bryn emerged the following morning, squinting in the brightness, his hair sticking up in wild clumps. Rosa had set a place for him and the smell of excellent coffee beckoned.

'How was your first night in Buenos Aires?' Rosa smiled with amusement, her gaze taking in his dishevelled clothes from the night before.

Bryn reached for the coffee pot. 'What a fantastic city you live in, Rosa,' he rasped, his mouth as dry and rough as a sheet of sandpaper. 'I can't imagine why anyone would ever want to leave.'

'*Sí,*' said Rosa. '*Los porteños* certainly know how to enjoy life but it is not always easy, you know?'

Bryn sipped his first cup of coffee gratefully. 'What do you mean?'

Rosa beckoned him close, lowering her voice conspiratorially. 'We had a great man in charge one time. He made things better for the worker, for the poor man and for women. He gave women the vote and his wife was a great lady who did much to reduce poverty.'

Bryn raised his eyebrows, his curiosity piqued by her secrecy. 'So, what happened?'

Rosa hesitated and glanced at Scaff, who gave her a quick nod. 'The rich people and the military, they didn't like this, so they staged a *revolución* and he was sent into exile in Spain. His poor wife died young. Oh, how the streets were filled with flowers…' Rosa closed her eyes momentarily, lost in the memory. 'And now we have a cruel military regime. The police – "*la cana*", we call them – can do as they please, kill or torture whoever they want, and people live in fear.'

Bryn was lost for words, his cup of excellent coffee suspended halfway to his mouth. 'My God!' he exclaimed, wide-eyed with disbelief. 'The police actually torture and kill people here? Really?'

He turned to Scaff, who was gazing at Rosa with naked adoration.

Rosa's chin jutted and her eyes glittered. 'Juan Perón is a good man and the ordinary people want him back. We will do whatever it takes,' she said. 'We will fight for our freedom!'

Bryn helped himself to a pastry as he took in her fearless words. She was certainly a feisty lady and he had no doubt she meant everything she'd said.

After Rosa went to open the bookstore, Bryn and Scaff lingered over their coffee in the dappled shade, vivid green parakeets chattering noisily in the branches overhead. A bold mockingbird foraged around their feet, searching out its own breakfast of seeds and insects, as a family of tiny brown lizards rustled among the understory.

'What a great lady,' said Bryn. 'She's so fiery, so passionate about life. I can see why you like her so much.'

'Yes, I absolutely adore her.' Scaff's candour took Bryn by surprise. 'I would do absolutely anythin' for her, and I mean *anythin'*.'

Bryn noticed the fierceness in Scaff's voice. A furrow formed between his brows. What was it they were not telling him?

A haze of blue smoke, pungent with the enticing aroma of grilled meat, lured Bryn into the courtyard just after midday, where he found Scaff wearing a long apron as he attended to the stone-built barbecue, brandishing a long pair of tongs. The slabs of steak that sizzled temptingly above the coals were more than twice the size of anything Bryn had ever seen in the butcher's window in Aberavon.

'What's the occasion?' Bryn asked, salivating like a hungry dog.

'No occasion, mate. It's siesta. Everything closes between noon and four, when it's too hot to work. This is an *asado*,' Scaff pointed at the steak with his tongs. 'Just you wait till you taste it. It's nothing like the crap we get in Britain.'

He cut off a thin slice and handed it to Bryn. 'Try that.'

Bryn put it in his mouth and chewed, savouring every mouthwatering moment.

'Good, innit?' Scaff gave a throaty chuckle. 'Best steaks in the entire world, in Buenos Aires.'

With his mouth full of the juiciest, most tender meat he'd ever tasted, Bryn could only nod his agreement.

'It's why they export so much of the stuff to Britain.' Scaff liberally seasoned everything on the griddle. 'But it's not the same when it gets there, all frozen solid. Loses its flavour in transit. And we don't cook it properly in the UK either.'

Bryn cast his mind back to the hundreds of frozen beef carcasses he'd seen being loaded as he left the ship. Of course! The *Buenos Aires Star* was a refrigerated meat carrier! He'd not given it a second thought on the outward journey when the ship was loaded with textiles for export.

Rosa's smiling face appeared at an open window overlooking the courtyard, just as Scaff was proudly handing Bryn a beautiful hand-painted ceramic plate of steak, cut across the grain, the lightly charred slithers oozing pink juices. It was a mouthwatering work of art. 'When you have finished your *asado*, we will begin your lessons,' she said. 'But don't rush – *buen provecho!*'

Rosa's lessons quickly became the high point of Bryn's day. In the coolness of the lush sub-tropical courtyard, surrounded by scores of tiny fluttering mariposa and entertained by the antics of wall lizards, Bryn soaked up knowledge with a thirst he'd never known in the austere classrooms of his childhood in South Wales. Within two weeks, he'd mastered basic vocabulary and could string together simple sentences. He filled several exercise books with line after line of useful Spanish phrases, to help him find a job.

'You are a quick learner, Bryn,' said Rosa one afternoon as they shared a plate of exquisite homemade spicy chicken *empañadas* and a jug of fresh orange juice, clinking with ice and laced with *maté*. 'You have a good ear for accents. Now, I think it's time for you to learn about my people.'

Bryn was utterly swept up by the drama as he sat listening intently to Rosa's passionate telling of the story of Juan Perón and Eva. Her fervour was captivating. It was like watching a thrilling piece of theatre enacted before his very eyes. Rosa's powerful storytelling brought the actions of the *Uturuncos*, a daring resistance group fighting to restore Perón to power, alive in his mind. The fearless guerrillas had raided a police station several years before, stealing a cache of machine guns and other weapons to equip the resistance. On the edge of his seat, Bryn was enthralled by Rosa's vivid and dramatic account of this bold and daring act of rebellion – until she spoke about the brutality with which the military junta suppressed opposition. Government sponsored kidnappings and murders were an everyday occurrence. Young men, and even boys, were dragged away from their families, never to be seen again.

Horrified by her words, Bryn found it almost impossible to reconcile the beauty and sophistication of Argentina's capital city with the ugliness of its politics. Now he understood why the people so desperately wanted Perón back from exile.

'D'you know what I'm thinking, Bryn?' Rosa said one afternoon about a fortnight later as they packed away their textbooks. 'I'm thinking you're ready.'

'Rosa,' Bryn took her beautifully manicured hand in his calloused one, 'you have been marvellous. I don't know how I can ever thank you enough for your generosity, patience and time.' He brought her hand to his lips and kissed it chivalrously. 'Scaff really is a very lucky man to have found you.'

Bryn told Scaff of his plans to go job hunting, the following morning over breakfast.

'Well, well, well!' Scaff's leathery face creased into a

smile. 'So, you've passed your eleven plus! Miss Mendoza says you're ready, does she?'

'I'm not exactly a native yet,' said Bryn, gathering up the dirty cups and plates, 'but I can get by.'

''Ere, let me give you an 'and with that.' Scaff reached behind his chair for the tray propped there. 'So, what's yer plan for today?'

'Well, I was thinking about taking a walk over to the British Embassy first,' said Bryn, loading the crockery onto the tray in precarious piles.

Scaff stopped what he was doing and stiffened perceptibly. 'What d'yer want with the embassy?'

Scaff's sudden mood change took Bryn by surprise. 'Oh, it's nothing to worry about, Scaff. It's just something I've been meaning to do since I got here.' He explained to Scaff about finding Gryff Morgan's passport and how he'd forgotten to hand it to the captain. 'I thought I could drop it off at the embassy while I'm out today.'

Scaff shrugged. 'Personally, I wouldn't bother if I was you. That Morgan bloke was a scumbag who doesn't deserve your time. But if you insist, I'll take you there meself – but it'll 'ave to be tomorrow. I'm off to see some business associates today.'

Bryn's ears pricked up. 'Business associates? Perhaps I could come with you. Maybe they could give me a job?'

Scaff scowled and avoided catching Bryn's eye. 'These ain't the sort of people you would wanna be working for.'

Bryn's neck prickled uncomfortably at the menace in Scaff's words. Perhaps these associates were part of the mystery between Scaff and Rosa. But he was a guest in Scaff's home, so it was none of his business. With a strong sense of foreboding, Bryn watched Scaff ride off on Rosa's motor scooter in a haze of blue exhaust fumes. There was definitely something going on. He returned to the bookshop, where he found Rosa up a ladder, sorting a high shelf.

'*Puede usted* – lend me – *un libro de mapas, por favor?*'

Rosa climbed down and rewarded him with a wide smile.

'Not bad, El Gecko, *no malo*. The verb you are looking for is "*prestar*". Yes, of course I can lend you a map book. Where are you going?'

Bryn explained to Rosa his plans to go job-hunting and drop by the embassy to hand in Gryff Morgan's passport. He'd decided to save Scaff the trouble of taking him there the next day.

Rosa flicked through the Buenos Aires city guide until she found the right page for the embassy and marked it for Bryn. 'If you are going to look for work, don't forget to take the captain's testimonial with you,' she said. 'A reference that good will improve your chances.'

Taking Rosa's advice when he returned to his room to get his jacket, Bryn slipped the envelope containing the captain's testimonial and Gryff Morgan's passport into the inside pocket. He grabbed the guidebook and went out via the narrow back alley, emerging cautiously into the street, as Scaff had shown him.

Bryn set off along the wide avenue with purpose in his stride, marvelling at his surroundings and brimming with optimism that getting work as an engineer on a construction site would be straightforward, given that Buenos Aires was in the middle of a building boom with new forty-storey *rascacielos* going up all over the city. But he hadn't allowed for the xenophobia of the gruff swarthy site foremen, who told him to *vete a la mierda* the moment he opened his mouth.

The blazing sub-tropical sun was directly overhead and everything was closing for siesta when Bryn decided he'd had enough. Sitting on a park bench in one of the countless immaculate plazas, he removed his boots and rubbed his throbbing feet. The cool municipal fountains bubbled invitingly, but as nobody else seemed to be cooling their feet in the water, he decided against it. He was ready to quit but still hadn't been to the embassy.

Despite keeping to the leafy shade of parks and plazas wherever possible, Bryn's shirt was soaked with sweat by the time he arrived at Dr Luis Agote Street, where the graceful, cream neo-Baroque embassy building dominated the corner plot, surrounded by high walls topped with wrought iron railings. A pair of padlocked wrought iron gates guarded the entrance. Bryn cursed under his breath. He hadn't imagined for a moment that the embassy would be closed for siesta too. It was very un-British. He scratched his stubbly chin and looked around for somewhere shady to sit and wait. Glancing at his watch, he realised with dismay that the embassy was not due to reopen for another three hours.

The sight of the antique gold timepiece on his wrist unexpectedly brought back a flood of memories. It had been a gift from his mam on his twenty-first birthday two years ago, a family heirloom passed down from her father. He pinched his nose and blinked rapidly, a silent ache in his heart as visions of his special birthday celebration came to mind. His mam had even arranged for a professional photographer to mark his passage into adulthood. What would his mam think if she could see him now?

With a resigned sigh, Bryn abandoned his efforts at the embassy for the day. With Scaff's scathing words ringing in his ears, he even briefly considered tossing Gryff Morgan's passport into the nearest bin, but he couldn't risk a British passport falling into the wrong hands. With a weary groan, he set off back in the direction he had come, the prospect of a cold drink and a plate of spicy *empañadas* with Rosa the only thing keeping him going. He could hardly wait to put his sore feet in the courtyard fountain.

Striding along Calle San Martín an hour later, he was so lost in thought that he almost didn't notice the commotion ahead. A stationary police car blocked the road at the junction where he needed to turn left to reach the bookstore, the flashing light still revolving. A uniformed police officer with his cap on the back of his head and a gaucho moustache stood beside it, scowling at onlookers, a heavy-looking rifle slung across his belly.

Bryn stopped dead in his tracks. *What in the name of God?* This had to be trouble for Scaff and Rosa; he just knew it – but he needed to be sure. Fear coiled like a snake in his stomach as he attempted to blend in with the crowd of onlookers. The scene along the street from the corner where he stood was chaotic. The police were everywhere. Three vans blocked the road outside the bookshop, their rear doors wide open. Smashed glass and broken books littered the pavement, not a single window in the bookshop remained intact and the elegant glass door hung off its hinges. With mounting dread, he saw two cops loading long narrow wooden crates into the backs of the vans while other officers toting machine guns stood guard. It was like something out of a movie, but this was all too real. It was clear something terrible had happened to Rosa and Scaff.

'Does anyone know what's going on?' Bryn asked a middle-aged woman in huge sunglasses, who seemed to have a lot to say to the people grouped around her. All eyes turned to him uncomprehendingly.

Bryn cursed under his breath and tried again. *'Sabe… alguien… qué está pasando?'*

'Es una redada policial,' said the woman in sunglasses, with obvious relish.

A police raid? On a bookshop? Bryn's mind spun as he tried to make sense of the crazy idea.

'Dicen que la mujer y el hombre son Uturuncos.'

Bryn's blood ran cold. *Uturuncos!* It was the only word he understood in the entire sentence: The guerrilla resistance! There must be some terrible mistake. Scaff and Rosa weren't guerrillas. Or were they? Suddenly, it all made sense: the secret looks they exchanged, the unexplained 'business'.

Bryn mingled with the group of gawping rubberneckers with his thoughts in turmoil, keeping his head down and straining hard to understand what they were saying. He picked up a few odd words, including *'carga de armas',* which he suspected had something to do with guns. Bryn circled around the back of the crowd, desperate to get a glimpse of Rosa or Scaff, but couldn't get a better view along the road. 'Dear God! Please let them be safe,' he prayed under his breath.

Suddenly, his blood ran cold. All his possessions were still in the cabana, including his passport and reward money! The cops would have found everything by now and would be looking for him, too. They would think he was a revolutionary guerrilla! He knew all too well from Rosa's stories what happened to the enemies of the state. The thought of being shot as a terrorist paralysed him with fear. He had to get as far away as possible, as quickly as possible. But how? He had no money and no passport, and he had no friends in Buenos Aires other than Scaff and Rosa – and who knew what had happened to them?

A line of sweat broke out on his brow. His body shook no matter how hard he tried to stop. The more he clenched his fists and jaw, the more intense the trembling became. To make matters worse, he was drawing attention to himself. The woman in sunglasses and the bystanders around him were staring at him with a mix of concern and alarm.

What should he do? Without any money, he was stranded. All he had were the clothes he was standing up in and his precious watch. He clamped his opposite hand over the watch protectively. He could never sell it – the idea was unthinkable. He'd have to come up with a better plan to get hold of some cash – no question about it.

Slowly, he began to edge away from the crowd to give himself space to think clearly without drawing more attention. He spotted a stone bench in a shady spot across the busy road and casually made his way towards it. From there, he could still keep an eye on what was going on.

He took a deep breath to steady his racing thoughts. He had to come up with a plan and fast. The embassy seemed like a logical choice, but Rosa's warning about informants being everywhere kept echoing in his mind. Could he trust the authorities to keep him safe? He couldn't take that risk.

Back across the road, sunglasses woman was talking animatedly to the moustachioed, gun-toting cop and pointing in his direction. The cop was looking over, the sunlight reflecting off his mirrored shades.

Bryn's stomach clenched as the cop raised his rifle and began to stride in his direction, calling out something he didn't understand. The other cops turned their heads.

It was time to go. He stumbled away from the bench, his legs turning to jelly. Suddenly, there was a loud crack and something zipped past his head like a giant buzzing locust. He had to move fast. Before he knew it, he was running like a gazelle, leaping over low hedges and through flower beds, expecting at any moment the burning thud of the bullet hitting his back and tearing through his flesh.

He was a marked man and he knew it.

EIGHT

S weat crawled down Bryn's spine with every passing truck as he dodged into doorways or crouched behind stinking dumpsters, fearing the screech of tyres at any moment, followed by rough hands throwing him to the ground at gunpoint and spiked manacles biting into his wrists like angry alligators. Terror clamped his heart in its snapping jaws at the prospect of a brutal ride in a Black Maria with a gang of bloodthirsty militiamen.

Stepping warily out of the shadows, Bryn pulled his thin canvas jacket about his shoulders with a shiver, his cold sweat-soaked shirt clinging to his skin. The growling sound from his belly was a painful reminder that he'd not eaten since breakfast, while the soles of his feet burned from the endless friction between his socks and boots with every step he took. As the colour drained from the day and the world slipped into black and white, even familiar landmarks became unrecognisable.

Bryn kept walking, his shoulders hunched, his hands shoved deeply into the pockets of his borrowed denims, as if perpetual motion would help him make sense of the chaos in his head. As the brightly lit shops and raucous bars gave way to windowless warehouses and rusting hangars, he hobbled into the desolate shadows in search of a bolthole for the night. Inside his head, a deeper darkness took hold.

Everything that had happened was his fault; he could see that now. He'd prayed for punishment and his prayer had been answered, but at what cost? Scaff and Rosa were likely dead because of him. Was it fair or just that his friends should pay the ultimate price for his crime? He sank his face into his hands, shocked at the cruelty of the Almighty's indiscriminate retribution for Emlyn's death. He'd lost his mam, his fiancée and his home, but now without his money and his passport, his actual life was in jeopardy. His suffering was absolute, just as he'd prayed for, but why did his friends have to suffer, too? Guilt ate into his soul like acid.

He slumped against the wall of a large warehouse, his strength ebbing away as he slid down the corrugated steel until he was crouched in a gully of stagnant water. Holding his pounding head in his hands, the sound of his laboured breathing echoed in his ears. He remained there for what seemed an eternity until the sound of distant drunken singing gradually penetrated his exhausted mind. Slowly lifting his heavy head, he struggled to get his bearings. The noise sounded like it was coming from a bar. *All those happy people, drinking and dancing without a care in the world. They didn't know how lucky they were.*

The knot of hunger in his guts tightened as his senses strained in the pitch dark, picking up clues to his whereabouts: the rhythmic lap of water, the stink of marine diesel, the salty tang of brine on the breeze. It was the unmistakable signature of the quayside. Somehow, in the pitch dark, he'd found his way back to the port.

He must have been led there by a divine hand. The tension that gripped him melted away and a feeling of weightlessness spread through his soul. The soothing sound of the sea's eternal ebb and flow called to him, and he rose to his feet as if he had awoken from a deep slumber. Drawn irresistibly towards the inviting call of the water, he approached the edge of the seawall and gazed up at the stars, drinking in the cool clean air. Every nerve ending tingled with exhilaration and, suddenly, everything became clear. It all made perfect sense. No one would ever know and no one would miss him.

He dropped his jacket to the ground as his eyelids closed with heavy finality.

A gentle breeze caressed his skin and whispered in his ear. *You promised... you promised...*

The hairs on his arms sprang up.

Emlyn was running towards him along a sunny beach, a bucket of crabs in his hand, his hair tousled and sandy.

A comforting warmth spread through every fibre of Bryn's body. He remembered this lovely day in Tenby. Emlyn must have been four, maybe five. Joyfully, he put his arms out to sweep his adorable brother into his embrace... but he was a mirage of sand.

You promised... you promised... whispered the breeze.

Bryn's arms fell to his sides as he opened his eyes. Stinging tears spilled through his lashes and coursed down his cheeks. He took a pace back from the edge of the sea wall and lowered himself carefully onto the cold concrete, his feet hanging above the restless ocean as his tears fell into the waves.

'Oh, Emlyn!' he sobbed. 'I'm so, so sorry for everything. Please forgive me. Someday I *will* make you proud. I promise.'

Bryn lost all sense of time as he sat in the inky darkness on the sea wall, with only the gently crashing waves for company as he waited for fate to deal him the next card. A distant intrusive sputtering sound reached his ears. The noise grew louder and closer until it was all he could hear. When the noisy scooter drew alongside him, he scrambled to his feet, scarcely able to believe his eyes.

It was a sign from heaven that everything was about to change.

Scaff killed the ignition and kicked out the side stand. 'Where the bloody 'ell 'ave you been?' he demanded. 'I've been worried sick about you! I've been riding around looking for you for hours!' Scaff's eyes were hollow and his face was deeply etched with lines of fatigue.

Bryn threw his powerful arms around Scaff's wiry frame and hugged him fiercely. 'You're alive! Thank God!' A tsunami of relief crashed over him.

'Steady on, mate.' Scaff lowered his voice to an urgent whisper. 'We ain't got time to muck about. We can't be seen together, right? Make yer way to this address.' Scaff shoved a piece of paper into Bryn's hand. 'It's a safe house with a green door. They'll let you in if you knock and say you're El Gecko. They're expecting you. I've got some urgent business to attend to but I'll be there later to explain everything. I promise.'

Bryn nodded as he dried his eyes on his shirt sleeve. 'I'll be there.'

As Scaff rode off in a cloud of two-stroke fumes, Bryn fumbled in his jacket, dazed by the incredible turn of events. Luckily, Rosa's city guide was still there. As he pulled the book from his inner pocket, an envelope fell to the ground. Bryn stared at it for a second, his mouth open with disbelief. *Gryff Morgan's passport! Another sign!*

'Thank you, thank you, thank you, Lord!'

He snatched the envelope and ducked into the shadow of the warehouse. The Almighty had finally thrown him a lifeline. Scaff would know someone who could doctor a passport photo, he'd lay money on it, and he'd be able to leave Argentina and escape the clutches of the murderous authorities who were hunting him down. It was nothing short of a miracle.

It was a second chance at life.

***

Wilting from hunger and exhaustion, Bryn's skin prickled as he approached the safe house above a scruffy tobacconist shop. The boulevard was eerily quiet except for the occasional noise of a car engine in the distance. Tall palm trees cast long ominous shadows on the pavement, adding to his unease. He stood on a dark corner for a while, scanning the street and watching the premises, until he was as sure as he could be that he wasn't being watched. Looking from side to side, he crossed the street to the green door, hidden away in a dark alleyway stinking of rotting garbage. His palms were slick with sweat and his stomach was in knots as he knocked. His pulse raced as the door creaked open.

'Me llamo El Gecko.'

The door opened further and he was pulled inside by a young man with a long gaucho-style moustache and thick wavy hair that reached his collarbones. He smelled of cigar smoke and stale sweat.

Bryn followed him in silence up a narrow, unlit flight of stairs to a high-ceilinged room overlooking the boulevard, furnished with a threadbare sofa and a heavily stained armchair. A thick blue haze hung low in the air and an ashtray overflowed with used butts on a low table, liberally marked with cup rings. A small television flickered in the corner of the room.

Bryn swept his gaze around the shabby room. Scaff was already there – and so was Rosa!

'Thank God!' Bryn strode across the room and took her in his arms. Her hair smelled of cigarettes. 'I thought you were dead, Rosa!'

Rosa's face was ashen. 'We are all in grave danger, Gecko, make no mistake.'

'Where 'ave you been?' A pulse throbbed in Scaff's temple. 'I thought the cops had picked you up. You'd better sit down, mate. We've got a lot of explainin' to do. I'm so sorry you got mixed up in this business. I honestly never meant for that to 'appen.'

Bryn dropped heavily onto the sagging sofa. His hands began to tremble, and stomach acid rose in his throat as hunger and exhaustion finally overwhelmed him. While Rosa spoke, Scaff disappeared down a short passage to a small kitchen.

'For several years,' she began, a tremor in her voice, 'we have been using the bookstore as a front for a safe house for the *Uturuncos*. To begin with, I tried to keep Scaff out of it, this is not his fight—'

'Oh yes, it is, *querida*,' said Scaff, returning to the room and placing a dish of *alfajores* and three small glass cups of coffee on the table. 'If it matters to you, then it matters to me.'

Bryn took a bite of biscuit and a swig of the bitter black liquid and almost threw up. The room spun horribly.

'But it was impossible to keep secret from him,' she continued, clasping and reclasping her hands in her lap. 'The cabana makes a great hiding place for the resistance, as it can't be seen from the street, and it's so overgrown even the neighbours don't know it is there.'

Scaff flopped beside Bryn on the sofa. 'It's been a while since anyone stayed there, so I thought it would be ideal for you till you got on your feet.'

Bryn groaned. That explained all the cloak-and-dagger coming and going through the secret passage.

'The only problem,' Rosa continued, 'was that the *Uturuncos* recently brought the haul of stolen guns from the police station raid I told you about and hid them in the cellar of the cabana. They have to keep them on the move, as *la cana* has many informants. Scaff has been away for three months, so he did not know this.'

Bryn hung his head and covered his face with his hands, desperate to wake up from the nightmare he found himself in. Discovering his friends were guerrilla sympathisers was a sucker punch to the gut, adding to his deep unease. Even in the relative safety of the safe house, he was jittery. Rosa's stories of informants had him constantly on edge.

'I'm sorry, Gecks. I wouldn't 'ave put you on top of a pile of guns if I'd known. But once you were there and you got on so well with Rosa, learnin' the lingo and everythin', we decided to risk it, just for a month.'

Bryn nodded, remembering those halcyon days. 'So, what went wrong?'

'I was stupid,' said Scaff. 'It was all my fault. After the accident on the ship and you saved my life, I decided to jack it in. I'm getting too old for this malarkey and I've got a good sum put by. I decided to retire and spend all my time with Rosa.'

Bryn frowned. 'I don't get it. Why was that stupid? What aren't you telling me?'

Scaff glanced at Rosa. She gave him a nod. 'You have to tell him, Scaff. He's in this now, like it or not.'

Scaff ran a hand through his greasy hair. 'You're not going to like this, Gecks.'

'Just tell me.' Bryn blew his cheeks out. It had been a hellish day and he wanted answers, not riddles. Anyway, what could be worse than a pile of guns?

'I'm the money man.' Scaff rubbed the back of his neck uncomfortably. 'It's me who's funding the resistance. I've been shippin' kilos of cocaine to Liverpool, packed into the frozen beef carcasses. I'm actually a small cog in a big machine but I get a decent cut of the profits.'

Bryn groaned and put his hands over his face again. Not only was Scaff a terrorist, he was a drug smuggler as well!

Scaff drummed his fingers on his knee. 'It all works great till the small cog stops. Then the whole machine stops. My business associates were not impressed when I went to tell them I'd retired.' Scaff's hands trembled as he rubbed his face. 'The 'eavy mob only let me get away alive when I promised to recruit my replacement on the *Buenos Aires Star*. The Ol'

Bill raid on the bookshop was a tip-off from the drug barons, I reckon. A warning to remind me not to mess with 'em.'

'Informants are everywhere.' Rosa's voice quivered. 'Luckily for me, an informant on our side rang and tipped me off about the raid. I've no idea who it was but they saved my life. I escaped through the narrow alley at the back as the cops came in the front. I've never been so terrified in my life.'

Bryn reached out to squeeze her fingers. How could these good people be mixed up with drugs and guns? Life in Argentina was so much more complicated than he'd ever imagined when he first arrived. But now he was on the authorities' hit list and maybe even the drug barons', too, for all he knew.

'How are we going to get out of this mess?' he asked Scaff, beginning to feel faint.

Scaff dragged a khaki canvas backpack from under the sofa, pulled out a thick wad of paper currency and slammed it down on the table with relish. 'With good old American dollars.'

Bryn's eyes widened at the sight of so much money. 'What on earth—?'

'I've been saltin' a bit of cash aside for fifteen years.' Scaff exposed his tar-stained teeth in a shifty grin. 'A sort of retirement fund, if you like. I keep stashes of it in secure locations across the city. Even Rosa don't know where it is, for her own safety. I've got enough for the pair of us to live like royalty for the rest of our lives.'

He shoved the backpack across the table to Bryn. 'An' that little lot is for you.'

Bryn's mouth fell open. 'I… I… I can't take your drug money!'

Scaff shook his head sadly. 'I know it's dirty money, Gecks, but I don't think you have a lot of choice,' he said. 'I got you into this mess and this is the only way I can help you out of it. You saved my life once and now I'm returnin' the favour.'

Bryn slumped back on the sofa and eyed the backpack bulging with cash. There must be thousands of dollars in that bag, and he was penniless and in mortal danger. Scaff was right – he had no choice and should at least show some gratitude for Scaff's generosity. He stuck his hand out. 'Sorry, Scaff, I'm just being stupid.'

Scaff took the proffered hand and shook it. 'So, it's a deal. First thing you'll need is a new identity, Gecks, and that won't come cheap. A fake passport will probably be a few 'undred bucks, at least.'

'I might not need one.' Bryn pulled Gryff's passport from his jacket pocket. 'I've still got this.'

Rosa's eyes widened with disbelief. 'You didn't take it to the embassy?'

'Well, I did – but it was closed.'

Rosa erupted into hoots of laughter, clapping her hands with mirth as Scaff and Bryn swapped bewildered glances. 'That was an amazing stroke of luck, Gecko – amazing!' She wiped the tears from her eyes. 'I think you must have a guardian angel. Let me have a look. We will have to get it fixed for you.'

Bryn handed the passport over and Rosa flipped straight to the photo page. She looked closely at the grainy image of the shaven-headed, stony-faced Gryff.

'Do you know what I'm thinking?' she murmured. 'This could be you, Gecko.'

'You must be joking!' scoffed Bryn. 'I don't look anything like him, not even close!'

'Show me!' Scaff snapped his fingers for the passport. Rosa tossed it over to him.

'I think Rosa may 'ave a point,' said Scaff dubiously. "'E's not much older than you and, if you shaved your head, this could be you. Put on some specs to break it up a bit.' He gave a brief laugh. 'And of course, he is Welsh. The big difference is that he's an obnoxious tosser and you're Mister Nice Guy.'

'Of course!' Bryn exclaimed. 'I completely forgot! You knew him!'

'He owes me money,' said Scaff, sourly. 'In fact, I think he owes a lot of people money in these parts, so you may not want to 'ang around using his identity. I think he was on the run from that crazy Welsh lot in Patagonia, so you might want to avoid them, too.'

'I thought they were just an old wives' tale.' Bryn raised a quizzical brow. 'I think the best thing for me is to head north and leave Argentina completely. I might try my luck in North America.'

'Sounds like a plan,' said Rosa. 'But first, we have to shave off all your hair.'

'Look!' Scaff cried as Rosa stood up to fetch a razor. He pointed at the television set. 'Quick, turn it up!'

Bryn's face filled the screen. It was his passport photograph. A voice-over was commentating in Spanish and the words *Bryn Evans* appeared across the picture.

Bryn blanched. 'What are they saying?'

Rosa translated quickly. 'They say... you are a suspected foreign mercenary resistance fighter. The police want to question you about the raid on the police station where the guns were stolen. They say you are probably working undercover on a construction site, and that you are dangerous and not to be approached.'

They must have found his Spanish lesson notebooks. His mind raced, frantically flipping through phrases he'd practised, trying to anticipate how the police might twist his innocent words.

'Go and get that razor, quick, Rosa,' he said. 'I need to get rid of my hair.'

OCTOBER 1963

SOUTH WALES

The scenic 'Red and White' bus service rumbled along the winding coastal road on its route to Aberavon, carrying Lowri home from visiting her newborn grandsons at the maternity hospital in Swansea. The blustery breeze gusting through the driver's open window brought with it the plaintive cry of seagulls and the tang of salty sea air. Bright sunlight danced on the raindrop-beaded windows of the single-deck coach as it laboured up the impossibly steep hills that offered stunning panoramic views of the rugged coastline. Over Lowri's left shoulder, the navy-blue waters of Swansea Bay, striped with white-capped waves, reminded her the canvas deckchairs on the beach at Tenby where she and Evan used to take their boys crabbing in the rockpools when they were young. Her eyes tingled at the wonderful memory.

As the bus route turned inland, the coach plunged through the steep-sided woodland gullies of Cwm Coedig, an ancient forest on either side of the lanes leading into Aberavon. The centuries-old trees were a riot of fiery crimson and gold as autumn sunshine streamed through the dripping canopy, creating a dazzling display of freshly minted diamonds.

To Lowri's smiling eyes, the day was a masterpiece of nature's beauty – the perfect celebration of the arrival of Shirley and Bryn's twin sons, Huw and Rhys. There was no denying that the familiar weight of the newborn twins cradled in her arms on the maternity ward had brought back bittersweet memories of the beloved twin brothers and sisters who were taken by the white plague, not to mention the three sons she had borne who were no longer in her life. Filled with love for the new arrivals and a deep ache for the ones she had lost, the conflicting emotions were almost too much to bear. But as she looked down into the bright blue eyes of the two perfect black-capped baby boys, not even the absence of the proud father could wipe the smile from Lowri's face that day.

NINE

1965

CHARLESTON, SOUTH CAROLINA

A bright thread of molten copper on the horizon cleaved the charcoal grey of the earth from the indigo of the sky, as tramp freighter *MV Darwin* nosed its way through pungent marshes ripe with the scent of decaying sparling grasses and rotting crustaceans on the approach to Charleston Harbour. Deep below, the ship's engine thrummed quietly while on the forecastle deck, Bryn stood wrapped in a warm muffler against the chill of the night sea air. He took in his first, long-awaited breath of North American air – and it stank.

Leaning on the bow rail, a gentle vibration passed through his hands as he watched the hexagonal outline of Fort Sumter silently slide by to starboard. A shiver ran through his body as the first drifts of land-warmed air reached him and the twinkling lights of the distant seaport beckoned.

It had been four hours since he'd seen a soul, when he'd had a quick coffee with Gustav, the helmsman, to get some caffeine into his blood at the start of the midnight watch. He glanced at his watch – his relief was due any minute. With any luck, he should be able to get a couple of hours of sleep before docking. The noise from a distant small boat engine arrived on the gentle breeze, announcing the pilot's approach. A sharp spasm twisted his gut. He no longer trusted pilots. He panned the bow waves with his signal lamp as men's voices drew near across the water, straining to catch their words.

Someone tapped him on the shoulder. He spun round in terror, heart pounding, as a Swedish-accented voice said: 'Your watch is over, Gryff.'

He headed off to his berth, the metallic tang of fear in his mouth, his hands still trembling. Would he ever be able to stop looking over his shoulder? It was a question that haunted him. The prospect of spending the rest of his life on the run like a hunted animal was unbearable.

It was almost two years since he'd left 'Bryn' behind in Buenos Aires, shedding his former life like a snake sheds its skin, leaving no trace of his original self other than a garbage bag full of thick black curls. The torment of leaving his dearest friends in danger played on his mind constantly but there was no other choice.

That final night in Buenos Aires, plotting his escape using Gryff Morgan's passport, was burned into his memory. Scaff was adamant that traveling by sea would be less risky, as border control at cargo ports was notoriously lax compared to airports. But there were two major issues that threatened to derail the plan. First, he couldn't use his glowing testimonial to secure work on a ship as Gryff; second, there might be extradition orders or arrest warrants for Gryff's crimes, and Bryn could end up being held responsible. The thought of it was enough to make Scaff's face blanch. Even he had been afraid of the vicious Gryff. But Bryn was all out of options. He had to travel as Gryff and take the risk, and he'd have to alter his testimonial to match his false ID.

Alone in the darkness of his berth on the approach to Charleston harbour, Bryn grimaced with shame as he remembered how irritated he'd been at Rosa's laughter that night when she'd examined the handwritten document. He'd give anything for her company and wise counsel now. He dreaded to think what had become of her and Scaff after he'd left, and he had no way of finding out.

'Seriously, Gecko,' she'd said, 'I think you have a guardian angel.'

He would have sworn that the exact opposite was true at that moment. 'What makes you say that?' he'd snapped, tension getting the better of him.

'Take a look,' she'd said, returning the document to him. 'Don't you see? The captain doesn't mention your name in the letter, only on the envelope.'

'Don't be daft!' he'd replied scornfully. But as he'd examined the elegant penmanship, he had to admit that Rosa was right. It was an incredible stroke of luck. Rosa had also been right that without his hair, he would pass as Gryff Morgan, but his biggest test was yet to come.

North America and safety were in spitting distance, but he had to get through border control first.

Clearing customs without declaring the vast sum of money he was carrying was a risky undertaking, but Bryn had a plan. He would hide in plain sight, posing as a casual day tripper, taking only the canvas backpack of dollars. Timing would be crucial.

The air was thick with the aroma of coffee beans as the ship's cargo from Venezuela was offloaded onto the bustling dock. Amid a cacophony of groaning winches, rattling chains and clanging derricks, Bryn shouldered the well-travelled backpack, feeling the familiar weight settle against his shoulders. As he made his way down the gangplank of the *MV Darwin* for the final time, he was so focused on his plan that he barely registered the familiar seaport clamour.

The heat of the blazing sun that reflected from the concrete jetty hit him like he'd opened an oven door. He paused to catch his breath and take in his surroundings. Charleston seaport had a distinctly military appearance he hadn't expected. In the distance, imposing grey warships were moored at remote jetties and every building, from the sheds to the warehouses, was painted in a uniform military-style grey. Uncertainty wormed its way into his confidence. Maybe this wouldn't be such a cakewalk after all.

The narrow strip of shade cast by the *Darwin* gave Bryn a haven to bide his time, waiting for the right moment to make his move. Twenty minutes passed before Bryn saw what he was waiting for – a group of about ten swarthy sailors heading across the wharf towards the grey single-storey US customs and border protection shed.

He took a deep breath to steady his nerves and headed after them, adopting a confident swagger. Slotting in behind the pack, he listened to their lively banter about the bars they would be visiting and the *chicas* they would be screwing. Behind his sunglasses, his eyes darted from side to side, scanning for trouble as he crossed the open expanse of concrete, convinced that the passport in the back pocket of his denim jeans was a radioactive beacon, emitting an ominous glow that would instantly give the game away.

Despite his weathered complexion from two years at sea, and his freshly shaved head emulating Gryff's stubbly look, his heart raced and his palms were slick with sweat as he followed the gang of Venezuelans into the chilly air-conditioned customs shed. Goosebumps sprang up on his arms as he removed his sunglasses to let his eyes adjust to the darkness. Standing behind a low counter were two portly middle-aged customs officers, their shirt sleeves emblazoned with insignia. Both men bore sidearms in holsters on their belts.

Ahead of him, the Venezuelans heaped their bags on the countertop and rummaged noisily for their travel papers, creating just the sort of distraction he'd been banking on. Hanging back from the crowd, Bryn caught the eye of one of the border officers and waved his distinctive British passport over the heads of the chaotic group. If Scaff was right about British passports, it was the golden ticket to freedom. The officer beckoned him forward through the melee.

'I'm just going ashore for the day,' Bryn called above the din, swinging his shoulder around to show the officer that all he had was a backpack. 'Sightseeing.'

Reaching for the passport from Bryn's outstretched grasp, the officer flipped it open to a new page. Without even the slightest of glances at the photo, he thumped down the border stamp. 'Welcome to America,' he said on autopilot, before handing back the passport and turning his full attention to the boisterous group before him.

It had gone even better than Bryn had dared hope. The distraction had worked like a dream and now he was just yards from safety. If there had been an extradition order for Gryff, the border guard certainly hadn't checked. Despite the air-con, sweat poured down his spine as he strolled casually out of the opposite door.

Euphoria surged through his veins as his feet took their first official steps on US soil under an ultra-blue sky, but he didn't dare show it. Summoning every ounce of restraint he possessed, Bryn sauntered away from the seaport as if he didn't have a care in the world. Scaff and Rosa's plan had worked perfectly. If only he could write to tell them. A chasm of loneliness opened inside him. He'd made it to North America alive – but he had no life.

Bryn's shadow had almost disappeared by the time his adrenaline wore off. The top of his shaven head was red-hot in the blistering sun as the relentless heat beat down on him like a blacksmith's hammer. Beads of sweat formed on his forehead and ran down his face in rivulets. He desperately needed to find some shade and be quick about it, before the scorching sun took its toll. He looked about for a tree or a doorway, and took in his shabby surroundings: a foul-smelling municipal dump to his left and an old run-down cigar factory to his right. Even the automobiles rumbling by were rusty and old. His heart sank. The US was nothing like he had imagined. He'd been so focused on getting there, but what now? He had no plan and no place to go. There wasn't a scrap of shade to be found anywhere in the industrial wasteland, so he pressed on, ignoring the first flutters of panic in his empty belly.

The decaying commercial surroundings gradually gave way to dilapidated white clapboard houses. Struggling to put one foot in front of the other, Bryn could barely discern the blurry figures of people sitting on their stoops and verandas, fanning themselves in the stifling shade. Each blink to clear the sweat from his eyes only made the world seem more distorted. Despite the thick soles of his heavy leather work boots, the heat emanating from the concrete sidewalk scorched Bryn's feet and he staggered as the solid ground undulated with every laborious step. Gasping in the hot oppressive air, he struggled to fill his lungs, his shirt saturated with sweat. Leaning against a painted white stone wall, he hung his head and panted as waves of nausea washed over him. It was becoming painfully clear that he wasn't cut out for the punishing heat and humidity of Charleston at midday. He desperately needed shade and water, and he needed it fast. He just had to reach those houses—

Before Bryn could take another step, the sky came crashing down on him and, in an instant the world turned upside down. He pitched forward against the wall, crumpling onto the red-hot sidewalk. Within moments, strong hands under his armpits hauled him to his feet.

'My bag... I need my bag,' he mumbled, despite his confusion.

Surrendering completely to the mercy of his unknown guide, Bryn found himself being half-led, half-dragged to a cool place where the blazing whiteout in his brain was replaced with soothing shade. The relief was instant and merciful as he was lowered into a soft seat. A cool vessel was presented to his lips and he drank, gratefully.

'Slow down there, my friend,' drawled an earthy male voice. 'Take it easy, now.'

Gryff squinted dizzily about himself, trying to make out his surroundings. The faint waft of incense and candle wax, and the unmistakeable musty aroma of old books told him all he needed to know.

'Welcome to the Maurice Emmanuel African Methodist Episcopal Church, my friend,' said the same warm voice. 'You just had yourself a real close shave out there in the noon-day sun.' A cool hand covered his forehead. 'Lucky I found you when I did, Son. Now you jus' sit here quiet, and I'll get a cloth and a basin of cool water. You're burnin' up.'

The man's receding footsteps echoed as he left.

Bryn slumped forward, elbows on knees, and pressed the heels of his hands into his eye sockets as he marshalled his conflicting thoughts. He'd not set foot inside a church since the day of Emlyn and Tad's funeral, and he'd vowed he never would again. How could he ever again believe in an unmerciful God? But now it seemed the Lord had found him and saved him. It had to mean something. Opening his eyes, his unfocused gaze lit on a beam of sunlight filtering through a stained-glass window.

Inside his head, an insistent voice chanted a litany of Bryn Evans' failings:

Bryn Evans killed his brother.

Bryn Evans abandoned the women who loved him.

Bryn Evans was alone, thousands of miles from home.

Bryn Evans was on the run from a murderous military regime – which would never stop looking for him.

Faced with the harsh truths he'd been running from, everything became clear. 'Bryn Evans' had made a mess of his life and had reached the end of the road – and maybe that was a good thing. It was a sobering moment.

A shadow fell across him. He looked up, startled; he hadn't noticed the footsteps returning.

'What shall I call you, Son?' The bald-headed African-American reverend standing before him, holding a basin of water, wore a flowing purple floor-length tunic.

'Gryff', he replied without hesitation. 'You can call me Gryff Morgan.'

'Pleased to meet you, Gryff. I'm the Reverend Sylvester.' He placed a comforting hand on Gryff's shoulder. 'Rejoice with me, for I have found my lost sheep.'

TEN

Gryff hadn't realised how much he'd missed the finer things in life after two years working his way north along the South American coastal cargo routes through the vibrant, hazardous ports of São Paulo, Salvador, Recife, Georgetown, Caracas and Maracaibo. Little things such as clean sheets, home-cooked food and the company of people who didn't threaten to knife each other over dinner.

Although his room in Grace Freeman's house on Meeting Street overlooked the noisy six-lane highway, that didn't bother him one jot because the cotton bedsheets were crisp and fresh, and there was clean running water and reliable electricity. The simple room on the first floor was cheerfully furnished with a beautiful hand-stitched patchwork quilt on the single bed and colourful rag rugs adorning the black deeply glossy varnished floorboards. White cotton drapes floated at the two large sash windows, catching the slight sea breeze. On the nightstand, an American Standard Version of the Bible rested on a quilted placemat, matching the beautiful hand-sewn quilt on the bed.

Gryff found himself warming to Grace's serene unquestioning manner over dinner on the first night in his new digs. She was a widow and a lay preacher supporting the Reverend Sylvester's ministry, and she reminded him greatly of his mother. Breakfast and dinner were included in the room rate, and his mouth was already watering at the incredible aromas drifting from Grace's kitchen. He would need to brush up on his table manners if he was going to dine in her company regularly.

'It's gonna be a real treat to have a young man round the house once more.' Grace ladled a generous helping of traditional west African okra stew on his plate. 'My boy, Gus, is in the military. He's 'bout the same age as you. He's fighting communism in Vietnam right now.'

Gryff remained silent. He'd never heard of Vietnam but was afraid to show his ignorance. He hoped for Grace's sake that Gus's side was winning. Instead, he nodded, his mouth full of the fantastic flavours of Grace's childhood.

'Will you be worshipping with us in the mornin'?' She reached across the table to lay her birdlike hand on his huge coarse one.

Gryff stopped chewing, unexpectedly moved by the tenderness of her touch. It was a question that had been on his mind since he'd arrived at Grace's house. The congregation was Methodist, just like his church back home in Aberavon, where he'd been a choirboy as a child. But he wasn't sure he was ready yet. And besides, his would be the only white face. He didn't want to presume he'd be welcome, but on the other hand, he didn't want to offend the people who had taken him in and shown him such kindness. It was hard to know what to do for the best.

'Don't you worry, Son,' Grace said when he mentioned his concerns. 'That won't matter none. We live by our motto, "God Our Father, Christ Our Redeemer, Holy Spirit Our Comforter, Humankind Our Family." Everyone is welcome, regardless of where they come from.'

***

The following morning, Gryff made his way to the back of the church and took a seat in one of the pews, hoping to remain unnoticed. As the congregation filed past, spruced up in their colourful Sunday best, each member took time to say a few quiet words of welcome. Grace was right. His white face didn't matter one jot. To the churchgoing African-American folk of the East Side, he was just another lost sheep who had found his way home. Their generosity of spirit humbled him profoundly.

He cast his eyes around the Episcopal church for the first time since the Reverend Sylvester had saved him from sunstroke, looking forward to discovering whether the African-American Methodist service would be very different to the Methodist services in Aberavon's tiny village church. The Episcopal church building was nothing like any church he'd ever seen in South Wales, with magnificent soaring marble columns and an elegant sweeping balcony on three sides. It was practically a cathedral.

A hush fell over the congregation as the Reverend Sylvester entered the high pulpit, cloaked in dignity.

His sonorous voice boomed like a heavy church bell, reverberating into every corner of God's house. Gryff was amazed to hear the congregation joining in.

'We thank you, Lord, for those who are here with us today,' the Reverend Sylvester began. 'May we love one another. May we talk about love around our breakfast tables and our dinner tables.'

'Oh yeah,' voices called out from the pews with encouraging applause.

'Because Jesus loved us.'

'Jesus loved us!' echoed voices from the pews to more applause.

Gryff looked about with amazement. The church was filled to the brim with people paying rapt attention to the service. The sound of clapping and hollering filled the air as Reverend Sylvester delivered his message of love, and Gryff found himself inspired by the energy lifting the roof off the church. Despite the oppressive heat, the men in the congregation were dressed in their finest suits and ties, while the women wore traditional west African garments or brightly coloured dresses and adorned themselves with large, floppy-brimmed hats. From where he sat, the sea of pale palm fans being fluttered to keep the congregation cool resembled a cloud of white butterflies descending upon a vibrant and colourful wildflower meadow.

Gryff couldn't resist the urge to get to his feet when the church organ struck its opening chords. Energised by the lively music, he grabbed a song sheet from the pew to join in. The choir in the gallery burst into song and, with each joyous note, Gryff's spirits soared. The congregation's jubilant clapping and cheering only added to the infectious energy. He'd never heard a hymn like it. Compared to the stuffy hymns of his youth, it was a breath of fresh air. The entire congregation was on its feet, rocking and rolling energetically, and Gryff found it impossible to resist dancing along with them. He couldn't remember the last time he enjoyed himself so much. It felt like a new beginning.

After the service, Gryff walked with Grace along Meeting Street to the boarding house and thanked her for inviting him along.

'Don't thank me, young man, thank God. It was him who brought you to our door.' She flashed her perfect teeth in a wide sincere smile. 'How long you planning to stay?'

'As long as you'll have me,' he replied, returning her smile. 'Everyone has been so welcoming. But I'll need to find a job soon and get some new clothes.'

Gryff had been overwhelmed with gratitude when he'd counted the dollars in the backpack – but also regret. Scaff had given him far more money than he'd ever imagined, and he hadn't appreciated his friend's generosity at the time. Now he'd never be able to thank him. But the money had to last a lifetime. Getting a job would help him put down some roots and help him be part of a community again after so long at sea.

'I suggest a strong young man like you would have no trouble gittin' a job working on that new bridge they're building over the Cooper River,' said Grace. 'Why don't you go on by there tomorrow?'

He nodded. 'I think I'll do just that.'

***

The construction depot for the new three-lane-highway cantilevered bridge linking Charleston's East Side neighbourhood with Mount Pleasant was awe-inspiring. Inhabiting a vast shoreline compound, it was packed with gigantic construction machinery that left Gryff open-mouthed with amazement. Having seen some immense industrial cranes at ports in his journey along the east coast of South America, he thought he'd seen everything, but the machinery in this compound dwarfed anything he could ever have dreamed of. The chunky wheels on some of the heavy-load trucks were taller than a man. It was impressive kit and he'd love to get his hands on it.

Gryff could see the bridge already taking shape across the river like an enormous stegosaurus bestriding the land. The upright piers were already in place all the way across to Mount Pleasant via a small midstream island, and the cantilevered freeway sections reached almost halfway. Donning a hard hat and steel-toecap boots handed to him at the security gate, Gryff made his way to the foreman's shack, not knowing what to expect. The sign on the door told him he was in the right place: *Foreman – Al Moreno*.

Al Moreno was sprawled in a chair behind a desk littered with technical charts and plans, plastic coffee cup in hand and heavily booted feet resting on a low filing cabinet. The thick folds of flesh on the foreman's face were unshaven and grimy with sweat and sand. He assessed Gryff's appearance in one sweeping glance.

'Br— Gryff Morgan,' Gryff held out his hand and silently cursed himself for nearly giving the game away. Moreno's heavy jowls sagged into a disdainful sneer until Gryff let his unshaken hand drop to his side.

'Have you been here lookin' for work before, Son?' Moreno's eyes narrowed mistrustfully.

'No, sir,' Gryff replied, alert for signs of trouble. 'I've just arrived in Charleston, sir.'

Moreno grunted. 'You sure look familiar, somehow – and I never forget a face. Your name sure rings a bell too, for some reason.'

Gryff stiffened, and he studied his boots as he groped for something innocuous to say. After a flat silence, Moreno grunted and shrugged dismissively. 'So, what sort of experience and skills you got?'

Faking more confidence than he felt, Gryff explained his experience working with heavy machinery on tramp freighters for the past two years. He took a sheaf of papers from his bag – references in the name of Gryff Morgan that he'd diligently collected from every ship he'd worked on the coastal route and the testimonial from Captain Cruikshank. Moreno flicked through them as Gryff talked.

'We get a lot of you boat people around here.' He eyed Gryff with unconcealed suspicion. 'Most don't last long and cause a lot of trouble. So, you tell me, what makes you different from all them others?'

Gryff hesitated. This job was a perfect fit for his skills and he wouldn't have to work underground, which was a big plus. But he didn't like talking about his former life, not wanting to merge his old Bryn identity with the new Gryff persona he was developing. The silence hung in the air like a bad smell.

Gryff took a deep breath and exhaled slowly. 'I used to be a colliery mechanic at a coal mine in South Wales,' he said. 'I have a lot of experience repairing and maintaining specialist equipment used in shifting rock in difficult conditions.'

Moreno's sour expression softened as he quizzed Gryff about his mining mechanic apprenticeship. 'Okay, I'll take you on as a fitter,' he growled. 'Three dollars seventy-five an hour. Sign on at the office over the way. You'll have to join the union, too.'

'That's no problem.' Gryff turned to leave. 'You won't regret it.'

The sun was directly overhead by the time Gryff finished signing on at the site office. His belly rumbled as he walked out of the compound into Johnson Street, where he spotted a diner across the highway. Dodging the lunchtime traffic, he hop-skipped across the busy road and dived into the cool dark interior of the Cabana Seafood and Oyster Bar. His mouth watered at the delicious smell of fried fish as he stood and let his eyes adjust to the low light.

The diner was U-shaped, around a central bar with a well-stocked rack of optics and a mirrored shelf laden with dozens of brands of American whisky. One side of the diner had a shuffleboard table, and a low platform equipped with a microphone and piano; the other was dedicated to eating and drinking.

He slipped into a leatherette booth and picked up the laminated menu, glancing around the dining room. There were about a dozen other tables occupied, he guessed, and only one overworked teenaged girl, her dark chestnut hair tied back in a swinging ponytail, waiting table. She flitted about busily with a glass coffee pot but he couldn't catch her eye.

Gryff resigned himself to a long wait and studied the menu. Most of the dishes had names he'd never heard of. He recognised gumbo, a delicious soup of okra, tomatoes and onion, which Grace had prepared for dinner one evening, but what on earth was Hoppin' John? Or purloo?

'Howdy, stranger. What can I get you?' The young waitress had materialised at his table as silently as smoke, catching him completely off guard.

He scanned the menu, searching for something recognisable to order quickly.

'Um… er, I—'

'How about some she-crab soup to start, thirty-five cents for a cup or sixty-five cents for a bowl, then I would recommend the Hoppin' John – it's my favourite,' the girl suggested in a singsong lilt.

He looked up from the menu to put a face to the lovely melodic voice and found himself looking directly into the steady gaze of her violet eyes, her long lashes covered in thick mascara.

MY NAME IS GWENNA declared the plastic name badge pinned to her breast.

Her skin was as pale and flawless as porcelain, her lips irresistibly full, with a dark rosy sheen, and her dark chestnut hair was glossy, with loose strands framing her perfectly oval face. She was the image of Shirley. His mouth opened but words simply wouldn't form. Ridiculously, he scanned her face for signs of recognition but, of course, there were none. The girl looked on with an amused smile as he struggled to compose himself.

'Um, Gwenna, er, yes… what a lovely name… sounds a bit Welsh, actually. Um, yes, I'll have whatever you just said,' he stammered, still wrestling with the illogical half of his brain that expected her to know him.

She giggled sweetly. 'You're not from round here, I can

tell. That Hoppin' John? It's just rice and beans. You'll love it.' She flitted away as noiselessly as she had arrived, without writing anything down. 'I'll bring you a soda,' she called out as she disappeared into the kitchen.

Gryff gazed after her, the heat in his face gradually subsiding. She may have looked like Shirley, but that was where the resemblance ended. The fluidity of her movements and the sound of her voice were uniquely her own. Her lilting southern accent – the way she pronounced *rah-yes ay-end be-yans* – was music to his ears. He couldn't wait for her to come back and talk some more.

His pulse quickened when Gwenna returned with his food, but disappointingly, she was too busy to stay and keep him company. 'There you go, darlin'.' She deposited the soup bowl on the table, the contents slopping over the side. 'I'd love to stay and chat, but I gotta get a lick on, or my boss'll pitch a fit.'

The creamy crab soup, tinted orange with crab roe, was divine, and Gryff mopped the bowl clean with a hunk of yellow cornbread. The Hoppin' John was even better: cowpeas and bacon simmered in a pot, with rice absorbing all the lovely flavours. He sat back replete, finishing off the last of the soda. It was quite possibly the most delicious meal he'd ever eaten.

Gryff's eyes followed Gwenna's retreating figure as she disappeared into the kitchen for the umpteenth time, laden with a tray piled with dirty dishes. There was something irresistible about that girl and he'd like to get to know her better. Rising to leave, he put three one-dollar bills on the table, tucked under the sugar jug.

He glanced over his shoulder one last time as he reached

the door and caught Gwenna's eye as she emerged from the kitchen with her empty tray.

'Come again soon, stranger,' she called out to him with a dazzling smile.

Something melted in his belly and he crossed the freeway with a newfound bounce in his step. Maybe he could ask her to show him around sometime?

ELEVEN

Gryff soon discovered that bridge building in the blazing sunshine was even more brutal than hacking coal from deep underground seams as he battled to stay hydrated and keep his fair, Celtic skin from burning. His brush with sunstroke was a lesson he wouldn't forget in a hurry. His Guatemalan co-workers, with their mahogany tribally scarred skins as tough as animal hides, could work bare-chested all day without breaking a sweat. They were incredible.

Already considerably brawnier than when he left Aberavon, the heavy work on the Silas N. Pearman site made the muscles in Gryff's legs, arms and shoulders fill out even further, giving him a powerfully athletic build. His problem was that he'd come ashore with only his rucksack and the clothes he'd been standing in. He'd been getting by with old shirts and faded denims that Grace had found for him in Gus's wardrobe. That was all very well for working in, but not respectable enough for church. It was time to invest in some new clothes for his new physique.

Charleston's fashionable quarter was buzzing with life on Saturday afternoon when Gryff and Grace walked a couple of blocks in the bright sunshine along King Street to the Kress department store, with its imposing art deco façade. Grace had kindly offered to help him pick out some new clothes when he'd confessed he didn't know where to begin. But as they wandered together around the menswear department, Gryff couldn't help noticing the disdainful looks and muttered comments of the exclusively white clientele. Even as he peeled off a week's wages in dollar bills for his purchases at the checkout, he was outraged at the contemptuous look the young white cashier gave Grace.

'Now, look here—' he began, bristling with indignation.

Grace's gloved hand on his forearm stopped him in his tracks.

'Pay no heed, Son,' she said with composure. 'It's the law now – I got the right to shop here, whether they like it or not.'

Gryff grabbed his shopping bags angrily and shot a dirty look at the cashier as he stormed away, but held his tongue out of respect for Grace's wishes. Her poise and dignity made a profound impression on him. Once she'd finished helping him with the remainder of his purchases, he invited her to afternoon tea in the elegant antebellum tearoom on the top floor of the department store – his treat.

The genteel clink of china and the low buzz of discreet conversations greeted them as they took their seats among the potted palm fronds that added to the old-world charm. The ambience brought back memories for Gryff, reminding him of the time his mam took him for tea at Howells department store in Cardiff when he was a small boy – probably the last time he'd been in a fancy tearoom, come to think of it. The memory of that special day – his ninth birthday – was so fresh and vivid that he could hear his mam's voice as clearly as if she were sitting next to him. What was she doing at that very moment? The tightness in his throat made it hard to breath as he pushed the thought away abruptly.

Grace ordered for them both. The Earl Grey tea arrived in a graceful teapot with delicate china cups and there was moist hummingbird cake on matching china plates. Gryff took a tentative forkful of the tropical fruit gateau.

'My word, Grace, this is delicious!' He licked cream cheese frosting from his lips. 'I hope it wasn't made from real hummingbirds, though.'

Grace's laugh was breezy and relaxed as she assured him it wasn't. He couldn't get over her lack of rancour about the earlier incident, still playing on his mind.

'I'm so embarrassed I had no idea about segregation before I came here,' Gryff admitted to Grace when they had finished their tea. 'It's just so un-Christian. It doesn't make sense.'

Grace set her cake fork down on the side of her empty plate. 'The new civil rights law has made some difference but there's still a long way to go. At least it's no longer illegal for me to sit here with you, and enjoy tea and cake now.'

Gryff shook his head with disbelief. How was it possible that having tea here with a friend whose face was black could have been a crime less than a year ago? The strength of this tiny birdlike lady's determination to enjoy her hard-won rights humbled him.

He regarded Grace with even greater respect.

***

The diner was already half-full later that evening when Gryff settled himself in his usual booth and scanned the menu, more for something to do with his hands than reading it. His mind was elsewhere, rehearsing his invitation to Gwenna for a walk along the promenade after her shift finished that evening. He'd thought of little else all day.

'Well, look at you in your new finery!' Gwenna's broad smile lit up her face as she came to take his order. 'And you look so much more handsome now you've grown your hair. You should keep it like that.' Her gently teasing laughter filled his ears. 'You'll have all the gals chasing you now, so watch out!'

Gryff's hair had grown back as glossily thick and curly as before, and his new lightweight, slim-fit trousers and pale-yellow short-sleeved polo shirt clung to his powerful physique. He smiled inwardly, secretly pleased with Gwenna's complimentary words. He'd begun to enjoy her company at the diner in the three months since arriving in Charleston. Sometimes, on a Tuesday if he was lucky and it was not too busy, she'd sit with him in the booth, graciously allowing herself to be regaled by his comically exaggerated exploits at sea. She was a great listener and laughed in all the right places. The night she'd taught him to play shuffleboard, they'd laughed so much that it hurt.

'Are you headin' straight home this evening?' Gwenna

asked before he'd had a chance to think of a suitably modest reply.

'Um... no. Why d'you ask?'

She fiddled nervously with her apron. 'I'm playin' here tonight after my shift. It's my first live gig. I brought my guitar in, especially, and Rudy is payin' me an extra five dollars.' Her beseeching eyes scanned his face. 'I was hopin' you'd stay and watch. I could do with all the support I can get.'

Gryff sat back in his booth with astonishment, his rehearsed invitation forgotten. Gwenna performing in the diner? She'd never mentioned she could play guitar. Come to think of it, she'd not told him very much about herself at all. How could he not have thought to ask?

'I would be delighted, Gwenna.' He gave her an encouraging smile. 'I had no idea you played the guitar – you never said.'

Gwenna caught hold of her ponytail and twisted it around her fingers, the colour fading from her face. 'Well, my mamma – God rest her soul – used to tell me I came outta her belly singin'.' Her smile was thin and distant. 'I taught myself to play guitar by the time I was twelve.'

Gryff caught the faintest tremble in her voice. There was something she wasn't telling him but that was for another day. Besides, there was a lot he wasn't telling her.

'That's incredible,' said Gryff, lightening the moment. 'I love singing, too. In fact, I've just started singing in the choir at the African Methodist Church.'

She chuckled sweetly. 'I know ya have. Folks on the East Side cain't talk about nothin' else. You're the famous white gospel singer!'

Heat rose in his face and he gave an embarrassed smile.

'Well, I don't know about that,' he said. 'Perhaps we could do a duet?'

'Maybe another time, darlin', I don't wanna be upstaged on my first night!'

'Okay, if you insist. But would you mind if I walked you home after? It'll be pretty late by the time you finish.'

'That would be mighty kind of you. I surely do appreciate that.'

Gwenna was almost unrecognisable as she perched on a bar stool behind the microphone on the low stage, with her dark hair loose around her shoulders, wearing a slim-fitting checked blouse with pearl buttons, and pale-blue denims tucked into tooled-leather cowboy boots. She was breathtaking and he couldn't help but stare. A single spotlight picked out her delicate features. How slender and vulnerable she looked! The urge to protect her was so intense it left him gasping.

At that moment, it hit him with the force of a wrecking ball. He was completely and utterly in love with Gwenna.

A sudden hush fell over the diner as Gwenna strummed her first few chords and the crowd settled down for the show. As she sang, her warm, melodic voice filled the room with such passion that Gryff could almost believe she was the heartbroken wife, abandoned by her no-good husband, leaving her penniless with a bunch of kids.

She was mesmerising.

As the night went on, Gwenna's confidence grew and so did the applause. When her final note faded away, the diner erupted in a storm of whoops, cheers and whistles; some folks even stood on chairs to applaud. Gryff was blown away.

Beads of sweat ran down Gwenna's face and she was breathing hard as she came over to Gryff clutching her guitar, a huge smile on her face. 'How was I?' she gasped, taking a big gulp of Gryff's soda.

'You were amazing, Gwenna!' He took hold of her shoulders and kissed her warmly on the cheek. 'You could be a professional singer with talent like that.'

Gwenna's proud smile lit the whole room. 'That sure is my dream, one day,' she said breathlessly. 'Let me just get myself a soda and then I need to be gittin' home. My landlady locks the door after ten thirty, so I cain't be late.'

Gryff returned to his booth to wait for Gwenna, mulling over what he'd learned about her that day. There was a lot more to Gwenna than he'd given her credit for. Sure, he'd thought of her as funny, charming and great company, but now he realised that she meant so much more to him than that. If he was honest with himself, he'd probably been in denial about his feelings for her from the moment he met her. Hopefully, she'd open up more about herself as he walked her home.

'Come with me out the side door, Gryff,' she called to him from the kitchen. 'Staff ain't supposed to use the customer entrance.'

He followed her as she pushed open the fire escape and stepped out into an unlit service alley, her guitar slung on a strap across her back. A pale moon shone weakly through broken clouds, barely illuminating the industrial garbage bins on either side of the doorway.

Gryff's pulse raced when Gwenna linked her arm through his as they carefully picked their way along the pitch-black alley towards the main street lights, Gwenna chatting excitedly about her performance. She smelled of cherry blossom and perspiration, and the urge to kiss her was almost impossible to resist.

Ahead of them, a bulky, hooded silhouette in a long cape-like coat appeared at the end of the passage, blocking the way. Gryff stopped dead in his tracks, jerking Gwenna to a sudden halt by her arm. His heart pounded as he tried to figure out what was happening. 'What's up?' she asked, seemingly oblivious to the danger lurking ahead.

'Hey, Morgan!' growled the grim reaper lookalike. 'I heard you were back in town.'

The hairs on the back of Gryff's neck prickled as he recognised the South American accent. His throat tightened and he could barely breathe as rising panic gripped him.

Backing away quickly, he dragged Gwenna with him, scanning the alley for escape routes. 'What's going on?' she yelped.

As he looked over his shoulder, a second shadowy figure stepped out from the garbage bins behind them, blocking their retreat. They were trapped.

'Who are you and what do you want?' Gryff wrapped his arm around Gwenna and pulled her tight against his body, hoping she hadn't noticed the tremor in his voice.

The grim reaper figure took a pace forward, his hands hidden among the folds of his coat. 'You owe me *mucho dinero, gringo* – and I'm gonna make you pay.'

Gryff frowned. They wanted money from him? That didn't make any sense. What about the extradition? Could these man-hunting mercenaries really be bought off? He hesitated as he grappled with the confusing demand, unsure of what to do next. But then it came to him in a flash of realisation. They were looking for the *real* Gryff Morgan! His blood ran cold. How badly had Gryff cheated these men? Enough for them to kill him? Or could he try to settle the debt to protect Gwenna and escape with their lives? An icy tremor ran through him. Extradition was the soft option compared to this nightmare situation.

Desperately thinking on his feet, Gryff struggled to come up with a plan but something just didn't add up. If the real Gryff had double-crossed these criminals, surely they would realise they'd got the wrong man if they could just get a good look at him? He needed to get into better light somehow. His and Gwenna's lives depended on it. He had to stall for time.

'*Lo siento, amigo*,' Gryff faked a relaxed and friendly tone. 'I'm sorry, but you seem to have the wrong man.' He pulled Gwenna closer to his chest and began to back away with her. She whimpered quietly but had the good sense to say nothing. The sound of heavy footfall to the rear and the reek of stale whisky told Gryff the second villain was right behind them.

'Don't you move a muscle, *gringo*.' The air crackled with tension as the menacing figure advanced towards them, his hood casting a deep shadow over his entire face. 'You're a thieving *bastardo*, Gryff Morgan, and you're gonna pay big time for keeping me waiting for my money. Nobody messes with *El Cabrón* and gets away with it.'

The threat in his words tore through Gryff like a chainsaw. Time was not on his side. 'Look at me!' he yelled. 'Can't you see I'm not the man you're looking for? As God is my witness, I don't owe you anything.'

A gobbet of phlegm hit the ground with a stomach-churning splat. 'Don't gimme that God shit!' The figure raised both arms like a sinister archangel of vengeance and pushed back his hood with chilling deliberation. A shudder ran down Gryff's spine. Gwenna gasped and buried her face in Gryff's shoulder.

The thin moonlight cast an eerie glow on a completely shaven head and an empty eye socket with a thick vertical scar running through it from temple to chin. 'People change the way they look in ten years, asshole. I used to have a left eye ten years ago before you stuck a knife in it and ran off with my money.' He took a pace forward, his face a few inches from Gryff's, swamping him in a stinking fog of rotten teeth, tobacco and whisky. 'Did you think I wouldn't come looking for you, eh? You weren't hard to find, Morgan, you stupid *pendejo*. Everyone on the East Side is talking about you. I can't ever get my eye back, but now that you're mine, you can give me one of yours – and the money you owe me – or the girl gets it.'

Gryff recoiled from the stench, vomit rising in his throat. He swallowed hard, his palms suddenly slippery. So that was how they found him – through his own carelessness. He was a dead man, no question about it, and Gwenna's life was in danger too – and it was all his fault.

'Look, here, take this. It's all I've got on me.' Gryff pulled out a wad of dollars from his pocket. 'There's twenty bucks there, but I can get you more—'

The hoodlum hawked repulsively once more and spat thick slime on Gryff's boots. Gryff's stomach lurched and threatened to empty over his tormentor's feet, but he forced himself to swallow again, gagging on the sour taste in his mouth.

'*Hombre*! You owe me two-thousand dollars and you're gonna pay me in full. But first, I'm gonna teach you and your doll a little lesson you won't forget.'

Gryff heard a click and saw a flash of moonlight on metal. With a piercing shriek, Gwenna was wrenched away from behind. Gryff lunged to one side to avoid the strike, grabbed the thrusting forearm with both hands and brought it down hard across his raised thigh with a sickening crack. As the arm bone snapped, the hoodlum screamed in agony and crashed to the ground, the switchblade clattering to the floor, lost in the dark shadows. Behind him, the second villain was crushing Gwenna against the alley wall, grinding her face into the brickwork with his filthy hand on the back of her head, his face close to her ear as he growled obscenities at her.

Gryff launched himself at Gwenna's attacker with a primal roar of rage and kicked him in the base of the spine with all his might. The thug pitched forward, smashing his head with a resounding crack on the alley wall. He crumpled to the ground, dragging Gwenna down with him, splattering her in his blood. Trapped under his body weight, Gwenna screamed and struggled desperately to free herself.

Gryff grabbed hold of Gwenna's outstretched arm and hauled her from underneath the motionless body. Blood streamed from her deeply grazed cheek and her lip was a pulpy mess. Her legs buckled as she tried to stand and the neck of her guitar was broken.

'Bonnie!' she wailed at the sight of the damaged guitar. 'They broke my Bonnie!'

'Leave it!' shouted Gryff, propping her up with his shoulder under her armpit. 'We've got to run!'

Gwenna clutched the broken guitar across her chest with the other arm. 'I'm not leaving Bonnie,' she screamed. 'I'd rather die!'

As Gwenna staggered forward, the one-eyed thug struggled to his feet with a furious roar.

'Take that, you bastard!' Gwenna landed a hefty kick on his dangling forearm with the toecap of her stiff leather cowboy boot. He crumpled to his knees, bellowing like a mad bull and clutching his loose arm to his chest.

'Come on, Gwenna, leave him!' Gryff grabbed hold of Gwenna as she made to kick the thug again. 'We've got to get out of here.'

Gryff and Gwenna staggered out onto the busy main street, where Gryff tried to flag down a cab – but no taxi driver was ever going to stop for a frantic madman and a woman with a bloodied face. Looking anxiously over his shoulder, a roaring commotion from the alley told Gryff that the enraged thug was coming after them.

'Run, Gwenna, run!' Gryff grabbed Gwenna's hand and dragged her into the road. 'He's coming!'

Horns blared, and tyres screeched as cars swerved to avoid them. They dashed to the opposite side of the road and stumbled away into the crowd, scattering horrified people in their wake. They turned down a dark side street almost immediately, where Gwenna staggered and fell against a building, her left eye nearly closed with the swelling. 'I cain't... I cain't run... anymore,' she gasped, her mouth full of blood.

Gryff bent over to scoop her up but the broken guitar made it impossible. 'You've got to leave the guitar, Gwenna, please!'

Gwenna groaned. 'I'm not leaving Bonnie. I can hide. You go on without me.'

Gryff glanced over his shoulder, expecting to see their assailant at any moment. 'I can't do that, Gwenna, I can't leave you!'

From the road behind them came the deafening blast of a truck's air horn, followed by a long screech of tyres and a sickening thud. Women screamed, men yelled and then there was a deathly silence. Gryff's mind reeled as he processed what had just happened. With a mixture of horror and relief, he realised that their pursuer had been stopped dead in his tracks. He could hardly believe it.

'Come on, Gwenna,' he said gently, supporting her as she clutched her precious guitar. 'I'll help you; just lean on me. We don't have to run any longer.'

Holding Gwenna round the waist, with her arm over his shoulder, the pair hobbled slowly away, leaving a scene of carnage on the highway behind them.

After about half a mile, Gryff stopped and lowered Gwenna onto a wide doorstep. 'How bad is it, Gwenna?' He took her face lightly by the chin to examine her injuries. She looked like she'd been hit by a car. His face flamed with shame; this was all because of him. The skin on Gwenna's cheek was shredded and oozing blood, her eye was closing, and her lip was swollen and purple, but at least she was conscious and responsive.

'Where are we?' she mumbled through her split lip.

Gryff looked around. The road was deserted but seemed familiar, even in the darkness of the night. With a jolt of relief, he realised where he was. Help wasn't far – the African Methodist Church was just a few streets away. With the last of his strength, he scooped her up and headed towards the church. 'Nearly safe, Gwenna, nearly safe.'

Although it was almost ten thirty when Gryff tried the handle on the church's front door, the door swung open smoothly. Grateful beyond belief and staggering with exhaustion, he carried Gwenna inside the peaceful dark sanctuary and lowered her semi-conscious body carefully to the floor. Her cheek had swollen like half a pomegranate. 'Wait here, Gwenna, don't move. I'll get help.'

'Not goin' anywhere,' she groaned bravely.

Gryff stumbled down the nave towards the Reverend Sylvester's private entrance and hammered his fist on the carved wooden door. 'Reverend, are you there? I need help! Please!'

There was a shuffling sound behind the door and, after a few moments, an elderly lady in her nightgown opened it.

'I need to see the Reverend!' he gasped. 'I need help.'

'The Reverend ain't here, Son. He's outta town for a few days,' she replied in a wavering voice. 'Best you come in, though, and I'll see what I can do.'

'It's my friend – she's hurt. I'll go and get her.'

'Well, get on with you. I'll be right here.'

When Gryff returned, carrying the semi-conscious Gwenna, the woman showed him into the Reverend's private apartment in the adjoining rectory and took him to a guest room, where a single bed was covered with a yellow candlewick counterpane and the bedside lamp was already glowing. A large crucifix hung on the wall above the bed.

'Put that poor girl on the bed so I can get a good look at her,' the woman said. 'What should I call her?'

Gwenna groaned as Gryff lowered her gently onto the bed. 'Her name's Gwenna,' he said.

'Well, you can call me Mary. I'm Wesley's mamma. Now let me have a good look at Gwenna and let's see what we can see.'

Gryff's shoulders drooped with exhaustion and relief. 'I'm so grateful to you, Mary, for helping us like this. I've never been so scared in all my life,' he said. 'We were attacked by a couple of thugs and I've no idea where the hospital is.'

'No point going to the hospital anyway, 'less you got yourself some insurance,' said Mary, turning to examine Gwenna.

'Gwenna, can you hear me?' Mary carefully loosened Gwenna's collar and checked her pulse. 'I'm just gonna check you over, my darlin'.' She moved the lamp to get a clearer look at Gwenna's injured bloody face, tutting to herself. 'Lemme know if anything I touch hurts,' she said, gently pressing along Gwenna's arms and legs. Apparently satisfied, she turned to face Bryn. 'S'cuse me, young man, I need to check she ain't got no bodily injuries.' She ushered him from the room, closing the door behind him.

Gryff drifted listlessly into the Reverend's kitchen and filled a glass with cold water. He sat down on a stool, put his elbows on the kitchen table and sank his face into his shaking hands. What had he done to Gwenna? The situation couldn't be much worse and it was all his fault. He'd been a fool for thinking he could ever live a normal life. He should never have let Gwenna get mixed up with him. How could he have been so selfish and stupid?

After a few minutes, Mary came into the kitchen.

'Gwenna ain't gonna need the hospital. She's gonna be okay in a bit, once I get that face cleaned up, give her a few stitches in that lip.' She filled a bowl with water and poured in a handful of salt. 'Looks worse than it is. Won't be winnin' no beauty contests for a few weeks, though.'

'You're going to stitch her lip?'

She patted Gryff kindly on the shoulder with a sad smile. 'Don't you worry none, Son, I've had a lot of practice.' Gryff wondered what she meant by that but was too exhausted to ask. 'Go and lay on that couch in the living room, Son,' she continued. 'I'll bring you a blanket. Try and get some sleep. It won't seem so bad in the mornin'.'

As she left to bathe Gwenna's wounds, Gryff called after her. 'Thank you so much for all your help, Mary. I don't know what we would've done without you.'

'Don't thank me, Son. Thank the Good Lord who brought you to my door.'

TWELVE

Mary sat up with Gwenna through the night, keeping watch on her vital signs. 'Us old folks don't need much sleep anyhow,' she explained to Gryff early the following morning as he sat on Gwenna's bed, stiff from his night on the couch and aching with concern for her. He reached for her hand and caressed her fingers gently. He'd give anything to swap places with her.

Mary gently placed a cool damp cloth across Gwenna's forehead. 'She may have a bit of concussion,' she said. 'She took quite a blow to her head, I reckon, looking at that swelling on her face. I'll just stay sittin' with her till she comes round good and proper. You can sit with her now, though, while I go get her some iced tea.'

Gwenna's eyelids flickered but the swelling was too much on one side for her eyes to open. 'Where am I?' she groaned. 'Where's Bonnie?'

'Don't try to speak, Gwen,' said Gryff, perplexed that her first thought was for her guitar. Why was Bonnie so important to her? She'd been ready to die to keep hold of it last night. It made no sense. 'We're safe, Bonnie's safe. We're at the church. Mary has been taking good care of you. You'll be okay in a week or two, but you need to rest now.'

'Wha' happened?' she mumbled, her neatly stitched lip thick and purple.

'I'll explain everything later, Gwenna, I promise.' Gryff was already dreading the moment when she would look at him with disgust and it would all be over. He owed her a proper explanation – it was the least she deserved – but he couldn't face it, not yet. 'Just get some more rest now. Is there anyone I should call to let them know you're safe? Your folks, maybe?'

'Just my boss, Rudy, at the diner. I don't wanna lose my job.'

'Don't worry about the diner, Gwenna. I'll go and speak to Rudy today myself. It'll all be fine, I promise.' He'd already decided that, if necessary, he'd pay Rudy to hire a temp to cover for Gwenna. There was no way he'd let her lose her job because of him.

'Time for you to leave this young lady to get some rest,' said Mary, returning with the iced tea and a folded newspaper. 'Here, take this down to the kitchen.' She handed the newspaper to Gryff. 'I'll be down directly to fix us all some eggs.'

When Mary returned to the kitchen, Gryff was sitting at the table, the newspaper spread out before him.

TWO DEAD IN SUSPECTED NARCOTICS DEAL

Two Argentine nationals died last night on the East Side in what law enforcement agencies believe was a narcotics deal gone wrong.

One man was found dead with head injuries in a service alley; a switchblade was recovered nearby. The other man was struck by a truck and killed as he tried to flee the scene of the crime.

Unconfirmed sources say that an Interpol arrest warrant exists for one of the men regarding the 1958 murder of Conrad Müller, a Swiss banker, and that the second man had recently completed a prison term for trafficking cocaine. Both men were carrying a large amount of cash and narcotics at the time of their death. So far, officers have been unable to trace any witnesses willing to assist with the inquiry and are appealing for...

Gryff didn't need to read any further. They were lucky to be alive. Those men really were ruthless killers. He'd feared as much last night in the alley but hadn't truly believed his instincts. Now they were both dead – it said so, right there in black and white – and they wouldn't be coming after him or Gwenna ever again. He was surprised how little guilt he felt.

The big question now was: who else was out there hunting for the real Gryff Morgan? His temples throbbed as he tried to figure out what to do next.

'What you should do next,' said Mary, cracking eggs into a basin, 'is buy yourself some time to think. Get down to the diner and tell Rudy that Gwenna walked in front of an automobile by accident last night – real bad luck, nothin' more than that, won't be in for a week or two – and then get yourself off to work this morning, like nothin' happened.'

Gryff stared at Mary in amazement. It was as if she'd been reading his mind and had come up with the best plan he'd heard all day. She truly was one savvy old lady.

***

When Gryff arrived at the diner, he expected to see the street cordoned off and police vehicles everywhere. Instead, traffic flowed freely, and a single uniformed officer leaned against the wall at the head of the service alley with a clipboard in her hand, looking bored.

The sign on the glass door read 'closed', but Gryff could see Gwenna's boss, Rudy, inside, looking pale and exhausted. Used coffee cups were strewn across every surface and dirty plates were piled high on a cutlery dresser. Gryff tapped on the glass.

'Cain't you read, asshole? We're closed!' yelled Rudy.

'Rudy, it's me, Gryff.'

Rudy's irritated expression disappeared at the sight of his most regular customer. He opened the door just enough to speak through. 'Sorry, Gryff, I'm closed. Been a hell of a night. Got a lotta clearin' up to do.' He swept his arm around the scene. 'Cops have been in all night, eatin' and drinkin' for free. Darn near cleaned me out! Couple of dead guys on the street last night. Real scumbags, the cops say.'

'A terrible business.' Gryff lowered his voice so the cop couldn't overhear. 'Can I come in? I need to speak to you about Gwenna.'

A look of worry passed across Rudy's features. 'She okay?' He stepped aside to let Gryff in and wiped a hand across his face wearily. 'I could do with her here right now to help clear up this mess.'

'Gwenna got hurt last night in the street,' Gryff began, telling the story he'd rehearsed with Mary. 'I left the diner with her last night after her show to walk her home and we were right there when that lowlife got hit by the truck. She got hit by a Buick that swerved off the road. It was nobody's fault, just enough to knock her off her feet.'

'Gee,' said Rudy. 'That's real bad luck on Gwenna. She gonna be okay?'

'She hit her face pretty badly on the sidewalk, so she's got a nasty black eye and a cut lip,' Gryff explained. 'Her face is swollen and she can't talk very well, so she isn't going to be able to wait tables for a few weeks.'

'Damn!' said Rudy. 'I feel real bad for her. She's a good worker, one of my best.' He picked up a tray and began to stack it with dirty crockery. 'So, if you were there, did you see what happened? The cops ain't got any witnesses,' he nodded towards the officer beside the door, 'but they ain't lookin' real hard. Last night the cops in here were saying those two dead guys were real scumbags and no one's gonna miss 'em. They pretty much closed the case already. I mean, who gives a damn if two scumbags wipe each other out, right?'

'Right,' agreed Gryff, avoiding Rudy's eye. 'Who gives a damn—?'

Gryff's spirits soared. This was great news. The cops weren't interested, the bad guys were dead, and nobody would be looking for him or Gwenna. Should he feel bad about the dead guys? *Not a chance! It was us or them,* he thought grimly.

'Gwenna's worried about losing her job,' Gryff said, helping Rudy stack cups on his tray. 'She's going to be off work for a few weeks till her face gets better.'

Rudy stopped what he was doing and gave Gryff a reproachful look. 'She ain't got no worries about that. I cain't pay her while she's off, but she can come back whenever she's good and ready. I'd hate to lose her.'

Rudy's words were exactly what Gryff was hoping to hear. He clapped Rudy on the shoulder with relief. 'She'll really appreciate that, Rudy.'

Rudy gave a tired smile, his eyes drooping with fatigue. 'Don't mention it, bud. She's a great gal and she's got a great voice. She sure knows how to play that beautiful Gibson. I ain't seen a guitar as lovely as that in years. Must be worth a fortune.' He stuck out his hand to Gryff. 'Tell her I hope she gets well soon.'

Gryff shook his hand warmly. 'Thanks, Rudy, you're a star.'

***

Gwenna was sitting in the kitchen, polishing off a bowl of Mary's homemade cherry ice cream when Gryff returned that evening. She wore a clean bathrobe, and her shiny hair smelled sweet and fresh when he kissed the top of her head.

'How'd it go with Rudy?' she asked anxiously through

swollen lips, as Mary dished up a bowl of chicken soup for Gryff.

'It went great, Gwen.' Gryff broke off a hunk of Mary's homemade bread to dip in his soup. 'Rudy says the cops aren't interested in the case and don't have any witnesses. It's practically case-closed already. The cops think the bad guys killed each other.'

Gwenna's eyes welled up. 'Thank the Lord! I've been worried sick. Those men were gonna kill us, Gryff, I just know it. Do ya really owe them thousands of dollars?' Her lips trembled. 'They knew your name. I don't understand what's goin' on…'

Gryff chewed slowly on his bread. What should he say? The moment of truth seemed to have arrived. He couldn't put it off any longer.

Gryff led Gwenna by the hand to a low stone bench under the shade of a tall, gracefully arching rice-paper tree in the lush semi-tropical churchyard garden, with the resignation of a man on his way to the gallows. Deep blood-red petals, fallen from a Confederate rose bush pooled around their feet on the gravel path as a pair of brightly coloured hummingbirds hovered, wings buzzing gently, busily seeking out the last of the rich ambrosial nectar. Gryff sat silently for a second or two, soaking up the last sweet moments when Gwenna still thought he was a good man. When he could put it off no longer, Gryff took a deep breath and dived into the deepest recess of his mind, where he kept the locker of painful memories. Once opened, there would be no going back. With a dry mouth, Gryff gathered his courage and began.

'My brother Emlyn was only ten when I killed him…'

Beside him on the bench, Gwenna sat as motionless as an alabaster statue, silently attentive as Gryff poured out the litany of misfortunes that had irrevocably changed the course of his life.

'So, you see, Gwenna,' he mumbled as he reached the end of his story, utterly wrung out with the emotional toll of reliving the worst moments of his life, 'I've been lying to you all along. I'm not Gryff Morgan at all. It was a dreadful mistake to assume the identity of a terrible man to escape from a junta that kills its enemies. Now, everyone wants to kill me, whether I'm Gryff or Bryn. I'll never be anything but a danger to you.'

He hung his head in desolation, fearful of the disgust and rejection he was sure to see on Gwenna's face.

Gwenna took both Gryff's calloused hands in hers, twining her fingers through his. Her voice was gentle and sorrowful when she finally spoke.

'My heart breaks for you, Gryff… Bryn…' She gave a small wry laugh. 'But you are not to blame for any of those terrible things that happened. Don't you see?'

She was softening the blow of rejection – he knew it. He steeled himself for what was coming next. In his coarse hands, hers were soft and pale, her fingers slim and straight, each fingernail a perfect oval. Her breathing was gentle, every inhalation long, every exhalation slow. The sweet scent of cherries lingered faintly on her breath. The silence between them seemed to stretch on for an eternity until her melodic voice broke the stillness. It was barely audible but her words were clear.

'I blamed myself when my momma died but that wasn't really my fault either.'

THIRTEEN

'I grew up in Daviess County, Kentucky,' Gwenna began softly. 'My younger brothers, Ray and Roy, are twins, and I have a li'l sister, Martha Junior… she's named after my ma. Pa grows tobacco on Jack Jepson's plantation. Mister Jepson breeds and trains racehorses up at Buena Vista. Did you ever hear of Red Admiral – Jack's Kentucky Derby champion? Or Jimmy Knox, his champion negro jockey? No, I don't s'pose you did. That's just me bein' stupid, as usual. Jack's a good man, and his wife, Greta? She's a saint, in my eyes.

So it all happened when I was twelve and the boys were just six when a plague o' bugs hit Pa's crop. Me an' the boys picked bucket loads o' them fat sticky hornworms off Pa's crop by hand and we were doin' just fine till I got in trouble for falling asleep in class. That's how Pa met Carol. She was just my teacher – Miss Luther – back then. She drove up to our cabin to tell on me. After that, Mister Jepson came to our rescue and lent Ma and Pa some o' his field hands, free o' charge, and that saved Pa's entire t'bacca crop from bein' eaten by the bugs…'

***

Auction day couldn't arrive quickly enough; it was almost more exciting than Thanksgiving. Gwenna and her brothers were awake before sunrise, noisily whispering under the bedcovers until their ma finally let them get out of bed. Ma looked real fine in her navy-blue church dress, the one with the red-ribbon trim, as she brushed Gwenna's hair till it shone like jet and braided it into a long tail, tying it off with a red ribbon to match her own. Ray and Roy buzzed around madly in blue shorts and checked shirts, just like their pa's.

When it was time to leave, the whole family bundled into Wendell's battered old green Chevy truck. Gwenna sat up front on the bench seat between her pa and ma, who had Martha Junior in a basket across her knees, while Ray and Roy sat in back on top of the first bound canvas bale of precious tobacco leaves. Five more giant bales sat in the barn, waiting their turn for the fifteen-mile drive to the Big Independent auction warehouse in Owensboro.

'You hold on tight, boys!' Martha called to her two flush-faced sons. 'I sure don't want you two bouncin' right out the truck at the bridge over the creek.'

'Yes, Ma'am,' they chorused, dissolving into childish giggles.

'Are we gonna do well at the auction today, Pa?' asked Gwenna as Wendell cranked the ignition. For once, it started first time.

'I surely do hope so, darlin',' said Wendell. 'I reckon we picked 'bout two-thousand pounds o' baccy per acre. After working my magic on them leaves, I reckon I got us a mighty fine cure, maybe even my best ever.' The old truck groaned as Wendell released the clutch with a grimace. 'I'm hopin' we'll get as much as sixty cents per pound.'

Gwenna's eyes widened as she did the math in her head and on her fingers. Martha's hazel eyes sparkled with amusement as she watched her daughter's expression. 'Pa!' exclaimed Gwenna. 'That's more'n seven-thousand dollars! We're gonna be rich!'

Wendell's lean, tanned face creased into a wide smile. 'Sure does sound a lot, Honey, but that's gotta last a whole year, get us a new truck for one thing, and invest in next year's crop. Seven-thousand bucks won't last long, what with you varmints eatin' me outta house and home like a bunch o' hornworms!'

As they crossed the creek and reached the highway, Gwenna couldn't recall a time when she'd ever been so happy.

***

The air crackled with excitement at the auction warehouse as hundreds of folks in their Sunday best crowded the rows while gangs of little boys clambered like colourful raccoons on the stacked tobacco bales. As Wendell inched the truck forward in the slow queue for the weigh-in, the sing-song voice of the auctioneer rose above the excited clamour. Gwenna joined in, improvising her own tune.

Wendell glanced sideways at his little girl. 'You always find the music in everything, my angel.' He patted her knee fondly. 'Some folks say the chant of an auctioneer can sound as good as a song and, when you walk down the rows, you can almost dance to the tune of the sale.'

Gwenna squirmed on the old Chevy bench. 'I feel like dancin' already, Pa.'

Martha smiled at her overexcited daughter. She opened the truck door and took hold of Martha Junior's basket. 'Let's climb out here, fidget-pants, so we can get a place for our rug under that tree before someone else gets there. You boys can stay in the truck with Pa for the weigh-in round back.'

Gwenna rested her head on her mother's lap as they sat in the dappled shade of the holm oak with Martha Junior, whose blue eyes serenely reflected the patches of sky peeping through the tree canopy as she kicked and burbled happily in her basket. Martha made a daisy chain coronet for Gwenna's shiny hair, while Gwenna pulled the petals off a dandelion before making a wish. The aroma of hotdogs and onions filled the air, competing with the deliciously familiar vanilla and oak of the tobacco bales. Gwenna's mouth watered so hard that she could scarcely wait to start their picnic of Ma's homemade beaten biscuits and country ham.

Wendell and the boys returned from the weigh-in with great big grins on their faces. Roy and Ray were both eating sticks of bright-pink cotton candy and had most of it in their hair. Settling himself down on the picnic rug beside Gwenna, Wendell handed her a shiny dollar coin. 'Go and treat yourself in Owensboro today, Pumpkin, and get yourself that ice cream sundae you've been hankerin' after.' He tugged her braid playfully. 'It's gonna be a good day.'

Gwenna's smiling cheeks felt fit to burst. A dollar all to herself! She could get a butternut crunch and cherry syrup ice cream sundae with extra whipped cream for a quarter at 3-D's and still have some left over to buy a kite, a hot dog and a soda! Her pa was the best!

Wendell turned to Martha and wrapped his arms around her slender waist, kissing the tip of her nose. 'That first bale weighed in at two-thousand pounds, darlin', and has gone for grading. The weigh-in guy said it was the finest quality bale he'd seen so far and should get top dollar.' He produced a five-dollar bill from his wallet and handed it to her ceremoniously. 'I've been savin' this for you to spend on yourself in Owensboro today while me and the boys wait for my baccy to be auctioned.'

Martha took the bill hesitantly, her cheeks rosy. 'Are you sure you can afford this, Wendell? Shouldn't we wait till we know?'

Wendell's pale-blue eyes disappeared into a nest of weathered creases. 'Martha, my angel—' he brushed her hand with his lips '— you deserve this for sticking with me through thick and thin. In fact, you deserve much, much more. When I think of everything you've sacrificed for me and the kids...' He pinched the bridge of his nose, his eyes glistening. 'Now get on into town with Gwenna, and go and buy yourself something beautiful.' He handed her the truck keys. 'Me and the boys will be just fine here, won't we, boys?'

'Yessir!' yelled Ray and Roy in unison.

'Well, if you insist!' Martha kissed the boys on the tops of their fuzzy fair heads. 'You be good now!' Her lips lingered on Wendell's as she gathered up Martha Junior in her basket. 'Ray, you're in charge!' she joked.

Ray stood to attention and threw her a salute. 'Yes, Ma'am!' They all laughed at his earnestness.

***

That evening, Martha drove the family truck back to the auction house from Owensboro along unfamiliar, unlit country lanes under the deep-blue velvet cloak of darkness. Gwenna was asleep along the bench seat, full to bursting point with ice cream and soda, and Martha Junior's basket was in the passenger footwell. A fancy box tied with a ribbon was beside her. Martha smiled at her sleeping daughters. It'd been such a lovely day and she couldn't wait to show Wendell the beautiful emerald dress she'd bought with the five dollars he'd given her.

Rounding a blind bend, Martha had no time to react to the unlit forklift tractor coming her way. The giant forks speared the windshield of the old Chevy with a splintering crash and carried the truck for a full fifty yards. Gwenna was showered in broken glass, cutting deeply into her bare arm, neck and shoulder, narrowly missing her vital arteries. By some miracle, Martha Junior was completely unhurt in the shelter of the footwell.

When Martha's broken impaled body was removed from the half-crushed truck, her navy church dress soaked black with blood, it was a mercy, the rescuers said, that Gwenna was unconscious, to spare her the sight of her mother's catastrophic fatal injuries.

Word of the tragedy reached the Baptist pastor of Whitesville that same night, reported by Dooley Fox, a fellow sharecropper travelling home from the auction.

'I recognised Wendell's truck in that ditch as quick as a flash,' Dooley told Pastor Cloyce Burnett, his voice thick with worry. 'I didn't know who else to tell, 'cept you.'

Frantic telephone calls to the Owensboro police department through the night eventually confirmed Cloyce's worst fears. Martha was dead and Gwenna was unconscious in the hospital. The whereabouts of Wendell and his other young'uns was unclear. The congregation gasped when Pastor Cloyce broke the news at Sunday worship the following morning. As he led the prayers of remembrance, the good Baptist folks of Whitesville sobbed openly in the pews.

Jack Jepson gripped Greta's hand tightly as they hurried away from the church after the service towards their shiny new Chevy Task Force pick-up. Greta stumbled, blinded by her tears, while their only son, Jerome, in the same grade as Gwenna at school, trailed behind with a dumbfounded look on his face.

'Hurry along, Jerome!' Jack snapped with uncharacteristic impatience. It was a fearful situation, and Wendell and his kids needed help right that very minute. There was no time to lose. Jack floored his new truck, sending up a spray of sand and gravel as he wheel-spun out of the parking lot and headed out along the highway towards Owensboro General Hospital.

'Slow down, Jack.' Greta placed a steadying hand on his forearm, her eyes swollen and red-rimmed. 'We don't want to wind up in the hospital, too.'

Jack and Greta found Wendell sitting on a scuffed plastic chair in a dingy yellow corridor. His hollow eyes were black and unfocused, and his face was a deathly shade of grey. Jack called Wendell's name three times before he responded.

'Jack...' Wendell stood up slowly, dazed and confused like a man waking from a bad dream. 'What are you doing here?'

'Where are the kids, Wendell?' Jack grabbed Wendell by the shoulders, determined to shake him out of his stupor long enough to find out what he needed to know.

'The kids?'

'Yes, Wendell. Where are Ray and Roy, and... the baby?' Jack faltered. *Oh, dear Lord!* he thought with dismay. *That poor child shared her dead mother's name.*

'The County Sheriff's Department took 'em away.' Wendell's voice was slow and slurred like a drunkard. 'The sheriff brought me here himself.'

Jack blew his cheeks out with frustration. He needed answers fast but Wendell was clearly unable to think straight. 'Where's the sheriff now, Wendell?' he snapped. 'We need to find your young'uns as soon as we can.'

Wendell looked around the corridor in a daze as if he had misplaced his gloves. 'He was here a minute ago.'

Jack couldn't afford to waste anymore time. 'Greta, get down the stationhouse now and see what you can find out.' He threw the truck keys to Greta. 'I'll stay here with Wendell till we can find out what's happening with Gwenna.'

Greta caught the keys expertly. 'I'll do my best,' she said, stopping to wrap her arms around Wendell before leaving. 'We're here for you, Wendell. Whatever you need.'

***

Jerome stayed in the truck while his mother marched resolutely into the Daviess County Sheriff's office stationhouse in Owensboro. If ever there was a time to wield the full power of the Jepson name, she'd said on the way over, now was it. He'd never seen her so fired up and, he had to admit, it scared him a bit. He couldn't decide what to think about any of it. Would Gwenna still be the same, when she came back to school? *If* she ever came back to school, now her ma was dead. Guiltily, he thanked his lucky stars it wasn't *his* ma who'd been pulled from a crushed truck.

After about fifteen minutes, the stationhouse door burst open. Jerome looked on with astonishment as his mother emerged with a purposeful stride, holding Ray and Roy – trotting to keep up with her – by their hands, their little faces pinched with fatigue. A deputy carrying Martha Junior's basket hurried along close behind. The baby's high-pitched wail reached Jerome's ears, even with the truck doors closed. His mother's face was set in an expression of grim determination, the like of which Jerome had never seen before.

'Jerome!' Greta snapped heatedly as she flung open the truck door. 'Sit in back with the boys and hold the baby's basket good and steady while I get us out of here.' Alarmed by the urgency in his mother's voice, Jerome scrambled into the back seat to do as ordered,

'What's happening, Ma?' Jerome's insides turned over as Greta accelerated away from the stationhouse in a cloud of dust, with Martha bawling furiously. He'd never seen his mother so angry.

Tears streamed down Greta's face. 'Those people make me so mad!' she cried. 'These poor little souls have had nothing good to eat or drink all night, and they've no idea what's going on. Just look at them, Jerome! They're scared half to death.'

Jerome glanced at the two little figures sitting beside him, clutching each other's hands tightly. Roy had his thumb in his mouth and both boys' matching shorts were stained with wet patches. He wrinkled his nose. They looked so small and vulnerable; his heart went out to them.

'The sheriff's department was looking to foster them out for the next few weeks – with complete strangers!' Greta's knuckles were white as she gripped the steering wheel. 'As if these kids haven't been through enough already. What on earth were those stupid people thinking?'

'Do you mean they don't know what's happened to their ma?' Jerome looked at Ray and Roy's dirty tear-stained faces with even greater pity.

'Not now, Jerome,' warned Greta in a stern voice. 'Let's get everyone home and deal with that later.'

Greta kicked off her pumps in the elegant family sitting room and collapsed onto a mammoth Chesterfield sofa with a weary groan, taking the crystal tumbler of bourbon offered by Jack. As she put her feet up, Jack slumped into a grand armchair, nursing his own shot of bourbon. The soft chimes of an elegant polished walnut grandmother clock told her it was eight o'clock. It felt more like ten.

Greta's feet and head throbbed with equal intensity. 'What next?' she asked. She'd already opened Jerome's old nursery and had two extra cots moved there so the three children could stay together. After a simple supper of buttery spoonbread in Inga's kitchen, she and Inga had carried the two urchins to their beds. Inga's daughter,

Hattie, who'd be standing in as nursemaid for Martha Junior until a permanent solution could be found, had already put the baby down to sleep. Greta had sat with the boys, reading from Jerome's old book of Br'er Rabbit, till their eyes closed and their breathing came slow and steady.

'You did a great job with the children today, Honey,' said Jack. 'Wendell is in no fit state to look after himself and his little girl Gwenna is all cut up. Nothing that won't heal in a month or two, thank the Lord.' He took a sip of his bourbon with a thoughtful look on his face. 'This is gonna take one heck of a lot of sortin' out, Greta, and it needs sortin' right now. There's still ten-thousand pounds of Wendell's tobacco to get to auction – and that truck o' his is finished.'

'What are you thinking?'

'Number one, take care of Wendell at the hospital. He's got a room there as long as he needs it and they're gonna bill me for it.'

Greta nodded her approval. That was a big relief.

'Next up, I got some of my boys loadin' up all that baccy on one big rig tomorrow and gittin' it down to Owensboro. Dooley Fox has agreed to oversee the auction on Wendell's behalf.'

'Uh-huh, he's a good man for that job.'

'And lastly, I'm thinking that Wendell can have our old truck till he gets back on his feet. A man cain't manage a family without a truck.'

'That's a great idea, Jack.' Greta cupped her cool hand across her throbbing forehead. She was so proud of Jack. He was doing the right thing for that poor soul Wendell and his family. They would all be in her prayers that night.

She reached across to the armchair and took Jack's hand, pressing his fingers softly between her own.

Jack swirled his bourbon ruminatively. 'It won't bring back his darlin' wife, though.'

***

Gwenna's physical lacerations had almost healed but her mental scars were deep when she was released from the hospital a month later. A never-ending loop played over and over in her head, tormenting her with memories of her non-stop begging for her ma to drive into Owensboro because she wanted that ice cream sundae so darned much. It was all her fault. God was punishing her for her greed and selfishness.

With the boys and Martha Junior still being cared for at Jack and Greta's, Gwenna withdrew deep inside herself in the empty stillness of the cabin and her voice completely deserted her. She'd barely spoken for weeks in the hospital and now she simply had nothing she wanted to say. The silence, she decided, was all part of God's punishment and had to be endured – wordlessly.

Wendell poked his head around her bedroom door, his face a picture of worry. 'I'm drivin' up to Buena Vista this mornin', my darlin'. It's high time I collected Martha Junior and the boys. Would you like to come for the ride?' Gwenna shook her head and returned to gazing out the window, punishing herself in the only way she knew how.

Sitting in her cavernous modern kitchen, Greta listened sympathetically as Wendell spilled his worries about his daughter.

'It's going to be a terrible loss if Gwenna never speaks again.' She rested a comforting hand on Wendell's forearm as he demolished a plate of succulent fried buttermilk chicken. Gwenna had such a wonderful voice; the very idea of never hearing her beautiful singing in church again broke her heart.

'Even getting her to speak would be a miracle.' Wendell's voice cracked with hopelessness. 'She's so deeply disturbed by losing her ma in such a horrible way.'

Greta covered her mouth with her hand as horrific images flooded her mind. It was unthinkable what that poor girl had endured. There must be something that could be done to reach her. 'Have you tried playing music?'

Wendell scratched his stubble. 'D'you think it might help? I don't play any instruments, and we don't own a record player or even a radio, come to that.'

Greta scolded herself for her thoughtlessness. The poor soul could scarcely feed himself and his children. How could he possibly afford such things? She could kick herself sometimes. But she did have one idea.

'I may just be able to help you with that, Wendell,' she said. 'I own a guitar that I cain't play.' She sighed ruefully. Jack bought it for her a year or two back when she was trying to learn, but she really didn't have a musical bone in her body. She was hopeless, even when Jack paid for a private tutor. 'That lovely guitar has been sitting around gathering dust – perhaps you'd like to take it home for Gwenna? It might help to distract her from her painful memories?'

'I'll try anything, Greta, absolutely anything,' said Wendell gratefully. 'It really is kind of you to do this for Gwenna – and for me. I don't know what I would've done without all your help.' He turned his crumpled face from her. 'It's been good to know that Martha Junior and the boys were safe here with you. I'm sorry if they were a bother.'

'The children have been no bother, Wendell.' Truth be known, the boys were really coming out of themselves and Jerome had been teaching them how to ride a horse. Martha was coming along nicely, too. She was such a sweet-natured baby; Greta was really going to miss her. A shadow of sadness passed fleetingly over her face. 'It is such a mercy that Martha Junior will never remember anything about the car wreck.'

Wendell's eyes welled up. 'But she will never remember anything about her mother either, except that she shares her name.'

***

Gwenna was lying on her bed staring into space when Wendell arrived home later in the afternoon bearing Greta's gift. The guitar that Jack Jepson had bought for Greta was a custom-built mahogany Gibson J-45 with a beautiful ebony teardrop pickguard inlaid with mother-of-pearl butterflies, a matching ebony fretboard with mother-of-pearl position markers, and a sunburst finish on spruce. Wendell knew nothing about guitars but even he could tell this one was extremely special.

'Hey, darlin',' Wendell's voice brimmed with love and concern. 'How are you feelin'?'

Gwenna sat up and shifted her bottom up the bed, propping herself up on her pillows. Her long dark hair covered the scars on her neck, but the angry scars on her left arm and shoulder were raised and red. Wendell tried not to wince whenever he saw them.

'I brought ya somethin' special, darlin'.' He lifted the guitar for Gwenna to see. 'I hope ya like it.'

Something changed in Gwenna's face when he handed her the stunningly beautiful instrument. A light appeared in her eyes as she caressed the polished mahogany and spruce with reverence.

'It's beautiful,' she said. 'Thank you.'

Wendell's face crumpled at the sound of Gwenna's first words in over a month.

Thank you, Greta, he thought gratefully, wiping his eyes on his shirtsleeve and laughing through his tears. She'd brought them a miracle.

He kissed Gwenna on her forehead. 'You're welcome, my darlin'.'

***

The shadows had begun to lengthen in the church courtyard as Gwenna reached the end of her story, releasing one of Gryff's hands to wipe away the tears coursing down her bruised, swollen cheeks.

'If we had never gone to Owensboro for ice cream, the car wreck would never have happened, and my wonderful momma would be alive today. For all these years, I've blamed myself; I wanted that darned fancy ice cream sundae so much.' She squeezed his fingers and gave a small, tight smile. 'So, you see, I do understand exactly how you feel. My momma's death was as much a tragic accident as your brother's. I can see that now.'

Gryff pulled Gwenna gently into his arms and kissed the top of her sun-warmed head. He'd never heard anything so sad in his life. How was it possible that he had stumbled across someone who could truly understand his guilt and grief because theirs was as painful as his own? As he held her to his chest, her gentle sobs catching in her throat as she rested her swollen face against him, he was overcome by a powerful urge to protect her for the rest of their lives. The problem was – he was the source of her danger.

They embraced in silence for a time, until Gryff eventually released her from his arms so she could wipe her eyes. 'I had no idea,' he said. Her obsessive devotion to her guitar and her crazy refusal to leave it behind when her life was in danger made complete sense now. He'd been asking her to give up the one thing she truly lived for. He vowed to find the best guitar shop in the land if he could, to get Bonnie repaired as good as new. But what still didn't make sense to him was why she had run away from home and her lovely family, and why the guitar was called Bonnie. He had a feeling Gwenna's sad tale wasn't over yet. Something she mentioned about her teacher at the beginning of her story bothered him.

'So, what do we do now?' Gwenna looked at him expectantly as the last of the daylight faded from the sky.

That was a good question. Gryff hadn't thought of any future past his confession. He'd been convinced that Gwenna would despise him for all his lies and deceit, not to mention dragging her into his dangerous world. Making plans had seemed pointless, but everything was different now and he needed to think fast. Gwenna was already ahead of him.

'The way I see it, you are in trouble whether you are Bryn or Gryff,' she said, succinctly putting words to his fears. 'You used Gryff's papers to get out of Argentina alive. You had no choice. Don't ever lose sight of that, Gryff. Those people in Argentina think Bryn Evans is a terrorist, so you cain't ever be Bryn again, in case the authorities come for you. Like you said, they want to kill you – you're their enemy. The problem with being Gryff—'

Gryff raised his hand to interrupt her '—is that *everyone* wants to kill him.'

'Well, we don't know that for sure,' she said. 'Those two bad guys only caught up with you because you made such a name for yourself in Charleston.'

Gryff rubbed his chin. She had a point. He didn't know much about the real Gryff other than that he was a Welshman who worked the East Coast cargo routes, gambled, and got into fights. If he could stay away from seaport towns and keep his head down, he could carry on as Gryff and keep out of trouble. Gryff Morgan's passport was his only documentation, so the truth of the matter was he had no choice. Gryff Morgan – gambler and criminal, had to become Gryff Morgan – good citizen.

'What do you suggest?' he asked, impressed with Gwenna's clear thinking.

She was silent for a moment before releasing a slow, heavy sigh.

'When I ran away from home, I came to Charleston for the Country Music Festival. I thought it was the place to get talent-spotted, and become rich and famous.' She laughed quietly to herself. 'It seems so stupid now, but I didn't know any better then. I shoulda gone to Nashville.'

'So, what are you saying?'

'I think Nashville would be a better place for us to start

over. Nobody will know you there and it's a big crowded city, easy to blend in – or get lost, whichever.'

Gryff's heart sank as the truth of her words hit home. It was the safest thing to do, but the thought of leaving Grace and his friends at the Episcopal Church, who had been so good to him, was gut-wrenching. But it would mean he'd be with Gwenna, which was the most important thing.

'Come on, Gryff, don't look so down', she pleaded. 'It'll be amazing! They don't call Nashville the Music City for nothin', ya know. I could get discovered by RCA or even Decca!'

He could barely see her face in the unlit courtyard but he could hear the excitement in her voice. He needed to stop being so selfish.

He cupped the uninjured side of her face in his palm and kissed her forehead. 'I'll go wherever you want as long as I can be with you, Gwenna.'

FOURTEEN

NASHVILLE, TENNESSEE

Gryff and Gwenna emerged from the Romanesque arches of Nashville's elegantly castellated railroad station, yawning and stretching their stiff limbs, squinting painfully against the bright glare of the fierce noonday sun. Gryff's empty stomach growled as Gwenna rummaged in her purse for the huge sunglasses she'd been using to conceal the remains of her bruises. It'd been a gruelling twenty hours since they'd said their tearful farewells to Grace and Mary at Charleston, and all he wanted now was to find some decent food and a cheap place to stay.

Gryff shouldered his canvas rucksack of cash and Gwenna's precious guitar case as they scoured the Broadway vista for a homely-looking diner. Across the freeway, a red-and-white canopy shading tables and chairs on the sidewalk looked promising. Gwenna grabbed Gryff by the hand and hauled him across six lanes of slow-moving traffic.

The moment he saw the hand-painted gold lettering on the glass door of Valerio's Diner, he knew she'd found the perfect place for them. As she pushed open the door and he followed her in, the cool shady interior that greeted them was a welcome respite from the harsh sun outside. The tantalising aroma of freshly ground coffee beans filled the air. He took a deep breath, savouring the inviting scent. Over in the corner, a jukebox was playing *Dark Moon*.

Gwenna's face split into a huge smile. When she removed her sunglasses, her violet eyes sparkled in a way that Gryff hadn't seen for days. 'I love it here already,' she declared, with laughter in her voice as she settled into a window booth. 'They're playing Bonnie Guitar!'

Gryff slid into the seat opposite her, stashing his rucksack on the floor between his feet and putting Gwenna's guitar case on the padded bench seat. What the heck was she talking about? Bonnie Guitar was right there beside him.

'She's my all-time favourite', Gwenna continued. 'I had her picture on my bedroom wall, along with Loretta Lynn and Johnny Cash, when I first began to play. I even taught myself *Candy Apple Red* for the Daviess County Talent Contest – but Carol wouldn't let me enter on account of my poor grades.

The happy smile of moments earlier melted from her face, the instant the words were out of her mouth. She reached quickly for her sunglasses and put them on, turning towards the window. It was clear she was trying to hide whatever was bothering her.

Gryff reached across the table and grasped her hand. 'Is everything all right, Gwen? You look pale all of a sudden.'

Gwenna squeezed his fingers in return. 'It's nothin', I'm just bein' silly.'

'D'you want to talk about it?'

'Not really, it was just some silly ol' memories comin' back outta nowhere,' she murmured. 'I'll be fine in a minute.'

Gryff sat back heavily in the booth. He hated seeing Gwenna like this but he didn't want to push her on it, if it upset her. Something was going on with her that he didn't understand and he had no idea what to do for the best. 'Let's order!' He grabbed the laminated menu, energetically. 'I'm starving!'

Gwenna ordered biscuits and gravy for them both, on account of Gryff not recognising anything on the menu. Gryff grimaced comically at her choice, screwing up his nose and poking out his tongue, and was rewarded by the return of her radiant smile.

'You've got no idea how grotesque that sounds to me, Gwenna, but I'm trusting you not to poison me.' He chuckled softly to himself as he took hold of her hands across the table. It was a relief to have cheered her up so quickly.

Gwenna turned one palm upwards with an amused pout. 'Have you got a dime?' she asked. 'I wanna play *Candy Apple Red,* so's you know my favourite tune.' She slid out of the booth. 'Of course, I wasn't as good as Bonnie Guitar when I learned to play it, 'cos she's got a beautiful singin' voice, as you're just about to find out.'

Something in Gryff's head clicked as the cogs fell into place. So Bonnie Guitar was the name of a singer! *Now,* it all made sense. Gwenna had named her beautiful guitar after her favourite recording artist! He grinned inwardly, pleased to have solved part of the mystery without making too much of a fool of himself – for once.

Bonnie Guitar's honeyed tones filled the diner as Gwenna returned from the jukebox, her eyes lit up with delight. Before he knew it, Gryff was on his feet, with his arm around her waist. They floated together between the tables, the warmth of her body permeating his, moving in perfect sync with the rhythm of the music. It was utter bliss. As Bonnie crooned her love song just for them, Gryff buried his face in Gwenna's silky raven hair and inhaled the scent of cherry blossom and almonds. Longing burned inside him, and time seemed to slow down as he held her close and savoured every sweet second of her being in his arms.

As Bonnie's final notes died away, Gwenna clung to him for a few more moments before pulling away with flushed cheeks. 'Why, Gryff Morgan', she said with a soft giggle. 'I had no idea you were such a hopeless romantic.'

She was teasing him but he didn't mind. It was good to see her so happy.

When they returned to their table, their food had arrived, and they fell on it ravenously. Gryff's cheeks bulged with sausage and he had a smear of white sauce on his nose. One of his glossy curls had broken free from his slicked-back locks and hung cutely over one eye. Gwenna smiled to herself. Gryff had no idea how unbelievably handsome he was and that was just how she liked it. There was not one scrap of vanity about him. She'd go so far as to say he was the least self-conscious man she'd ever met – unlike Jerome. Her smile faded as memories of Jerome invaded her thoughts. It was little wonder she was thinking about him, seeing as the last time she'd played *Candy Apple Red*, she'd been with him at Panther Creek. She remembered it clearly. It had been a beautiful day.

***

Lime-green sunlight filtered gently through the canopy of poplar, oak, chestnut and sycamore. The roots of the ancient trees lay twisted and exposed at the edge of the creek, where Gwenna sat dangling her bare feet into the crystal-clear swirling water and noodling on her precious Gibson guitar. Catfish lurked under the stones, emerging only to snap an unwary iridescent damselfly from the surface, while blue jays squawked overhead in the yellow poplars. An earthy aroma of damp moss infused the shady glade.

Gwenna's laughter mingled with the bubbling of the small cascades as Panther Creek tumbled through Wendell's backyard from Jack Jepson's lake and down yonder into the Ohio River.

Jerome chewed a long stem of bluegrass as he lay in a bright clearing, drying off in the warm sun. 'Play something special for me.'

'Here's somethin' I've been practisin' for a while.' Gwenna gave a shy smile. 'It's for the Daviess County talent contest in May. I hope you like it.'

Jerome lay back on the grass as Gwenna began to strum the chords on the guitar. Her voice was pure and sweet as she sang her favourite love song – *Candy Apple Red*.

Jerome applauded and whooped as the last note hung in the air.

'My, oh my, Gwenna, that sure was lovely! You sure

could give Bonnie Guitar a run for her money if she was playing at the county fair.'

Gwenna's cheeks flushed with pleasure. 'Well, lucky for me, she won't be there. Although I'd love to meet her,' she said with a dreamy look in her eye.

'Well, I think you sing every bit as good as them ladies and you were born to play that lovely guitar.' Jerome idly tossed a pebble into the stream. 'Ma is real proud that you taught yourself to play it so beautifully, as it was just sittin' there goin' to waste after she quit learnin'.'

Gwenna gave the guitar a playful hug. 'When I think of my lovely Bonnie sittin' there doin' nothin', it makes me wanna cry. She's my best friend, ain't ya, Bonnie?'

Jerome reached out and tucked a strand of her hair behind her ear. 'Ma wants to know if you'd like to come by for supper this evening. We're having burgoo and Inga's making Derby pie. Bring Bonnie with you – Ma would love to hear you play. It's been a while.'

Gwenna loved Inga's home-style cooking and Derby pie was her favourite. Her mouth watered at the thought of the chocolate and walnut tart with crisp sweet pastry, but her face clouded over. 'Thank your ma from me, Jerome, but I cain't come this evenin'. Carol's real mad with me that my grades are slippin' and she blames Bonnie.' Gwenna's face creased into a deep frown. 'I cain't even practise at home no more 'cos she gets so mad.'

Jerome put a steadying hand on Gwenna's shoulder. 'She's got a point, Gwen. It's only six more weeks till we both graduate high school. Then you can leave and get a job and spend as much time with Bonnie as you like. Just hold tight a little longer.'

Gwenna hated school and was a poor student. Unlike Jerome, who was destined for Cornell in central New York State, she wouldn't be going to college or university after graduation. Her time in hospital after the car wreck had put her far behind her classmates, who'd formed new friendship groups and moved on without her. She was a misfit and it didn't help her popularity that she was the teacher's stepdaughter.

Ever since Carol Luther had wed her pa, she'd been on at Gwenna the whole time to improve her grades. 'Martha is doing so well in third grade, Gwenna,' Carol often said. 'Why cain't you be a bit more like her?' Gwenna gritted her teeth whenever Carol compared her to Martha. Nobody called her Martha Junior anymore. Martha was bright and intelligent, just like her ma – who'd wanted to be an author before she met and married Wendell. Martha's prized possession was her ma's old typewriter, which had pride of place on her desk in the bedroom she shared with Gwenna. She was constantly clattering away on it. It drove Gwenna mad.

'At least Carol's agreed you can sing at the talent contest,' said Jerome, tossing his strand of bluegrass into the stream.

'I haven't asked yet,' Gwenna replied sulkily. 'She's just gonna say no, I know it.

***

Gwenna took a bite from her biscuits and gravy with a sigh, pushing aside her bitter memories of the woman who'd stolen her father's heart and made her life a misery. Luckily, the food was delicious and her spirits perked up. Gryff seemed to be enjoying his, judging by the goofball look on his face. There was something about Gryff that made her insides flip. She felt safe with him, which was pretty crazy, seeing as how everyone was after him. It truly broke her heart, how so many bad things had happened to such a good kind man. She couldn't begin to imagine how terrible he must have felt for shooting his brother, especially as they were just burying his pa. No wonder he couldn't face his family any longer. She knew exactly how that felt.

And as for his poor ma! The suffering that woman must have endured losing two sons and a husband didn't bear thinkin' about. Gwenna would give anything to have her ma back, and it grieved her that Gryff's ma was still alive but he couldn't be with her. He must be missin' her something terrible. But right then, he looked so happy tucking into his food that she decided not to press him on it. That could all wait for another time.

The waitress refilled her coffee cup as Gwenna put her fork on her empty plate and gave Gryff her full attention. 'That was lovely. Now all we have to do is find someplace cheap to stay while we find ourselves jobs.'

As she spoke, hot coffee splashed on the table narrowly missing Gwenna's arm. She flinched and cried out as the waitress grabbed a handful of serviettes from the tabletop dispenser in a panic and began to mop up, saying '*Mi dispiace*! So sorry! So very sorry!'

'Don't worry, I'm fine.' Gwenna swept her hand down the front of her skirt to check for dampness. 'It seems to have missed me.'

'*Bene, bene.*' The waitress gave Gwenna an apologetic gap-toothed smile. 'I was overhearing you talking. You're looking for someplace to stay, *sì?*'

'Well, yes,' said Gwenna. 'But we've only just arrived in Nashville, so we've no idea where to start.'

The waitress wiped her hands on her apron. 'Look no further! My mama runs a rooming house upstairs, just fifteen dollars a week, including the best breakfast in town!'

Gwenna smiled ruefully. Renting above a terrific diner would be perfect but they couldn't afford fifteen bucks each per week, leastways not until her singing career took off.

'I think we can just about afford that if we both find work quickly,' said Gryff, his eyes lighting up at the mention of the best breakfast in town. 'Don't you think, Gwenna? This would be a great place to stay and fifteen bucks each sounds like a good rate to me, right?'

The waitress slid into the booth next to Gryff. 'Call me Gio, please. The room rate is for you both, not each,' she explained with an encouraging smile.

Gwenna felt the heat rush to her face. It was an awkward moment, as she and Gryff hadn't discussed their sleeping arrangements yet.

'That sounds just grand, Gio,' said Gryff. 'But I think it's best to have two rooms until we are married. I'm happy to pay for the extra room till then if your mam has two rooms available?'

Blood thundered in Gwenna's ears like a herd of galloping horses. It was all she could do to keep a calm exterior. *Until they were married? He wanted to marry her?* She rummaged in her purse, more to conceal her whirlwind of emotions than anything else.

Gryff rested a firm hand on her arm. 'What are you looking for, Gwenna? Don't worry about the money. I've got a bit put aside that will tide us over for now.'

Her flesh tingled, and goosebumps sprang up at his touch. She still couldn't believe it. *He wanted to marry her!*

Gryff reached into his rucksack, pulled out a roll of cash and said to Gio, 'Here, let me give you a month in advance.' He peeled off a dozen ten-dollar notes.

Gwenna gasped quietly at the size of the bankroll. A hundred-and-twenty bucks, handed over to Gio like it was nothing! How much more money was in that backpack of his, she wondered, and where had it all come from? The more she thought about it, the more she realised that the bag was always with him, never out of his sight. She hated mysteries and was dying to ask about it, but now wasn't the right time. It was all very intriguing.

'We have a deal, *signore*.' Gio held out her hand to Gryff. 'Let me show you to your rooms. You'll love it here and Mama's going to adore you two lovebirds!'

They gathered their belongings and followed Gio upstairs to their rooms while Sonny James crooned *You're the Only World I Know* from the jukebox, providing the perfect soundtrack to a time she would never forget. A warm glow suffused her body to the very ends of her fingers and toes as she replayed the moment Gryff let slip that he wanted to marry her. She had a great feeling about Nashville. The Music City was the perfect place for her – the stars were aligning in her favour, at last!

She could hardly wait to find out what the future held in store.

FIFTEEN

L ive music blared out of every shabby doorway along the
buzzing neon-lit strip of Lower Broadway when Gryff
and Gwenna stepped out of Signora Valerio's rooming
house, locking the street door behind them. Thick clouds
obliterated the moon and stars, adding to the feverish
humidity. The atmosphere crackled. It looked like there
might be a storm coming.

Delicious aromas of fried chicken, griddled steak and
onions drifted from open café doorways along the strip.
Gryff's mouth watered as the familiar smells transported
him back to his childhood, and the rugby matches his father
had taken him to as a lad. They'd shared the illicit pleasure of
a greasy burger from the open-sided van under the spectator
stands, the savoury onion juices seeping through the paper
wrapper. They'd had to lick their fingers. 'Don't tell Mam!'
Tad had said, but he couldn't remember why. He could
still feel the reassuring strength of his father's hand on his

shoulder, steering him to their usual place directly behind the uprights. Those were the very best of days, unrepeatable days. His eyes tingled at the powerful emotional tug from the past and he squeezed Gwenna's hand. He would make some new 'best days' with Gwenna – he'd make sure of it.

The teeming sidewalks hummed with activity as Gryff and Gwenna threaded through the crowds. Young musicians in sweat-stained tasselled shirts and Stetsons, carrying guitars and fiddles, rushed from one honky-tonk bar to the next while young couples just like Gryff and Gwenna strolled hand in hand, enjoying the razzmatazz of the strip. And then there were the older folks, many of them on their own, simply reliving their heydays through the lens of timeless good music. Everywhere Gryff looked, there were smiling faces of every hue adding to the welcoming atmosphere. A palpable excitement filled the air as Gwenna tugged Gryff along by the hand, in search of the *best* bar playing the *best* music.

In many ways, Nashville reminded Gryff of Buenos Aires, with its vibrant street culture, but his fond memories of tango night in Argentina were tainted by the crippling guilt he felt whenever he thought of the friends he'd left behind, abandoning them to an unknown fate. He was banking on Scaff's wiliness to have made good their escape but he would give anything to know for sure they were safe. He couldn't allow himself to think they may be languishing in some barbaric prison – or worse. Lagging behind Gwenna as he tried to force the lid back on his personal Pandora's box, he stopped to watch the performance of a glowering dark-haired youth giving a very passable Johnny Cash rendition. He really was terrific and it distracted him from his worries.

'But, Gwenna, this guy is incredible!' he protested as she tried to drag him away from the gathering crowd.

'That's the thing about Nashville, darlin',' she said, tugging at his hand. 'Just about everyone here is "incredible". I'm tellin' you right now, it sure ain't gonna be easy, making it big in this town! There's so much competition.'

Gryff wrapped his arms around her waist and pulled her to him, effortlessly hoisting her off her feet as she laughed with delight.

'You're going to knock 'em dead, my lovely, once we've got Bonnie back in action.' He found her warm lips with his, encouraged by her keen response.

'I'm so afraid that she'll never be the same again,' she said, pulling away from his embrace with a tremor in her voice, which Gryff couldn't decide was fear or pleasure.

She dropped onto her tiptoes as Gryff relaxed his grip and looked down into her worried face. The repair would cost a lot of money – money he knew Gwenna thought they didn't have. He could put her mind at rest by telling her about his rucksack of cash from Scaff, but that might worry her more, especially seeing as how the money was drug money. He'd only just come to terms with that himself, now that he was beginning to understand what he'd be missing out on by having to spend the rest of his life on the run. He swallowed hard at the thought of the happy family life he'd grown up taking for granted, all made possible by his parents' stable marriage. They'd been content with so little. He'd never even heard them exchange an angry word. How had they managed? He sighed heavily.

'Don't you worry about a thing, my angel.' He stroked her silky raven hair, which shone like polished jet in the streetlights. 'Some things in life are worth every penny, and getting Bonnie professionally repaired is an investment as far as I'm concerned – in your career and our future together.' Gwenna's trusting ravishing smile pierced his guilty heart and he hated himself for not being straight with her.

'*Candy Apple Red!*' she cried turning suddenly towards the sound of a female vocalist and the chords of an acoustic guitar from the nearest honky-tonk. She grabbed Gryff's hand and dragged him into the dark interior of the purple-painted brick building decked in flashing neon. The stink of stale beer and cigarette smoke choked him as the roar of a hundred conversations competing with the amplified music deafened him. It was all he could do to resist the urge to run for the door.

As his eyes adjusted to the low light in the narrow deep room, he began to make out a low platform to his right, where a young woman was perched stiffly on a tall bar stool, wearing a tight-fitting low-cut dress. Lit by a single dim spotlight and cloaked in swirling blue smoke genies, a giant microphone obscured her face so that only her heavily made-up eyes could be seen. Her voice was sweet and true, as she sang and played her guitar, but nobody seemed to be paying her any attention. Gwenna was yelling something at him but it was pointless trying to hear above the din. A smattering of applause followed the woman as she disappeared into the crowd at the end of her song.

Her replacement on the stool was a grizzled old cowboy in a sweat-stained Stetson, clutching a battered guitar in one hand, with a tumbler of amber liquid and a lit cigarette in the other. He swayed like a rotten oak in a windstorm as he tried to balance on the stool while finding a ledge for his glass. Tucking the cigarette into the corner of his mouth, he raised the guitar and began to play.

Wild applause and whooping greeted his opening chords. The crowd clearly knew this tune and loved it. Gryff was transfixed by the magical sound from the guitar, which seemed to reach straight through his chest and grab his soul.

The room fell silent as the cowboy began to sing, completely under the spell of his gravelly voice. Boy, did he yearn for the good times he'd wasted and ache with regret for the harm he'd done and the people he'd lost. The room erupted in applause as the final chords faded away. As he looked towards Gwenna by his side, Gryff was astonished to see glistening streaks on her cheeks as she clapped and hollered with the crowd.

The cowboy was starting on his second song as Gryff steered Gwenna towards the door, desperate for a breath of fresh air.

'Well, that was something else!' Gryff said as they emerged into the street.

Gwenna dried her face on her sleeve. 'That was Chip Muldoon!' she replied breathlessly. 'He used to be someone. What I mean is, he made it into the Billboard Hot One Hundred a couple o' times. I cain't believe I just saw him for real!'

Gryff had never heard of the Hot One Hundred, but it sounded impressive. Gwenna was clearly star-struck by the old cowboy, with his extraordinary ability to connect with the crowd – completely unlike the girl with the sweet voice before him.

'What about the stiff girl wearing too much makeup?' Gryff stepped off the sidewalk to avoid a musician toting a double bass case. 'What did you think of her?'

Gwenna giggled. 'You mean that girl right behind you with her guitar case, the one who sang *Candy Apple Red*?'

Gryff looked over his shoulder as the colour rushed from his neck to his face. 'Yes, that's the one!' She was leaving the honky-tonk by a side door, a shapeless grey trench coat thrown over her skin-tight dress; her tight-lipped expression was grim. He sincerely hoped she hadn't heard his unflattering words.

'Let me just go tell her how much I enjoyed her performance!' Gwenna dashed away before Gryff could stop her.

Gryff leaned against a streetlamp on the corner as he waited for her to return, watching the world go by – a pastime he was learning from Gwenna. She called it 'people watching'. And what a cosmopolitan world it was, as vibrant as some of the South American ports he'd seen on his travels but without the lurking sense of threat. Gwenna was right; this was a great place to come for him to disappear. Nobody would ever find him among these colourful crowds, especially if he began to dress more like the country and western folks around him. He was smiling to himself at the thought of what a fool he'd look wearing a Stetson and cowboy boots when the sight of Gwenna's crestfallen face brought him out of his daydream.

'What's the matter, Gwen? What did she say?'

'Well…' she said slowly, with a sad pout. 'She calls herself Corinna Coward – that's her stage name – and she seems like a real nice lady, but she wasn't too encouragin' when I asked what advice she would give to someone just startin' out.'

'So, what did she say?'

Gwenna blew out her cheeks with a look of utter dejection on her face. 'She told me to go home and find myself a nice husband.'

'What?' Gryff's voice rose in outrage. How dare she crush Gwenna's dreams so casually? Gwenna didn't deserve that! Just because Corinna wasn't talented enough to make it in Nashville. The lukewarm applause for her performance was proof of that. She was probably trying to undermine the competition, most likely. And besides, Gwenna was way more attractive than her; it was no wonder Corinna wanted Gwenna to leave town!

'Yep. Her exact words were: "Go home, have some kids, sing at the church and enjoy a nice happy life".'

Gryff's jaw tightened. He cracked his knuckles, the way his father used to when he was exasperated. He felt like going after the woman and giving her a piece of his mind. 'Did she say why? What did you say?'

'I told her I already got me a nice fiancé and that you were right here in Nashville with me, and she said: "Get out now before it destroys you." Can you believe that?' Gwenna threw her hands up in dismay. 'She said Nashville's crawlin' with talented wannabes with guitars, and country and western is a tough business for women to break into. She's been playing the honky-tonks for two years for tips, and the A&R reps just want her to sleep with them to get a record contract and, even then, only if she's got her own original material.'

She propped her hands on her hips and stared at the ground despondently, scuffing her foot on a bright-yellow weed growing through the sidewalk cracks. 'And I don't have my own material,' she said flatly. 'I just teach myself everyone else's tunes and copy them. I don't know how to write songs or even read music – and I certainly ain't about to start sleepin' with people to get on. I'm finished before I even got started.'

The ground shifted under his feet before she'd even finished speaking. Had she really told Corinna he was her fiancé? Gryff's heart leapt for a fraction of a second until the sight of her wretchedness brought him back to earth. Whatever she'd meant by it, it would have to wait. She didn't deserve to be kicked in the teeth on her first day in Nashville. For all Corinna knew, Gwenna might be the most talented new solo female vocalist in town and she'd just destroyed her confidence. *So much for sisterhood*, he thought, bitterly. Corinna had better watch out if he saw her again – he might just tell her a few home truths. But right now, the most important thing was for Gwenna to understand that Corinna was just being mean and bitter, and that she, Gwenna, was indisputably the most amazing and talented woman in the world.

The jostling stream of passers-by forked around them as Gryff reached for Gwenna's hands and drew her close, aching to comfort her. He could almost taste the scent of cherry blossom and almonds on her warm skin, and feel the gentle breeze of her sweet breath on his face. His senses reeled with intoxication from her nearness and he knew he couldn't wait – he *had* to know what she meant. 'Did you really tell Corinna I was your fiancé?' he murmured, kissing her fingers one by one.

Gwenna's cheeks flushed rosy-pink. 'Well… yes, I s'pose I did, but I didn't mean nothin' by it—'

He gazed into her sparkling violet eyes, flecked with glints of sapphire and amethyst, searching for the truth. He was sure she would never have said such a thing to Corinna if it meant nothing. Could it be possible that she felt the same way about him as he did about her? She was so brave, strong and utterly incredible. Was he even capable of being all those things and more, for her? He wasn't sure he was good enough to be the man she deserved but when would he ever be if he wasn't good enough now? He'd have to put his heart on the line to find out. What did he have to lose other than his stupid pride?

A line of sweat broke out above his lip and his armpits became suddenly clammy. 'Would you *like* me to be your fiancé?' he ventured, giving her an easy way out if he'd misjudged things. She could just make a joke and tell him to stop being a fool.

Gwenna's mouth opened but no words formed. Her blush deepened to crimson and her pupils dilated into bottomless pools.

Gryff's subconscious read her instinctive reaction and, suddenly, he understood. She loved him! She truly was his soulmate, the only person in the world who could ever understand what it was like to be him. His life would be worthless without her – he was certain of it! He needed to act now.

The strains of *You're the Only World I Know* drifted from the nearest honky-tonk as Gryff sank to one knee on the cracked sidewalk among the cigarette butts and empty beer bottles, garishly bathed in pulsing yellow-and-blue neon. The jostling flow quickly reached a standstill around them until they were an island in a sea of expectant spectators. He clasped Gwenna's hands to his chest and held his breath to steady his trembling nerves.

Gryff's world slowed on its axis. The crowd receded into the background as Sonny James faded to a distant murmur. The neon signs fused into soft halos, gently framing Gwenna's startled expression. A bead of sweat appeared beside the tiny scar on her brow as her rosy lips trembled and the thick lashes of her violet eyes glistened with the half-shed tears of her earlier frustration. He could barely hear the words forming inside his head above the drum of his heartbeat. His mouth moved and the words spilled out, filling the space between them with the resonance of a church bell.

'Gwenna Martha Garland... will you marry me?'

A single second stretched into eternity as her mouth formed a perfect 'O', and her eyes widened, spilling the half-shed tears down her porcelain cheeks. Gryff's world focused on her perfect lips as they formed the word that would alter the course of his life forever, praying for that word to be 'yes' with every fibre of his being.

In that elongated second, her head began to nod and a smile crept into her eyes as her answer gained momentum inside her. She fell into his arms, put her mouth to his ear and whispered the word he'd prayed for.

With perfect timing, the oppressive storm clouds parted and a bright strawberry moon shone down on them, locked together euphorically in their sweaty inner world. The crowd's celebrations erupted around the oblivious couple. Strangers pumped each other's hands like they'd won the $64,000 question and ladies with mascara-streaked faces dabbed at their eyes with handkerchiefs. It seemed that even in Nashville, marriage proposals in the street were not an everyday occurrence.

As the newly engaged couple were helped breathlessly to their feet by kind hands, a voice in the crowd yelled, 'What about the ring?'

Gryff's heart skipped a beat. He needed a ring! He had to give Gwenna something, a symbol of his love for her, to seal his promise. Frantically, he patted his pockets as if a diamond solitaire was likely to be lurking in his denims. Apart from a couple of bucks and a fistful of dimes, all he had was a folding pocketknife and the key to the rooming house, attached to a wooden fob *by a brass ring*. Prising the ring from the fob with his knife, he took hold of Gwenna's left hand and brought it to his lips with a rueful smile.

'Please believe me, Gwenna, when I say that you mean so much more to me than a brass keyring can ever say.' He slipped the ring onto her third finger. 'But I hope you can accept this ring as a token of my promise and my undying love for you until I can find something more beautiful.'

Gwenna cocked her hand this way and that as if admiring a sparkling gem. 'It's perfect', she said with a playful giggle. 'I'll treasure it all my life'

After shaking what felt like a hundred different hands, Gwenna and Gryff finally found themselves alone as the congratulatory gathering broke up. They linked arms and followed the crowd of revellers heading along Lower Broadway towards the Cumberland River, lured by the bright lanterns festooned along a short pontoon, where an old-fashioned paddle steamer was moored. Up-tempo music came from a six-piece jazz band of exclusively black musicians in dapper cream suits playing on the upper deck, while exclusively white folks dressed in their stiff evening finery could be seen settling in at round dining tables on the open-sided decks below. The memory of the disdainful treatment meted out to Grace at Kress's in Charleston still rankled Gryff, despite her calm refusal to be excluded. With a clenched jaw, he hoped Gwenna wouldn't ask to go aboard for a special dinner to celebrate their engagement.

'Look at those fancy folks, Gryff!' Gwenna pointed at the diners and laughed. 'What a bunch of stuffed shirts! Don't ever take me to a place like that when we are married!'

Gryff snorted and took hold of her hand. 'No chance of that,' he said, leading her toward the irresistible aroma of fried bacon that reached him on the warm breeze. 'Come on, Gwen, let's follow that lovely smell and see where we end up. I always think of Sunday morning breakfasts in the valleys, with my mam and tad, and all my brothers, when I smell fried bacon. It's the smell of home.'

'That's a wonderful memory and a wonderful thing to say, Gryff.' She hugged his arm and rested her cheek against his massive bicep. 'I promise I shall cook you bacon for breakfast every Sunday for the rest of our lives.'

Half an hour later, Gryff and Gwenna sat thigh to thigh on a wooden bench beside the river, eating their engagement dinner out of a paper bag. Brightly coloured festoon lights twinkled on the inky flowing water and the ragtime tunes from the *General Jackson* reached them on the stifling breeze.

Gwenna's mouth was full of fried baloney sandwich when she suddenly remembered something important she'd meant to mention to Gryff before his proposal. She chuckled to herself. No wonder she'd forgotten all about it!

She chewed faster so that she could tell him what she was bursting to say.

'I forgot to mention. That lady singer – Corinna – she said to go to Cressy's on Eighth Avenue to get Bonny fixed like new. They're real craftsmen, she reckoned. Been there forty years. Nowhere better in the whole of the USA.'

Gryff's eyes flickered with annoyance. 'That was helpful of her,' he said with heavy irony. 'She crushes your dreams on the one hand, then gives you good advice on the other. That's one classy dame. But I promise we'll go there first thing in the morning, without fail. Bonnie will be as good as new before you know it.'

Gwenna sighed with contentment as she leaned against Gryff's shoulder, licking the last traces of fried baloney sandwich from her fingers and wiping her lips with a paper serviette.

'I cain't wait to get Bonnie repaired.' She took a swig from her bottle of PBR beer. 'I've missed her so much. By the way, d'you realise this makes me an outlaw in this town? I'm still a minor in Nashville,' she added with a chuckle, snuggling against his broad chest. 'I can get married, but I cain't drink alcohol. How crazy is that?'

'I guess that makes us both criminals on the run,' Gryff murmured, finding her face with his soft warm mouth, kissing her eyebrows, the tip of her nose and then her lips. His tongue tasted of caramelised onions and beer. She shivered with pleasure and a jolt of electricity speared her groin. She gasped and pulled away sharply. 'How soon can we get married?' she panted, astonished at how urgently she wanted more of the kind of pleasure that Gryff could give her.

'Not soon enough!' He slid his hand down from caressing

the outline of her breast to a more respectable position on the front of her thigh.

They tossed their engagement dinner wrappings in a trash can and walked the short distance back to the rooming house, her arm around his waist and his arm across her shoulders, making plans for the next day. Her angry frustration from talking to Corinna was gone and in its place was a deep satisfied contentment. She'd finally made it to the Music City, where, despite what Corinna said, the A&R reps would spot her incredible talent, and she'd get a recording contract – because with Gryff at her side, anything was possible. And besides, her precious Bonnie was gonna be fixed the next day and she was gonna marry the kindest, handsomest and most decent man she'd ever met – other than her pa. What more could a girl possibly ask for?

The nightly street party of Lower Broadway was just getting started as they reached the rooming house. Gwenna would've loved to stay up touring the honky-tonks until they closed at 3am but it had been a long and exhausting rollercoaster of a day, and she was desperate for some beauty sleep.

As Gryff wrapped her tenderly in his arms in the corridor outside their opposite bedroom doors, her goodnight kiss burned with longing for the time when they would only need one room.

Sweating profusely in his singlet and shorts, Gryff opened his bedroom window, hoping to catch a breeze. Instead, all he caught was an endless soundtrack of Johnny Cash, Willie Nelson and Merle Haggard playing into the night. Neon patches flashed hypnotically on his ceiling as he tossed and turned restlessly on his single bed in the small simply furnished room. His thoughts turned to the flicker of worry he'd been suppressing all evening. Proposing to Gwenna was, without a doubt, the best decision of his life, but it left him with a messy situation that he couldn't put off any longer.

Shirley.

He would have to end their engagement. He felt terrible about it, but what choice did he have? If he was honest with himself, he had never truly loved her. He had been too young and foolish to understand what love was back then.

He closed his eyes and groaned aloud at the thought of the pain he was already responsible for – and that which was yet to come. He could almost see the sorrow in his mother's dove-grey eyes and feel the guilt he always felt as a child whenever she looked at him that way. He counted his lucky stars that his father wasn't alive to witness his shameful behaviour, although he'd still have to face him in the afterlife. He snorted to himself with derision – if he carried on like this, he wasn't going to the same place as Tad anyway.

Unable to get comfortable, he rose from the bed and crossed to the washstand where he sluiced his sweating face and neck with water. As he stared at his reflection in the small washstand mirror, a wave of indecision washed over him. What would Tad do in his position? Somehow, he never seemed able to measure up to the standards set by his father.

He wandered over to the window and leaned on the wooden sill, his senses assailed by the aroma of spicy chicken and the happy clamour of revellers in the street carrying on without a care in the world. Luckily, Shirley was still young. She had her whole life ahead of her and could easily find someone better for her than him. He was sure of it.

He would write Shirley a letter. That would be best. But what would he say? And what if the authorities found out and discovered where he was? The police would question his family once they received the extradition warrant in his name – if they hadn't already!

The realisation hit him like a bucket of cold water. Shirley and his mam may already think he was a terrorist! They'd all be worried sick. He could kick himself that he'd not thought about this already. He cursed his own stupidity. He was still bringing trouble to their door, even in his absence. They would all be so much better off if he'd died at sea.

Then, at least, they could all get on with their lives.

SIXTEEN

1966

Gwenna removed her key from the door latch silently, so as not to disturb the sleeping household above the diner. She couldn't go on like this much longer, getting home at three in the morning with her hair and clothes stinking of cigarette smoke and the buzzing in her ears that wouldn't go away. She couldn't hear herself think – not that she could think straight by that ungodly time of the morning anyway. On top of all that, she constantly had the mother of all sore throats – and then having to get up a few hours later for the breakfast shift at the diner? It was too much. She'd lost weight in the past three months, not that she had any to spare in the first place, and those circles around her eyes? They were getting deeper and darker with every passing week.

She hung her coat wearily on the rack of hooks behind the door and stood for a time, eyes closed, head pressed against the wall as she summoned the energy to climb the steep staircase to her single room. Corinna was right all along. She'd been a fool not to take heed. If she weren't so darned tired, she'd laugh at the stupid optimism she'd felt about her singing career when they first arrived in Nashville six months ago. And she was luckier than most – at least her looks got her a honky-tonk slot every night, unlike the poor souls on the street corners, buskin' for nickels and dimes. Although at least they got to breathe clean air and didn't get to go home feeling like they'd swallowed a porcupine every night.

Sure, it had been great at first, when Bonnie was fixed as good as new. Gettin' Bonnie back was like the first day of spring when the new buds appeared after the snow, and you realised the long winter was over and anything was possible. That seemed like a lifetime ago. Gryff came to her shows back then. But with her tips barely covering the cost of his beers and what with him getting so mad when the audience didn't love her as much as he did, they'd agreed it was probably best if he stayed away.

Her problem was that the Nashville crowd was such a tough bunch to impress. They'd seen and heard it all before, and she had nothing new to give them. The chances of being talent-spotted by an A&R rep were less than nothin', especially since she'd given the booker at the Purple Bricks a piece of her mind when he suggested she might have more luck if she wore a low-cut figure-hugging dress and be more willin' to share her favours. She wasn't selling her body; she was selling her music! But no one was interested in buying. She needed some original songs, but she wasn't a songwriter and she couldn't even read music. There sure as heck wasn't anyone giving away new tunes for free in the Music City.

She opened her eyes and rolled her shoulders with a deep sigh, steeling herself to haul her weary bones up two steep flights to her room, opposite where Gryff was sure to be sleeping soundly. His job at that shabby, no-good auto-shop on the edge of town was dead-end, poorly paid and way below his skill level, but it was the only work he could get in the Music City besides being a barman. Nashville wasn't cut out for men like Gryff, she thought sorrowfully. Seeing him wasting his talent, never complaining and making the best of the situation to support her and her foolish dreams was heartbreaking.

Between the pair of them, they were barely making enough to cover the cost of their two rooms at Signora Valerio's boarding house.

Something had to change.

***

Something had to change. Gryff wiped his oily hands on a rag before removing his thin boiler suit and hanging it on the hook behind the locker room door at the auto-shop, where he spent his days servicing an endless stream of family station wagons.

Gwenna was burning herself out working day and night at the diner and in the Honky Tonks, and he couldn't bear it. They scarcely saw each other, and when they did, she looked thin and tired. They were passing like ships in the night. They simply couldn't go on like this. It was time to use Scaff's money for its intended purpose – to set himself up for the future. There was no point in scrimping and scraping, with Gwenna making herself ill when he had enough money for a small family home, in someplace where he could get a proper job to make the money go further. He'd been so sure she'd make it in Nashville and was willing to do whatever crummy job it took to support her, but somehow, Nashville didn't love her as much as he did. He could only hope that things would get better once they were married.

As he trudged along the edge of the highway back into town, he pondered for the umpteenth time the problem that had been giving him sleepless nights. It wasn't Bryn Evans who'd be marrying Gwenna Garland – it was Gryff Morgan. No matter how hard he tried to convince himself that a name was just a name, he couldn't bear the thought of Gwenna bearing the family name of that thieving lowlife scumbag who'd almost got them killed. Who knew where Gryff Morgan came from and what sort of people his family were? Probably all thieves and scoundrels, for all he knew. He couldn't let Gwenna be tainted by that association and, even more importantly, his children must never carry the name 'Morgan', either. He just couldn't countenance it. If his children couldn't bear his real family name, at least they could bear Gwenna's – and be true to their American heritage. It was the best plan he could come up with.

He'd even invented a plausible explanation for Gwenna keeping her unmarried family name. One day, she would be famous, he was sure of it, and 'Gwenna Garland' would look better in lights than 'Gwenna Morgan' ever would.

***

On their wedding day at the Nashville First Baptist Church, Gwenna wore a simple yellow summer dress with fresh flowers in her hair. Gryff wore the pale linen suit Grace had chosen for him to wear to church in Charleston. They were a handsome couple, radiating happiness on their special day. But behind their happy smiles, they each carried a hidden sorrow for their mothers, absent from the most important day of their lives.

Signor Valerio baked a wonderful wedding confection of vanilla sponge with coffee, chocolate and whipped cream, with a delightful Italian name that Gryff kept forgetting. It was so delicious that Gwenna declared she had truly died and gone to heaven! On their wedding night, when exhausted Gwenna snuggled into Gryff's warm embrace in their marital bed for the first time, her eyes quickly closed and she was asleep within minutes. Gryff couldn't begrudge his new bride a decent night's sleep. He stroked her raven hair and lay awake most of the night, trying to figure out how to make life better for her.

***

Gwenna's dream of Nashville success ended when her missed period and early morning sickness confirmed what she already suspected. Bringing up a baby surrounded by drunks and drifters was not going to happen. Gwenna was adamant about that. Babies needed families and Gwenna knew the perfect place. All she had to do was swallow her pride and admit what a rotten brat she'd been to her poor pa and long-suffering Carol. And there was no getting away from it – she had been a brat. It was crazy how becoming a mom changed your outlook on life, she thought, with a new understanding of why Carol and Pa had gotten together. It made her want to hang her head in shame.

She had her plan all worked out before she broke the news to Gryff: Kentucky was a big coal-mining region and the Blackstone Coal Corporation was always hiring. Jobs at the mine came with a small corporation house and would be perfect for Gryff's skills. It would solve all their problems in one go; she just knew it. They could raise their family and be truly happy there.

Gryff's joy about Gwenna's fantastic news quickly turned to despair. He'd sworn never to work underground again when he lost his beloved Tad to emphysema. But now here was his pregnant young wife pinning all her hopes on him doing exactly that. Plastering a smile on his face, he kissed her forehead and told her it was a perfect plan. What on earth was he going to do?

SEVENTEEN

1967

WHITESVILLE, KENTUCKY

Gryff settled into the bulls-blood red leather chair at
Joel's Barbershop on the edge of town, marvelling at
the display of motor racing paraphernalia plastered
on every visible surface that wasn't a mirror or a window.
Every inch of wall space was hung with faded black-and-
white photos of grimy-faced men with white goggle marks
around their eyes and broad grins, holding shiny trophies.
Overhead, colourful race-day bills threatened to meet across
the ceiling. He could barely keep his head still for the scissors.

It was Gryff's first Saturday afternoon in Whitesville,
Kentucky, and he was a nervous wreck. He had two
important interviews coming up: one for the mining job
that Gwenna was banking on for their future and the other
was an audition for the role of son-in-law – with failure

not an option. The risk of his father-in-law's disapproval, especially as he hadn't asked permission to marry his daughter, weighed heavily on his mind. They were meeting for the first time that evening over dinner and he had to make a good impression. Hopefully, a good shave and a decent haircut would help.

Joel was lathering a dish of soap when a deep earth-shaking roar sent a tremor through the very foundations of the building. Gryff leapt to his feet, his colliery instincts firing on all cylinders, his heart banging like a traction engine, convinced that an earthquake was about to swallow them whole. As he dashed for the door in fear of being buried in rubble, he caught sight of Joel collapsing in tears of laughter against the washbasin, strangely unbothered by his imminent death.

Gryff drew up sharp – something wasn't right. It looked like the ground wasn't about to swallow him up after all, although now he wished it would. 'What the hell is that noise?' he yelled above the ongoing roar, hoping his embarrassment wasn't too obvious.

Joel jerked a thumb toward a steep bluff across the road. 'Race day,' he replied, his shoulders still shaking with mirth. 'Warm-up laps.'

Gryff could hardly believe what he was hearing. There was a racing circuit right there? In Whitesville? That certainly explained the memorabilia.

'The SCCA motor speedway circuit is just on the other side of that bluff, which was built to reduce noise.' Joel rolled his eyes. 'You'd never know it.'

Gryff had never heard of SCCA but reckoned he could figure it out. He could scarcely contain his impatience to investigate as Joel painstakingly scraped his face and tamed his unruly thick black curls.

The moment Joel was finished, he leapt to his feet, settled his bill and sprinted across the road to where a dense blue cloud of exhaust fumes hung low over the bluff. The pungent aroma reminded him of people and places he loved but hadn't seen for years. In a heartbeat he was a kid again, back in the green hills around his home town, watching his eldest brother, Tomos, riding his two-stroke Greeves scrambler in the Aberavon Motor Cross Club hill-climb. The air was filled with blue exhaust fumes and the distinctive high-pitched whine of motorcycle engines. A wave of nostalgia washed over him and he swallowed hard. All the Evans brothers were avid motocross fans back then – all except Dylan, who preferred to spend the day baking with their mam. Gryff could never smell engine oil – or freshly baked bread – without thinking of his brothers. An aching void opened inside him. God! How he missed them all.

From where he stood, clinging like a curious possum on the circuit's chain-link fence, Gryff had a great view of the colourful stock cars as they made their way in a pack around the quarter-mile banked asphalt track, jostling like thoroughbred horses in the Grand National. The sight of the wide-wheeled oversized autos emblazoned with giant race numbers and painted logos filled him with the same envy and longing to join in that he'd felt watching Tomos all those years ago. As he walked back to their rented rooms in town, along the dusty highway, an idea formed in his head that was so exciting, he could hardly wait to tell Gwenna.

Gwenna had been jittery all afternoon. Her pa was coming at 5pm sharp to collect them for dinner at the home she'd run away from three years earlier, so it was no wonder she was as much of a nervous wreck as he was. Gryff decided to keep quiet about his exciting idea until a better moment.

Wendell had barely knocked when Gwenna opened the front door and hurled herself into his arms.

'Oh, Pa! You have no idea how much I have missed you!' She buried her tear-streaked face in the shoulder of his soft kidskin jerkin. He hugged his daughter close and lifted her clean off her feet, seemingly overcome for words, before turning to Gryff with an outstretched hand.

Gryff was surprised to feel his own hand tremble with emotion as he shook hands with his father-in-law for the first time. Up close, Wendell's lean face was deeply tanned, and his goatee beard was short and neatly clipped. He had a muscular wiry physique and a confident handshake. He seemed to be assessing Gryff's appearance every bit as much, if not more. Gryff was relieved to see a look of approval in the older man's pale-blue eyes as they released their grasp. It was a good start.

During the short drive back to her childhood home, Gwenna chatted non-stop, barely drawing breath. Gryff could tell she was nervous about meeting Carol again.

As the truck crunched to a halt on the loose gravel outside the cabin, the front door opened and a girl of about twelve, whom Gryff assumed was Gwenna's little sister, Martha, rushed out to greet them. Two lanky blond teenage boys appeared in the doorway and leaned, arms folded, against either side of the frame like a matching pair of Greek columns, looking decidedly unimpressed. They must be the twins, Ray and Roy, Gryff thought, with a knot in his stomach. He took a deep breath to steady his nerve. These folks were strangers to him, but to Gwenna, they were family. It was vital to make a good impression, as they were now his family too, and they all needed to get along for the sake of his unborn child.

Behind them, a slim woman appeared in the doorway, untying her apron strings. She could only be Carol. Gryff was astonished at how youthful and attractive she was, entirely at odds with the impression he'd formed from Gwenna's stories. Had she painted Carol as an ogre or had he assumed that for himself? Whichever it was, that impression couldn't be further from the truth.

The two women locked eyes. It was a tense moment.

It was Carol who spoke first. 'Hello, Gwenna.' A warm smile spread across her face. 'It's good to have you home. We've all been so excited to see you and meet your new husband since we got your letter.'

Gwenna stepped forward and took a deep breath. She was visibly trembling, but Gryff couldn't tell if it was fear or emotion. He held his breath, wondering how Gwenna would respond to the woman she resented so bitterly.

'Hello, Carol.' Her voice was steady as she returned Carol's warm smile. 'Thank you for having us over for dinner. I really appreciate your kindness. I owe you and Pa a huge apology for being such a brat when I ran away. I've learned a lot of lessons since then and I'm mighty sorry for the pain I must have caused.'

Tears of pride sprang to the corners of Gryff's eyes. He knew how hard that must have been for her; she'd carried it off with dignity.

Carol smoothed her skirts and looked Gwenna squarely in the eye. 'Let's hear no more about that and get inside before the food goes cold,' she said, steering them into the cabin with a welcoming hand.

The ice was broken and Wendell's relieved face spoke volumes.

Once inside the cabin, Gwenna couldn't help but admire the modern, well-furnished interior. Carol had gone to great lengths to create a comfortable home for her husband and stepchildren, and Gwenna was furious with herself for the way she'd judged Carol in the past. She'd been selfish and immature. Carol had been a blessing to her father as he struggled to raise a young family without a mother – she could see that now. Reaching across the table, Gwenna discreetly sought Carol's hand and gently squeezed it, exchanging knowing smiles.

After everyone had helped themselves to food, Gwenna was delighted to see how effortlessly Gryff and Wendell fell into conversation, discussing the Kentucky motor speedway scene with great enthusiasm and hearty laughter. It was obvious that Gryff was passionate about motorsport and Wendell was thoroughly enjoying himself. She couldn't believe how well everything was going, better than she'd ever imagined. She caught Gryff's eye across the table and blew him a discreet kiss. The sparkle in his gorgeous blue eyes made her insides melt. She'd made the right choice, for once in her life.

For most of the evening, Martha monopolised Gwenna, chatting excitedly about her love of writing, and proudly regaling her big sister about the magazine competitions she'd entered and won. Gwenna was astonished by the maturity and complexity of the stories her little sister read out to her. Her little ladybug was growing up to be a great talent and she'd almost missed it. Hugging her sister, her eyes welled with pride that she was following in their mother's footsteps. It would be a wonderful legacy if she fulfilled the dreams their ma never got the chance to.

Gwenna noticed Carol's loving and benevolent smile whenever she looked at Martha. As Carol placed her hand fondly on Martha's shoulder, mixed emotions welled inside Gwenna.

'We are so proud of this young lady, Gwenna,' Carol said. 'She's top of her class in everything at school and I just know she's gonna do something special when she grows up.'

Carol's pride in Martha was evident; she was her teacher and stepmother, and it was good to see her sister thriving, but she couldn't help remembering herself at the same age, lying in a hospital bed, torn to ribbons by flying glass, silently locked into her grief. She pushed aside the unwelcome memory and smiled warmly at the woman who had replaced her mother in her sister's affections.

'With you by her side, Carol, I'm sure Martha will achieve everything she sets her mind to.'

Gwenna sighed with relief as she crawled into bed. It had been a long and eventful day. She'd had a wonderful evening, but now her pregnant belly ached and she could barely keep her eyes open. Gryff seemed uncharacteristically pre-occupied as he got ready for bed, but she was simply too tired to find out why. Maybe the evening hadn't gone as well for him as she'd thought, but her aching back and swollen ankles were her biggest problem at that moment. Anything else would have to wait until morning.

***

Gryff and Gwenna had just finished their breakfast coffee when Wendell pulled up in his truck outside the window of their rented rooms. Gwenna was still in her nightgown, and Bryn in his vest and shorts.

'Get your hat, young man.' Wendell's eyes crinkled with merriment as Gryff hopped about on one leg, hastily pulling on his shirt and trousers while searching for his boots and combing his hair. 'We're on a mission today. I've got something to show you that you might find interesting.'

Gryff hurriedly kissed his wife's cheek. 'I'll explain later,' he said as he grabbed his jacket, ran his fingers through his hair and headed for the door.

'Where are we going?' Gryff asked as they drove out of town in a cloud of dust.

Wendell gave Gryff an enigmatic smile that, for a split second, reminded him of his own father. He shook his head, bemused. The two men looked nothing alike, yet something in Wendell's presence was reassuringly familiar, almost comforting. He'd missed the company of decent men – men like his tad – but hadn't realised how much until just then. Sitting beside Wendell on the bench seat of his old truck, the tension vanished from his shoulders and he relaxed for the first time since he could remember.

Wendell's gravelly Kentucky accent was more pronounced than Gwenna's and Gryff had to listen harder to understand what his father-in-law was saying. 'There's a run-down t'bacca barn between here and Evansville that I want you to see,' Wendell drawled.

A tingle ran down Gryff's spine and he shivered involuntarily. Had he heard correctly? Did Wendell really just say *Evans*ville? After travelling more than ten-thousand miles, could fate have brought him to a town bearing his family name? He shrugged and shook his head. He must have misheard.

Wendell glanced across at him expectantly.

'Um, great?' Gryff replied, unsure what Wendell imagined he'd want with a tobacco barn but not wanting to appear ungrateful for the older man's help.

'It's right on the main highway, only two miles from the speedway racetrack. I think it will suit your purpose real well.'

At the mention of the racetrack, the penny dropped. Wendell's 'mission' was to help him realise his dream for the future – his own auto repair and service workshop. He would specialise in stock cars, family saloons, farm machinery and anything else with an engine. They'd talked about it the previous night but he'd not expected his father-in-law to act so decisively. He opened his mouth but words failed him.

Wendell glanced at him sideways. 'I know you must be worried, Son. It's a big risk for a young fella just startin' out. You'll need a big loan from the bank and a ton of graft to get this project off the ground.' Wendell pressed his lips into a firm line. 'But with my help, I think you can do it.'

Gryff didn't doubt for one minute that surefire success would be his with Wendell backing him. Nothing Gwenna had told him about her father had prepared him for the discovery that he had the drive and energy of a tornado. But how would he explain to someone as astute as Wendell that he didn't need a bank loan? Maybe he should apply for one anyway? It would look less suspicious and he could stash his cash for a rainy day. There was a lot to think about but the idea of keeping secrets from Wendell was deeply uncomfortable.

Shadows were thin on the ground, and the inside of Wendell's truck was like a furnace by the time Wendell and Gryff left the realtor's office later that morning. Wendell was right about the barn. It was in the ideal location on the highway, near the racetrack and would be an easy conversion to set up as an auto repair shop. Gryff looked at the older man and broke into a huge grin. It was achievable – the price of the barn and land was a fraction of what Gryff had expected. With Wendell's generous offer to act as guarantor and help him source workshop equipment at auctions to save money, Gryff's dream of being his own boss was within his grasp. It was almost too exciting for words.

'Well, Son, what do you say?'

Gryff looked at his powerful, calloused hands resting on his denim-clad thighs – hands that had killed two people. Could he finally put all that behind him? Could this truly be the moment he'd dreamed of, the moment he could finally reclaim his identity as a decent hardworking family man? He could never again be Bryn Evans but he could put these hands to good use and make 'Gryff Morgan' a byword for trust and respectability in this little Baptist town in the middle of nowhere. It was more than he could have hoped for. It didn't matter that this moment had arrived with so little fanfare and nobody else could understand its life-changing significance. He was in the company of a good man, a man he could look up to, just like his tad, and it didn't get much better than that.

He looked directly into Wendell's expectant blue eyes and smiled. 'It's perfect,' he said, his voice trembling with emotion. 'And best of all, I won't have to work underground ever again.'

The two men clasped each other's hands in a celebratory handshake. It was a deal.

***

Martha's typewriter seemed to glower at him from the breakfast table, where it had sat since Carol dropped it off that morning. She was taking Gwenna to register at the maternity clinic and then on to look for second-hand baby clothes at the community hall. They were getting along well, which was a huge weight off Gryff's mind. He had an appointment at the bank's head office in Owensboro later that afternoon to apply for the loan. Wendell had suggested that a typed application would help create a favourable impression. It was a convenient excuse to borrow the machine for its real purpose now that he would be alone for a few hours.

It was time to write the letter to Shirley.

It was a moment that had been a long time coming and he couldn't put it off any longer. He owed it to Shirley to release her from their engagement and had spent countless hours trying to think of the right words to soften the blow, but also to throw anyone off the scent who might be looking for him. He couldn't take the risk that the letter might fall into the hands of the authorities and be used to track him down. He had Gwenna and the baby to think about now.

He steeled himself as he retrieved Captain Cruikshank's

testimonial from his old bergen under the bed and slid the unused Blue Star Line headed paper from the envelope. As he fed the sheet of paper into the machine's roller, he held his breath to quell the sadness and finality rising in his chest. He knew the words by heart, having rehearsed them a thousand times since he had settled on his plan.

He began to type.

Dear Miss Jones— His fingers trembled violently, and he stopped to stretch his hands and forearms before continuing. Once this letter was sent, his whole family would believe him dead and buried at sea. He wished with all his heart that he could tell them the truth – that he was alive and well but wasn't ever coming home – but that would just make things worse for them. His death would be the end of their uncertainty and they were better off without him. Shirley would get over her loss quickly: she was still young, free and single, and would soon find someone new to make a happy life with, but his mam was another matter. He would never forgive himself for the pain he'd already caused her but nothing in this world would ever bring Emlyn back. His eyes and nose streamed as he continued to type.

Gryff intended to post the letter – sealed in a plain envelope – that afternoon during his trip to Owensboro, crossing the state border at the Ohio River into Indiana. With any luck, the Indiana state postmark would throw off anyone who might come looking for him.

The die was cast. Gryff had crossed the point of no return.

EIGHTEEN

ABERAVON, SOUTH WALES

In Shirley's opinion, the medical centre at the new colliery, with its state-of-the-art facilities for sick and injured miners, was miles better than the grotty old first-aid room at Aberavon and was a fantastic place to work, even though it was nearly ten miles further along the valley. If it had been around when her father first got sick, maybe things might have turned out differently. Of course, she understood the villagers' worries about their jobs when their old Victorian-era pit was closed for good, but she was relieved when the angry miners were soon won over when they saw the modern physiotherapy centre designed by Dr Dai Bevan. The provision of subsidised National Coal Board buses to ferry the workers to the new colliery, suggested by Dr Bevan, was a crucial step in overcoming the initial resistance. As far as Shirley was concerned, the mine and the men owed a lot to Dr Bevan.

And Shirley owed a lot to her tad and Lowri for supporting her through typing college, which enabled her to get the admin job working for the colliery GP when the clinic first opened. With it being just her and the doctor, it wasn't long before she was helping him with all sorts of duties. She even organised health clinics for the miner's wives and children. It was hard to believe that she'd only been there for a year but already she felt she was making a difference.

'Goodnight, Dr Bevan,' Shirley called out as she donned her coat and headscarf.

'Thank you for your work today, Shirley,' he replied through the open door of the consulting room. 'Get yourself home to your lovely boys.'

Her front door creaked on tight hinges as she let herself in, wrestling to get the Yale key from the stiff latch. Another item for the growing list of things that needed attention, she thought wearily, as she stepped on a letter lying on the doormat.

'Tad,' she called up the stairs. 'You didn't pick up the post.'

The house was unnaturally quiet, except for the ominous tick of the kitchen clock. Where were the boys? Panic rose in her throat like a tidal rapid until she remembered it was Lowri's turn to mind them that day. Nevertheless, the horrible jittery feeling remained. It wasn't like her to be so jumpy but she'd noticed lately that Tad had been spending more of his time sleeping, and it was becoming a struggle for him to mind the boys while she worked. His health was still declining despite treatment from Doctor Bevan and the prognosis was not good. Shirley was worried.

'Tad!' she called louder, making her way up the stairs to his room, still holding the letter.

She pushed open his bedroom door, expecting to hear her father's familiar rasping breath. Instead, she was met with deathly silence.

She dropped the unopened letter onto a side table and went to feel her father's pulse.

His flesh was as cold and lifeless as marble. He was dead.

Shirley came across the forgotten letter while cleaning her father's room a week after his funeral. It probably wasn't that important, anyway. She never got important letters, only bills, bills and more bills. The envelope was addressed to her and had a postmark from Indiana, USA. Her hands began to tremble. Finally, after four long years, it could only be a letter from Bryn. Lightheaded with nerves, her legs buckled and she sank into her father's armchair. She tore open the envelope and slid out the thick sheet of good-quality paper, headed boldly with the words *Blue Star Line*. Her eyes raced across the badly typed words, scarcely comprehending what she was reading. It took her less than a minute.

Bryn was dead.

They'd buried him at sea.

His cause of death was pneumonia.

Captain Cruikshank of the *Buenos Aires Star* sent his sincere condolences.

The letter slipped from her fingers and fluttered to the floor. Shirley sat in a dazed state for a few moments, her mouth open and eyes dry. A cavern of emptiness opened inside her. So that was it. All those months and years of waiting, running to check the post every morning full of hope, and for what? For nothing, that's what. She should have seen it coming. She'd been such a fool even to *think* he was coming back. And now this! The ultimate betrayal! How *dare* the stupid fool die and leave her poor blameless sons without a father? Every boy needed a father figure to look up to, to teach them how to be a decent man, and now her boys had nobody. How could he be so selfish and thoughtless? She would never forgive him – never!

She picked up the letter, took it to the warm grate in the parlour and shredded it onto the dying embers. *Let this be the end of it*, she thought, as the flames flickered briefly, releasing her from her long burden. Bryn was gone forever but now her life could begin again. Huw and Rhys had never enjoyed their father's presence so they wouldn't feel his absence. A single tear of pity for her fatherless sons slid down her cheek as she gulped down the lump forming in her throat. Her sons didn't deserve any of this. She should have known it would end this way. It was all too predictable.

As she watched the paper curl and turn to grey ashes, the emptiness inside her began to fill with sorrow. The stupid fool had passed away far from home. He must have felt so alone. How would she break the news to his mam? She'd seen for herself the stoicism with which Lowri had borne the double tragedy of Evan and Emlyn, but the death of another son? That would devastate most people. But Lowri was stronger than anyone Shirley had ever met, and it seemed that no sorrow was too great for Lowri to bear. What was it she always said at difficult times? Ah, yes: *'Agree with God and be at peace,'* that was it.

Perhaps now they could both *'be at peace'*.

1970

Dai Bevan had a great view of the stage from his seat in the front row, sitting next to Lowri at Shirley's graduation ceremony, where she was collecting her certificate in nursing. It must be over fifteen years since he'd graduated as a medical doctor at Swansea. Nobody had been there for him to witness his achievement and it still pained him to this day. He and Lowri applauded till their hands stung when it was Shirley's turn to stand awkwardly on the stage, gripping her certificate and smiling nervously for the photographer. He was delighted to be there for her and pleased that Lowri was there for her, too – the woman was like a mother to Shirley.

Dai tremendously admired Shirley's spirit. She had this indefinable quality that made you feel like anything was possible around her. From the very start, it was obvious that her talents were wasted as a typist. It took him ages to convince her to enrol as a trainee nurse, even though she was well aware there was an acute shortage of qualified nurses in 1967. The problem was her lack of self-confidence. She simply had no idea how flipping marvellous she was. Establishing the popular new family clinic for miners' wives and children was virtually all Shirley's work. Her unstoppable determination hurdled every obstacle in its way. Without her, the clinic would never have got off the ground. He was incredibly lucky to have her working with him.

'I'm so proud of you, my love.' Lowri kissed Shirley on both cheeks and admired the framed certificate as they mingled with the other proud families at the reception afterwards. 'You've achieved so much and you're still only twenty-three.'

'I can hardly believe it myself, Mam,' Shirley replied, brimming with excitement. 'The only thing that could have made the day any better was if Tad was here to see it.'

The fine lines in Lowri's soft cheeks creased as she gave Shirley a warm smile, her arm around Shirley's waist. 'Don't worry, my lovely, he knows. I'm sure of it.'

Shirley's violet eyes sparkled like amethysts as she turned to face Dai. His heart skipped a beat. He felt alive in ways he couldn't put into words when she looked at him like that. 'I don't know how I can ever thank you enough for believing in me, Dr Bevan.' She took hold of his hand and clasped it in both of hers. 'I could never have done any of this without you.'

Sudden warmth coursed through his body as if he'd just sipped a smooth vintage whisky. He longed to tell her how much she meant to him, but in his embarrassment, the words stuck in his throat. What would he say anyway? That he couldn't wait for the moments they spent together? That the memory of her lingered for days after they had parted? That the hours away from the clinic dragged until he could see her again? Or maybe that she was the most remarkable woman he'd ever met? None of these came remotely close to the feelings he was privately denying.

He cleared his throat and vigorously clapped his hands. 'Afternoon tea at the Castle Hotel, ladies! My treat!'

Dai spent that evening sitting in his library in a deep, glossy Chesterfield wing chair, surrounded by leather-bound medical books. The air was redolent with the smell of old paper and dust. On a small table, the facets of a cut-glass tumbler of amber whisky reflected the flicker of an open fire. He'd dismissed the housekeeper for the evening, declining

Mrs Lodge's offer of supper due to an excess of Victoria sponge cake that afternoon. Now he was alone, save for the company of his old Labrador. The metronomic tick of his ancestral grandfather clock resonated from the entrance hall, discernibly different from the click of Jasper's claws on the black and white stone tiles. The stillness was intense. An inquisitive black nose came to sniff the whisky as he reflected on the day. He caressed Jasper's warm, silky head absentmindedly.

It had been a splendid occasion for Shirley. He'd been privileged to be part of her professional development over the last few years, so why did he feel so melancholy? She wasn't leaving the clinic—in fact, she would be taking on a greater role. He took a warming sip of whisky and rolled it around in his mouth pensively. He couldn't put his finger on it, but it had something to do with the closeness between Shirley and Lowri. It was endearing to see their warm intimacy, but the stark contrast to his monastic life really hit home. He might as well have taken a vow of silence for all the conversation he had at weekends and evenings. He'd never really paid much heed to his reclusiveness before, choosing instead to bury himself in his books or the Sunday newspapers, but now it was becoming a worry. On his deathbed, Dai's father, a renowned surgeon, had made him promise that he wouldn't waste his life. He'd thrown himself into his medical studies, as he believed his father had wanted.

Approaching forty and still single, seeing life through the bottom of his whisky tumbler with only Jasper for company, he began to question whether he'd understood the true meaning of his widowed father's dying words.

NINETEEN

1972

'What's that you've got there, Mam?' Dylan emerged from the kitchen at the Bread of Heaven tearoom, removing his apron and drying his hands on a tea cloth. He took his heavy overcoat from a peg and shrugged it on to face the bitter March winds outside.

Lowri quickly slipped the small rectangular card into her handbag under the counter. 'It's nothing, my love,' she said with a fleeting smile. Today, of all days – the ninth anniversary of Emlyn's death – was not the day to confide in her youngest stepson, who remained resolutely unmarried at the age of thirty-four. Of all her three stepsons, she was closest to Dylan, mainly for their shared love of baking. It was Dylan to whom she planned to bequeath her father's treasured secret recipe for bara brith. With Tomos at the seminary and Wyn away teaching art in Swansea, Dylan was the only one still living at home. She prayed she wasn't the cause of his celibacy, and that they hadn't made some kind of ghastly pact for him to stay and take care of her. Perhaps he was just waiting for the right person to come along – or maybe he was simply the unlucky one who drew the short straw.

'I don't know why you come to work on the anniversary, Mam,' said Dylan. 'Plenty of the other ladies would cover your shift if you asked.'

He was right, of course. Any of the other Aberavon widows would have stepped in without a second thought to cover for her. She and her widow friends had been a tight-knit group ever since she'd set up the tea rooms as a support group for bereaved miners' wives, with the help of the Methodist Church, right after Evan died.

'Do you know, Dylan, I'm actually happiest here, serving customers, keeping busy and taking my mind off things.' She absentmindedly re-stacked a pile of teacakes before covering them with a glass dome.

'Oh well, just a thought. I've finished clearing up out the back, so I'll be shooting off now—' He bit his lip as soon as the words were out of his mouth. 'I'm so sorry, I… I… I didn't mean—'

Lowri patted him reassuringly on the arm. It was just a slip of the tongue. 'Don't worry, Dylan, love. You didn't mean anything by it.'

He kissed her soft cheek. 'Sorry, Mam. It was thoughtless of me.' He headed for the door, quietly cursing his tactlessness.

'I'll catch you up later,' she called after him as she locked up and turned to walk in the opposite direction. She pulled up her coat collar against the cold stiff wind and thrust her hands deeply into her pockets, hunching her thin shoulders to keep warm. She wouldn't be surprised if it snowed, even though it would be Easter in a few weeks. Her feet found their way along the high street and then turned off at the bottom of the hill to climb the well-worn stone steps into the Methodist churchyard, where Emlyn and Evan were buried in the same grave under the canopy of the ancient yew tree. It was a great comfort that they were together for all eternity and not lying in the cold hard ground all alone.

The rectangular remembrance card in her handbag tugged constantly at her thoughts. Sitting on her regular bench nearby, Lowri took the card from her bag and examined it again. It was a standard remembrance card, just like any other that she could buy locally, yet the envelope was postmarked from America, just like the three that had preceded it each year since the letter from America had arrived, informing Shirley of Bryn's death. It was too much of a coincidence not to mean something, but what? Lowri doubted that the sea captain who'd sent the letter was sending the anonymous remembrance cards, so who was? It was time to find out.

Lowri rummaged through her handbag and, after a few moments, found what she was looking for. It was a battered business card. She'd had kept it for almost a decade. She turned it over and hesitated, unsure of what to do. Detective Inspector Vaughan Davies had said to contact him if she needed anything but did he really mean it? People often said things they didn't mean just to be polite. Besides, it had been years since they last spoke. But then, the detective did seem sincere and kind. That was the clincher. Her mind was made up. She would write to him the following day. What did she have to lose?

The following day, after breakfast was cleared away, Lowri sat at the kitchen table with her notepaper to compose her thoughts, which were a jumbled mess. Was it too presumptuous to write to Detective Inspector Davies? Should she address him as 'Dear Vaughan', or would that be too personal? On the other hand, calling him 'Dear Detective Inspector Davies' might be too formal. In the end, she decided to use his first name, which he had insisted she call him. Through the lens of her grief at the time, she remembered him as a gentleman. It was unlikely he'd take offence.

Dear Vaughan,

I hope this letter finds you well and that you will recall your investigation into the accidental death of my son Emlyn almost a decade ago. It is this that I am writing about.

For the past four years, on the anniversary of his death, I have received an anonymous remembrance card, postmarked from the USA, as was the letter informing my son Bryn's fiancée of his death at sea. This has left me perplexed, and I am seeking your advice on identifying the sender. I would appreciate any help you can provide on this matter.

Lowri signed the letter with a brave flourish and quickly sealed it in an envelope to take to the post office immediately, before she could change her mind. She hoped that the kindly detective hadn't retired from the police force in the past nine years.

The old blue door had been repainted a cheerful glossy red to match the spotless front step, and a vase of early daffodils stood in the front window, framed with crisp white net curtains, their vibrant yellow a splash of springtime promise in a street of wintery grey. Contrary to what Vaughan had expected, the terraced stone cottage gave every impression of a well-run home. So often, in tragic cases, people let themselves and their homes become run down, having lost the will to carry on. He saw it all the time. But that was not the case here – not one jot.

Since receiving Lowri's letter the previous morning, Vaughan had thought of little else. He'd had precious little sleep last night.

She'd called him *Dear Vaughan,* and she wondered whether he recalled his investigation into her son's death. He gave a short bark of laughter when he read her words. She could have no idea how deeply her losses had affected him and how he had never forgotten her quiet dignity. He'd left her his card, hoping that there was something he could do for her but, as the years passed, his hopes of her getting in touch had faded, even when he'd seen the death notice for her missing son Bryn, which she'd posted in the local paper. It was a cruel end to a sad affair and his heart went out to her. So for Lowri to reach out to him after nearly a decade, something must have happened and he was intrigued by what it could be. Whatever it was, he would do his utmost to help, no question about it.

'Goodness me!' Lowri's expression was one of pure astonishment as she opened the door to his authoritative knock. 'I wasn't expecting to hear from you quite so soon,

Detective Inspector. I'm sure you are a very busy man.' Her warm smile crinkled the corners of her beautiful grey eyes, and her flawless skin looked soft and radiant. She smelled of sun-ripened peaches.

'It's actually Detective *Chief* Inspector now, Mrs Evans,' said Vaughan modestly. 'But do please call me Vaughan.'

'And please call me Lowri,' she replied, recreating their introduction from all those years ago. Vaughan was struck by a strong sense of déjà vu as they laughed together. But more importantly – s*he had remembered!*

The small kitchen hadn't changed much since his last visit and even the welcoming smell of fresh baking was the same. Vaughan hung his coat on the back of the kitchen chair as Lowri attended to two boys, still wearing their school uniforms, whose good looks were virtually identical. The boys' thick black curly hair and dazzling blue eyes immediately reminded him of her missing son, but how could that be possible?

Once the boys were settled in the parlour with a glass of milk and a colouring book each, Lowri returned to the kitchen and set about boiling the kettle. Her long raven hair, loose around her slender shoulders, was now thickly streaked with bands of grey. It was a strikingly attractive look. Vaughan hastily took out his notebook and became engrossed in it, hoping she wouldn't notice the flush in his face.

Lowri went to the kitchen dresser and removed a square metal tea caddy from a high shelf as the kettle heated on the stovetop. She took out four envelopes and placed them on the kitchen table. 'Please do take a look, Vaughan.'

Vaughan took out his spectacle case and propped his bifocals on the end of his nose to examine the papers closely, holding each one gingerly by the outer edge. Each envelope was typed with her name and address, and postmarked from America, in each case from a different state. Vaughan examined the envelopes and the remembrance cards. 'And what about the letter to his fiancée? May I see that too, please?'

Lowri's expression was downcast. 'I'm sorry, Vaughan, but Shirley burned that letter at the time. She was so upset, poor love, I don't blame her.'

Vaughan stifled a grunt of frustration. A comparison of the typewriter type would have been useful but it couldn't be helped. 'I'm not sure there's much that can be done, as my jurisdiction doesn't extend as far as America,' he said, 'but I'll have a dig around and see how far I get.' He was fairly confident he could trace the ship that Bryn had sailed on, and that would be a start, but he didn't want to give Lowri false hope. She was so fragile and elegant; it was as if she were made of bone china and he didn't want to be the one to smash her hopes into a million pieces.

Lowri's eyes sparkled vivaciously. 'That would be marvellous, Vaughan,' she said, clasping her delicate hands across her winsome breast.

Vaughan removed his spectacles and was replacing them in their case when she added, 'My theory is they are from Bryn. I think the letter was a hoax, for some reason, and he's still alive. I can feel it. What do you reckon?'

Words failed him. His mouth hung open as his brain raced to catch up with this alternative reality, the world in which Lowri was not a wilting widow made of bone china but a determined mother out for the truth. He looked at her with newfound respect and berated himself for underestimating her. He wouldn't make that mistake again.

PART TWO

Greer
Travis and Chase
Huw and Rhys

1984-2008

TWENTY

1984

Gryff was sharpening an axe in the front yard when he heard Gwenna yelling for him from the house. He removed his Stetson and wiped the sweat from his brow with his forearm.

'Honey! Jerome was just on the phone. Shelby's horsebox won't start and they need it tomorrow. He says can you get over there this afternoon? Shelby's real upset she might miss her competition, so it's kinda urgent.'

Gryff thumped the axe down into his wood-chopping block. It was Saturday afternoon and he'd hoped to get this pile of hickory split into firewood by sunset, ready for tomorrow's day of rest. But the Jepsons came first. The Jepsons *always* came first and most of the time, that was just fine. If it weren't for Jack Jepson, he wouldn't be standing there right now, in the yard of the modest family home he and Wendell built on Jepson land with Jack Jepson's personal approval, so that his kids could be a stone's throw from their grandparents. He paid a peppercorn rent on the land and all he had to do in return was be available at a moment's notice for mechanical repairs at the stables or on any of Jack's farmland. You couldn't say fairer than that.

Except for when it was Jerome doing the asking.

Gryff had a problem with Jerome. Whenever the two families got together for Jack's legendary summer barbecues at Buena Vista, Gryff could see Jerome's eyes following Gwenna's every move. It made his blood boil and there was nothing he could do about it that wouldn't upset the applecart.

With weary resignation, Gryff rolled down his sleeves and buttoned up his faded old plaid shirt, gathered up his wood-chopping equipment and headed to the tool shed to pack it all away.

His twelve-year-old son, Chase, looked up from dismantling his bike as he walked in.

'I'm heading up to the stables to look at fixing Shelby's horsebox. Fancy keeping me company?' Gryff knew full well that Chase would jump at any excuse to fix stuff with his pa. He grinned and ruffled Chase's tousled curls, which had grown long during the summer break.

Chase grinned back and leapt to his feet. 'You bet!' He wiped his oily hands on the legs of his dungarees. Like father like son, Gryff's customers often said to him whenever the pair of them pitched up together to get a tractor running again or fix a hay bailer. And they weren't wrong – Chase was indeed a chip off the old block, completely at home covered in grease, with a spanner in one hand and a screwdriver in the other. As they strolled to his truck, Gryff put his arm across his boy's shoulders, enjoying the warmth of the afternoon and the pleasure of being with his son.

As he brought his truck to a halt in the stable yard at Jay Jay stud farm, Gryff caught sight of the retreating figure of his other son, Travis, pushing a barrowload of horse muck out of the yard towards the muck stack behind the newly built showjumping ring. The twin brothers might be impossible to tell apart, but their personalities were like chalk and cheese. Travis was the serious one, hard-working and sensible, whereas Chase was an easy-going prankster. Nobody could fathom how identical twins could be so different, to the extent that sometimes-brooding Travis seemed unknowable compared to his extrovert brother. In many ways, Travis reminded Gryff of his own father and he loved him all the more for it. He watched his son's progress with the barrow, noticing how it wobbled as Travis drew level with the ring, where Jerome's ten-year-old daughter Shelby was riding a small white pony. He chuckled to himself as Travis set down the barrow and stood looking on.

'Go and give your brother a hand, Chase.' Gryff didn't want Chase around when he was dealing with Jerome.

'Sure thing, Pa.' Chase's eagerness surprised his father. He scampered off to join Travis by the horse ring without a backward glance.

As Gryff unloaded his tools from the truck, he was struck by how his two sons standing side by side at the ring were a perfect mirror image of one another. Their unruly black curls shone in the bright sunshine, and they both had their hands on their hips and legs apart like a pair of matching trestles, equally fascinated by the sight of Shelby who was wearing a navy velvet riding jacket and white jodhpurs, cantering her pony around the ring. Her features were arranged in an expression of intense concentration and her strawberry blonde ponytail flowed out from under her hat.

The thought came from nowhere and it hit him like a train.

His sons looked just like Emlyn.

Poleaxed by the notion, he leaned against the truck, and ran a calloused grimy hand over his face, blowing out his cheeks. Where had that come from? His throat tightened as the once-familiar wave of guilt and panic surged inside him. He coughed a few times and stamped his feet in the dust to distract himself, which usually worked. It wasn't the first time this had happened but it had been a while. The sudden attacks had waned over the years and, at times, he thought they'd gone. And then one came out of nowhere, just like this. He could see why his brain had thrown a hand grenade at him this time, though. Travis and Chase were nearly the same age as Emlyn had been, and with their usually cropped raven hair grown out into long summer-break curls, just like Emlyn's, it was impossible *not* to see the similarity. As the panic ebbed, he headed to the stable yard office to get the keys for the horsebox and helped himself to a leftover cold coffee. It tasted like mud but was better than nothing.

He already had the hood up and was inspecting the engine compartment when Jerome's bright-red Jeep Cherokee sport wagon crunched to a halt beside him. It was so new that the black walls of the tyres were still shiny. Either that or Jerome had them washed every day. The relief on Jerome's face spoke volumes as he climbed out of the spotless wagon, dressed like nobody ever dressed at a stable in a blue blazer, a white shirt open at the collar, dark-navy jeans, and tan suede Gucci loafers with tassels on. Gryff's eyes lingered on the tasselled loafers.

'Thanks for coming out, Gryff.' Jerome spread his arms expansively and plastered his face with a warm smile. 'Shelby has been obsessed with showjumping since we got back from Los Angeles and she doesn't want to miss tomorrow's gymkhana.'

Gryff felt his hackles rising already. The man had only been here thirty seconds and was already banging on about the Olympic Games. Chase had said the same about Shelby and her brother Tyler, but they were kids and their parents had bought them VIP passes for everything, so it was no wonder they wanted to brag about it.

'Some Jay Jay horses were competing in eventing,' Jerome explained as if someone had asked. 'The moment Shelby set eyes on the showjumping and the dressage, that was it. She was hooked. We couldn't tear her away from the ring and now she's got one of her own to play with.'

Gryff grimaced. Even he knew Shelby wasn't 'playing with' her new showjumping ring. She was serious about horses, like her Grandpa Jack. If there was one thing everyone around these parts knew about Shelby – apart from her own father, or so it seemed – it was that when Shelby put her mind to something, she was soon good at it. Gryff admired that determination in a girl. Greer was just the same with her music. His daughter had perfect pitch, so he was told. If she got into music college next year, as she hoped, she'd be the first person in his family ever to go to college and Gwenna had a big surprise lined up for her as a reward.

Jerome was still talking, something about the Olympics, no doubt, as Gryff tuned back into his one-sided conversation. ' —and Joseph Fargis let her sit on *Touch of Class and* wear his Olympic gold medal. That was an exceptional day for Shelby.'

Gryff had had enough of Jerome and slammed the horsebox hood shut, relishing Jerome's flinch. He was glad Chase wasn't there to see him being such an ass.

'All fixed. Loose alternator cable,' he said through gritted teeth, turning his back on Jerome as he gathered his tools. He truly was being a jackass and he knew it, but he couldn't help himself. Jerome always brought out the worst in him.

Jerome sounded happy with the news, but then he always did. 'Thank you so much, Gryff,' he said. 'I'm sure Shelby will be so grateful. In fact, we are all grateful for everything you do for us, Gryff, me and the whole family. You're a good man to know and have around. Thanks once again.' Jerome stuck out his hand.

Gryff pressed his lips together so firmly that they turned white. Was Jerome honestly so thick-skinned that he hadn't noticed Gryff's surliness? He eyed Jerome's proffered hand, weighing up whether he could get away without shaking it.

'No problem, Jerome. Anytime.' He grasped Jerome's hand firmly. It was all part of being a good husband and father. Now, where had those boys got to?

Chase bobbed in the warm lake, his feet feeling the tickle of stonewort rooted in the sludge far below. He was waiting for Shelby and Tyler to come down from the big white house on the crest of the hill, where three generations of Jepsons lived together under one immense roof. Buena Vista always reminded him of a giant wedding cake and the perfectly striped lawn that extended from the house to the edge of the lake looked like a vibrant green tablecloth. Back at the ring, he'd suggested that he and Travis go for a swim with Shelby and Tyler, but Travis had other ideas, as usual, and went off on his own. Chase was fuming with his brother at first, but he soon got over it. He was planning to pull a practical joke on them all, which he'd been practising all summer. There was nothing Chase loved more than a practical joke, and this was a good one. He couldn't wait to see their faces! He'd just have to catch Travis out another time.

After what seemed like an eternity but was probably just five minutes, Shelby and Tyler appeared at the top of the hill. They ran hollering down the slope towards him, their thin legs flailing. Carrying their swim towels bundled under one arm, they made a beeline for the pontoon, where they always leapt into the lake with excited screams. Shelby's hair streamed behind her as she raced to keep up with Tyler, who was two years older than her and the same age as Chase.

Chase waved his arms wildly to attract their attention. He needed them to see him in the water.

Her free arm waved back and her happy giggle reached him through the still, warm air. It was the moment he'd been waiting for.

Chase breathed in deeply and then breathed in some more. With his lips tightly sealed, he slipped below the surface, barely leaving a ripple and struck out strongly using underwater breaststroke to pull himself silently towards the island in the middle of the lake.

Chase was confident he could make it. It was a good sixty yards away and no one would ever expect a twelve-year-old kid to be able to swim that far underwater. Even so, his lungs were fit to burst as he pulled himself the last few yards through the murky water. Gasping quietly, he surfaced alongside a thick patch of undergrowth, out of sight of the shore and pulled himself onto dry land. As he raked his fingers through his mop of slick curls, he heard Shelby's cries of alarm from the shore with a satisfied chuckle.

'Chase! Chase! Where are you? Chaaaase!'

Everything was going according to plan. Any minute now, they would think that he'd drowned. He stifled his laughter and waited patiently as the panicked cries grew louder. Just as Tyler was being sent to get help, he burst from the bushes and revealed his miraculous survival with a triumphant cry. The effort was worth it for the angry looks on their faces.

'That's not funny, Chase!' yelled Tyler, throwing a rock in his direction. He jumped off the pontoon and thrashed across the lake, clearly intending to start a fight. Chase laughed so much that it hurt and collapsed onto the gravel, clutching his stomach. There was no way Tyler would have enough left in him for a fight by the time he got to the island, and that made Chase laugh even harder. As Tyler crawled out of the water, panting and exhausted, Chase helped him out, and they both slumped onto the narrow gravel shoreline. 'You gotta admit, Tyler,' gasped Chase as he wiped tears of laughter from his face, 'that was an amazing trick! Sixty yards underwater! I'm gonna be a stuntman in the movies when I grow up.'

'*If* you ever grow up,' Tyler retorted, grinning despite himself. He punched Chase hard on the forearm, scrambled to his feet and flung himself back into the water. 'Last one back is a bozo!'

Shelby sat pouting with her feet dangling off the pontoon, her legs too short to reach the water below. The two boys swam up to her, grabbing at her ankles and pretending to pull her in.

'I hate you, Chase Garland, scarin' me like that!' Shelby's bottom lip trembled as she pulled her feet out of their reach. 'I thought you wuz drowned!'

Chase felt a brief pang of guilt. He always forgot that Shelby was only ten years old and easily frightened. He may have even apologised to her if Tyler hadn't chosen that moment to jump on his back and push him underwater in a flurry of bubbles. Shelby's laughter rang in his ears as he emerged from the water, spitting out algae and bellowing for revenge.

They spent the rest of the afternoon playing pirates at the lake, taking turns to row the small rowboat that was kept there and making each other walk the gangplank off the end of the pontoon. As the sun began to set and the temperature dropped, Shelby and Tyler grabbed their grassy towels and headed back, just as Jerome appeared on the veranda and called out to his kids to come and eat. 'Coming, Pa!' Tyler replied as they ran up the sloping lawn, rubbing their goosebumps. Shelby turned to wave to Chase but he had already disappeared underwater, practising for when he could scare the living daylights out of Travis – if he could drag him away from his precious horses.

Travis was captivated by the rich timbre of Jimmy Knox's soulful voice rising and falling against the background chirrup of crickets as he sat astride the stable door, watching the older man lovingly groom his glossy chestnut mare, Zelda, in her stall.

The way Jimmy told it, his songs went back generations, originating from his great-great-grandma, who worked the cotton fields as enslaved labour till the day she died. Travis couldn't help but wonder what Jimmy's great-great-grandma would think of him now – a celebrated Kentucky Derby-winning champion jockey and owner of a beautiful racehorse in his own right. Zelda was the granddaughter of the first mare named after her, his reward from Jack for bagging him a record-breaking sixth owner win at the Kentucky Derby on Red Admiral almost thirty years before. It had made legends out of both Jimmy and Jack, now immortalised in the Kentucky Derby Hall of Fame. Some of the older folks who lived in Whitesville, Grandpa Wendell included, still spoke of that day with a faraway look. Travis's admiration for Jimmy was boundless. The older man knew everything there was to know about horses and Travis wanted to learn it all. The more reason he had to be at the stables where he could help Shelby with her pony, the better. He'd only ducked out of Chase's suggestion for a swim because he couldn't bear to hear Shelby giggling at Chase's stupid pranks – but she was only ten and easily impressed by his show-off brother so it wasn't hard to forgive her.

From the corner of his eye, Travis spotted movement in the twilight shadows at the edge of the stable yard. He sat bolt upright, fully alert.

'Jimmy! Hush up! I've seen something moving. It might be a black bear!'

Jimmy reached smoothly for the lever-action Winchester shotgun resting on the frame above the stable door. 'No bear is gonna have himself a feast in *my* stables.'

Travis held his breath as the undergrowth rustled once again. 'If that bear's lookin' for trouble, he's found it,' said Jimmy, checking both barrels for cartridges.

The shrubbery rustled some more, and Travis and Jimmy gave each other worried looks. Without warning, Chase burst through the dense foliage, skinny and pale, barefoot and without a shirt. His hair was dripping wet and his teeth chattered in the cool evening air. Travis and Jimmy both exhaled in relief.

'Hey, jackass!' Travis shouted. 'You could have gotten yourself shot just then!' He tossed a horse blanket in Chase's direction. 'Catch this. It should keep you warm until you get home.'

Chase grinned sheepishly. 'Thanks, Trav. Can I have your boots too?' He scooped up the dusty blanket, shook it out and wrapped himself in its itchy smelly warmth. Travis kicked off his boots and threw them over to his idiot of a brother, knowing he had spares in the tack room.

Jimmy wheezed with laughter as he watched Chase's retreating figure disappear towards the lights of home. 'When will that damn fool boy ever get some sense into his head? Are you sure he's your brother? He ain't got the sense he was born with!'

Travis snorted. Jimmy was right; Chase was always getting into scrapes because he didn't think things through properly or plan. He, Travis, was the exact opposite. Jimmy had set aside one corner of the tack room for Travis, and it was a treasure trove of spare kit and bits and bobs that might come in useful someday. You'd never catch Travis going swimming without a towel and some dry clothes to put on afterwards. Greer always said that he and Chase were the flip sides of the same coin, and that made sense. Because they *were* the same coin. He was the 'heads' to Chase's 'tails'. No matter how infuriating Chase could be, Travis loved him – second only to Shelby.

Jimmy grunted. 'Talkin' o' family, not seen much o' your sister lately.'

'That'd be about right, Jimmy. She goes to a special high school for music, way over in Owensboro so that she can get into music college someplace near Louisville. They're gonna teach her to be famous, so she says.' Travis snorted with laughter. 'That'll be the day.'

'I heard folks say she's got real talent,' Jimmy said, burnishing a high shine on the beautiful mare's coat with a soft goat hairbrush. 'Perfect pitch, I heard – whatever that means.'

Travis nodded. 'That's what Ma says and she should know.' His ma used to tell stories of how she played Bonnie Guitar to Greer in her crib the whole time she was a baby, but when he and Chase came along at the same time, two babies kept her too busy for guitar playing. It didn't bother him any. He was happy right where he was, in the stables with Jimmy.

TWENTY- ONE

1986

OWENSBORO, KENTUCKY

G reer settled herself on the stool, her acoustic guitar resting across her knee, and adjusted the microphone to face level. The only window in the Owensboro High School music studio looked directly into the control room, where her friend Misty sat at the digital audio workstation. The glare from the control panel illuminated her face, emphasising the dark hollows around her eyes, and made her huge metallic hooped earrings glow eerily green. Her back-combed hair looked wilder than usual. Greer supposed she was channelling her inner Tina Turner that day.

Audio feedback jarred deafeningly in Greer's earphones. She pulled a face and leaned towards the mike. 'Hey, Misty!' she barked. 'What the heck?'

'Sorry! – My fault!' Her best friend's voice in the headphones sounded distant. 'I'm not with it this morning.' Her tired sigh was amplified in Greer's ears. 'I was serving tables at the diner last night. I didn't get to bed till late.'

'Don't expect any sympathy from me,' joked Greer. 'You don't have to sit on the bus for two hours each way to get here every day, like I have to.'

'Yeah, but at least you can get some sleep on the bus,' retorted Misty, slumping in the controller's chair.

Misty was right about one thing: Greer did sleep the two-hour journey from Whitesville to Owensboro each morning to reach the only school in a fifty-mile radius good enough for a student with perfect pitch, but she used the journey home to study. Nothing less than a perfect score in her advanced placement music theory exam would be good enough for Greer, and everyone was expecting her to top the list of honours students. Privately, she thought the same, as no one at Owensboro High was even close to being as smart and hardworking as her – except maybe Misty. It would be amazing if they both got a place at the University of Louisville School of Music.

Misty's voice in the headphones interrupted her thoughts. 'Are you going to the UoL open day next month, Greer? We could go together if you like?'

Greer rolled her eyes and stuck her tongue out at her friend, enjoying the sound of her husky laughter in the headphones. Of course, she was going to the music college open day with Misty. She was amazed she even needed to ask.

***

Greer's application to the University of Louisville School of Music had taken weeks to prepare, but now worry was eating her alive. What if it wasn't good enough? She'd played and sung Ma's favourite Bonnie Guitar song – *Candy Apple Red* – at her audition, and it seemed well received, but there was so much riding on it, she wasn't sure she'd done enough. She was Ma's second chance at success and she knew it. Deep down, since she was in second grade, she'd known that Ma should have been famous but never got the big break she deserved, and it was all her fault. If she hadn't been born, maybe Ma would have got that break. Now, it was up to her to achieve the success Ma had always dreamed of.

Greer was eating grits with Travis and Chase in the kitchen when the mailman brought the letter. The plain brown envelope was addressed to Miss G Garland and there was no question what it was. She looked at the unopened envelope, hands trembling. These were the final moments of her life before everything would change, for better or worse.

'Travis, go and fetch Grandpa and Carol,' said Gwenna, 'and Chase, you run to the auto shop and get Pa. It's only right that everyone should be here when Greer gets her news.'

Greer propped the unopened letter against the coffee pot on the kitchen table with shaky fingers and chewed her grits in nervous silence, her eyes fixed on the letter as she waited for Pa and Grandpa to arrive. The grits tasted like sawdust and she could barely swallow past the lump in her throat. Ma pretended to go about her usual morning routine as if nothing was happening but you could cut the tension with a knife.

With everyone assembled, exchanging anxious glances, Greer braced herself to open the envelope. She might as well have been wearing boxing gloves, the way she fumbled to tear the letter open.

'Give it here,' Pa brandished his folding pocketknife. 'Let me do it.' The envelope was open with a single neat slice, and she only had to take the letter out and read it. But even then, it was like she was wading through glue. What was wrong with her?

With the letter finally in her hands, her eyes raced over the words. She only read as far as the first line before shrieking with joy. She'd done it!

A wild cheer erupted and a dozen joyful arms wrapped around her as her legs gave way. She collapsed onto a kitchen chair sobbing, her pent-up tension releasing like a burst fire hydrant. Five years of getting up at 5am for the two-hour bus ride had paid off. She was finally on the fast track to being the person she'd always dreamed of: *Greer Garland, country and western star*. She could already see her name in lights. The relief was so intense it was almost unbearable.

'Best thirty bucks I ever spent,' said Grandpa Wendell with a laugh, wiping his eyes on his shirt sleeve and patting the lid of the old upright Baldwin piano he'd bought Greer when she was just three years old and already showing signs of musical prodigy.

'I'll pay you back when I'm rich and famous, Grandpa, I promise,' joked Greer, regaining control of her breathing, wiping her swollen eyes and blowing her streaming nose on a handkerchief. 'I've gotta call Misty and find out if she got in, too,' she said hoarsely, reaching for the phone.

'Hold on just one second, young lady.' Gryff rested a calming hand on her shoulder. 'Before you do, I think your mam has something for you.'

Greer looked around. Ma was nowhere to be seen. How had she not noticed she wasn't there, celebrating with her? What was going on? Why was everyone wearing such goofy grins?

When Ma appeared at the kitchen doorway, she was carrying Bonnie Guitar like the Crown Jewels on a velvet cushion. Ma's cheeks were flushed and her eyes were glistening. Greer searched the smiling faces around her for clues. What was going on?

As Ma placed Bonnie in her arms, the symbolism of the moment was unmistakable. Greer cradled the precious guitar like a newborn baby, tears streaming down her face. The familiar scent of cherry blossom and almonds filled her senses as Ma leaned in to kiss her cheek while the rest of the family broke into wild applause. It was a moment she would never forget as long as she lived.

'She's all yours, now,' Gwenna whispered in her daughter's ear. 'Go and make us all even more proud of you than we already are, and take Bonnie along for the ride. She deserves it.'

As Greer excused herself to phone Misty and everyone else drifted away, Gwenna found herself alone with Wendell in the kitchen. She wrapped her arms around her father's waist and rested her cheek on his plaid-covered chest, savouring the familiar tobacco smells of vanilla and oak. He rested his bristly chin on the top of her raven hair, now streaked lightly with seams of bright silver, and held her close. Neither spoke as they swayed gently together, lost in their thoughts.

Several minutes passed before Gwenna extracted herself reluctantly from her father's warm embrace and dried her face on a tea towel. She adored her pa more than words could say, but they didn't hug often enough and none of them was getting any younger.

'You've done a great job with that girl, Gwenna.' Wendell pulled out a kitchen chair from the table and lowered himself stiffly onto it.

Gwenna waved a dismissive hand at him as she took the seat opposite and poured coffee for them both from the pot on the table. 'It was a team effort, Pa,' she said, 'and nobody worked harder than Greer herself. She deserves all the credit.'

Wendell grunted. 'You're doing yourself a disservice, Gwenna.' He pulled a face as he sipped his tepid coffee. 'I know how hard it is to raise a family, don't forget.'

Gwenna winced. He didn't mean anything by it, but she'd never quite forgiven herself for being a teenage runaway and the worry she'd caused her pa.

'Well, I've been luckier than most', she said. 'I've had a good man by my side who'd do anything for his kids, and I've had you and Carol backing me up.' She smiled and took hold of his weathered hand across the table. 'Thank you, Pa, for all your help. You *and* Carol. It seems like the sun is finally shining on the Garland family.'

***

Chase's blood raced with excitement as the brightly coloured cars zigzagged out of the pits, warming up their tyres. One of them, the pale blue '65 Oldsmobile Cutlass with 'Morgan Auto Repairs' emblazoned across the hood, was driven by his pa, looking like a spaceman in his helmet, goggles and thick padded gloves. Deafened by the roar of the engines and intoxicated by the aromatic clouds of exhaust fumes, Chase could almost believe he was at the Daytona 500 in Florida – *The Greatest Stock Car Race in the World* – and not watching a bunch of amateur weekend warriors at the Kentucky Motor Speedway circuit.

Chase watched with mounting tension from his vantage point in the pits as his pa navigated the 3/8-mile banked track and slotted in behind the pace car for the warm-up laps. It would be him behind the wheel one day and he could hardly wait.

The commentary through the crackling PA system was impossible to understand, but it was easy to tell the moment the green flag dropped when the pitch of the engines rose from a gut-shaking rumble to a brain-splitting roar, drowning out everything else. The drivers accelerated hard and the cars surged forward, jostling fiercely for the inside line. They were off! Pumped with adrenaline, Chase hopped about like a crazy frog, punching the air. 'Come on, Pa!' he hollered at the top of his lungs. Could anything possibly be more exciting than this?

As the clouds of blue exhaust smoke cleared, Zakrey Dunbar's Yellow Peril Chevy was ahead of his pa on the first lap. Chase kicked a pile of tyres with a flare of frustration, cursing Zak for having a better car than Pa, even though Pa always said stock car racing was like horse racing – you paced yourself until the finish line was in sight. Chase didn't give a crap about horses but he understood what Pa meant.

At that moment, a collective groan rose from the small crowd of spectators. Chase clambered on top of a stack of hay bales, desperate to get a better view of the far side of the track but dreading what he might see. His worst fears were realised – a thick cloud of black smoke was billowing from the Cutlass's hood. He looked on in dismay as the car lost speed and dropped out of the field, cruising into the pit on momentum alone.

'It looks like Gryff Morgan is out of the racing today, in the second lap of the first heat,' crackled the PA system. 'That'll be a big disappointment for him.'

Chase rushed over to his pa's car, his heart in his mouth, but he was pushed back by pit crewmen wielding fire extinguishers. Black smoke and the acrid stench of burning rubber filled the air.

'Get the hell outta the way, Chase, you'll get yourself hurt!'

'Pa! Pa!' he yelled, jumping frantically to see around the crewmen.

Through the sea of blue overalls, Chase caught a glimpse of his pa pulling himself through the glass-free side window, coughing and choking on the black smoke, before walking away from the car unharmed. Pa ripped off his goggles and crash helmet, and tossed them angrily onto the grass bank.

'You okay, Pa?' Chase called out, running up to him breathlessly.

'It's okay, Son, I'm fine.' Gryff turned to his son, revealing his blackened face with white goggle marks around his eyes. 'It's just not my lucky day today.'

Chase burst out laughing at the sight of his pa's comical panda face, the crushing fear of a moment earlier completely forgotten. Zakrey Dunbar flicked a quick wave as the Yellow Peril roared past at the front of the pack, which his pa acknowledged with the briefest of nods. For all their rivalry on the track, Chase knew that Zak and Pa were the best of friends after the race, sitting in the bar analysing each heat, corner by corner. Nobody wanted to see anyone get hurt.

'We'll have to get the old banger up on the ramp in the morning and see if we can work out what went wrong,' Pa said as he walked back to the pit with his arm over Chase's shoulder.

Chase could hardly wait until he was old enough to race for himself but, until then, he loved nothing more than helping his pa at the auto repair shop. There was simply no better way to spend a Sunday morning, monkey wrench in hand, covered in grease and being with his hero.

***

A gust of cold wind blew a flurry of dry leaves through the open doors of the old tobacco barn, which had served as the home of Morgan Auto Repairs for almost two decades. Every inch of wall space was covered with tool racks and shelves filled with every kind of car lube, spray paint and degreaser. On the oil-stained floor were stacks of spare tyres, replacement radiators and gas cylinders. The pale blue Cutlass stood amid the organised chaos, up on ramps, with its hood open and surrounded by tools and blackened engine parts. Viscous black oil dripped from the engine compartment into a shallow tray below. On the car roof, next to a coffee mug with no handle and a pile of torn cotton sheets stained with grease, Tammy Wynette's heartbreak blared from a transistor radio.

Gryff tossed his spanner into a large metal toolbox and wiped his oily hands on the trouser legs of his grease-stained coveralls. 'That's enough work for today,' he muttered as he slammed shut the hood of the ageing Cutlass. The darned car had overheated the last couple of weekends at the Kentucky Motor Speedway circuit, and he was tired of being beaten by Zakrey Dunbar. He would always beat Zakrey on the tight turns since he'd tuned the Oldsmobile for maximum grip, but the problem was that the price for grip — as everyone knew — was overheating. He couldn't seem to get the balance right, somehow. He hadn't finished the job, far from it, but he'd already sent Chase on home ahead to get washed up for Sunday lunch. He didn't want to be late and find himself getting a D-I-V-O-R-C-E.

An involuntary shiver passed through Gryff as he drove the short distance home from Evansville. The cool days of late February always left him feeling out of sorts as the anniversary of Emlyn's death approached. Gwenna understood his moodiness and knew better than to bring it up, and he was grateful for that, but his kids couldn't understand why their normally fun-loving dad became so blue, even though he tried his best to hide it from them. It had been over twenty years since the tragedy, yet the anniversary continued to haunt him. The shame he felt for his cowardice in abandoning his mam and brothers was a weeping sore, made worse by the letter he'd sent to Shirley, faking his death. He would carry the burden to his grave.

Climbing out of his truck on his driveway, Gryff patted the pocket of his heavyweight winter jacket. The envelope was there, already typed with the address of his childhood home in South Wales, words so familiar they could almost have been tattooed inside his eyelids. What would the old place look like now? Would anything have changed at all?

Maybe someone had painted the front door a different colour? He would never know. He was almost jealous of the envelope in his pocket for returning to his old home, a journey he would never make again. Was his mam even still there? A shiver ran down his spine. If anything happened to her, he would never know. He'd just have to pray for the best that she was still there and was receiving the anonymous cards he'd been sending for the past eighteen years. Most importantly, he prayed that she knew they were from him and that he was still alive. It was the only way he knew to tell her he loved her and was sorry.

He'd be posting the card at Beaver Dam this year, too darned close to home for comfort, but there was no stock car event for him to race in in another county at the right time. It would be a dead giveaway to post them from the same place every year, and there was no way Gryff was going to allow extradition to catch up with him, especially now that he had his children to think about.

TWENTY-TWO

8TH MARCH 1986

Chase lay on his sick bed drenched in sweat, his bedsheet a sodden twisted knot, and his pillow annoyingly hot and flat. Whichever way he lay, he couldn't get away from the lacerating pain in his throat, like he'd swallowed a handful of razor blades. At first, he'd thought it would be fun to spend a couple of weeks in bed watching movies on the new VCR player he and Trav had gotten for their fourteenth birthday the week before. But after he'd watched *The Terminator* so many times that he could recite the dialogue in his head and his feverish dreams were populated with unstoppable metal exoskeletons trying to kill him, the novelty had worn off.

He must have been asleep, because the sound of tapping woke him. His pa's greying curly head poked around the bedroom door with a concerned look on his face.

'Hey, Son. How are you feeling today? Any better?'

'Not really,' Chase croaked, barely audibly.

Pa winced with sympathy as he approached the bed and gently put his calloused hand, deeply engrained with auto-shop grime, on Chase's forehead.

'That throat sounds painful, Son, and you're still burning up. Can I get you anything? Some Tylenol? Some iced tea?'

Chase shook his head forlornly.

'I'm off to the racetrack shortly, Son,' Pa continued. 'I'll take that video cassette back to the store and get you a couple more, shall I? How d'you fancy *Ghostbusters* and the new *Indiana Jones*?'

Chase nodded. He didn't want to appear ungrateful for his pa's movie choices, but they wouldn't make up for not going with Pa to the track. A wave of self-pity washed over him and a tear slid down his cheek. He wiped it away quickly, embarrassed with himself. Luckily, Pa hadn't noticed – he was busily slipping his grandpa's antique wristwatch from his wrist. Placing it in Chase's clammy hand, he folded his son's fingers over it gently. 'Look after this for me, Son,' he said. 'I'll be back for it later.'

Chase grinned, despite the pain in his cracked and sore lips. Pa had remembered! Entrusting his precious watch to Chase's care was a pre-race superstition thing he normally did at the trackside – an unspoken promise to his son that he'd return safely to collect it. Chase turned the watch over in his palm and inspected the familiar faded gold face set with large ornate Roman numerals. Even before Pa told him it was 'an air loom' passed down to him on his twenty-first birthday by his ma and had once belonged to his grandpa, he was ready to protect it with his life.

Gryff leaned over and kissed Chase on his perspiring brow.

'Get some sleep, square eyes,' he said affectionately, ejecting the cassette from the VCR and putting it back in its box. 'See you later.'

Chase's eyes closed as his father left the room, pulling the door shut behind him with a quiet click. Stock cars raced across the inside of his eyelids as he drifted into a feverish slumber, his fingers still curled around his pa's precious watch.

***

The deafening roar of V8 engines at full throttle filled the air at the Kentucky Speedway track on lap fifteen, as the vintage Oldsmobile Cutlass descended the steep asphalt bank, the Yellow Peril in its sights. Inside the stripped-down cockpit, the heat was like a furnace despite the lack of windows, and sweat filled Gryff's helmet and ran down his face, coursing around his steamed-up goggles. Focused on his rival, Gryff searched single-mindedly for a chance to storm past him, leaving him trailing in a cloud of burning rubber and race fuel, but it was not happening. Out of respect for his scorching brake discs, Gryff eased off the gas on the approach to the next bend, just as the steering column began to judder uncontrollably. He wrestled with the unresponsive steering with everything he had but couldn't control the direction of travel. It was bad news and he needed to get off the track quick, but the car had taken on a mind of its own as it slewed sideways, tyres screeching in a cloud of burning rubber. The whole car shook violently as toxic black fumes poured from under the hood, obscuring the view ahead and filling the driver's compartment. Gryff couldn't see a thing, but he knew what was coming and there wasn't a damned thing he could do about it. *Thank God*

Chase isn't here to see this, he thought, choking on the acrid smoke as he slipped into unconsciousness.

WHITESVILLE EVENING NEWS: MONDAY, 10TH MARCH, 1986 MAN DIES IN SCCA CLUB RACING EVENT.

A racecar driver was killed in a horrifying crash at the Kentucky Speedway Track on Saturday, the first fatal accident in amateur club racing at the racing circuit in twenty-seven years.

Witnesses report seeing the Vintage 1965 Oldsmobile Cutlass driven by Gryff Morgan, 46, sliding sideways as it took off from the raised bank and somersaulted across the track before exploding in a thirty-foot fireball, sending burning wreckage spinning into the crowd. Screaming spectators fled for their lives, and one onlooker said it was 'a miracle' there were no other reported casualties.

No other vehicles were involved in the crash, leading crash investigators to speculate at this stage that mechanical failure may have been the cause.

Mr Morgan, owner of Morgan's Auto Repairs in Evansville, KY, leaves a wife and three children. Nobody in the family was available for comment. Mr Zakary Dunbar, also racing in the event, described Mr Morgan as a great driver and terrific friend who will be sorely missed.

***

The house was deathly quiet, save for the monotonous tick of the kitchen clock.

Sitting alone at the table, Gwenna contemplated the face of the woman in the creased black-and-white photograph in her hands. She looked about twenty years old, with dark glossy hair set in a sleek wave against her flawless porcelain skin. Her eyes sparkled, and the trace of a smile lingered around her lips. She looked serene and happy. On the back of the photograph, in faded handwriting, there was a single word – *Lowri*.

Gwenna found the photograph weeks ago in Gryff's wallet, just after the funeral. She hadn't been able to stop looking at it since. The woman in the picture had to be Gryff's mother, except – of course – that she'd have no idea who Gryff Morgan was. It was strange to think of Gryff as Bryn Evans, someone's son. It haunted her that Gryff carried this photograph yet never spoke of his mother, not even to her – his own wife. It must have been too painful for him. It was unbearable that he'd handled all that alone. What would Lowri think if she knew her son lay in a grave under a headstone bearing another man's name? It was an awful thought and Gwenna couldn't believe she'd let that happen. But what choice did she have?

Gwenna studied the photograph of her mother-in-law and ran her fingers through her thick hair, which she'd noticed lately was streaked with grey around the temples. Was Lowri even still alive? She'd be… what? Sixty-five, seventy, maybe? *Where are you now, Mrs Lowri Evans? Would you want to know the truth? Would you want to know your grandkids? Or would the truth hurt too much?* It was impossible to know the price they'd all paid simply because young immature Bryn Evans had been in the wrong place at the wrong time. But there wouldn't be any extradition to Argentina now, so was it time for the truth?

She sank her head into her hands and let out a low groan. She couldn't tell her kids the truth. Knowing that Pa was an imposter would break their hearts. She just couldn't do it. God knew the truth and that was what mattered most.

Gwenna reached for a pen and notepad in a maelstrom of emotions, and began to write. The words flowed effortlessly.

Time is a one-way street,
No chance of turning back.
How many people did I meet
Along life's twisting track?
Was I your son, your brother or your friend?
Did I break your heart or leave you cold?
Now I've reached my bitter end,
Will the truth finally be told?
I thought I could choose my life,
But my life chose me.
I tried fighting back,
Imagined I was free.
But the damage was done before I knew it.
The lies I told myself helped me through it.
I had great chances, but I really blew it.
If I had my time again, would I really do it?
Who will I be when I am dead,
Just a name on a stone above my head?
My time's behind me, no more ahead.
Is there anything else left to be said?

Gwenna enjoyed having Greer home from music college on weekends, bringing a burst of life and energy into the house, but she was unexpectedly lonely during the week. The twins had disappeared from her life as if their pa had been the magnet that kept them home and, without him, there was no pull to return. Travis spent most of his time after school and at weekends at the Jepson stables with Jimmy as if he'd moved in there, and as for Chase, no one knew where he was or what he was doing.

'What about his schoolin', Gwenna?' Carol asked as Gwenna sat next to Wendell at her dining table after Sunday lunch had been cleared away. Greer had gone out to find the twins, who hadn't shown up for dinner.

'He's still attendin' and scrapin' by, by all accounts,' said Gwenna, 'but Chase is not actually my biggest worry right now.'

Wendell reached across the table and took her hand. 'What is it, Gwenna? What can we do to help?'

'It's Greer's college fees, Pa,' said Gwenna. 'The auto repair shop was making good money before Gryff… passed away,' she faltered. 'He was sure we could afford to pay the college bills.' She rubbed her face wearily. 'But with the auto shop shuttered and no money coming in, I reckon I'm gonna have to sell up to keep Greer in college and feed the family.'

Wendell's brow furrowed. 'Isn't there any way you can keep it on? We all thought Chase would take it over when his pa retired.' His voice cracked. 'He's a great mechanic, just like his pa.'

'I would love to, Pa, but Chase has only just turned fourteen. He's got four more years of high school till he could take it over and, even then, he cain't run a business at that age.'

Wendell grunted. 'You're right of course, but selling the repair shop? It must be the last resort, surely?'

The porch door flew open and Greer stormed in, bringing the cold spring air with her. 'I cain't find either of the little varmints.' She propped her hands on her hips and tapped her riding boot with exasperation. 'I'm gonna write a note and leave it at the stables for Travis. Jimmy says he'll pass it on, maybe even try to encourage him to come home a bit more. He's a good man, that Jimmy.' She grabbed the notepad from the kitchen dresser and took it to her room.

Wendell lowered his voice. 'You'll need to find Gryff's papers, Gwenna. I know he took out a business loan to set up the repair shop.' He paused. 'I don't know if the business still owes money.'

Gwenna's blood turned to ice. It had never occurred to her that that might be the case. 'He keeps a box of stuff at the back of the wardrobe, Pa,' she said, trying to hide the panic in her voice. 'Shall I go get it now? Could you help me sort through it?'

She'd been dreading this moment for weeks, but she had to face up to it sooner or later. It would be a whole lot easier with the help of Carol and Pa, who knew a lot more about papers and running a business than she ever would.

The piles of statements and business loan documents on the dining room table grew steadily as Carol gradually emptied the box and sorted them into categories. At the very bottom of the box was an old passport with a black cover.

'Hey, look at that!' said Wendell. 'That must be Gryff's ol' British passport! I bet he looks real young in the photo.' He had it in his hand and was flipping through the pages before Gwenna could stop him.

'No!' she screamed, her hand flying to her mouth.

Wendell froze. Carol sat wide-eyed with surprise beside him. 'Hey, darlin',' said Wendell softly. 'I'm sorry. I didn't mean to upset you.'

Gwenna snatched the passport from Wendell's hand, her own hand trembling violently. 'Too soon,' she mumbled, her pulse racing and heat rising in her face. She hated lying to her pa, but if he took one look at the photo, the game would be up and she would have a whole lot of explaining to do. It would destroy their belief in everything they held true about Gryff and she couldn't allow that to happen.

Tucking the passport safely in her purse, she turned her attention back to the documents, her voice artificially bright. 'So, what do we have here?'

They worked steadily for two hours, sorting everything into date order.

'I don't rightly know what to say.' Wendell's face was a picture of astonishment as he held the earliest bank statement in his hand.

It was all there in black and white, Gryff's opening deposit, dated 1967.

Twenty-thousand dollars.

'Where did Gryff get his hands on a fortune like that?' gasped Carol, sitting back in her chair and running both hands through her hair.

Gwenna blew out her cheeks, lost for words. In hindsight, the twenty-thousand dollars looked like a lot of money and she'd never known Gryff's pay-off was that much, but the reality was that no amount of money could compensate for the loss of freedom and family that she, Gryff and their children had endured all because of that

238

stupid revolutionary plot. Just thinking about it made her angry.

'Wh... what happened to it?'

'Well, according to the most recent statements—' Carol flicked through the pile of papers—'it's all still there. In fact, it grew. It's now sixty-five thousand, six-hundred and twenty-eight dollars, and 74 cents!'

The blood rushed from Gwenna's face. Her hands shook as she took the statement from Carol. 'This cain't be real?'

'And there's more.' Wendell extracted a thick sheaf of papers from a stiff envelope. 'These are the title deeds to the auto repair shop. It looks like Gryff paid off all his business loans over the years. The repair shop is yours outright. He left you and the family in great financial shape, Gwenna. You won't have to worry about money for the rest of your life. There's more'n enough here to send all the kids to college if they wanna go!'

Gwenna's face crumpled. She'd been holding it together for weeks but this was just too much.

'Oh, Gryff!' She buried her face in her hands and sobbed. He must have worked harder than she'd ever imagined, paying off his loans without ever saying a word about it. Now, it was too late to tell him how much they all loved and appreciated him. Wracked with heaving sobs, Gwenna fell into her father's arms and cried like she was never going to stop.

In her bedroom, sitting at her desk, Greer opened the notepad. Her mother's familiar handwriting covered the top sheet.

Time is a one-way street...

As she looked around for Bonnie, the notes were already forming in her head.

***

UNIVERSITY OF LOUISVILLE, KENTUCKY

'Okay, Greer. Whatcha got? Let's hear it.' Will Dixon's confident Boston accent boomed in her headphones, interrupting her favourite daydream, the one where she was gigging with Crystal Gayle and Dolly Parton at the Grand Ole Opry. She noodled a few chords on Bonnie, mulling over what to play. Mr Dixon had asked for a simple acoustic session. She smiled to herself. She had just the thing.

On her tutor's cue, she strummed the opening chords, the guitar reverberating gently against her body as Bonnie came to life in her hands.

'*Time is a one-way street*,' she began, her voice soft and melodic, '*no chance of turning back, how many people did I meet, along life's twisting track.*'

She closed her eyes as the song's melancholy took hold of her, the words flowing from her heart in a stream of regret, her fingers skilfully weaving the mellifluous tune from Bonnie's strings. As the final chords faded, she smiled proudly and opened her eyes. On the other side of the recording studio glass, where her classmates were gathered for Mr Dixon's mixing tutorial, she could just about make out a sea of open mouths and wide eyes. There was radio silence in her headphones. Heat rushed to her face. What had she done? Had she made a terrible fool of herself?

Static crackled in her ears as she waited for the axe to fall. She could kick herself for using untested lyrics but she'd been showing off, so she deserved what was coming.

'Wow... pretty good actually, Greer,' said the Boston voice in her headphones. 'Did you write that yourself?'

Greer slumped forward on her high stool, giggling with relief. Thank God! He liked it! 'Yessir, um... no, Sir... well, maybe,' she stammered. 'It was a poem my ma wrote and I put it to music. I hope you don't mind.'

'Not at all, Greer. You did a great job, fantastic. Let's go again.'

***

That afternoon, Greer found a note in her pigeonhole, summoning her to Will Dixon's office. Her hands shook as she re-read the note. What had she done wrong? Maybe he didn't like her using her ma's poem after all? Perhaps it had to be all her own work? She hated the idea of being reprimanded. She hadn't let it happen even once, during the whole of high school.

Greer stood outside the door etched in gold with her tutor's name, closed her eyes, took a deep breath and knocked.

'Come!' barked Will's voice.

Greer pushed open the door and strode confidently into the room. Will Dixon was perched on the edge of his desk, his sleeves rolled up, exposing tanned forearms folded across his chest. His long denim-clad legs stretched out before him, crossed at his bare ankles, his feet clad in spotless white sneakers. At a guess, she'd say he was about thirty-five, trying to be twenty-five. She glanced around the room. She wasn't sure what she'd expected a music tutor's office to look like but this wasn't it. The scant furniture was utilitarian, the walls were bare, except for a cool Andy Warhol print of Elvis holding a gun, and a stack of unpacked boxes teetered precariously against one wall. She couldn't tell if he was moving out or moving in.

Will got straight to the point. He didn't even offer her a seat.

'We had an RCA talent scout in the studio this morning, Greer,' he said. 'I didn't introduce her, as I didn't want anyone to get nervous or self-conscious. She loved your performance and wants to take the recording back to her label. This could be an amazing break for you, Greer. What do you say?'

'I'm sorry?' Greer shook her head. Did he just say what she thought he'd said? Something about a talent scout. She wasn't sure she'd heard right.

'An RCA talent scout is interested in your song, Greer,' he repeated. 'This could be your big break.'

The walls and ceiling warped and closed in around her, and she felt herself crumpling to the floor. 'Are you okay, Greer?' Will sounded like he was underwater as he rushed to catch her.

The feel of his arms around her as he steered her safely to the floor, the heat of his body against hers, and the strong smell of cigarettes and sweat overwhelmed her senses. *I'm fine* was what she wanted to say, but her mouth was weirdly out of sync with her brain. Something cold touched her lips. She took a couple of tentative sips, relieved it was water and not something stronger.

After a couple of deep breaths, she opened her eyes. He was leaning over her, the crucifix on a chain around his neck brushing against her face. Through the open collar of his chambray shirt, she could see the texture of his skin and the tuft of dark hair at the hollow of his throat. Her pulse quickened. She placed her hands on the floor to steady herself and attempted to get to her knees.

'Whoa, steady on Greer.' Will had pulled away some and his grinning face was coming into focus. 'Take your time, Greer; that was a big surprise, I guess.' He got to his feet and held out his hand to her. She took it and he hauled her upright, carefully.

'I'm sorry I didn't handle that better. Come here.' He pulled her against him and wrapped his arms around her in a steadying hug. 'You're a great girl, Greer, and a talented musician – the best I've seen around here for a while. You deserve this.'

She leaned her face into his chest and inhaled his musky aroma, wishing the moment would last forever.

TWENTY-THREE

When Zak returned from the scrapyard, a transistor radio was blaring and Chase had a lawn mower stripped down in pieces on the workbench at Dunbar Automotive Services.

'Hey, Chase, can you lend me a hand,' he hollered above the music, leaning out of the driver's window as he reversed his flatbed truck to the auto shop barn doors.

'Sure thing, Uncle Zak.' Chase turned down the radio and wiped his greasy hands on his overalls. 'Have you been to the scrapyard? Looks to me like you brought back more'n you took.'

Zak laughed as he climbed out of his truck. 'It might look like scrap to you, Chase, but this here motorcycle frame is a timeless classic, in my eyes.' When he quit his job at the mine and took out a big bank loan to buy his best buddy Gryff's workshop, a big part of his thinking had been about keeping his buddy's son out of trouble. The boy needed a father figure who shared his love of grease and engine oil.

Chase flipped down the tailgate and sprang onto the back of the truck in one easy move. 'What is it?' He hauled up the dirty rusted frame and examined it. 'It looks like an old Harley to me.'

Zak grinned broadly. 'Dang me, Chase, you're good. It's a 1965 Harley Davidson Sportster. I thought you might like it. You can fix it up and, once you're done, it'll be all yours to keep.' He reached up and took the frame as Chase passed it down. 'What do you think?'

Chase jumped down from the back of the truck and rubbed a greasy hand through his slick wavy locks. 'I don't know what to say, Uncle Zak. I'd love to give it a go, but it'll cost a fortune in spare parts and I don't have that kinda money.'

Zak rested his hand on Chase's shoulders. 'Don't you worry about that, Chase. Most parts'll come cheap from auto-jumbles and you can save up your weekend wages for the new stuff. You have birthdays, don't you? Now we all know what to get you for the next ten years.'

Chase's ice-blue eyes shone as a smile crept across his face. 'D'you think I can do it, Uncle Zak? Will it really take ten years?'

Zak shoved him playfully on the shoulder, almost knocking him over. 'Quit your fussin', Chase. You know you can do this. You don't need me to tell you that. Your pa would have loved a project like this. He'd be real proud of you stickin' at something, even if it takes you a coupla years. What else have you got to do with your time?'

Chase nodded, his boyishly thin neck flushed red as he scuffed his boot in a patch of sand soaking up some spilled oil, wrestling with his thoughts. It was a sign of maturity and Zak was pleased to see it.

Chase looked Zak in the face with glassy eyes. 'I'll do it, Uncle Zak.' He wiped his nose on the back of his hand and sniffed hard. 'I'll do it to show Pa, and I'll save up every nickel and dime I get to make this the most beautiful Harley anyone ever saw'.

'That's terrific, Chase,' said Zak. 'Just promise me one thing, okay? Promise me that you won't skip on your schoolin', 'cuz that won't make your pa proud, you hear me?'

'You have my word.' Chase held out his hand to Zak like a proper businessman closing a deal.

Zak grasped the boy's hand and shook it solemnly, swallowing hard. If only Gryff could see what a fine young man his son was turning out to be. Zak was determined to be there for Chase as long as he needed him.

1990

Alone in the workshop, Chase lovingly polished the deep glossy custom paintwork on the newly fitted gas tank of his Harley Davidson, deep in thought. The stunning artwork of a fire-breathing red dragon was the final touch: the rebuild was complete. Four years of saving every dime and spending every spare moment combing scrapyards and autojumbles for spare parts with Uncle Zak were over. It'd been great fun, although it had been slow going at times. The custom paint job was his reward for graduating high school, costing

Grandpa Wendell a small fortune. He should have been elated, yet he was in a foul mood – all because Shelby Jepson was going to the prom with Dalton Brown. He could think of nothing else.

Shelby was wasted on Dalton. She was way too smart and funny for that knucklehead, and this was all her pa's fault. Jerome Jepson was behind the decision for Shelby to go to the prom with Dalton, no doubt about it. He could see why Pa hated Jerome so much. Chase never let on to Pa that he knew he hated Jerome but it had been as clear as day, even to a fourteen-year-old. Now that he was eighteen, he felt the same way his pa had. Before long, Jerome would marry Shelby off to some rich guy. Rich folks always stuck together in the end – they were all the same. Except for Jack and Greta, of course. How could Jerome be so different to his own pa? A horrible thought struck him and a viper of jealousy wriggled in his belly. What if Jerome was plannin' on marryin' Shelby off to Dalton Dickbrain? He didn't wanna stick around to see that.

He could hit the highway anytime he pleased now that school was over forever and the Hog was finished. Trav's idea of a great job was shovelling shit at the stables all day, just so he could be near Shelby. What a joke! Shelby barely noticed him and thought that he – Chase – was much more fun. Chase couldn't think of a duller job but that was Trav all over. It was hard to believe they were brothers sometimes if they didn't look so darned alike. Trav was just so sensible – *all the time.* Chase wanted some excitement, to have some adventures, to do somethin' that his pa would have been proud of. Greer had the right idea. She'd become famous, just like she always said she would, although he'd laughed at her at the time. Ma said Greer and her band were touring Europe, wherever that was. Somewhere near Paris, maybe?

Chase threw down his polishing cloth and fired up the motorcycle just for the sheer pleasure of hearing the ear-splitting roar and feeling that Harley rumble through the soles of his boots. His very own red dragon! He grinned from ear to ear. He might as well take the beast for a test ride.

The full moon of late May bathed the monochrome world in a metallic sheen, even though it was only after nine when Chase rode out of the auto shop. Every cell in his body vibrated in time with the thump of the twin-cylinder engine. The flat open farmland on either side of KY764 soon gave way to lush forest as Chase turned onto KY144, enjoying the freedom of the smooth empty tarmac as it wound its way gently into the hills. His unbuttoned shirt flapped behind him and it was colder than he'd thought it would be, but the thrill of his first ride on his hand-built Harley was enough to keep him warm. He whooped out loud with delight. Nobody was around to hear him anyway, so what did it matter? As he found himself approaching Whitesville towards the end of his circular route about a half hour later, he took a spontaneous turn off the highway onto the crunchy sweeping drive that led up to Buena Vista through the horse paddocks, reducing his speed out of consideration for the thoroughbreds. His head was clear and he'd worked out a terrific plan. Shelby deserved to hear it first.

He couldn't wait to see her face when he told her.

***

Shelby was already waiting on the front veranda when Chase brought his motorcycle to a halt on the drive below where she stood, dressed in her nightgown, her hair flowing loose around her shoulders. For a fleeting moment, she reminded him of a play he'd studied in class about a girl on a balcony who killed herself for love. He grinned despite himself. Shelby wasn't stupid enough to kill herself over a boy, even if that boy was him.

'Chase!' she scolded. 'What in tarnation are you doing out here at this time of night on that infernal noisy machine? It sounds like an army tank just parked on the lawn!'

Chase smirked. She didn't know how close to the truth she was.

'I want you to be the first to know, Shelby,' he called out to her, still sitting astride the Harley. 'I'm done with livin' in Dullsville. There's nothin' for me here since Pa died. I'm leavin' in the mornin' to join the United States Army.' His chest swelled with pride now that the words were out and he'd declared his intentions. It felt so good. Shelby couldn't fail to be impressed.

Shelby snorted back a laugh. 'Good luck with that, Chase. I'm not sure they take skinny rats like you!'

She meant it as a gag but he was furious. He'd declared himself a man and she'd mocked him!

Kickstarting the Harley into life, he roared off down the drive without a backward glance. He didn't give a damn about the horses anyway.

TWENTY-FOUR

1996

SARAJEVO, BOSNIA

The Hercules transporter approaching Sarajevo International Airport descended swiftly over the surrounding hills, which had bristled with snipers and heavy artillery emplacements until very recently. The cityscape of Sarajevo beneath the gigantic circling military aircraft was decimated, a vision of hell through the bleak grey March drizzle. High-rise apartment blocks slumped sideways, their inner floors exposed through gaping wounds in their sides, spilled intestines blackened by missile strikes; burned-out cars and buses lay strewn across every highway, already impassable with shattered building debris; the few remaining trees that hadn't been cut down and burned by the besieged population for firewood were charred stumps, and barely a pane of glass existed anywhere. The four-year siege of Sarajevo was over but, as the troop-carrying aircraft came into land, Chase was well aware there were no guarantees that hostilities wouldn't occur on this mission. Chase and his battalion were being deployed in the city as UN Peacekeepers, but it didn't look like there was any peace yet to preserve.

Chase's first patrol took in Dragon of Bosnia Street, a boulevard of once high-rise buildings heavily pocked with bullet holes. As his squad's two white UN armoured personnel carriers cruised slowly along, Chase noticed civilian women in their winter coats and headscarves, carrying shopping baskets, hurrying along beside them.

'Ask them what they are doing,' he called to the UN interpreter attached to his squad.

'No need to ask. They have to scour the city for food daily, risking their lives. Over two-hundred people have been killed in this street alone by snipers. See that sign there?' The interpreter pointed to bright yellow graffiti daubed on the side of a derelict petrol station. '*PAZI SNAJPER* – that means *watch out: sniper*. This street is known as Sniper Alley. Your armoured carrier acts as a screen to protect these women. They often wait hours for a UN armoured vehicle to come along before they can move. It's how they stay alive.'

Chase couldn't believe what he was hearing. How had these civilians survived almost four years of siege? He couldn't begin to imagine what they'd been through. This war was completely different to the Gulf War in '91, where he'd seen combat at Medina Ridge. It wasn't being fought across remote battlefields in deserts or open countryside. This war was being waged against the civilian population and yet he'd just seen wan-faced, hollow-eyed kids playing in the street. They'd been crawling around in craters and over hulks of burned-out vehicles so peppered with bullet holes they looked like rusting colanders. They didn't even flinch at the sound of gunfire.

He clenched his jaw, barely containing his outrage. The civilian population needed humanitarian aid and they needed it now. This posting wasn't the easy option he'd thought it would be – it was a crucial mission to save innocent lives.

***

Chase stripped off his dirty gear and collapsed onto his bunk at Camp Punxsutawney, where every day was Groundhog Day. He was deeply troubled. How could such a thing happen in the modern world? It was only twelve years ago when Sarajevo hosted the Winter Olympics, the same year that Los Angeles hosted the Summer Olympics. That was the year he'd gone to the stables with Pa to mend Shelby's horsebox. His throat tightened at the memory and he swallowed hard. The thought of a war breaking out in Los Angeles was unimaginable, yet there he was, patrolling an Olympic host city from the same year that had been ravaged by war. It was crazy.

His belly grumbled. He needed some food. Shame flooded through him at the thought of the vast 24-hour catering facility at the base camp. How much food, if any, did those women find for their families in Sarajevo today and how much uneaten cooked food would go to waste in the mess tonight?

A low hum of voices from the camp mess tent reached his ears as he crunched across the frozen mud, following the enticing smell of fried onions. Stepping inside, he quickly scanned the facility to find his squad but they were nowhere to be seen. He grabbed a tray and filled it from the hot buffet, steaming gently under bright catering lights, ashamed of the ridiculous mountains of food. He found himself a plastic chair at an empty table, as far from other diners as possible. After what he'd seen that day, he wasn't in the mood for chit-chat.

Chase had barely finished his tepid hot dog when a uniformed figure sat heavily in the opposite seat. Chase's heart sank. Hadn't he made it clear enough that he wasn't looking for company? He kept his head down and speared his fries savagely. With any luck, the soldier would pick up on the hostile vibe and clear off.

'Good evening, Sergeant,' said the interloper in a rich baritone. Chase couldn't immediately place the accent but it sounded strangely familiar. He grunted.

'I hope you don't mind me interrupting your dinner—'

Chase looked up. Sitting opposite him was a burly young private wearing British Army insignia alongside his UN peacekeeping badges. He fixed him with a steely glare from his ice-blue eyes.

'—but I just saw you come in and it's the strangest thing—'

The kid must have been about twenty but he could have passed for fourteen if it wasn't for his bulk. He wouldn't last five minutes in combat if he couldn't recognise hostility, Chase thought with a derisive snort. 'Listen, Soldier, no offence, but I ain't in the mood for socialisin' right now, so could you just leave me to finish my dinner in peace – pretty please?'

The young soldier's face flushed. 'Sorry, Sergeant. I'll keep it short. I just had to come over to tell you that you have a doppelganger – two doppelgangers, in fact.'

'A doppel-*what*?' Chase slammed his fork down so hard that his tray bounced on the table with a crash. 'Jeezus! Let me make it clear for you, Soldier. Get the hell outta my face and let me eat in peace.'

'Don't you want to know about your lookalikes?' the private asked hastily, getting to his feet. 'My half-brothers are identical twins and you could be their triplet! It's astonishing, the likeness, uncanny... freaky, in fact. Sitting here talking to you is like talking to them, except they're Welsh, of course.'

Chase, who was already on his feet preparing to grab the soldier and shove him away, stopped in his tracks. 'What did you just say?'

'Um, sitting here talk—'

'After that! Did you just say they're Welsh?'

'Yes, actually, I did. We're all from South Wales. Huw and Rhys are my half-brothers. Their tad died when they were young.'

'Their what?'

'Their tad – their father. Died at sea, apparently, in the mid-sixties.'

Chase's anger dissolved rapidly. 'Well, they say it's a small world and it surely is,' he said with an apologetic grin. 'I cain't say I was expecting to meet a Welshman this evening, slap bang in the middle of nowhere. My pa was a Welshman, too. He passed away ten years ago. The funny thing is, I'm also a twin – me and my brother, Travis. We're identical, too. How about that?'

'You are *kidding* me!' The private re-took his seat. 'That means there are four of you who are dead ringers! No way!' The young soldier laughed incredulously. 'This is wild. I've got a picture somewhere, of me with my mam and brothers. I'll bring it to show you tomorrow night if you like?'

'Sure, why not?' said Chase. Well, well, well, who'd have thought it? He and Trav were not as unique as they liked to think they were. 'So, what are you Brits doing here at Camp Punx anyway? What's your name, Soldier?'

Gareth Bevan introduced himself and the two men shook hands warmly. He explained that the British peacekeeping battalion's camp had caught fire, so they were billeting in the US base temporarily for a few days.

'I look forward to seeing your photo, Gareth,' said Chase. 'I think I may even have one of my own to show you, of me and Travis, from a while back though.'

Gareth stood up to leave. 'Great! See you tomorrow at dinner, then.'

'Sure thing,' said Chase as the two men shook hands again.

Chase lay on his bunk that night, staring at the ceiling, lost in thought. His conversation with Gareth troubled him, but he couldn't say why. It just seemed too much of a coincidence that two guys somewhere in South Wales looked exactly like him and Trav. Could they be related somehow? Or was it just something in their ancient genes? Perhaps everyone in Wales had thick black curly hair and pale blue eyes. Apart from his pa, he'd never met any other Welsh people. He rolled onto his belly, trying to get comfortable on his lumpy bedroll as he replayed the conversation in his mind.

What he found interesting was that Gareth's two half-brothers' pa died at sea in the mid-sixties around about the same time his own pa migrated from Wales on a ship. They might have even known each other at sea. Wouldn't that be something? Not that anyone would be able to find out for sure, though. It was as frustrating as hell that he hadn't thought to ask Pa about his past before he passed away. He thumped his flat pillow and rolled over again.

Maybe Ma knew something about Pa back when he was a kid in Wales. He'd have to ask her the next time he saw her. For all he knew, these guys – what was it, Hugh and Reese? – they could be his cousins. Maybe Pa had lots of brothers back in Wales?

Chase waited three hours in the mess the following evening for Gareth but he didn't show up. He asked around and it turned out the Brits had moved out unexpectedly. Chase returned to his bunk with the photograph of him and Travis standing with Pa next to a tractor, and slipped it back into his passport despondently. He'd been looking forward to seeing Gareth's photos and had even hoped they might give him something to go on, to find out more about his pa. But if he was honest, the chances they were related were less than zero. He'd just been kidding himself. It was no big deal.

TWENTY-FIVE

1998

WHITESVILLE, KENTUCKY

Greer studied her wrinkles in the softly lit magnifying mirror in her Italian marble bathroom, pulling her skin taut with her ring finger – now bare – to smooth them away. She'd be turning thirty this year. Where did that time go? She'd wasted most of it on that dumb bastard Dixon; that was where it had gone. The memory of their divorce still stung, even after five years. She sighed regretfully. If only she'd listened to her ma's advice. She should never have allowed Will to appoint himself as her manager when *Who Will I Be?* hit the top of the country and western charts and stayed there for sixty weeks, and she definitely should never have let him negotiate her recording contract with RCA. Little did she know he'd tied her into a three-album deal with million-dollar bonuses for him if they went gold or platinum. She'd be doing all the work and he'd be making all the money.

The warning signs started after her successful European tour when she was exhausted and needed a break, but Will wouldn't let her rest. He became toxic to live with, resorting to ever-nastier threats to coerce her into writing music until, eventually, the situation became unbearable and they reached breaking point. It was a day that would haunt her for the rest of her life.

It was gone noon, and Greer was still in bed. Will had been out all night and she didn't care. She couldn't shake off her crushing fatigue. Anyway, less time awake meant less time to endure Will's constant criticism.

She was sleeping her life away in a fog of depression.

Greer barely flinched at the crash of the bedroom door being kicked open. Her eyelids felt like they'd been stitched together. Heavy stumbling footsteps approached the bed and she assumed it was Will. She waited for the first blow. When the pain came, it wasn't what she expected. He was dragging her out of bed by her hair!

'Stop Will! *Stop!*' she screamed. Her legs buckled, leaving her entire body weight hanging from her scalp. The sound of her hair ripping from her flesh was something she would never forget.

She grabbed wildly at Will's hands as he screamed abuse at her, his spittle splattering her face and his breath stinking of vomit and sour whisky. Her feet scrabbled to find the floor as he dragged her by the hair across the room to the balcony doors and dropped her to the ground just long enough to get the doors open. He hauled her upright, using both hands around her throat until her face was level with his, enveloping her in a cloud of repulsive fumes. Gagging and choking, she screwed her eyes tight shut to block out the sight of his rage-contorted face.

Then it hit her – he was going to throw her over the balcony! The drop was at least thirty feet. And she didn't care.

'Do me a favour,' she rasped, her exhausted hands clawing feebly at his. 'Get it over with.'

Will threw her body against the balcony handrail, roaring with drunken rage, and reached down, grasping hold of her legs. With her body inverted over the railing, Greer's eyes finally burst open with the pressure of the blood rushing to her head. Between Will's legs, she could see movement reflected in the glass of the balcony doors behind them. Someone on horseback was galloping up the drive towards the house, yelling her name.

It was Travis.

'*Travis!*' she screamed. '*Travis!*'

At the sound of her scream, Will redoubled his effort to tip her over the balcony. But now Greer fought frantically to hold on – she had to last just a few more seconds. Help was on its way.

Travis burst into the bedroom, bellowing like a mad bull, and raced across the room to the balcony. She screamed at the sound of his horsewhip slicing into Will's skull and the splatter of Will's blood on her face, before being grabbed around the waist and hauled upright across the handrail, falling into Travis' arms.

An animalistic wail escaped from her as the last of her defences collapsed. Travis pulled her against his chest, rocking her and stroking her hair until her shuddering sobs began to subside. The motionless form of her husband was sprawled close by; his head twisted awkwardly, his one visible eye open and staring blankly, the white of his skull showing through an open laceration that sliced right through his wiry hair. Blood bubbled from one corner of his mouth. He was still alive.

Travis took off his soft plaid shirt and used it to wipe Greer's face and mop the vomit from her hair. He held her face steady in both hands as he examined her. 'You got burst vessels in both eyes, Greer,' he said gently, 'and there's blood on your head, where some hair is missing. You're in a bad way, darlin', but at least you're still alive.'

Greer let out a low moan, incapable of forming words, and raised her hand just enough to point a trembling finger at Will. Travis glanced at where she was pointing. 'He ain't goin' nowhere, Greer, least not until I call the sheriff's office and they take him away'.

He could die on her bedroom floor for all she cared.

Travis had saved her life. She owed him everything.

There was no prosecution; Will's injuries and cross-allegations of assault and battery against Travis saw to that. He didn't contest the divorce, although he pinned his behaviour on Greer for driving him to pills and booze, suing successfully for alimony. Even now, five years on, it still rankled bitterly that she had to pay off that manipulative sociopath with her hard-earned money. And to make matters worse, it took her two years of exorbitant attorney fees to extract herself from the punitive contract Will had tied her into at RCA.

Gazing at herself in the mirror, her jaw tightened as the memory of that shitty feeling came flooding back. With her thirtieth birthday approaching, and the fine lines around her eyes deepening, she was older and wiser now. She would never make a terrible mistake like that ever again. Five years on, she still had good days and bad days.

She clipped on a pair of emerald earrings that complemented her eyes and ran a brush through her lustrous honey-gold hair.

Today was a good day.

Today was the day Chase was coming home at the end of his eight-year commitment to the US army.

TWENTY-SIX

Travis had two palominos saddled up and ready for Greer and Chase as they strolled down the track from her elegant hacienda farmhouse. Her new stable block stood on land once occupied by Grandpa's old tobacco cropper's cabin – their ma's childhood home. The generous stable yard was shaded by the ancient hickory tree where Ma and Grandma Martha used to sit in the olden days, stringing together bunches of tobacco leaves onto poles for Grandpa to dry in his old barn. Travis had heard the old stories more times than he could count, and even though he'd never known his real grandma, the stable yard was where Travis truly felt his roots were, and his favourite place to sit and think was right there under that self-same tree. Along with the cabin, the tobacco barn and fields were gone, surplus to requirement as demand for cigarettes crashed.

Travis was gripped by a deep sense of foreboding as he watched the burly figure of his brother approaching, almost unrecognisable from the teenage runt who'd left eight years earlier; he'd thought of little else other than Chase's return ever since Greer sprang the news on him the week before. Chase running off to join the army had done him a big favour – it had cleared the decks for him to win Shelby's heart. But now Chase was back, just as he and Shelby were about to get engaged, and the last thing he wanted was his fun-loving twin brother muscling in on his fiancée-to-be. He would need to be very much on his guard when they were all together.

Chase's face lit up as their eyes met, and the two brothers hugged and thumped each other's backs vigorously.

'It's been a while, Brother.' Travis grinned broadly, forcing himself to sound pleased. 'It's great to have you back, but you'd better behave yourself. You might find life around here pretty dull after so long in the military.' He passed the reins to Chase. 'You sure you still know how to drive one of these?' he joked. 'Just remember, she's not an armoured tank – she has a brain of her own. Treat her with respect and you'll have her eatin' out of your hand.'

'Are you talkin' about the horse or Greer?' retorted Chase, doubling over with laughter.

Travis grinned despite himself. Chase was still a joker, even after serving in four war zones and killing God-knows how many men. He couldn't imagine taking a man's life, himself. It had to change you at some level, surely?

Greer rolled her eyes in mock exasperation. 'Will you two schoolboys ever grow up?'

Travis handed Greer her reins and patted the withers of the lovely horse he'd recently found for her. 'So, what's your plan for the afternoon?'

'I thought I would show Chase around the property, so

I can tell him my plans for the land and see if I can persuade him to become the estate manager.' She shielded her eyes from the bright October sunshine with her hand.

Travis took a pair of sunglasses from his shirt pocket and passed them to her. 'Sounds like a great plan.'

'Let's take a ride to the lake first,' said Chase. 'I always loved it there.'

'Sure thing.' Greer wheeled her horse around expertly. 'Don't forget to come on by for supper tonight,' she called over her shoulder to Travis, 'and bring Shelby with you if she's free.'

Chase had a glorious view of Buena Vista's sweeping landscape on the far side of the lake, as he sat astride his horse on the lake's southern shore with his sister beside him. 'So how come you persuaded ol' Jack Jepson to sell you a hundred acres of his land, Sis?'

'I just went and asked Greta what she thought of the idea and she said she'd fix it,' Greer replied. 'I never actually spoke to Jack. Personally, I think Greta wears the trousers in that household,' she said with a laugh. 'Do you wanna ride over to see Grandpa's new place?'

As the two palominos ambled along side by side, Greer outlined her plans to develop the estate. In addition to her lovely hacienda farmhouse, with its private stables and recording studio, there was their grandpa's brand-new smallholding and workshop, which they were on their way to see. If he wanted one, she said, she would also have a substantial, comfortable home built for Chase, not far from the one already being constructed for Travis. There would also be an organic vineyard and a small airstrip so that Greer could fly herself to concerts.

It all sounded like a dream come true to Chase. She'd come a long way since he'd joined the army, but he hadn't appreciated just how far until now. He hadn't even known she had her own pilot's license. 'What about Ma?' Chase asked.

'She's living with me, now we're both alone.'

Chase caught the downward inflexion in her voice. 'Yeah, I heard about Will, Greer,' he said. 'I'm really sorry to hear that happened to you. I'm mighty glad that Travis gave him the whippin' he deserved.'

'It's behind me now, Chase.' She pulled her shoulders back and straightened her spine. 'I'm glad to move on and it makes me real happy to have Ma around the whole time.' She paused, gazing into the distance. 'It's funny how ever since Pa died, she's started writing beautiful songs. I've recorded a dozen or more on my albums. Did you know that she wrote *Who Will I Be?*'

Chase's skin prickled inexplicably. He knew the words of Greer's melancholic first hit single off by heart but had never imagined his mother had written them. He found the thought strangely disturbing. What could Ma possibly know about lies and self-delusion? 'No, I never knew that,' he muttered uncomfortably.

'I make sure she gets her share of the royalties, Chase,' Greer said hurriedly. 'None of this would be happenin' if it wasn't for her.' She gestured with a sweeping arm. 'I even went back to college after… after Will. It was important to me to show her that she was right all along.'

'You went back to college? How did that work out?'

Greer laughed. 'I couldn't actually *go* to college, Chase. I was already too famous for that. Folks would never leave me alone! So, I had a college tutor come to me and hired a studio. *And* I passed all my exams. Ma was so relieved – you should've seen her face, Chase.' Greer chuckled. "No one's ever gonna take advantage of you again, girl!" she said to me, and she was right. I'm my own business manager now.'

As they emerged from the dappled shade of light woodland into a bright clearing, Chase saw an elegant low-profile property ahead. It had a generously proportioned central entrance and two wings sweeping out to either side; a pool was just visible to the rear. He gave a low whistle.

'My word, Greer, this is a lovely property. Is this Grandpa's place?'

'Sure is. Beautiful, ain't it?' She reined her horse to a standstill. 'I wanted him and Carol to have someplace special. It meant I could put my new stables near the hacienda. D'you know, Ma wasn't sorry when I knocked down Grandpa's old cabin – too many unhappy memories for her, she reckoned, back from when her ma died. It's a shame for Ma that none of us kids ever got to know our Grandma Martha, but Carol has been my grandma all my life and she makes Grandpa happy, so I'm happy for her to have this lovely place.'

Chase was struck by a thought. 'Are Ma's brothers and sister still around?'

Greer roared with laughter. 'Don't be a dumbass, Chase. I know you've been away and all, but that's a real dumb thing to say.'

Chase fiddled with his reins to cover his embarrassment, hoping Greer would carry on and forget what an idiot he was. Luckily, she did.

'Uncle Ray's a Baptist preacher over in Jonestown, but you knew that anyway, and Uncle Roy went and got his own tobacco plot in Evansville when Grandpa retired, not far from the old auto repair shop.'

Chase nodded; he knew just where she meant. He'd always liked his twin uncles, although neither of them ever said very much. Maybe that was what he liked about them.

'So, what about Aunt Martha?' He imagined her as the first-grade teacher at the local infant school.

'Really, Chase? You don't know about Aunt Martha?'

Chase shook his head. He had no idea. News didn't travel well to Basra, Sarajevo or Kabul.

'Aunt Martha lives in London, Chase. She's an internationally renowned author and playwright with a string of successful plays and novels. She calls herself Martha Haycraft now. It was Grandma's maiden name. One of her books got made into a movie. She's even more rich and famous than I am. I cain't believe all this has passed you by.'

Chase shook his head with astonishment. 'Jeez. I had no idea. That's unbelievable. So, did any of them get married? Have I got any cousins I don't know about?'

'Nope.' Greer shook her head. 'Not a one. Not one single cousin from among the lot of them.'

Chase frowned. It seemed odd that he didn't have any cousins. He'd always liked the idea of having a big family around him as he got older. 'That's a real shame,' he said. 'What about you, Greer? Are you plannin' on having any?'

The smile slid from Greer's face. He'd put his foot in it, as usual. 'Sorry, Greer, I didn't mean nothin' by it,' he mumbled apologetically. It was time to change the subject. 'Shall we call on Grandpa?'

'No point, Chase. He and Carol are in London with Ma to visit Martha and see her latest play on Shaftesbury

Avenue. She's booked rooms for them all at the Ritz hotel at her expense.'

Judging by Greer's tone of voice, that was something to be impressed about, but it meant nothing to Chase. His family sure had changed in the past eight years. Maybe if he'd shown more interest while he was away, none of this would have come as such a surprise to him.

'So, what do you think, Chase? Have I sold you the job of estate manager?'

Chase checked off the list in his head. He'd just left the military, he had no home of his own, no personal possessions beyond his rucksack of papers, his pa's precious watch and the clothes he stood up in, and he had no professional qualifications. He could fix a Sherman tank, rebuild a howitzer or shoot a man dead at one hundred yards, but he wasn't sure there was much demand for that sort of thing around these parts. It was a no-brainer, except for one important thing.

Shelby.

'It's a very attractive proposition, Greer,' he replied. 'Let me sleep on it.'

Later that evening, the sound of voices in the reception hall brought Chase out of his guest bedroom at the top of the stairs. Looking over the internal balcony, he could see the top of Travis's head with its familiar jet-black curly hair as he stood talking to Greer beside Shelby's strawberry-blonde mane.

Chase's heart skipped a beat. Shelby looked lovely in a plaid shirt tucked into denims with simple cowboy boots on her feet. Her slender figure leaned towards Travis slightly as they laughed with Greer about something Chase couldn't make out. Travis put his arm lovingly around her waist. He'd seen enough to know what was coming.

Chase joined in the applause and congratulations at supper when Travis announced his engagement to Shelby. It felt like a kick in the guts but it all made perfect sense if he was honest with himself. Travis and Shelby were passionate about horses, and Travis had been in love with Shelby since childhood – they both had. Chase vividly remembered the time when he saw Travis watching Shelby in her showjumping ring, and it was clear even then that they were a perfect match. They would live happily ever after. Travis was a hard-working and decent man, and a great brother to him. Now, it was up to him to accept the reality and move on. Deep down, he was genuinely happy for his brother.

Chase tapped his spoon against his beer glass. 'While we are in the mood for celebratin', I'd also like to make an announcement – I've decided to take the job as estate manager.'

Greer popped the cork on another bottle of champagne. 'Bravo!' she exclaimed. 'Welcome home, brother!'

Chase came out of the guest bedroom after eleven the following day to find Greer singing to herself in the kitchen. She was dressed in riding clothes that were already dusty, and grinding coffee beans. The sunny smile she gave him melted his heart – he'd always had a soft spot for his lovely sister. He embraced her in a brotherly hug, kissing the top of her warm golden head.

'Sleep well?' she asked, pouring the fresh grinds into a large cafetière.

'Like you wouldn't believe! I haven't slept in a bed as comfortable as that in my whole life. Your pillows must be stuffed with angel feathers!' Chase nodded as she gestured to him with the coffee pot and took a seat at her breakfast bar.

'So, when would you like to start?' She slid a cup of coffee over to him. 'I've been doing some thinkin'. You'll be needin' a bunch of new things after leavin' the military. Some new clothes, maybe? And some kind of truck?'

'Well, I was plannin' to check on the Harley at the storage depot this mornin', see if I can get her started after eight years.' He took a slug of his coffee to wash down a couple of painkillers. The coffee was terrific. 'So, if you can give me a few days to get myself sorted, that'd be great.'

'No problem, Chase. Let's say you start next Monday. That'll give you five days to find yourself a new truck and whatever else you need. Let me give you some cash to be gettin' on with.' Reaching into a roll-top bread bin, she withdrew a small paper sack about the size of a two-pound bag of flour and handed it to him.

'What's this?'

'Twenty-thousand dollars, in twenties.'

Chase gaped with astonishment. 'You keep twenty-thousand dollars in your bread bin?'

'Not usually, dumbass! I got this for you, for your truck and stuff.'

'I cain't just take this from you, Greer. I haven't done a day of work for you yet!'

'Consider it an advance, if you insist.'

'I do insist!' Chase pulled his big sister to him and gave her an appreciative kiss. 'Thank you for all you are doin' for me, Sis. It'll sure make leavin' the army a helluva lot easier than it is for most guys.'

Chase arrived at the storage depot, pleased that the padlock on his lock-up was caked in grime. It was a sure sign that nobody had opened the shutter since he left it. He put down his rucksack and took the key from the chain around his neck, where it had hung for eight years. With a gritty click, the padlock opened, and he heaved up the stiff heavy shutter with a powerful clean-and-jerk motion. He peered inside the unlit space, making out the ghostly form of a motorcycle covered in a sheet, exactly as he'd left it. He'd missed his treasured Harley and could hardly wait to ride it again, but as he whipped off the cover, the wave of emotion that swept over him caught him entirely off guard. That hunk of chrome, leather and rubber represented four years of his life when he'd learned to come to terms with losing Pa, under the guidance of the man he never even said goodbye to when he ran off like a jilted fool and joined the military. He'd been so thoughtless back then, and had taken his friends and family for granted. Christ, he'd been such a jackass. He'd be lucky if any of them still wanted to know him. He had a week to figure out how to make it up to his ma and grandpa before they returned from their trip to London with Carol.

He ran his hand appreciatively along the shiny gas tank and admired the red dragon custom artwork his grandpa had paid for. The machine still looked in good condition overall – a little dusty, maybe, but no rust. Unsurprisingly, the tyres were both flat and perhaps even a little perished, and there was a good chance the cylinders had seized, given they hadn't moved in eight years. He knew better than to try to start the engine before giving it a proper service. He'd need to borrow a few tools from Zak to get the motorcycle running again – if Zak was still talking to him after he'd left without a second thought. He had some serious bridge-building to do.

Chase gathered up his rucksack, preparing to leave, when it occurred to him that carrying around twenty-thousand dollars in cash and all his personal papers was probably not the wisest thing to do. Grabbing his painkillers and the keys to Greer's spare truck from the side pocket, he tossed the rucksack into the lock-up and brought the shutter down with a resounding crash.

As he walked back to the truck with the padlock key safely back on its chain around his neck, his thoughts returned to his ma and grandpa. What would he say to them once they got back from London?

'Sorry' didn't begin to cover it.

TWENTY-SEVEN

WESTMINSTER, LONDON

The sky over central London was murky grey and a saturating drizzle fell as Shirley Bevan, member of parliament, left the Palace of Westminster, teetering awkwardly in her high-heeled court shoes on the treacherously slick cobbles of Old Palace Yard. The Commons select committee on healthcare she chaired had overrun, so she was already late to meet her husband. The last thing she needed was to slip and break her ankle. She turned up the collar on her elegant Aquascutum raincoat and buttoned it at the neck to keep the rain out.

Abingdon Street was busy with slow-moving rush hour traffic and dawdling tourists. Dai was nowhere to be seen, having told her he would wait by the statue of King George V across the road.

'I brought an umbrella,' said a warm Welsh voice in her ear as an arm linked through hers from behind.

Shirley pulled away before realising it was him. 'Don't do that, you daft bugger!' she exclaimed. 'I thought I was being mugged! You almost gave me a heart attack!'

He leaned towards her and kissed her lips. 'At least I'd get to practise my CPR,' he joked. 'I'm getting a bit rusty since I retired.'

Shirley snorted derisively. 'I don't see how you can call yourself retired.' She tugged Dai's arm and steered him towards Parliament Square, sharing his umbrella. 'You seem to be working more hours as a magistrate than you ever did as a doctor. I wouldn't mind if you were getting paid for it but you do it for free. It's a bloody liberty, if you ask me.'

'Now *you're* being daft,' he said as they crossed the road opposite Westminster Bridge Tube station.

'What's the time?' asked Shirley, chuckling as Dai checked his watch.

Dai rolled his eyes. 'I fall for that every time, don't I?' He looked directly up three-hundred feet into the face of the world's most famous clock. At that moment, Big Ben chimed the quarter bell. 'It's five forty-five, by all accounts,' said Dai, with a sparkle of merriment in his eye.

'Great,' she said. 'We still have enough time for an early supper before the show starts.'

Shirley hugged his arm tightly as they hurried along Whitehall towards Trafalgar Square through the evening commuter crowds. It was his birthday and Shirley had planned an evening of his favourite things – a surprise meal in Chinatown followed by a Martha Haycroft play at the Lyric Theatre.

Turning the corner into Wardour Street, the first clues to their destination reached them on the chilly breeze – the fragrant aromas of Chinese five-spice and star anise. Despite the evening drizzle, the Chinese pagoda-style gateway into Gerrard Street was a cheering sight and Shirley's mouth watered as they wandered hand in hand along the pedestrianised road, festooned with bright-orange Chinese lanterns, admiring the enticingly lit glistening crispy roast ducks hanging in the windows.

'How are things at home?' asked Shirley as they settled into their table at the Royal Dragon restaurant. Dai passed a letter to Shirley over the basket of prawn crackers.

'I got this from Gareth on Monday,' he said. 'He's back in Bosnia again – peacekeeping.'

Shirley's jaw tightened. That was not what she wanted to hear. She admired their son for joining the British Army, but she hated the thought of what he was being exposed to in the Balkans. She'd much rather he'd joined the police to do his peacekeeping in the relative safety of Swansea town centre on a Saturday night, like his brother, Huw.

'What does he say?' she asked. 'Is he all right?'

'Yes, he's fine but he says nothing has improved in the three years since his last deployment there.'

'And there's still no end in sight.' She pressed her lips together firmly. 'Have you got any good news from home to cheer me up?'

'I was saving the best till last,' Dai grinned. 'Huw has finally been promoted to inspector!'

'Oh, hooray!' Shirley clasped her hands with pleasure. 'It's only taken four years since he passed the promotion exam.' The moratorium on police promotions was a sore subject for Shirley, as it had significantly held back Huw's career prospects. Before the moratorium, he'd hoped to have reached the rank of chief inspector by now. 'Has he been posted yet?'

'Yes, he got the posting he wanted – he's back in the public order branch, running his own unit.'

'I'm so pleased for him', said Shirley, 'That's exactly what he was hoping for. He loved it there when he was a PC.'

Dai nodded, his mouth full of prawn crackers. 'Vaughan reminded me that was where Huw and Cheryl met.'

'Of course it was,' murmured Shirley, looking at the menu. 'I'd forgotten that too. So, when did you see Vaughan?'

'I had dinner with him and Lowri last Tuesday. Vaughan is dead chuffed for Huw. He remembers the day he got promoted to inspector. He reckons it's the point in your police career when you can say you've made it and anything more is a bonus.'

'Doesn't stop Vaughan calling Huw a "wooden top" and Huw calling Vaughan a "suit" though,' joked Shirley. The legendary rivalry between the uniform and CID branches played out between her son and her father-in-law was a bit of a family joke, every time there was a get-together. It was all very good-natured – she hoped.

'No, I guess not,' said Dai. 'The cops can call each other what they like, as long as they behave professionally in my courtroom.'

'Everything okay with Mam?' asked Shirley after the waiter had taken their order. 'I haven't had a chance to ring her this week; I've just been so busy with the extra committee work.'

'Oh, you know Lowri – keep calm and carry on, and all that,' said Dai. 'She read Gareth's letter and, of course, she was over the moon for Huw. Her only complaint is that she's not heard from Rhys for ages. He's too busy saving the world to send a postcard from God Knows Where.'

'I know how she feels,' muttered Shirley as their crispy duck and pancakes arrived in a cloud of aromatic five-spice. 'I've got no idea where he is either; last thing I knew, the Rainbow Warrior was in Polynesia somewhere.'

Dai helped himself to a pancake and slathered it in plum sauce. 'I know you say not to, but I blame myself for how he turned out. I was a doctor, for goodness' sake. I should have spotted his depression sooner,' he said.

'Oh, bugger off, Bevan!' snapped Shirley, dumping a generous portion of duck on her pancake and rolling it briskly. 'He was away at Bangor, studying his favourite subject – and doing well at it, too, don't forget. How were you to know he was taking climate change personally?'

'Well, he gave us plenty of clues, Dear.'

'Like what?' she asked through a mouthful of food.

'Like every Christmas, he'd come home and lecture us about plastic bottles, and how the oceans are the bellwether for the health of the planet, or how we were all sleepwalking into Armageddon. Pretty damning stuff, don't you think?'

'Come off it, Dai. He was a typical student with a holier-than-thou attitude. They all spout that sort of nonsense at uni. None of that was good reason to think he'd try to kill himself. Listen to me, Dai – It was not your fault.' Shirley put down her pancake and reached for Dai's hand across the table. This was not how she wanted him to spend his birthday, arguing over one of her twins. Rhys was always the sensitive one; if anything, she was to blame for his insecurities. She knew he'd never forgiven her for allowing his father to leave when she was pregnant. 'The main thing is he's happy now, saving the planet with Greenpeace. He'll come back when he's ready.'

***

The Lyric Theatre was packed with eager theatregoers, spilling out onto the street under a rococo-style glass canopy, creating a noisy stir of anticipation. The genial buzz of excited voices reached Shirley and Dai as they hurried along Shaftesbury Avenue in the persistent drizzle, keen to get out of the rain and take their seats in the theatre box Shirley had booked for Dai's birthday.

The foyer was densely crowded with well-heeled patrons and, as they threaded their way through the crowd, Dai could feel the excitement in the air. He was almost beside himself when he spotted Martha Haycroft mingling among the crowd unnoticed. He'd read all her works and was a huge fan. It was incredible to think she was raised in poverty on a tobacco farm in Kentucky.

'I do believe I just spotted the playwright herself,' Dai murmured in Shirley's ear as he took off his damp raincoat. 'I'd love to meet her, given half a chance. Here, let me take your coat, Shirley love,' he said, noting with gratification Shirley's impressed expression. 'I'll go and find the cloakroom. You wait here.'

It took Dai longer than expected to reach the cloakroom, drop off the coats, and make his way back through the dense crowd to where he had left Shirley, but when he arrived, she wasn't there. Standing on tiptoes to look around the crowd, he saw her by the box office – chatting to Martha Haycroft! Dai smiled to himself. He should have known

Shirley would seek out and introduce herself to the actual playwright.

Dai weaved adroitly through the crowd and lightly touched her elbow to signify his return without interrupting her conversation. She turned to face him with a polite smile.

'Can I help you, Sir?' she said with a strange drawl, her sparkling violet eyes matching her amethyst earrings.

Dai frowned. What the heck was she playing at? Was she drunk already? He even briefly considered she might be having a stroke. Then something clicked. Amethyst earrings? Shirley wasn't wearing amethyst earrings that evening. What on earth—?

With a jolt, Dai suddenly realised that the woman whose elbow he was holding was not his wife at all.

'I… I… I'm so sorry!' he stuttered, releasing his grip. 'I… I seem to have mistaken you for my wife. You really are her absolute image…' He trailed off, staring at Shirley's identical twin in disbelief.

The lady gave him an amused smile and said sweetly in her musical drawl: 'There's no need to apologise, Sir. I hope you find her before the show starts. Allow me to introduce myself. I'm Gwenna Garland and this is my sister, Martha Haycroft.'

Dai's face burned and his palms were clammy as he smiled at Gwenna and shook Martha's hand. 'Yes, yes indeed,' he stammered. 'I'm very pleased to meet you. I'm terribly sorry but I must find my wife.' He cursed his foolishness as he backed away, bowing ridiculously like a nodding dog.

Pushing his way back through the crowded foyer, he spotted Shirley emerging from the ladies' room.

'Shirley, you won't believe this,' Dai exclaimed. 'I just ran into Martha Haycroft at the box office and she was talking to a woman who looked exactly like you. I thought it was you at first. She was your spitting image, like your identical twin. You should take a look for yourself!'

He turned to direct Shirley's gaze towards the box office, but Martha and her sister had vanished. Shirley gave him a withering look. 'They were just there a moment ago...' he spluttered forlornly.

'Never mind,' said Shirley, linking her arm through his. 'Come on, it's your birthday. Let's get up to our box. I've got a bottle of champagne on ice waiting for you. Maybe you'd like to invite your new friend Martha to join us for a glass?' she added with a chuckle.

Dai felt like royalty as he ascended the sweeping red-carpeted staircase, which afforded a magnificent view over the sumptuous foyer. The elaborately panelled walls and ceilings were smothered in lavishly gilded curlicues, evoking images of the interior of Buckingham Palace. The prospect of the chilled champagne awaiting him in Box A only heightened his sensation of grandeur.

As they settled into their red velvet seats, Shirley popped the champagne cork and poured two glasses. The bubbles sparkled like diamonds under the stage lighting and Dai's worries melted away. He really was a lucky chap to have such a fantastic wife. Shirley had worked her way up from the nursing ranks to becoming an MP, via local government in South Wales, entirely on her own merit, championing the healthcare agenda the whole way. She was a force to be reckoned with and he was incredibly proud of her.

'Cheers, my darling,' she said, clinking glasses with Dai. 'Happy birthday!'

As Dai raised his glass, he caught sight of the occupants of the box opposite.

'Look, Shirley,' he whispered excitedly. 'There they are – Martha Haycroft and her guests, directly opposite. That's her sister, the one with the dark hair. I don't know who the older couple are but doesn't she look just like you? I told you so!'

Despite the mellow pre-show lighting, Dai and Shirley had a clear view across the auditorium. The woman seated opposite turned to face them as if drawn by some unseen magnetic force. They were separated by fewer than twenty metres. Dai looked on with fascination as the two women locked eyes and exchanged amused smiles. Their incredible similarity was undeniable.

Gwenna raised her glass in their direction and Dai raised his in return. Nobody spoke, but inside, he was elated.

The lights went down at that moment and the heavy velvet stage curtain swept back majestically.

'I told you she looks just like you!' whispered Dai, delighted to be vindicated.

'Can't see it myself,' teased Shirley in a whisper, with a muffled chuckle.

TWENTY-EIGHT

MANORBIER, PEMBROKESHIRE

Lowri was deadheading the last of her roses in the front garden of her limestone cottage overlooking the beautiful twelfth-century castle at Manorbier Bay when Shirley arrived in her battered four-by-four. The car's back windows were smothered in nose-art from Shirley's two golden retrievers, Ben and Jerry. At seventy-eight, Lowri had retained her youthful elegant frame, but her tumbling mane had thinned slightly and was now the colour of slate from the Preseli Hills, shot through with broad streaks of pure snow. She gave a welcoming smile as Shirley unlatched the front gate and walked briskly up the garden path. Ben and Jerry milled behind her, their plumy tails wagging, searching out sniffs.

'Hello, Mam.' Shirley embraced Lowri and kissed her soft pale cheek. 'Making the most of the last of the good weather, I see.'

Lowri slipped her secateurs into the pocket of her gardening tunic and took Shirley by the hand. 'Yes, they're forecasting rain for the rest of the week. Come inside, I'll get the kettle on. I've just made a fresh plate of Welsh cakes.'

'Ooh, lovely!' Shirley salivated at the thought of Lowri's famous baking. Having run the Bread of Heaven tea rooms in Aberavon for almost two decades before retiring to buy the cottage and run it as a B & B with Vaughan, Lowri had recently begun to hint that she may be ready to pass on her father's secret recipe for bara brith. Quietly, Shirley hoped it wouldn't be to her, as she was hopeless in the kitchen. As she walked through the low door frame into the slate-floored hallway, she was greeted by the welcoming aroma of baking. 'Great timing!' she exclaimed, looking about the kitchen for the man she called her stepfather.

'Where's Vaughan?' she asked. 'Is he out with Muttley and Tess?'

'Yes, he's taken the dogs down to the beach with Alys.' Lowri smiled fondly, but Shirley frowned, unexpectedly peeved. Nobody had told her that her granddaughter was staying with her mother.

'It's half term,' Lowri explained in response to Shirley's puzzled expression. 'She's been here all week. Huw's coming for her sometime today. You might catch him if you're lucky.'

Shirley made a face. She should have known that. She didn't spend nearly enough time with her granddaughter and her son had to depend on his elderly grandmother for childcare during school holidays when his police shifts clashed with his wife's. With Lowri being a couple of years shy of eighty, Shirley wondered if it wasn't all a bit much. Maybe she should just retire and take over caring for Huw and Cheryl's children, just as Lowri had done for her when she was busy building her career. It would be great to spend more time with her family, especially with Lowri – before it was too late. Which reminded her of the reason for her visit.

'How do you fancy a night out at the theatre in Swansea, Mam? I took Dai to see the new Martha Haycroft play in London last weekend for his birthday. We had a great evening,' she said. 'I thought of you. You'd have loved it.'

Lowri looked up from laying the table for tea and cake. 'I'm sure I would have, my love, but I can't manage those long train rides into London anymore,' she said, wistfully. 'I do still enjoy her work, though,' she added. 'I've just finished reading *The Smokebush*, actually. It's a family saga about a tobacco-farming dynasty in Kentucky in the eighteenth century. So engaging and beautifully written.' Lowri laughed lightly. 'I often think someone should write a family saga about us.'

Shirley snorted. 'Good luck with that, I'd say! We're a right bunch of misfits.' She chuckled to herself as the memory of Dai's encounter came back to her. 'We actually met Martha Haycroft at the theatre – well, Dai did, not me, although I saw her across the auditorium. It was the strangest thing – she was with her sister, who looked a bit like me. Dai keeps saying she was my absolute double, but I'm sure that's only because he thought she was me in the foyer.' Shirley's shoulders began to shake with laughter. 'He actually went up and grabbed her, thinking it was me. Good job he didn't grab her bum or he'd have got a slap for his troubles.'

Tears streamed down the two women's faces as they laughed about Dai's innocent mistake. 'Oh, I wish I'd seen his face!' said Lowri, wiping her streaming eyes on her pinny.

Lowri and Shirley were still laughing when the back door flew open. Two Alsatians and an eight-year-old girl whirled in like a tornado, followed more sedately by Vaughan, removing his tweed cap and straightening his thinning faded gold hair with his fingers.

'Nanny!' shrieked Alys ecstatically, hurling herself into Shirley's arms as she crouched to greet her granddaughter. Intense love washed over Shirley as she embraced the little girl and breathed in her chilly fresh-air scented hair.

As she stood up to hug Vaughan, Shirley noticed through the kitchen window Huw's brawny figure striding down the garden path towards the cottage. He was wearing a civilian jacket over his police shirt and trousers, and was still wearing his heavy-duty public order boots.

'Huw's here already, Mam!' she exclaimed, rushing to the door to let her son in. 'Get another cup out.'

As she opened the door, the sight of Huw's exhausted face and sweat-flattened hair spoke volumes. He'd obviously just finished a tough night shift, even though it was gone noon.

'Look at the state of you,' she said affectionately, reaching up on tiptoe to kiss him, even though he was stooping over to hug her. 'Bit of a late one, Son?'

"Fraid so, Mam. Swansea were at home to Millwall last night and there were running battles in the town centre. Don't go into Swansea for a few days if you can help it – all the shop windows have been put in. I've been dealing with prisoners all night. Football fans are morons – the lot of them.'

His massive form practically filled the tiny kitchen as he stooped to scoop up Alys in one of his enormous muscular arms. The little girl looked like a ragdoll against his vast chest. 'It's lovely to see you, Mam,' he said, pecking Shirley on the cheek. 'But I can't stay as I've only got a few hours to get some sleep before Cheryl has to leave for late turn.'

Shirley's heart sank. 'You've come all this way and you can't stop for a cup of tea with your old mam? I've not seen you in ages.' She cringed inwardly at the desperation in her voice.

Huw's shoulders slumped and he rubbed his face wearily with his free hand. 'I'd love to, Mam, but I've got to get Alys back home and it's a long drive. School term starts tomorrow.'

He turned to Lowri and hugged her gently with his spare arm, kissing the top of her head as she handed him a bag of Alys' things. 'Say thank you and goodbye to Mam-gu and Tad-cu,' he said to Alys as he ducked through the door, taking his daughter with him.

'Goodness me,' said Vaughan once he'd finished waving them off. 'What an exhausting way to live. I don't remember it being that bad when I was in the CID.'

'That was over twenty years ago, Vaughan. Policing has changed,' said Shirley. 'And you didn't have to juggle a career with being a husband and father.'

He slipped his arm around Lowri's waist. 'Good job, too,' he said, 'or I would never have won the heart of the woman of my dreams.'

Lowri's letter asking for his help solving the mystery of the remembrance cards changed Vaughan's life. He'd been determined to do his utmost to help her, but ultimately, he'd failed her. He'd never been able to trace Bryn or identify the sender of the anonymous cards, yet she still welcomed him into her life and made him feel like the luckiest man alive.

Through old-fashioned policing methods, he'd successfully followed Bryn's trail as far as Liverpool. There, he found a waiter in a café at the station who remembered meeting Bryn, and from him Vaughan learned of Bryn's plans to go to sea. He then spent weeks painstakingly checking maritime archives in the Wirral until he found Bryn's name as a passage worker on a ship bound for Buenos Aires. The ship was captained by Marcus Cruikshank. It had been a breakthrough moment for Vaughan, and he thought he was getting somewhere at last – that is, until he discovered that, infuriatingly, Captain Cruikshank had passed away only weeks before, having contracted deadly Argentine haemorrhagic fever. He was sure that if he'd been able to interview the captain, he would have uncovered vital leads.

Crucially, though, there was no record in the captain's log of the death of any crewmember on that passage, casting fresh doubt on the authenticity of the letter to Shirley. Even more interestingly, Captain Cruikshank had recorded a major incident towards the end of the voyage, where the ship was involved in a collision with another freighter in the Rio de la Plata and a man's life had been saved, having fallen overboard. It was a fascinating story and Vaughan was gripped by it. At first, he wondered if the 'man overboard' could have been Bryn until his eye alighted on the name of the rescuer – Bryn Evans!

With his heart in his mouth, Vaughan read with astonishment the captain's account of Bryn's heroic actions as he rescued Able Seaman Paul Holding from drowning. It was an unexpectedly moving moment and he was glad no one was there to see the tears in his eyes as he hurried to the Gestetner copying machine in the Wirral archive's admin office. He'd already shown his police warrant card to be authorised to produce a replica of official records *for police purposes*. This find was a breakthrough, which proved Bryn had made it alive to Buenos Aires, but it also put Bryn beyond the limit of Vaughan's policing jurisdiction.

Vaughan knew that Lowri treasured the copy of the captain's report he'd given her and chose not to share it with Shirley to avoid unnecessarily raising her hopes. She reasoned that if Bryn had faked the letter, there had to be a good reason. Privately, Vaughan suspected the opposite but kept his thoughts to himself.

Lowri believed that Bryn was still alive for almost twenty years, while the anonymous remembrance cards continued to arrive from America. But when they stopped, only God was privy to her thoughts. Every year, on the anniversary of Emlyn's death, Vaughan noticed that she placed an extra garland of seasonal flowers on Evan and Emlyn's grave.

As Vaughan watched Huw's burly figure striding away from the house carrying Alys, he silently counted his blessings. This lovely family considered him one of their own and saved him from becoming a lonely old fossil. Meeting Lowri was undoubtedly the best thing that had ever happened to him.

TWENTY-NINE

Chase descended the double-width staircase naked, enjoying the freedom of an empty house. The Hacienda was in complete silence, other than the echo of his bare feet around the vaulted ceiling as he padded across the terracotta tiles, making his way to the kitchen for a cup of coffee. It was Sunday morning and he had the entire day to himself. Greer was away in Louisville, planning a concert tour with her promoter, and Travis had gone on a business trip to look at a new stud horse for Jack Jepson. His mother was still in London with Wendell and Carol, which meant he was alone to explore at leisure.

But first, he needed that coffee. A cup of the incredible freshly ground stuff that Greer drank would have been great, but he had no idea how to make it, so he searched the kitchen for a jar of instant instead. The trouble with the vast kitchens of the super-rich was it took forever to find anything, he decided, based on his extensive experience. It was a wonder that she didn't have staff. But then, she kinda did. Travis was her stable manager, although she shared him with the Jepsons; Ma was more or less her live-in housekeeper and he'd just agreed to become her estate manager. He grinned to himself. She sure knew how to look after 'the help'.

Chase took his steaming mug out onto the terrace and basked in the gentle warmth of the mid-autumn sun on his bare skin, taking in the magnificent view of the expensively landscaped parkland sloping towards the lake. It was still hard to believe that all this belonged to his sister. Buena Vista was just about visible on the far side of the lake, commanding its own magnificent views. Greer wasn't quite the equal of Jack Jepson for wealth just yet, but he reckoned she wasn't far off – despite her divorce from that blood-sucking bastard, Will Dixon. It was lucky for Dixon that it was Travis and not him who had been there to save Greer that day a couple of years back, or things may have turned out very differently for him. If there was one thing Chase despised, it was men who abused women.

He put his angry thoughts about Greer's ex-husband aside and stretched luxuriantly. The sun felt good on his throbbing hip. A thick red welt ran from just below his rib cage to the outside of his upper thigh, a permanent reminder of the Battle of Medina Ridge. He was lucky to still have the leg, having been struck by a massive hunk of red-hot metal from an exploding tank that had taken a direct hit. He avoided thinking about that hellish time and he certainly didn't talk about it. Some nights, he would wake up in a feverish sweat from a vivid nightmare, reliving the deafening noise of shell fire, the blast-furnace heat, and the stench of hot sand drenched in blood bubbling out of a ragged hole in his body. He downed a couple of painkillers with his coffee. They should kick in quickly, with any luck.

He drained his mug and rinsed it in the butler sink before wandering downstairs into the entertainment room. The room was his idea of heaven. He potted a few balls on the billiard table before he noticed the giant movie screen rolled up above a bare wall. He searched for the remote and soon had the big screen lowered into place, flicking through the hundreds of channels on Greer's satellite TV.

He soon discovered a good football channel and sank into an oversized comfortable sofa to watch it. He'd been too skinny as a kid to join the high school football team but he reckoned he'd be an excellent linebacker now. His stomach growled loudly as he got engrossed in the game. He looked around the room and saw a vast double-door refrigerator built into a short set of kitchen units in an alcove. He would bet his bottom dollar that it was filled with beer. A quick search of the cupboards produced a plentiful supply of supersized bags of chips. He chuckled to himself. It was a good thing Ma wasn't around to see him having beer and chips for breakfast.

Chase spent several hours relaxing, feeling like the King of Kentucky as he flipped through football channels, munching on chips and sipping Bud, but eventually, the dull ache in his hip became a burning pain from sitting in a soft seat for too long. No matter how he shifted about on the thickly padded cushions, he couldn't ease the pain. He needed to go outside and stretch his sore joints. He cracked open his painkillers and swallowed a couple with a mouthful of beer.

Chase stepped out onto the sunny terrace and took a couple of deep breaths of clean Kentucky air to clear his beery head. His mouth felt like a skunk's nest but at least the painkillers would soon take the edge off his sore hip. It was a gorgeous day and he was wasting it sitting inside watching TV. In fact, it was the perfect day for a ride. Should he drive over to Evansville and take out his newly serviced Harley or just wander down to the stables and saddle up a horse? He couldn't decide. He flipped a coin in his mind and the horse won.

Chase dressed and had a Kentucky mountain horse saddled up within half an hour. He didn't have a particular direction in mind, so he let the horse do the thinking. He had a bit of a headache behind one eye, which wasn't surprising, seeing as he'd had booze for breakfast. He fished in the pocket of his denims for his painkillers and crunched a couple dry, grimacing at the bitter taste. At least it would take the edge off his headache.

In the warmth of the afternoon, with a belly full of beer, Chase was soon lost in daydreams. The horse ambled on, its rhythmic motion soothing him, until he was almost half asleep. There was Tyler, still twelve years old in Chase's mind's eye, throwing rocks at him at the lake for being a jerk and Shelby was giggling on the end of the pontoon, bathed in golden sunlight. And there he was, showing off and being an idiot, desperate to impress her, as usual. He'd wanted her to choose him for as long as he could remember. But she chose Trav and he didn't blame her – because Trav was perfect for her. He'd had to become a grown man to realise that.

After a while, he noticed the horse wasn't moving. Where the hell was he? His eyes slowly began to focus and things became clearer. He was at the lake, under the shade of an enormous ash tree whose leaves were just starting to display the tell-tale signs of autumn. It was almost as if the horse had read his mind.

He dismounted the saddle and fell in a heap as his legs gave way beneath him. He roared with laughter. Warm sunlight filtered through the golden leaves and the last of the crickets chirruped softly. The horse wandered off a few steps, happily ripping up mouthfuls of long bluegrass. His pain was gone and he was floating on cloud nine. He looked around, bathed in bliss, and noticed an old wooden rowboat upturned on the gravel shore of the lake. Could it possibly be the same one they'd used as kids to play pirates or Amazon explorers?

He wandered over to check it out, expecting to find a rotten hull, but it was in good condition with a fresh coat of paint. He gathered up the oars, pushed the little boat out onto the water, and stumbled in, swaying dangerously for a moment. He burst out laughing once again – he'd almost given himself a dunkin' then and there.

With just a few minutes of easy rowing, he reached the middle of the lake. It seemed so small compared to when he was a kid, yet as he leaned over the edge of the boat, the darkness of the depths below was impenetrable, which was hardly surprising as the lake had once been a gravel pit.

He was toying with the idea of stripping off and leaping in for a skinny dip when he saw a figure on horseback approaching the northern shore.

It was Shelby.

His heart leapt and his pulse quickened. By God, she looked beautiful. Her strawberry-blonde hair was longer than ever, cascading down to her waist in glossy waves.

She wore a pure white blouse that skimmed her slender figure, paired with cream jodhpurs and shiny black knee-high riding boots. She was a vision of perfection.

'Hey, Chase!' she called out, waving happily. 'I thought it might be you.'

'Shelby! Great to see you. Wanna join me?'

'Sure, why not? For old time's sake,' she said with a warm laugh.

Chase rowed across to Shelby's side of the lake in a couple-of-dozen powerful strokes and held a hand out for her. Taking it demurely, she stepped nimbly into the little boat, barely causing it to rock.

'Well, this is an unexpected pleasure.' She settled herself on the wooden plank seat, facing him.

'I was just thinkin' about you, as it happens.' Chase grunted with exertion as he pulled away from the shore. 'You and Tyler, and how we used to mess about here all summer. I loved those days. I haven't seen Tyler around since I've been back. What's he doin' with himself?'

There was silence for a moment as Shelby twisted a tress of her beautiful hair around her fingers. 'Oh, this and that.'

This and that? What did she mean by that? He raised a quizzical brow and looked at Shelby as if to say, '*This is me you're talking to*'. She was now clasping and unclasping her hands in her lap, a picture of discomfort.

'Oh well, you know how these things are, Chase,' she said. 'Things didn't work out so well here for Tyler.' She paused, looking down at her hands, clearly having second thoughts about what to tell him. What could be so bad?

Her shoulders drooped. 'Pa and Grandpa were training him up to take over the stud farm one day.' She sighed forlornly. 'But horses aren't his thing like they are for me.'

'Everyone knows that!' Chase exclaimed. 'So, what happened?'

'Well, he was always artistic, if you recall.' She smiled weakly. 'There was a blazing row one day, and he just upped and moved to New York to take up sculpture.' Her liquid amber eyes filled and glistening droplets sparkled on the ends of her lower lashes. 'He made quite a splash, by all accounts. The art scene loved him and now he lives in a gorgeous apartment with his... his... boyfriend.' She hung her head, avoiding Chase's eye, her shoulders beginning to shake. 'He hangs out with rock stars and supermodels these days.'

Chase put a comforting hand on her shoulder. 'Hey, Shelby, please don't get upset. I'm sorry I asked. It sounds to me like Tyler's having a great life and doing what makes him happy, right? That's what's important, ain't it?'

Shelby's shoulders began to convulse. He doubted she'd be able to hold herself together much longer. 'But then Ma went too!' She began to sob out loud. 'Turns out she never liked horses – or Pa – very much either.' Her adorable face twisted with anguish as she choked on her tears.

Chase gasped. Her parents had split up! Jerome and Erin had always seemed as solid as a rock – no wonder Shelby was upset. The sight of her pain was unbearable. He just had to comfort her.

He dropped the oars in the bottom of the boat and swivelled around to sit alongside her. There was just enough room if they squeezed together. He put his arm around her waist. 'Hey Shelby, you poor darlin',' he said gently. 'I didn't know. I'm so sorry for upsettin' you.' The warmth of her body radiated into his and her skin smelled like sweet honeyed mimosa. He couldn't stop his mouth from watering as she leaned her cheek on his shoulder, weeping like her heart would break.

'Oh, Chase, it was so awful, the screaming and the rows—'

He had to make her pain go away. 'Hush now, baby,' he soothed, taking her in his arms, stroking her hair and kissing the top of her fragrant head. He cared so much about this darlin' girl. He always had. She smelled so beautiful; her lovely face was so close to his—

As his lips met hers, a jolt of electricity shot through him. He pressed bodily over her, craving the taste of her skin. Her breast was soft to his touch outside her silky blouse as the steel inside his trousers surged against her groin. He'd yearned for this for as long as he could remember—

Her muffled screams pierced his ecstasy.

Pain exploded in his groin, white lightning searing his brain. He reeled backwards in shock and agony.

As he tumbled overboard into the inky depths, the last thing he saw was Shelby's contorted tear-streaked face as she held a bloodstained oar.

***

Travis had just returned to the Jepson stables from his business trip and was hanging up the keys to his Silverado in the wooden cabin that served as his office when he heard galloping hooves approaching.

What now? He crossed wearily to the cabin door. It had been a long tough trip, and he was looking forward to a good dinner with Shelby and a relaxing beer.

It was Shelby on horseback, hurtling towards him across the stable yard. His stomach lurched with fear. Her long wet hair was plastered to her shirt, her clothes were saturated and sticking to her skin, and her face was twisted in torment. What the hell had happened? He sprinted out to the yard and expertly caught hold of the bridle of the foaming horse, bringing it to a shuddering halt. She slid off the horse to the ground, her body shivering and convulsing, and let out a tormented wail. Releasing the horse, Travis threw his arms around her, his mind racing. She was shaking uncontrollably. Icy fear gripped his guts.

'What's happened, Shelby? He pulled her tightly to his chest. 'Did someone hurt you?'

'Chase... it's Chase...' she gasped. 'I... I think I killed him.'

She was practically incoherent and making no sense at all. She couldn't have killed Chase; that was ridiculous. 'Tell me exactly what's happened, Shelby.' He gripped her shoulders to get her to focus on his face. If someone was hurt somewhere, he needed to act fast.

Her voice came out in stuttering gasps. 'W... w... we were in the rowboat. I... I think he was drunk. He... he...' She faltered, her face contorting with anguish.

'What is it, Shelby? Tell me!' Travis's heart pounded with dread. Were his worries about Chase's return about to be confirmed?

'He f... forced himself on me, Travis!' she wailed. 'I was so scared! I... I thought he was gonna... gonna r... rape me, so I... I hit him... with the oar.'

Her words ripped a hole in his soul. It was worse than he'd feared. 'Where is he now, Shelby?' he yelled, a murderous rage boiling up inside him.

'I don't know,' she cried. 'He fell in the lake and just sank. I think he was unconscious. I... I did try to save him, Travis – honest, I did. I swam down as deep as I could.'

Travis couldn't believe what he was hearing. Chase had tried to rape her, yet she'd wanted to save him? She'd risked her own life to save his? He suppressed a cry of impotent rage and clasped her tightly to his chest. He'd have killed Chase with his bare hands if he'd been there. *Damn you to hell, Chase!* he thought. *I knew you were gonna be nothing but trouble!*

There was no time to waste. Travis pulled a fresh horse blanket off a shelf and wrapped Shelby tightly in it, hugging her close to his body while his racing mind planned his next move. If Chase really was dead, it would be hellish for Shelby. The sheriff would want to know everything and they might not believe her. It'd be her word against a dead body. But if there was a chance his brother might still be alive, he should try to save him so that he should be the one to face the consequences, not Shelby.

Travis was torn between caring for his shivering fiancée and searching for Chase. Shelby was a courageous girl but she was clearly traumatised, whereas Chase might be dying somewhere – and ought to be the one to face justice. It was the toughest decision of his life. 'Shelby, listen to me, okay?' he said, 'I need to try and find Chase. He might still be alive. Can you make it back to the hacienda on your own? Nobody is around, so you can take a hot shower and put on a warm robe, and I'll be back as fast as I can. Is that okay with you?'

She nodded wordlessly, her eyes black holes of shocked incomprehension. He almost changed his mind for a moment, but then she said in a cracked voice: 'Don't worry about me, Trav. Just go and find your brother.'

Travis ran to the cabin to get the keys to the Silverado, amazed at Shelby's bravery. She didn't deserve to be in this mess. He'd do whatever it took to protect her.

The haunted look on her face as he helped her into the driver's seat killed him. He kissed her firmly, desperate to reassure her. 'Remember just one thing,' he said with grim resolve. 'This is *not your fault*. I love you, Shelby, more than anything. Everything's gonna be all right, I promise.'

***

Shelby was sitting in Greer's kitchen, wrapped in a thick white towelling bathrobe, both hands around a mug of hot coffee, when Travis returned from searching the lake. Her face was as pale as the robe and she was still shivering. Travis crossed the kitchen in three paces, enfolded her in his arms, and kissed her hair and face.

'I cain't get warm, Travis, no matter how hot I made the shower.' Her teeth chattered as she rested her cheek against Travis's sweat-soaked chest.

'I think that's probably shock, my darlin'.' Travis gently removed the coffee cup from her hand. 'I don't think this will help any.'

'Did you find anything?'

Travis had ridden down to the lake but the short autumn evenings meant it was already dark when he arrived. Even though he'd thought to take a heavy-duty flashlight with him and had rowed out to the middle of the lake, it was an impossible task. He'd made sure to put the boat back where it always was, under the big ash tree, so that no one would ever know it had been taken out, and had rounded up Chase's horse and led it back to the stable. As far as he could tell, nothing would ever link Chase's disappearance to him and Shelby.

'I didn't find a thing,' he said, struggling to keep his voice low and calm. He didn't want to upset Shelby all over again. 'I'm so sorry he did this to you, my darlin'. You don't deserve any of this mess. This is all Chase's fault. Don't ever forget that, Shelby. They do say that war does terrible things to men. It changes them in ways you cain't see and, deep down, Chase was a different man when he came home. I reckon he is at the bottom of the lake and he can stay there as far as I'm concerned. Nobody needs to know about this, Shelby. Nobody!'

Shelby's haunted eyes scanned his face. 'But shouldn't we call the sheriff? Folks will be lookin' for him.'

Travis blew his cheeks out. They could take that risk but, if they got it wrong, the consequences for Shelby were unthinkable. 'You could get into a whole lotta trouble over this, Shelby, and that's not fair. Chase did this, not you. If anyone asks, you say you never saw him at all today. We can say he must have taken off out of jealousy that you're gonna marry me, not him.'

Shelby looked at Travis with astonishment. 'What do you mean?'

Travis took her pale cold face in both hands and looked into her hollow, dark-ringed eyes. Did she really not know that Chase had loved her as much as he had, since their childhood? That their competing love for her was what had driven an unspoken wedge between him and his twin brother all those years ago? Travis hugged her tightly. 'It doesn't matter now. The main thing is that you're safe and nobody is going to get into trouble with the law. Agreed?'

'Well, if you are sure, Travis,' said Shelby uncertainly.

'I am, Shelby. Never been surer of anythin' in my life.'

THIRTY

Travis sat in Greer's dimly lit kitchen, his eyes fixed on the rustic oak table that had been at the centre of so many joyous family gatherings. But today, there was no warmth in the air, no celebration, no laughter. Gone were the candles, the bottles of wine and the plates of food. Instead, the sombre faces of his relatives were etched with worry as they joined him at the bare table, speaking among themselves with muted voices. It was as if they already knew that Chase was dead.

Wendell and Carol were the last to arrive. Greer scraped back her chair on the tiled floor as they settled into their seats and rose slowly to her feet. The overhead lighting cast dark shadows on her makeup-free face, emphasising the deep creases around her mouth, and making her look tired and older than her years. Her unwashed hair was scraped up into a severe ponytail. The atmosphere in the room was tense as they waited for her to speak. Her hollow dark-ringed eyes

302

told Travis she'd barely slept in the seven days since Chase had gone missing. One glance in the mirror would tell him he looked even worse.

With any luck, everyone would assume his drawn appearance was because he was worried about his missing twin brother. But it was Shelby that he was really worried about. In the space of a week, her peachy cheeks had become shrunken and sallow, and the life had gone from her eyes. Her clothes seemed to have doubled in size, hanging loosely from her shoulders and hips as if she wasn't inside them at all. Whenever she closed her eyes, she'd said, she saw Chase's white face sinking to the bottom of the lake and imagined the carp eating his flesh from his bones. Her torment and his powerlessness to do anything about it ate away at Travis constantly, like a rat nesting in his guts.

'Now that you're all here, I've got something important to say,' Greer began.

There was an anxious silence as everyone at the table waited for the news. Travis thought he might throw up. They'd found Chase's body; he was sure of it. He took a big gulp of coffee to conceal his agitation. He clamped the inside of his cheeks between his teeth as tension got the better of him, relishing the pain and adding the metallic tang of blood to the acrid taste already in his mouth.

Greer leaned on the table and swept her gaze around the worried faces. 'I've hired the best private investigator in the business to find Chase,' she announced. 'Justine Cornelius is a former NYPD police captain, a specialist in kidnappings, hostage-taking and missing person cases. She'll want to interview you all individually immediately, as the sheriff's office has already wasted valuable time. There's nothing for anyone to worry about, though. It's standard procedure in missing person cases to speak to the family first.'

Travis gasped along with everyone else around the table, his eyes darting between their confused faces. He trembled, his armpits becoming clammy as the seriousness of his and Shelby's situation hit him. Sweat ran down his spine like someone had cranked the thermostat to full blast. He unbuttoned his jacket and loosened his shirt collar from his sweat-soaked neck. It was one thing to lay a false trail for the local sheriff's office to follow – if they'd even cared enough to look – but now, with a private investigator involved? It was an entirely different story. The confidence he'd had in his hastily conceived plan vanished in an instant as he grappled with the new development. He should have known Greer would spare no expense and bring in the big guns! Could he have been more stupid?

Carol was speaking – something about her and Wendell being in London with Ma at the time – but he wasn't really listening. 'What about the sheriff's office?' he burst out, interrupting Carol before she'd finished. 'What do they say about it?'

'The sheriff's office has been worse than useless, Trav.' Greer's eyes flashed with anger. 'They won't investigate Chase's disappearance because they say Chase isn't a vulnerable person and there are no suspicious circumstances. They reckon war veterans do this sort of thing all the time, just take themselves off and then turn up when they are good and ready. They've recorded him as a missing person, but that's all.'

'What do they mean by "suspicious circumstances", darlin'?' asked Grandpa Wendell. 'It all looks pretty suspicious to me that a man fresh home from the military should just up and leave of his own volition before he even got to say hello to his ma and grandpa!'

Across the table, Ma nodded in agreement, her pinched white face contrasting starkly with her dark hair. The dim overhead light made her look strangely spectral. 'It's just so out of character,' she said, her voice trembling. 'He wrote me before I went to London, sayin' how much he was lookin' forward to comin' home and seein' us all. It just doesn't add up.' Her face crumpled and she fished a tissue from her sleeve.

Travis' anger grew. Chase didn't deserve Ma's sympathy after what he'd done to Shelby. She was wasting her love on a monster who'd tried to rape his own brother's fiancée! He gritted his teeth, seething with rage. She must never find out about what Chase had become – it would destroy her. He cursed Chase for bringing so much misery upon his family. It would have been better for them all if he'd stayed away.

Grandpa Wendell put a comforting arm around Ma's shoulders. She rested her head against her father's chest, a look of utter desolation on her face. The sight of her distress was unbearable. He had to say something.

Travis looked around the table, his face set in a grim expression. 'That might have been true in the past, Ma, but don't forget Chase has been in the army these last eight years and has seen and done some terrible things. He's not the same Chase we knew before.' Travis paused. 'He's changed.'

Ma's pale face looked even more pinched. 'What makes you say that, Son?' she asked. 'In what way was he different? Only you and Greer can say what he was like when he came home. Nobody else saw him.'

He had to think quickly. He needed them to believe Chase had come home in an unbalanced frame of mind to make his sudden departure seem more believable. 'Look, Ma', he said gently. 'I don't want to upset you but we must look at the facts. We know he was drinking heavily from the way he almost emptied Greer's refrigerator of beer before he left and then there's the pills he was swallowing like candy, which must be a cause for concern. That was no scratch he got in Basra. He's in a constant pain.' He stopped abruptly, seeing his mother's eyes well up again. He'd gone too far and hated himself for it, but he had to protect Shelby at all costs. 'Sorry, Ma, but it has to be said. The detective will want to know all this anyway.'

'But I still don't get why any of that would make him want to leave,' cried Greer, banging her clenched fist on the table. 'If anything, it's a reason to stay. He was excited about the fresh start – a new job, new house, new truck – and he was insistent that the cash I gave him was an advance, not a gift. That doesn't sound like a man planning to leave.'

Travis cursed inwardly. Things weren't going the way he'd hoped. 'And where is that money now, Greer?' he snapped. 'Tell me that!' He regretted the words as soon as they left his mouth. Attacking his sister was unforgivable.

Greer stood up from the table and stormed out of the room without saying a word, her expression stony. Gwenna followed her, shooting Travis a dirty look as she went. He hung his head. He'd gone too far yet again and he knew it. He could hear their voices in the reception hall, Greer's angry tone and his mother's placating one. He closed his eyes and clenched his fists under the table, consumed with shame and frustration. They needed to believe Chase had left of his own accord. He didn't want to use the story he'd concocted to protect Shelby, but it was looking like he'd have to. The stakes were high – his family's trust in him was on the line, so he had to be convincing.

He took a deep breath and opened his eyes, steeling himself to lie to his family for Shelby's sake. He chose his words carefully to avoid casting himself as the villain. 'I didn't want to say anything before because I didn't want to upset everyone,' he said, adopting a conciliatory tone. 'But the truth of the matter is that Chase couldn't bear to stay once he found out I'd gotten engaged to Shelby.' He cast his eyes down towards the table, his heart pounding. Would this story be enough to convince them, or would it all come crashing down around him?

'What are you talkin' about, Travis?' Carol gripped Wendell's hand tightly. 'Greer told us how pleased he was for you both.'

Travis hated himself for what he was about to say, but everything was riding on this and it was all Chase's fault.

'He wanted her for himself,' he said bitterly, reflecting how true this part of the story was. 'He always did, since we were kids. He was as jealous as hell. It was torture for him to see me and Shelby together.'

The shock on their faces tore a jagged hole in his heart.

Goddamn you, Chase, for putting us through this, he thought. *Goddamn you to hell!*

Gwenna's eyes lingered on the black-and-white photograph of her mother-in-law that she had found in Gryff's wallet after his funeral. She'd put the treasured image in a silver frame and it now held pride of place on her dressing table. She picked it up and studied it carefully, trying to imagine what kind of woman her mother-in-law had been.

'Lowri Evans,' Gwenna murmured. 'Are you still out there somewhere, missing your son the way I'm missing mine?'

Gwenna's flight home from London with Carol and Wendell had seemed to last forever once they'd been told of Chase's disappearance, as if her being in Kentucky instead of London would change anything. At first, she was convinced it was all just some silly misunderstanding and that Chase had simply forgotten to mention an unplanned trip. But as the hours turned into days without any word, she began to fear the worst.

Greer's announcement that evening was a huge relief. Finally, someone professional would take Chase's disappearance seriously and actively search for her son. So much valuable time had been wasted waiting for the sheriff's department to investigate, but they'd done nothing.

She unclipped her earrings and ran a brush through her hair as she prepared for bed, not that she was expecting to get any sleep. Chase could be hurt somewhere, desperately waiting for help to arrive. It didn't bear thinking about. Hearing Travis describe Chase's drinking problem and terrible injuries had come as a shock to her and she was furious with him for shouting at Greer when all she was trying to do was help. But it seemed a lot had happened to Chase that she didn't know about. She sighed sorrowfully. When did her open and honest little boy become such a complex man with so many secrets?

Only now could she fully appreciate the pain and anguish of Gryff's mother. She must have spent years desperate to know her son's fate. Her eyes welled up with regret for not doing enough to persuade Gryff to reach out to his ma. How Lowri must have suffered. Maybe was still suffering, for all she knew. Was it too late for her to bring closure to Lowri's loss, if she could find her?

***

The scene was set for the photoshoot in Greer's spacious music room, where vast picture windows framed the breathtaking view of the verdant bluegrass pastures that led down to the sparkling lake. The photographer from *The World* magazine had already positioned her tripod, with reflective screens carefully arranged to diffuse the lighting for Greer's portrait photograph. The image would be part of *The World's* series of 'candid and revealing profiles of newsworthy individuals'. With her status as an A-list celebrity and her brother's mysterious disappearance, Greer certainly fitted the bill.

Greer's private investigator had recommended that she agree to the interview. In her twenty-year experience with the NYPD as a hostage negotiator, Justine Cornelius had investigated numerous high-profile kidnappings and missing person reports with an enviable success rate. She firmly believed that worldwide publicity of this calibre would yield much-needed new leads. Greer usually avoided the promotional interview circuit like the plague, but she was prepared to sacrifice her privacy if it meant finding Chase.

Greer was fuming when she emerged from the adjacent yoga room, which was acting as a makeshift dressing room for the photo shoot. The hour she'd just spent with *The World* magazine's fashion stylist being dressed from a rack of high-fashion clothes was pure torture. She was wearing a ludicrously expensive black lace blouse, so delicate it might tear at any moment, skin-tight black leather jeans that she could hardly breathe in that made her look like a teenager going to a rock concert, and skyscraper boots that even a supermodel would struggle to walk in – especially on a Kentucky farm. To complete the look, she wore a chunky silver chain-link necklace that was so heavy it could double as a weightlifting accessory. Did anybody actually wear this 'designer' gear? Would anyone really go out and buy one of those itchy two-thousand-dollar blouses because they believed that Greer Garland owned one? The sooner she could get out of the ridiculous outfit and change into something she could wear to ride a horse, the better.

A makeup artist flitted around Greer, putting the finishing touches to her complexion with a big fluffy blusher brush. Her honey-gold hair had been blow-dried to perfection in big bouncy curls, which tumbled past her shoulders and glowed with a fabulous sheen, thanks to an artfully placed halo lamp. Once the photo editor's airbrush had done its work, she would look like a flawless goddess in the finished pictures. It was all so superficial and artificial, and she was annoyed at herself for going along with it. But she couldn't back out now, not when finding Chase was at stake. With *The World* magazine's worldwide coverage, there had to be someone out there who had information about her missing brother.

Greer slipped into her comfy denims and cowboy boots for the dreaded interview the minute the photo shoot was over. 'So, Greer,' the interviewer began, 'tell me about your childhood. Let's start with your parents.'

As memories of her pa flooded back, Greer braced herself for an emotional trip down memory lane.

THIRTY-ONE

1999

Travis stood on the concrete footings of his farmhouse, the unfinished wooden framework against the azure sky a glimpse into his family's dream home. With just a month until the baby's arrival, he had to make the most of the dry weather and get things moving. The intense heat of the day had already set in and he wiped the sweat from his brow with his shirt sleeve, grateful for the cool breeze that provided some relief.

Since the wedding, he and Shelby had been living in a comfortable apartment at Buena Vista, but the wait for their new home was proving almost too much for Shelby. She was desperate for her own private space, where she didn't have to watch every word for fear of giving the game away about Chase.

It hadn't been difficult to find an explanation for Greer as to why he and Shelby no longer wanted the new house to overlook the lake: the new plot of land was closer to Greer and Ma and would cut down on the amount of new road, saving time, money and the landscape. Greer had accepted the explanation without question, just as she'd accepted his suggestion to shelve plans for Chase's new house – *until he was home safe.*

Travis's thoughts turned to the security upgrade for Greer's estate. That night back in October, when Greer introduced her private investigator to the family, the detective had mentioned that if foul play was a factor in Chase's disappearance, the lack of physical security or CCTV surveillance on the estate had made the felon's job a whole lot easier and her job a whole lot tougher.

'What you need to consider, Ma'am,' Justine had said gravely, 'is that while you have an army of loyal and adoring fans who mean you no harm, there are also freaks and stalkers out there who have access to the internet and can find out all sorts of things about you. You need to have complete peace of mind in your own home.'

A knot formed in Travis's stomach. He swallowed hard and volunteered to manage the installation of cameras and electronic gates.

But Justine had shaken her head and poured cold water on that idea.

'That won't be enough for a high-net-worth individual such as yourself, Ma'am,' she said to Greer briskly. 'I recommend that you engage the services of a professional security company to install a state-of-the-art security system. An estate this size needs a dedicated on-site security team twenty-four-seven. It will be an investment in the safety of every member of your family for years to come, especially when there are children around.'

Travis grimaced – all that expense and disruption was needless. 'Does Greer need to go to those lengths? Maybe we should all just move down the road into Fort Knox,' he joked.

Justine looked at him levelly. 'If you can be sure, Mr Garland, that your brother's disappearance was not the work of an intruder and that Miss Garland and the rest of the family are not at risk, then an electric gate and a few cameras may do the trick. But can you be sure of that, Sir?'

Travis's spine prickled. Was he just imagining it or did the woman seem to have a sixth sense? He took a few deep breaths. There was nothing to worry about – it was just his conscience playing tricks on him. He rolled his shoulders, straightened his back and said: 'No, I cain't be sure of that, Miss Cornelius. I'll get right onto it, if you can recommend a security company.'

The relief on the faces of his ma and sister that evening was plain to see. Justine had pressed the right buttons; the security of the next generation of Garland children was non-negotiable as far as the women were concerned.

He unhitched his horse from the frame of the house and set off around the estate's perimeter to check on the progress of the security installation before the day got too hot to bear. The more he thought about it, the more aggrieved he became. Just how much of a fortress did this place need to be?

***

Travis helped himself to the buffet in Jack's elegant air-conditioned breakfast room while waiting for Jack to arrive for their daily planning meeting. The past ten weeks had been a living nightmare. The heat grew more intense each day and the parched earth cried out for relief that never came. The once-lush bluegrass pastures were now barren wastelands and the crops had withered away to nothing. Travis had never seen anything like it – even the trees were dropping limbs to stay alive. State authorities had declared an extreme drought warning and water restrictions had been implemented.

Travis looked up at the sound of approaching footsteps. Jack's wiry tanned face was grim as he joined Travis at the buffet. Jack's champion horses were worth millions but their lush pastures had shrivelled away.

'Where are we with the supplemental water supply, Travis?' Jack asked, helping himself to ham and eggs.

Travis had worked round the clock to find a haulier big enough to ship in the volume Jack and Greer needed to keep their horses alive. 'I've done it,' he said wearily. 'The competition was tough, Jack, but combining your buying power and Greer's, I managed to see off even your biggest rivals.' Travis rubbed the back of his neck, painfully aware the buying power he wielded was pushing up the price of water and forcing smallholders out of business. 'It's costing, though, Jack, and that's gonna start hurtin' sooner or later.'

Jack grunted. 'Let me worry about that, Son,' he said. 'You just keep the water coming for those horses. The rest of us'll just have to cut back some more. When I was a boy, my pa only took a bath twice a year, once on his birthday and once at Thanksgiving. It didn't do him any harm.'

Travis laughed despite himself. Jack was great company and he looked up to him, especially since his pa died. 'I bet he didn't have many friends, though,' he said as Jack gave him a wry smile. It was good they could still find something to laugh about.

'Shall we wait for Shelby or just get started on the meeting?' Jack asked, mopping his plate with a slice of toast.

Travis's job had become much easier since Shelby's pa, Jerome, had finally given up the pretence of being interested in horses and shipped himself out to California, where he lived with his new wife. It had been a terrible time for Shelby, but good sense had prevailed, and she'd become Jack's chosen successor to run the family business. It was a relief to everyone who'd ever worked with Jerome that the future of the stud farm and stables was now in the hands of someone who cared intensely about horses.

'Let's wait, Jack', said Travis. 'She'll be right down. I know she had some ideas to tackle the grassland fires you might be interested in.' As he spoke, the sound of his wife's bare feet coming laboriously down the stairs could be heard. With just a month to go of her pregnancy, and shoes being too uncomfortable for her in the heat, Travis reckoned Jack's cool tiled floors must have been a blessing for her.

'I don't think we can cope any longer just with beaters,' said Travis as his wife joined them, kissing him and her grandpa on the cheek. 'There are too many fires at once for us to cover and those we miss get out of control real quick.'

'What about firebreaks?' suggested Shelby. 'We can get a 'dozer to scrape a ten-yard strip around each homestead so there's nothing to burn – that should slow things down.'

'Good call, Shelby. I can get that done right away,' said Travis. 'What else?'

Jack nodded. 'That'll work up to a point, but if the wind picks up, flying sparks will still reach the houses, which are tinder-dry.'

All except the hacienda, which is stone and terracotta, Travis thought as he went to the buffet for second helpings. He'd teased Greer mercilessly about her outlandish design for a Kentucky farmhouse but he'd be eating his words any day soon. Shelby joined him at the buffet, filling a glass dish with fresh fruit salad.

'So, what are you suggesting?' Travis took a seat across the table from his father-in-law.

'Well, I reckon that now the horses are all back in the stables under shelter, we could round up all the water bowsers from the pastures, fill them with whatever water is left in the lake and bring them on up to Buena Vista to put out any fires that make it across Shelby's firebreak. What d'you think?' Jack looked at Travis expectantly.

Over by the buffet, Shelby's dish hit the tiled floor with a crash. Her knees buckled and she fell into a swoon among the broken glass.

Both men were on their feet in an instant. 'Shelby!' Travis scooped his unconscious wife from the floor, blood trickling from a glass cut to her cheek.

'Get her over to the couch, Son,' said Jack. 'I'll get her some water – It must be awful being pregnant in this heat, poor girl.'

'Yes! Yes, of course,' said Travis, grateful for the obvious excuse for Shelby's collapse. With any luck, Jack would be distracted from his idea of emptying the lake. Once the lake was drained, the game would be up for him and Shelby when Chase's remains in the mud at the bottom were revealed. He shuddered, a knot of terror forming in his gut.

Jack held a glass of cool water to Shelby's lips as she started to come round, while Travis held a serviette gently to her cheek to stem the blood flow.

'How are you feeling, Shelby?' Jack asked. 'You just passed out in this heat. I think you might be overdoing things in your condition.'

Shelby raised her hand to her cheek. 'I'm not feeling so good, Grandpa,' she said. 'Did I cut my face?'

'You sure did, Honey. I think we should get you checked out at the hospital. Don't wanna be takin' any chances at this stage,' Jack stroked her hand gently. 'I'll ask Greta to drive you. I'm sure she'll be just as worried about you as I am, my darlin'.'

As Shelby left the room, carefully leaning on the arm of her concerned grandma, Jack resumed his conversation with Travis. 'So where was I? Oh yeah – filling the bowsers from the lake.'

A spasm shot through Shelby's chest and she gasped for air, crushed by the weight of the terrible secret she was harbouring. Her life was a living nightmare and it was never going to end. Going to prison had to be better than this – a life sentence of lying to the people she loved. Admitting everything and getting it over with would be such a relief. Did pregnant women even get sent to jail? Every fibre of her body trembled with fear.

Greta's gentle hand steadied her as she helped her into the air-conditioned luxury SUV waiting on the front drive.

'Don't you worry about a thing, darlin',' said Greta, 'We'll get you checked over in no time, but you'll have to leave the firefighting to the men.'

Gwenna rushed to the Owensboro County Hospital as soon as she got the news. Greta had already checked Shelby into a private room and was sitting at her bedside, holding her hand tenderly. The two women hugged each other tightly, the memories of the past flooding back, when forty years ago it had been young Gwenna in the bed, in the self-same hospital, with Greta holding her hand, her flawless young skin latticed with glass cuts. It was a bittersweet moment. They'd been through so much together.

'How's she doin'?' Gwenna whispered so as not to wake the dozing patient.

'Her blood pressure is too high,' replied Greta, 'she needed a couple of stitches in that cut and she's suffering with this heat, so they are keeping her in for observation for forty-eight hours.'

Gwenna flopped into the armchair beside Shelby's bed as her worry for Shelby and her unborn baby began to ebb away. 'Well, thankfully, she's in the best place.'

Greta was almost a second mother to her but Shelby's baby would be the first child to unite the two families in blood, bringing her and Greta even closer. It was wonderful having something so marvellous to look forward to.

Shelby lay still on the bed, her eyes half-closed, hooked up to various monitors. The room was silent except for the faint whispers of Gwenna and Greta as they discussed the ongoing drought. Shelby drifted in and out of consciousness, but as their conversation inevitably turned to the topic of Chase, she found herself listening intently.

'Has there been any word at all?' asked Greta. 'Any

new leads from Greer's interview with *The World* magazine, maybe?'

'Nothing,' replied Gwenna. 'It's been eight months and I still believe it will be a matter of time. We just have to wait and something will happen. I know Chase is alive – call it mother's instinct.'

Shelby fought back the tears that threatened to spill over as she listened to the two women supporting each other with kindness and love. They meant so much to her, but Gwenna's son was dead and she, Shelby Jepson, had killed him! So many people were suffering because of Chase's disappearance and she held the key to ending it all. If only she could take responsibility for her actions, even if it meant going to jail for involuntary homicide.

She opened her eyes and let out a weary groan. Greta and Gwenna rushed back to her bedside.

'I have something to tell you,' Shelby said in a rasping voice.

Jack and Travis sat beside the lake in the comfort of Jack's top-of-the-range SUV, with the air-con set to max. Nobody was riding horses any longer – it was banned on both estates to protect the animals from the scorching sun. The horizon shimmered in the heat, intensifying the surreal experience for Travis.

'I ain't seen the lake like this before in all my seventy years on this land,' said Jack, shaking his head at the depleted water level. All the lush vegetation around the lakeside had collapsed and a shelf of parched cracked mud dropped away steeply into the middle of the old gravel pit. All that remained of the water was a stagnant pool about fifty yards wide, buzzing with flies.

'We mined this pit for the gravel for all the roads on the estate back in forty-five,' said Jack, his eyes gleaming with reminiscence. 'My ma planted up the bullrushes and reeds to make it into an ornamental lake once we were done with it,' he continued. 'All the generations of kids since then have loved this lake. Lots of very fond memories.'

Travis was experiencing anything but fond memories seated beside him, his pulse racing so fast he was sure that Jack must be able to see it through his skin. His stomach clenched with dread at the prospect of draining down the stagnant puddle into Jack's bowsers, revealing all that was left of the brother he'd shared his mother's womb with. With any luck, the remains would be just bones; anything else would be just too grisly for words. He deliberately slowed his breathing to present a calm façade to Jack. 'Why don't you leave this to me, Jack?' he said. 'Once our guys get the pumps going, I can have the filled bowsers up at the house by suppertime.'

'Sure thing, Son. Call me if you need anything.'

Travis jumped out and collected his rubber boots from the flatback, his heart fluttering with relief. 'Thanks, Jack. I'll let you know if there are any problems,' he said as casually as he could muster. He thumped the side of the truck as Jack drove away, in a show of bravado. Once the need for pretence was gone, his shoulders slumped. Keeping up appearances, when inside he was screaming, was killing him.

He pulled on his boots while his men set up a generator and pumps nearby.

Alone at last, he took a deep breath and clambered into the pit, bracing himself for the horrific scene he was sure to find.

***

'Telephone call for you, Mrs Garland.' The brisk nurse bustled into Shelby's room, bearing a telephone handset, which she plugged into a socket by the bed. As Gwenna stood up to take the call, the nurse exclaimed, 'Sorry, I meant the other Mrs Garland,' and passed the receiver to Shelby.

Gwenna's face flushed pink. 'I still have to get used to that!' she said, with an embarrassed chuckle, as Shelby took the call.

'Shelby, it's me.' Travis's voice was urgent on the line. Shelby tensed. Why was he phoning her in the hospital? Didn't he realise she just couldn't take any more bad news? She was done with covering up Chase's death and wished more than anything they'd just told the truth in the first place.

'Are you alone?'

'No, Gwenna and Grandma are here.'

'Okay, it's imperative that you just listen to me and don't say anythin'. Can you do that?'

She nodded. 'Uh-huh.'

'I've been at the lake all day today,' he said in a hoarse whisper. 'Me and the boys completely drained it into Jack's bowsers. There was nothing there, Shelby! Chase isn't at the bottom of the lake. I'm certain of it! I searched it myself, pretendin' I was lookin' for some old treasure chest we threw overboard as kids… Shelby?'

The phone slipped from Shelby's hands. She hadn't killed Chase! Her stomach tightened and a fountain of vomit sprayed over the bed.

Gwenna grabbed the receiver. 'Is that you, Travis? Sorry, darlin', we cain't talk now. Shelby's just been real sick. She's sufferin' with this pregnancy, poor darlin'. I'll call you later when things have calmed down a bit. Bye, darlin'. Love you, Son!'

A pair of nurses materialised out of nowhere. One nurse whisked Shelby away for a shower, and by the time she returned, the other nurse had stripped the bed and remade it with fresh clean linen and fluffy new pillows. It was almost too good to be true. She sank into its soft sweet-smelling embrace and closed her eyes, letting go of all the fear and anxiety that had weighed so heavily on her for the past nine months. The nightmare was over and the sweet dreams could begin again.

Her grandma's concerned voice penetrated her thoughts. 'Now then, darlin', do you feel any better? You look it.'

Shelby opened her eyes and beamed at her two favourite ladies. 'I feel much better, thank you, Grandma. In fact, I feel like a million dollars right now. Never better.'

'That's good, darlin'. Now, what were you going to say earlier before Travis called?'

Shelby's eyes widened. That was a close call! She'd been about to confess everything to Grandma and Gwenna!

'Um… I cain't seem to remember' she said. 'I have terrible baby-brain right now, Grandma. You'll have to forgive me. It probably wasn't anything important.'

THIRTY-TWO

Travis stood outside the imposing wooden gates that marked the entrance to Greer's estate, admiring the expensive new security features. The place would sure give Fort Knox a run for its money. The gates had CCTV cameras that sat like a pair of curious crows atop double-thick brick pillars on either side and were enhanced with automatic number-plate recognition, which opened the gates for family and friends. Inside the estate, a uniformed security guard monitored a bank of screens in a self-contained office while two plain-clothes agents patrolled the perimeter in a truck.

In his hand was a remote-control fob, which he was testing for sensitivity. It would be a useful device to give to estate staff if he could get the darned thing to work. Pacing backwards and forwards, he could only open the gates from one spot. He pressed his lips together, his temper as frazzled as the dry grass, and was about to throw the useless fob on the dirt and stamp on it when a cloud of dust kicking up along the estate access road, just off the freeway about a half-mile away, caught his eye. With Greer and Ma away performing in Las Vegas, and Shelby and their newborn son, Beau, cocooned in their newly built home inside the estate, Travis wasn't expecting visitors.

The cloud of dust grew like an approaching desert sandstorm as Travis stood and waited. Within a minute, he could make out an old-style pick-up. Within two minutes he could tell it was a Studebaker Champ that had seen better days. Within three minutes, the rusty old Champ was crunching to a halt beside his glistening Silverado, smoking heavily from under the hood.

From the ear-splitting grind of metal-on-metal, Travis surmised that the driver was trying to get out of the vehicle, but the dented rusty door on its dry hinges wouldn't open wide enough for him to haul himself out. In no mood to parley with the old hobo, Travis strode around to the driver's door and jammed it shut with a hefty shove.

'No hawkers, no cold-callers and definitely no snake-oil salesmen,' he growled through the half-open window.

'Good day to you too, Mr. Garland,' the scruffy visitor smirked. 'That's no way to greet an old family friend. In fact, I'd say I'm more like a family member than a friend, now I come to think of it.'

Travis stared at the ground for a moment, hands on hips. The trouble with having a famous sister was that every crackpot within fifty miles knew your name. 'I don't know who you are, old man,' Travis snapped, 'or what you want, but I don't like the look of you, and I certainly don't like the smell of you. You got no business around here, so get movin'' before I get my shotgun from the wagon and send you on your way with an ass full of lead.'

For a second or two, Travis was alarmed by the old man's wheezing and gasping, until he realised it was laughter – noxious, foul-breathed laughter. He turned his face away in disgust.

'Well, ain't you the son-of-a-gun,' the hobo sneered. 'Or should I say – the son of an imposter.'

Travis blew his cheeks out. Enough was enough. He'd had it with this grimy old man and his pointless riddles. Reaching through the window with one hand, he took hold of the vagrant's filthy shirt by the neck and twisted it tightly under his chin.

'Listen to me, old man. I don't know what cock-and-bull ideas you've got in your head, but I'm not interested in them. Now get off my property, and don't ever come botherin' me or my family again.'

The man's phoney bonhomie vanished abruptly. 'You might want to take your hands off me when you know who I am, Son.' His eyes narrowed as he spoke and his voice took on a menacing tone. 'My name's Gryff Morgan, and your old man was a fake and an imposter – and I can prove it.'

The mention of his father's name landed like a left hook. Travis released his grip and staggered back from the truck, the hairs on his arms prickling. This guy was no random weirdo. He clearly had some axe to grind with his pa.

The old man gave the door a couple of hefty barges with his shoulder and climbed out of the truck with surprising agility. In his hand was a worn copy of *The World* magazine.

He was taller and burlier than Travis had imagined. Despite his filthy grey hair, grimy skin, and clothes that reeked of stale sweat and piss, he was not as old as Travis had first thought. In fact, he was a physically intimidating presence. Travis's glance took in the hands the size of hams, the missing half ear and the deep faded gouge down one cheek, and recognised the hallmarks of a hard life. He looked like he ate trouble for breakfast. Thank God the estate gates were closed and the CCTV was operational!

Travis took a step back. 'What is it you want from us?'

The man who called himself Gryff Morgan scratched his stubbly face with filthy black nails, casting his yellowing, red-veined eyes to the sky as if deep in thought. 'Well, it would be nice to have my passport back, if that's not too much to ask.' His voice was heavy with sarcasm. 'Oh, and half-a-million dollars for my troubles,' he added. 'That's pocket money for you rich bastards. You people made good on the back of my suffering.' He waved *The World* magazine in Travis's face with a thunderous scowl. 'I read all about your rich sister and her "beloved pa", *Gryff Morgan*. Made me wanna puke. Your old man owes me and, now that he's dead, that debt is yours – and I'm here to collect.'

'Half-a-million dollars? For your troubles?' Travis shook his head incredulously. The bizarre situation he found himself in was quickly spiralling out of control. None of it made any sense. 'Are you completely insane? D'you honestly think I'm just gonna stump up half-a-million dollars to every crazy stranger who pitches up on my doorstep?'

Gryff's revolting leer turned Travis's stomach. 'While you're thinking about it, let me tell you a little story about a ship called the *Buenos Aires Star* and all who sailed on her.'

In the CCTV control room, Justine Cornelius rewound the tape for what seemed like the twentieth time. 'There's some good-quality footage here, Mr Garland. We can follow up on the truck's licence plate and get a useful still of our perp, which might throw up an ID if this guy has a US driving licence.'

Travis looked at the images on the bank of screens overhead. 'I gotta say, Justine, I doubt very much if he does. He had an accent that didn't come from any state that I can think of and he didn't seem the type to bother with respectin' authority. He made my skin crawl – I don't want him anywhere near my family.'

'What did you make of his story?'

'That's the awful bit, Justine.' Travis's brow furrowed. 'It's real credible. He knew things that couldn't have been made up. And that accent? It reminded me somewhat of Pa's. But the worst of it is, he made me realise I know next to nothing about Pa before he came to the US and I cain't understand why I never thought to ask.' His shoulders sagged despondently. 'When I was a kid, he'd tell me stuff like he came on a ship from Wales and, one time, he even said it was called the *Buenos Aires* something. But there were never any details and I never thought to ask. Why would I? He was just "Pa".'

Travis had thought of nothing else since the hobo drove off in a cloud of dust and burning engine oil. It wasn't the crazy extortion attempt so much as the dawning appreciation of his father as a man with a past that was eating away at him. It was too late to talk to Pa, so Justine was his best hope for getting to know what Pa was like before he settled down with a family.

'Do you think your mother might be able to help?'

Travis pondered for a moment. 'Possibly... I'm not sure, but I don't want Ma or any of my womenfolk to know a dangerous individual is lurkin' around. He didn't say when he would be back for the money, just that he would be and that I'd better be ready!'

Justine propped her hands on her hips and gave him one of her looks – the one that made him think she could read his mind. 'You do realise you can't pay off these sorts of people, if that is your plan? They just keep coming back for more,' she said. 'He might be linked to Chase's disappearance. You said he had a copy of *The World*? Your family all have a right to know about this threat for their own safety and I've got to follow this up. Miss Garland is my client, after all.'

'Okay, you're right, of course, you're right.' Travis twirled his sunglasses by the arm. 'How about this? You follow up on this creep as part of your Chase enquiry without mentionin' to Ma or Greer that he's calling himself Gryff Morgan, but you also take a separate commission from me to look into Pa's background.'

'Are you seriously giving this man credence?' Justine asked. 'And I'm not sure I could take on such a secret commission if that's what you're asking.' Her eyes searched his face questioningly. 'There wouldn't be much to go on if I couldn't talk to your mother. She would be the main source of information for developing lines of enquiry.' She pressed the rewind button again and the whole scene quickly played out backwards. 'As a matter of interest, why is the family name not Morgan if that was your father's name?'

Travis breathed on his Aviators and polished them against his sleeve before replacing them on his face, preparing to leave. 'Oh, there's nothin' mysterious about that. Ma was a promisin' singer back in '67 when they got married. They decided to keep Garland instead of Morgan, as "Gwenna Garland" would look better up in lights when she got famous – but she never did.' He chuckled to himself. 'But they were right – just imagine now if Greer Garland, country-and-western superstar, had been called Greer Morgan. I don't think things would have worked out so well for her, somehow.'

'And everyone just accepted that without question?'

'Well, yes… the rest of the family were all called Garland, so why not? Why would Ma and Pa lie?'

Justine peered at him over the top of her bifocals. 'That's what I need to find out.'

THIRTY-THREE

Gryff Morgan stumbled across the parking lot in the painfully bright sunshine of late afternoon and patted the inside pocket of his leather jerkin, checking on what was left of the bottle of Wild Turkey bourbon he'd splashed out on at the Red Rooster tavern on Kentucky Route 54, to celebrate his morning's work.

It was sheer dumb luck he'd finally tracked down the thieving bastard who took his passport and left him rotting in a black hole in Argentina for five years, sharing one filthy mattress between ten and waking next to the wasted corpses of those who succumbed to the drugs, disease and venal intentions of others. He'd have probably died there, too, if there hadn't been some political coup, which emptied all the prisons. The vengeance he planned was barbarous beyond belief, gnawing away at him like a cancer for decades, without knowing who to blame. But now he had his man within his sights, thanks to that dumb magazine. Or at least, he would have if the stupid *boludo* hadn't blown himself up in a speedway fireball. But he was still gonna make that asshole pay for the five years of his life he'd lost, even from the grave.

Gryff yanked drunkenly at the battered old Studebaker's door handle until it almost came off in his hand. He hawked his lungs and spat a mass of thick phlegm in the dust. 'Useless heap of junk,' he muttered as he climbed aboard. He'd get himself a spanking new truck, a Hummer maybe, or even a big stretch limo, complete with a uniformed driver calling him 'Sir'. In his days at the orphanage in Carmarthen, he fantasised about his rich father arriving in a chauffeur-driven Rolls-Royce to whisk him away to a life of luxury. It helped him endure the beatings handed out to curb his rebellious behaviour until he eventually ran away to sea on his twelfth birthday. Unsurprisingly, nobody at the orphanage tried to stop him from leaving.

He foraged in the glove box for some smokes before finding a packet tucked into the sunshield. He squinted in the dazzling light, his head throbbing from the effects of his liquid brunch. The goddamn sunshine was driving him mad. He almost longed for a black hole to swallow him up, anything to escape the torture of the sun.

An eighteen-wheeler blasted its horn as Gryff pulled the Studebaker out onto KY54. '*Cabrón!*' yelled Gryff, sticking one digit out the window while gripping his cigarette between his teeth. The thundering truck quickly disappeared into the distant heat haze, shimmering and jumping wildly on the horizon. As bloody usual, blue smoke billowed from under the hood and he sucked on his cigarette to cover the foul taste of engine fumes. He tried using his wipers to blow the vapour away, but that didn't help at all. Maybe the fan would do it – if only he could remember which of the goddamned knobs it was.

As Gryff scrabbled at the dash controls in a boozed-up haze, his cigarette slipped unnoticed from his fingers into the passenger footwell, littered with empty takeaway coffee cups, cigarette cartons and his tatty copy of *The World* magazine. As the magazine smouldered, the thin wisp of blue smoke went unnoticed by Gryff, preoccupied with following the jumping road through clouds of blue engine fumes with sweat pouring from his brow into his stinging eyes. Tall yellow flames were jumping and dancing in the footwell before he noticed the heat on his right leg.

'Holy shit!' he yelled, swatting wildly at the blaze with his Stetson as the Studebaker drifted across the highway into the path of an oncoming RV. It took a moment or two for the scream of brakes and the screech of rubber skidding on concrete to register with Gryff before he looked up – at the very moment the RV drove through his windshield. The impact was like a bomb going off, sending shockwaves through his body. The Studebaker flipped onto its side, propelled by the RV along the road surface in a shower of sparks, spilling a trail of shattered glass behind it. In a billow of blue engine smoke, it came to a crunching halt in a roadside gully. The nearside wheels spun serenely, the bearings clicking in the blisteringly hot quiet air.

Dazed but conscious, Gryff lay on his side inside the blazing cabin, covered in shards of broken glass. He kicked frantically at the jammed door but it wouldn't budge. His belly was saturated and he clutched at it, expecting to see blood on his hands. Wild Turkey bourbon vapour wrapped him in its warm embrace as he surrendered to his fate, flambéed in his favourite liquor.

And so ended the misspent life of Lowri's long-lost firstborn son.

The traffic on KY54 was a nightmare as Justine headed back to Louisville. She had a ticket to the Kentucky Symphony Orchestra that evening, and she still needed to file an official report on the hobo's extortion attempt and get an APB out on the man claiming to be Gryff Morgan before she did anything else. She fiddled with the radio, looking for a classical music station. It wouldn't be the first time that her job had screwed up her plans and it sure wouldn't be the last. But what did it matter? She was going to the concert alone, so it wasn't as if she was letting anyone down. With a state police trooper guarding a detour barrier across the highway ahead, it looked like she would be sent down a minor road, taking her miles out of her way. The chances of making it to the concert on time were getting slimmer by the moment.

'What's the problem, Officer?' she asked through her wound-down window as she finally reached the front of the queue, squinting to prevent her eyeballs from frying in the heat.

'There's a vehicle fire along the highway, Ma'am,' the trooper replied. 'A couple of hundred acres are ablaze, what with everything being so tinder-dry in the drought. The smoke is so thick that the road is impassable and most of the road surface has melted anyway. It's gonna be a while before we get this road open again.'

Some poor bastard was having a bad day, she thought, suddenly feeling a whole lot less bothered about missing her concert. 'Everyone okay?'

'Difficult to say at this stage, Ma'am, but it's not looking good.'

Justine thanked the trooper and turned off the main highway along the detour. She'd lost count of the times she'd broken the news to the families of people who'd died suddenly, often doing stupid things which made it their own fault. Some poor detective was going to have to deliver the inevitable death message for this car wreck and she was glad it wasn't her any longer. She'd done her fair share of consoling the inconsolable.

The desk officer at Police Post 23 looked about twelve years old and possibly hadn't even been born when Justine joined the NYPD. She felt unspeakably ancient as she showed her ID to Trooper Vanda Warburg and placed the CCTV images on the counter, explaining her interest in the Studebaker.

'No problem. I can get an APB out on that automobile right away,' said Trooper Warburg, cheerfully. 'Let me run the licence plate first to see if any other agencies are interested in it.' Justine smiled at Trooper Warburg's helpfulness as she went off to get the checks done. She was obviously a rookie.

She alleviated her boredom by examining the wall posters for lost dogs and crime prevention advice, uncomfortable at being on the wrong side of the desk. She felt naked without a police badge in her pocket and a sidearm on her hip, but her work as a private investigator gave her a lot more freedom and was better paid. It was just a shame she had no time to spend the money and nobody to share it with. She was more or less resigned to being alone as she approached her fiftieth year, as the idea of being some man's compliant wife filled her with horror. In her experience, guys were all in favour of equality for women, just not *their* woman.

The return of Trooper Warburg interrupted her glum reverie.

'Well, I've got some amazing news for you, Ma'am!'

Her excitement confirmed Justine's suspicions of her rookie status. 'This automobile was involved in a car wreck this afternoon on KY54. It's still burning.'

Justine could hardly believe what she was hearing. 'No kidding!' she said. 'I just got caught up in the detour. What happened to the driver?'

'Dead, Ma'am.' Vanda's youthful features rearranged into a grave expression. 'We thought we had ourselves a John Doe till you just came in. Now we know who he is, thanks to you.'

Justine took out her notepad. 'Is he a known felon?'

'Sorry, Ma'am. I'm afraid I cain't tell you that.'

Justine grinned. She knew that already but hoped the rookie cop might have let it slip. It was worth a try. She thanked the trooper and walked outside to where her rented sedan was parked, and kicked one of the tyres. Just when she thought she had a possible lead on the Chase Garland missing person inquiry, the chief suspect went and got himself killed in a car wreck, just hours after attempting to extort half-a-million dollars from her client's brother. Now, that was a remarkably coincidental chain of events, if ever there was one. You could even call it good luck if you happened to be Travis Garland, who'd just saved half-a-million dollars and a whole lot of hassle. There was something about Travis that triggered her 'cop radar', but even a guy as wealthy as him couldn't magic up a professional hit that quickly. It was a crazy idea and she dismissed it, but she couldn't shake off the feeling that Travis Garland knew more than he was letting on.

THIRTY-FOUR

Six months later, Justine sat on the front drive of Greer Garland's multi-million-pound hacienda, with her automobile windows wound tightly, the air-con going full blast against the oppressive heat and the uplifting tones of Vivaldi's *Four Seasons* coming through the stereo speakers. Something about this case didn't add up but, for the life of her, she couldn't work out what it was. She ran through her search strategy one last time before seeing her client with her closing report, just to satisfy herself that there was nothing she'd missed in her investigation.

She'd interviewed every member of the Garland family, except Martha Haycroft in London, to establish Chase's last-known movements, his character and any friends or foes, but they all said the same thing – he'd been away in the army for eight years and back for less than a week. He was a virtual stranger to most of his relatives. Only Travis and Greer, who had spent time with him that week, knew anything more about him, and they gave Justine conflicting accounts of his state of mind.

Travis painted a picture of a hard-drinking, opiate-addicted war veteran struggling to adjust to civilian life. In contrast, Greer described her missing brother as a thoughtful laid-back guy looking forward to reuniting with his family and starting a well-paid, responsible job on her estate. She'd even given him twenty-thousand dollars in cash to get settled, which he'd refused to accept unless it was an advance on his salary. Nobody could account for the whereabouts of that money, nor of the vintage motorcycle that Chase had restored as a teenager. Frustratingly, any chance of tracing the vehicle through official records was lost, as it hadn't been registered for over eight years.

On the night of the disappearance, every member of Chase's family had been out of town or out of the country, and the neighbours on the Jepson estate hadn't seen him at all since he returned home from the army, other than Shelby Jepson, who saw him just the once earlier in the week, at dinner at the hacienda. She and Greer both recalled how delighted Chase seemed at the news of her engagement to his twin brother.

Her trip out to Fort Campbell had been just as futile. Chase's battalion commanding officer had nothing but glowing words to say about Sergeant Garland and confirmed that he was popular with the men. He couldn't think of any reason his army colleagues would wish him harm.

Closer to home, she quickly established that there was no CCTV within a twenty-mile radius of the Garland estate in Daviess County, Kentucky, and her enquiries and a poster campaign in the surrounding towns had drawn a blank.

Chase's photograph adorned every bar in Daviess County, but nobody had seen him.

Her next move was to have the entire estate searched by a highly trained search-and-rescue team, who left no stone unturned. It took weeks to scour the one-hundred-acre estate painstakingly. Luckily, she hadn't needed to bring in a dive team, as the lake had obligingly emptied itself during the drought, saving her the time and trouble.

She'd arranged local radio and TV appeals for information and sightings, with a dedicated phone line for tip-offs, which remained unused, and an international appeal via *The World* magazine had only succeeded in generating an extortion attempt by a hobo, who claimed to have the same name as Chase's father, before dying in questionable circumstances.

The only thing of any note other than the arrival of the aggressive hobo was that Dunbar Automotive Services, where Chase had worked as a teenager, had a break-in on the night Chase disappeared. According to the owner, Zak Dunbar, kids had sprayed juvenile graffiti around the premises before making off with the contents of the medicine cabinet. Luckily for Zak, there was very little actual damage, so it looked like he had got away with it lightly, all things considered.

Justine conceded that Chase may have committed the break-in himself if he had gone on the run voluntarily for whatever reason. However, as the premises were smothered in his fingerprints anyway, it would be impossible to prove, and why would he have needed to? Was the graffiti a cover story for the medicine cabinet raid? Was he injured and unable to seek medical help for some reason? These questions remained unanswered and every medical establishment within a hundred miles had returned a negative response to her enquiry.

The case of Chase Garland was proving a tough nut to crack, mainly because some folks weren't being straight with her. People expected private investigators to act like they did in the movies – breaking into private premises at night with a torch between their teeth, rifling through files, hacking into computers, accessing private financial information and government databases at the drop of a hat. Sadly, the reality was way more tedious. The private investigator's stock-in-trade was the personal interview and this avenue had been exhausted in Chase's case.

Justine's hunch that Chase's disappearance and the arrival of the man claiming to be the real Gryff Morgan were somehow connected was her best shot, but as he was permanently out of the picture, that left no leads she could follow up. Even a police search of his motel room failed to locate any personal papers or possessions that may have shed any light on the man or the extortion attempt. And what was it he'd said to Travis? He wanted his passport back? What on earth was that about?

To her lasting disappointment, the only open avenue for tracing Chase Garland remained the National Database of Missing Persons, where he was low-risk, non-active case number 83/967128/MPB00098. Justine had submitted a sample of his DNA from his toothbrush for inclusion in the file in the event that a body was found somewhere, but she hoped it wouldn't come to that. She'd become surprisingly fond of this family from humble origins, pretty much like her own. She told herself that it was because Greer had treated her with dignity and respect, even insisting upon first-name terms, unlike other super-rich clients she'd had, who treated her like something they'd trodden in.

But it was more than that. She'd spent a lot of time in Greer's company over the past six months and could not recall a time she had ever felt so relaxed and comfortable around another person. Greer's mere presence was enough to make her day and she often found herself seeking the solace of her kitchen, where they frequently shared a bottle of wine at the end of a long tiring day as she briefed her client on progress – or lack of it. But if she was honest with herself, she probably felt that way because Greer was her only friend. She didn't doubt it would be a massive wrench to move on from this case but her investigation had reached the end of the road, for now.

Justine picked up the manila dossier from the passenger seat, unable to shake off the feeling that something was still amiss. The Garlands, as they called themselves, had all shared the same story about their name being up in lights, but her gut instinct told her that there was more to it than that. Maybe the father, who called himself Morgan, had been impersonating someone all along? The hobo's claim that he was the real Gryff Morgan added weight to that idea. Getting hold of Gryff Morgan's passport would be pivotal now that she was free to dig deeper into Travis's private commission – if she chose to take it. But how could she lay hands on the passport without raising suspicion? The answer was clear: she would need Travis' help. But what would they discover once they had the passport in their possession? The possibilities were endless and intriguing.

As Justine stepped out of her automobile, a large splat of water struck her on the forehead, then another and then another. By the time she reached the grand portico of the Hacienda, she was soaked to the skin. The heavens had opened – the drought was over.

THIRTY-FIVE

2008

WHITESVILLE, KENTUCKY

The deep-orange sun climbed heavily over the reddening sugar maples by the lake, repainting swathes of night sky with hues of purple and turquoise, as the tenth anniversary of Chase's disappearance dawned. Greer rubbed the sleep from her eyes and silently made her way to her stables. Only the company of horses would do at a time like this. The promise of a beautiful October day helped to lighten the weight on her mind.

She swung open the stable door and was greeted by the comforting aromas of clover and sweet timothy, along with the earthy musk of dung. The velvety muzzle of Kya, her palomino Kentucky Mountain saddle horse, nibbled gently at her ears as Greer tacked her up. She rested her cheek against Kya's smooth warm withers and inhaled deeply, calmed by the much-loved scent.

They crossed the bluegrass paddock towards the lake in silent commune, the smooth rhythmic percussion of Kya's ambling gait soothing Greer's restless thoughts. Chase was still out there somewhere and there had to be something more she could do to bring him home. As they passed through a copse of tulip poplars along the shoreline, the tightness across Greer's shoulders eased as she took in the yellow-and-gold hue of their stunning autumn foliage, backlit by the rising sun. A cloud of migrating monarch butterflies descended, resplendent in their orange-and-black wings, alighting on every surface. It was a magical moment and Greer murmured a quiet prayer of gratitude for the seven-hundred acres that now belonged to her. The redundant tobacco fields she was rewilding were already teeming with new life. Since she'd recognised the terrible environmental impact of touring, she'd put her days of jetting around the globe with a vast entourage, performing in Paris, London and Rome, firmly behind her.

She checked her watch; Ma would be waiting for her in her recording studio to lay down some backing vocals for their new album. In the ten years since Chase vanished, their country and western partnership had fulfilled all her ma's youthful dreams of stardom. Yet, despite their great wealth and success, even the most joyful family celebrations were still overshadowed by the unspoken sadness that someone important wasn't there. Maybe the tenth anniversary was the right time for another push to find him.

A curly-topped boy was busily refilling the hay manger in Kya's stall when Greer rode into the stable yard. He looked up at the sound of approaching hooves.

'Hey there, Aunt Gigi, d'ya have a good ride?'

Greer's gut twisted with love at the sight of nine-year-old

Beau's cheeky smiling face. Folks all said he looked so much like his father but, to her mind, his prankster personality gave him an even stronger resemblance to his missing uncle.

The sun was in the final throes of its arc across the sky, bleeding out across the horizon and saturating the land with a vermillion hue when Greer led Kya back into her stall after her evening ride. At the far side of the stable yard, she noticed Travis leaning against the deeply furrowed bark of the enormous hickory tree that had stood there for generations. He had a cigarette dangling from his lips – a tell-tale sign that something was bothering him.

Greer swept the fringe from her eyes as she approached him and fixed him with a steady gaze. 'I reckon you've been avoidin' me today, Travis Garland.' She couldn't keep the disappointment from her voice. 'You said you'd come by for lunch with me and Ma.'

Travis ground out the cigarette with the heel of his boot and looked out across the horizon. 'That's not fair, Greer. I'm a busy man, you know that. Stud farms and stables don't run themselves. I cain't drop everything just because it's lunchtime.' He removed his Stetson and wiped the sweat from his brow with a dusty forearm. 'Tell Ma I'm sorry and I'll try harder to get over tomorrow instead'.

Greer took off her riding hat and ran the brim pensively through her hands. Tomorrow wouldn't do and Travis knew it. The invitation to lunch was to mark the anniversary of Chase's disappearance and it was important for Ma to know they all still had him close to their hearts. Like Greer, Ma had never given up on Chase. Travis skipping the lunch was a slap in the face to them both.

'Why don't you come over for supper with Ma and me tonight instead?' She scanned his face, willing him to look her in the eye. 'It would mean a lot to her.'

Travis examined the scuffs on his boots intently. 'How are you gettin' along with that new palomino?' He nodded towards Kya's stable.

He was being evasive, just as she'd expected. Travis had barely spoken of Chase's disappearance in the past ten years but being in denial about his missing twin was clearly eating him up. The pain was etched deeply in the creases around his distant pale blue eyes, but she pressed on. If she could only get him to open up, it might help him find some measure of peace.

'Kya's perfect, Travis. Thank you for finding her for me. I love her.' She raised her hand to touch his face but something in his expression made her think better of it. She hesitated, not willing to give up that easily. 'So shall I tell Ma you'll come for supper?'

He dug his hands deeply into the pockets of his sun-faded denims and aimlessly kicked a rock into the long bluegrass of the paddock. Greer waited, tension building with the passing seconds.

Travis exhaled slowly, like a punctured tyre. 'If you insist.'

It was a minor triumph but a triumph, nonetheless. She patted him on the forearm encouragingly. 'Thanks, Trav,' she said. 'I know it's been hard on you these past ten years, him bein' your brother an' all.'

Travis pulled his arm away sharply. 'Don't hang that on me, Greer,' he snapped. 'He was your brother, too.'

His words stung like a hornet, and she was speechless for a second or two. She'd only meant that it must be harder for him, being Chase's twin, but it had come out all wrong. 'He still is my brother, Travis,' she explained. 'But I always think of him as bein' especially yours. You two always had that special twin bond goin' on—'.

She stopped abruptly, Travis's twisted features telling her she'd made things far worse. It was obviously still too painful for him. How could she have been so clumsy?

'Travis, wait!' She reached for his arm as he spun away from her, anger contorting his weathered face.

'I'm sorry,' she called after him as he strode away. 'Oh, Travis, I'm so sorry.' She couldn't let him leave like this. 'I've got somethin' to tell you. Travis, please listen.'

She ran after him and grabbed him by the arm before he reached the tack room. He stopped in his tracks with his back to her, hands on hips. 'What do you want from me, Greer?' he yelled at the crimson sky. 'What do you want me to say?'

She'd never seen him like this and it scared her, but there was no turning back now. She took a deep breath and held it for a second, before saying, 'I know you must miss him and think about him every day, Travis. We all do. But I cain't stand the nightmares any longer, so I've decided. I'm gonna hire Justine again. D'you remember her? The private investigator? I wanna give it another try for the tenth anniversary.'

Travis's shoulders stiffened visibly, and his pale-blue eyes were icy as he turned towards her. 'Give it up, Greer, for Christ's sake. You'll never find him,' he snarled. 'The investigation dried up years ago. Chase is gone forever – and you need to let it go!'

Greer took a step back, shocked by the intensity of his anger. Somehow, she'd gotten him all wrong. Where was the gentle reliable Travis she adored, the Travis who once saved her life? Surely, he'd welcome another push to find his beloved brother? Her mind teemed with questions until an uncomfortable realisation dawned on her.

Travis knew more than he was saying.

Travis kicked open the wooden barn door and strode into the shady interior, throwing his hat onto the hay-strewn floor once he was out of Greer's sight. She'd hit a nerve with her plan to re-hire Justine and he'd gone off like a hand grenade, frightening his blameless sister and making him even angrier with himself than he already was. When would he ever stop hurting the people he loved the most?

It was true what she'd said, that the past decade had been hard for him, but not for the reasons she thought. He'd made such a mess of everything back then and put Shelby through so much stress – and for what? His selfish desire to get Chase out of the picture, that's what. He'd been so ready to believe the worst of Chase and assumed that he'd tried to rape Shelby, but it turned out he'd been wrong. When the lake had been drained and it was clear that Shelby hadn't killed Chase for trying to rape her, she was horrified to discover that he had ever thought that of his brother. She said it was just a clumsy drunken pass that made her afraid he might rape her – but he didn't actually try. Shelby's biggest regret was that she struck him so hard in her panic. With hindsight, she was sure if she'd just pushed him off, he would have stopped.

The revelation didn't stop Travis from being angry with Chase for making a pass at his fiancée, but his conscience hadn't given him a moment's peace ever since for cruelly misjudging his twin brother so badly. And to compound his guilt, he'd had to live with the anguish of his mother and sister as they mourned the loss of Chase for ten years. Travis had lost count of the times he wished he could turn back the clock and do everything differently.

Greer's plan to rehire Justine was like having a knife stuck into an old wound. Greer had never known about his secret commission to investigate their pa, and he was glad – because it had come to nothing. His insistence that Justine couldn't interview their ma and his inability to find Pa's old passport had left Justine with no leads to follow. They had parted on amicable-enough terms, but it wasn't going to be comfortable having her back on the scene.

Travis threw himself down on a stack of haybales and gazed at the dust motes whirling in the beams of sunlight that streamed between the loose planks of the barn walls. Life would be so much easier for everyone if he simply admitted everything and wiped the slate clean, but that was a foolish pipe dream that would probably destroy his family once and for all.

With a deep sigh, he resigned himself to a lifetime of purgatory entirely of his own making.

***

Greer poured two frosty glasses of white wine and passed one to her mother, who was relaxing after supper in an elegant lounge chair in the comfortable family room, her bare feet resting on the matching leather and wood footstool.

Gwenna took the glass with a warm smile. 'So, what happened to Travis?' she asked. 'Wasn't he supposed to be comin' for lunch today?'

Greer took a sip of wine and thought about her unsettling conversation with her brother. She rolled the wine around in her mouth pensively. What should she say to Ma? The anniversary was distressing enough without telling her about Travis's bizarre behaviour.

Greer raised her glass. 'Let's make a toast – to Chase, wherever you are.'

Gwenna raised her glass and clinked it against Greer's. 'To Chase, wherever you are'.

They both sipped their wine in reflective silence. It was Greer who spoke first.

'D'you realise, Ma, that Beau's coming up on ten in a couple o' months?'

Gwenna smiled fondly. 'He's the image of his father.'

Greer raised an eyebrow at her mother. 'And his uncle.'

'Well, of course he is, dummy.' Gwenna gave a snort of laughter, but stopped short, her head tilted questioningly. 'What are you driving at?'

'Well, have you noticed what a prankster Beau is, just like Chase at that age?'

'How could I ever forget the pranks that boy used to pull?' Gwenna smiled, her eyes lighting up at the memory. 'Do you remember how we all thought he would be a stuntman? He was forever leapin' off high things and ridin' fast motorcycles.'

'I do remember that!' said Greer. 'It was incredible how he rebuilt that Harley all by himself. He used to say he was doing it to make Pa proud. Strange how we never found any trace of that motorcycle.'

Gwenna nodded in agreement. 'It's part of what makes me think he's still alive,' she said. 'He had transport and enough cash to leave; I've just never been able to fathom why he would want to go so suddenly – and stay away so long.'

'I've been thinkin' about that a lot lately, too.' She was venturing into dangerous territory, discussing her worrying theories with her ma, but Ma was the only person she could trust to take her seriously and hear her out.

'I had a very strange conversation with Travis today,' she began, hesitantly.

Gwenna's lilac eyes widened with surprise. 'You got him to talk about Chase? My goodness, Greer, that was a breakthrough.'

'Maybe, maybe not,' said Greer. 'He tore my head off like a wild bear when I told him I'm going to re-hire Justine to see if there's anythin' new that can be done. I know she didn't solve the case ten years ago, but there's so much more information on the internet today. He was so angry, he frightened me!'

Gwenna gasped and put down her wine glass. 'Travis frightened you? That's not like him at all.'

Greer nodded sadly. 'It got me thinkin', Ma. The way he refuses to talk about Chase? His fury this afternoon? I hate to say this but I'm sure he knows more about Chase's disappearance than he lets on.' She swirled the wine in her glass meditatively. 'My theory is they had a terrible row and it had to be about Shelby. There's nothin' else they ever competed for, as their interests were so different. I always used to say they were opposite sides of the same coin.'

Gwenna's face settled into a thoughtful frown. 'But that's what Travis said at the time, that Chase left because he was jealous.'

'I know, Ma, but I just don't buy that. Even if he *was* jealous, he would have waited for you and Grandpa to get back from London before leaving. No, it had to be something more, something unforgivable.'

'Like what?'

Greer held her breath for a moment, then took the plunge. 'Do you think it is a coincidence that Beau was born almost exactly nine months after Chase vanished?' she asked. 'And that Beau is so much more like Chase than Travis?'

'Greer!' Gwenna's eyes widened. 'Are you really sayin' you think Chase is Beau's father, and that's what Chase and Travis argued about? Really?'

'Oh, I don't know, Ma, but it certainly would explain a lot.' Greer rose to her feet and began to pace about. 'I think that Travis has been keepin' a terrible secret for the past ten years and it's eatin' him up – and probably Shelby too. Me gettin' Justine back on the case would be a huge threat to them and he would do anythin' to protect Shelby. That would explain why he was so angry with me today. The funny thing is, I'm looking forward to having Justine around again. I missed her when she was gone.' She turned to the window, a faraway look on her face. 'We used to sit and drink wine together in the kitchen. She was the first person I felt I could trust to be myself with, after Will...' Her voice tailed off.

Gwenna sat in silence and contemplated her empty wine glass for a long moment.

'Men keepin' awful secrets and women payin' the price,' she murmured, barely audibly. 'Where have I heard *that* before?'

THIRTY-SIX

2008

ISLINGTON, LONDON

Rhys shut down the computer monitor on the hot desk in the open-plan office of Greenpeace UK HQ and stared out the window, disturbed by the media coverage of the Cwm Coedwig Rail Link protest. He'd often walked those woodlands as a boy with his tad-cu Vaughan. The magical feel of the place and its wild beauty were spellbinding, even to a child. He was horrified that the ancient trees were going to be ripped out to make way for a rail link nobody wanted.

Since he first read of the protest, he'd been obsessed with the idea that his Greenpeace evidence-gathering skills could help save the precious woodlands from destruction. The problem was that securing a court protection order would require a long-term scientific effort and there wasn't time for that. But in the short term, he could document and record the eviction operation, forcing the authorities to do everything precisely 'by the book', which should slow things down considerably.

The urge to get involved tugged constantly at his conscience but it would mean returning to South Wales, which he'd vowed never to do again. It was a dilemma he'd been wrestling with for weeks.

It wasn't that he didn't love his family – he just couldn't stand their politics. They were all 'establishment' figures: a member of parliament, a justice of the peace, *two* policemen and a soldier. Their law-and-order political views clashed with his liberal left-wing beliefs, particularly around climate change and environmental issues where they just wouldn't listen to reason. He was so sick of being ganged up on at family gatherings that he just stopped going. He couldn't remember the last time he went home for Christmas.

At first, he had the perfect excuse – being at sea on the Rainbow Warrior working as a marine biologist. It was his dream job and took him to some of the most remote oceans on earth. But as the years passed, he'd been promoted to a strategic role and transferred to Greenpeace's UK headquarters in Islington. It somehow slipped his mind to tell his family, not even his beloved Mam-gu Lowri, who'd practically raised him when his mother was working long hours. Lowri was the only one who understood him. They all still thought he was working in far-flung locations and, until recently, that suited his purposes just fine.

For the past five years, he'd been living with his partner Sam in a flat in an impressive Victorian House in trendy Hackney, just a few miles across town from his mother's parliamentary second home in Clapham – without her knowledge.

Rhys had a problem with his mother. She should never have let his father leave. It was a Freudian classic, according to the therapist he saw after his botched suicide attempt at uni.

Unlike Huw, Rhys had never accepted her explanation about his father's death at sea before he was born and couldn't forgive her for not telling his tad about her pregnancy in the first place. How could she possibly have failed to convey that crucial message? His father would never have left if he had known and would still be alive today. She should have tried harder. She should have made him stay. It was all her fault.

To make things worse, the Evans family tragedy was part of Aberavon folklore and at school he was taunted for having a father who ran away. The kids called his tad a coward and their words cut into Rhys like the lashes of a whip. The therapist helped him understand his emotional scarring was utterly justified.

But if he was honest, he needed a kick up the backside to go home and build bridges with his family, for Sam's sake. Sam was raised in social services care and was desperate to be part of a big happy family. With Christmas approaching, the Cwm Coedwig protest gave him the perfect excuse to return to South Wales, making his reappearance on the family scene seem just a normal part of events and not the big homecoming deal he dreaded.

His stomach knotted with apprehension, even as the idea formed in his head. He cursed himself for his spinelessness. He'd always been 'the sensitive one' in his family, a label he loathed, but now he was a man in his forties and it was time to grow up. Whichever way he looked at it, it seemed that powerful forces were aligning to drag him back to his roots and, if he didn't read the runes now, he never would.

Rhys grabbed his rucksack from under the desk. His mind was made up. He ran down to the basement property store, carried along on a surge of resolve as irresistible as the Bristol Channel tidal bore, and signed out a field kit grab bag. The bag contained everything he'd need for evidence gathering, including a mobile phone, a video camera, tape recorder and microphone, digital SLR camera and chargers, plus a luminous green hi-vis Greenpeace jacket.

As he logged online on his new smartphone to book a train ticket from Paddington to Swansea, he was struck by the irony that his mission to halt the development of a high-speed rail link would begin with a journey on a high-speed train. Even so, he was fairly certain that the three-and-a-half-hour journey back to face his family would feel like the longest journey of his life.

***

Acting Chief Inspector Huw Evans stood at the podium in the windowless briefing room at the South Wales Police Headquarters in Bridgend, his eyes firmly fixed on the notes in front of him. It was 0430 hours, and the air was already hot and stale as he prepared to deliver the supervisors' briefing for Operation Carya – the most extensive policing operation in South Wales since the miners' strike of 1984.

The stakes were high and Huw knew it. More than five-hundred police officers were assigned to the operation – more than a quarter of the entire South Wales police service

– to help bailiffs enforce a High Court eviction order. All that stood in the way of a billion-pound high-speed rail link development was a sustainable living commune in ancient woodlands near Aberavon. Police intelligence gatherers had established that seasoned environmental activists and anti-capitalists had arrived in their droves, bringing the latest protest tactics with them. The once peaceful commune had been transformed into a heavily fortified forest fortress, complete with booby traps and a labyrinth of tunnels.

As operational commander, call-sign 'Silver', it was Huw's job to develop a policing plan to ensure the court bailiffs could execute the eviction order by safely dismantling the fortifications and barricades at the protest site. Failure was not an option. It was a complex and risky operation, and the responsibility lay squarely on his shoulders. Months of planning and countless hours of unpaid overtime had gone into drawing up a plan with contingencies and safety measures, but even with all his preparation, the weight of responsibility hung heavily over him. If anyone was killed or seriously injured on this eviction operation, Huw could be held personally responsible and face criminal prosecution, or worse, imprisonment. The pressure was immense.

Yet even as he went over every detail of his plan, Huw couldn't shake off the conflict he'd been wrestling with for months. The beautiful woodlands, where he and Alys often walked their dog Jessy, were about to be destroyed and many of the officers under his command were local residents who would doubtless be feeling the same. How would he ever explain to Alys that he had played a fundamental role in destroying something they held so dear? How could he even look at himself in the mirror?

As Huw stood before the bleary-eyed officers, unease settled in the pit of his stomach like a lead weight. The operation would require a lot of physical and emotionally draining effort. The greasy operational feeding breakfast hadn't done much to lift their spirits and he could already detect apathy among his team. Nevertheless, he had a professional duty to uphold the gold commander's strategic intentions and values. His promotion prospects and the future financial security of his family depended on it.

He rolled his shoulders back and straightened his folio of papers on the podium. Switching on the overhead projector, he cleared his throat and began the briefing with a heavy heart.

THIRTY-SEVEN

CWM COEDIG, SOUTH WALES

Sycamore lay awake beside her partner, Digger, in the earthy darkness of their turf-roofed roundhouse, in the bed that Digger had built from reclaimed timber, quietly seething at the party going on outside. They were due to take the 5am look-out shift in one of the new watchtowers around the makeshift fortress and she'd hoped for some sleep first.

The influx of eco-warriors and professional activists had changed everything. The peaceful self-sufficient family commune she loved was gone and, in its place, the new Cwm Coedig hummed with activity around the clock. Most nights, there were noisy gatherings, singing and dancing around flickering wood fires to the hypnotic beat of African djembe hand drums, with the distinctive aroma of weed hanging in the air. It wasn't that the newcomers hadn't brought fresh hope. Without them, the commune could never have survived as long as it had, but the loss of their identity was a high price to pay. She hoped it would be worth it if it saved the ancient woodland.

'I don't want to be ungrateful,' Sycamore murmured, 'but I miss getting a decent night's sleep since they all turned up. Do you think they will stay after all this is over?' She buried her face into Digger's shoulder as he put his arm around her. 'I just want to go back to the way things were.'

Digger kissed the top of her head. 'I'm sorry to disappoint you, my lovely,' he said, 'but it's a pretty safe bet that things will never be the same again around here, whatever happens.' He hugged her to his body to keep her warm, even though they were both fully dressed in outdoor clothing and boots under their pile of hand-knitted woollen blankets, ready to spring into action at a moment's notice.

'I hate to say it but some of these kids are just here for the lark,' she whispered, as if they could hear her.

'What? Like you were when you first arrived?' Digger teased gently.

Sycamore slapped him playfully on the shoulder, but he was right. A decade earlier, she'd been a spirited teenager with red dreadlocks and a pierced septum, determined to reject the society that had placed her in social services care. Now, she still had the red dreadlocks and pierced septum, but with the heritage skills she'd learned in the commune, she supplemented their income selling hand-made Celtic silver jewellery to the tourists visiting the Black Mountain region. Digger earned his living as a mobile mechanic, touring the farms and villages of South Wales in his forty-year-old hand-painted converted Commer horsebox, fixing tractors, threshers and balers. They'd been blissfully happy living off-grid in the commune – until the bulldozers arrived.

She suppressed a giggle. 'I know, I know. I was just like them once. But things are different now. We just wanted to drop out and be left alone; half of this lot are out-and-out adrenaline junkies who are in it for the confrontation.'

'You may well be right, love,' said Digger. 'But as long as they stick to passive resistance, they can cause a lot of useful disruption and delay. It takes a lot of gumption to lie down in front of a moving bulldozer, don't forget.'

She nodded in the darkness, accepting the wisdom of his words. Sometimes, she found it hard to believe that the pony-tailed, thickly bearded, peace-loving bear of a man she adored had once been a soldier. She just couldn't picture it. But his army skills made him the obvious choice to lead 'the resistance' and so that was what had happened. They lay without speaking for a moment, the flames from the compound's fire throwing lively shadows around their walls, the rhythmic pounding of goatskin drums getting on her nerves.

Sycamore sighed heavily. 'You're right – as usual. We've had much more success blockading the developers lately.'

Digger propped himself up on one elbow, his warm breath brushing her cheek. 'And that's what it's all about, my love.'

'But will it actually work?' she asked, resisting the urge to kiss him. She'd much rather stay in bed with her lover than spend the next two hours up a watch tower. 'Will they honestly just give up and go away if we cost them too much money?'

They'd discussed it endlessly and Digger's view was that with a general election looming, it was a good time to stall major infrastructure projects in the hope an incoming new government would abandon the plans of the last – but she wasn't so sure.

Digger grunted. 'It's worked abroad,' he said. 'Anyway, what have we got to lose?'

He was right, again. They were in a no-win situation, so whatever they did was better than nothing. Sycamore yawned. 'Is it time yet?'

'Not quite, but we might as well get up, as we won't be getting any sleep at this rate,' said Digger. 'If we can't beat them, we may as well join them.' Outside, the ragtag bunch was now huddled around the dwindling fire, hugging each other as they swayed in time to a woman playing the guitar. Her melancholic voice carried as clearly as a bell in the still night air as she sang *Those Were the Days*.

They pulled on their furry trapper hats and gloves, and grabbed a hand-knitted blanket still warm from the bed to wrap around their shoulders. Their breath billowed like ice-breathing dragons as they ventured into the freezing compound. The circle of oak, ash and chestnut trees that towered like sentinels around the original commune now resembled a prison, enclosed within a barricade of wooden hoardings, forming the outer wall of the 'fortress'. Four constantly manned scaffolding watchtowers stood at the compass points, providing a clear view in every direction. Arborist rope dangled like Tarzan's vines from several mature trees, ready for climbers to rapidly ascend to the treetops when the bailiffs arrived. When Sycamore first volunteered to 'tree-sit', along with a dozen or so other people, it seemed like a great idea at the time. But now, she worried she might freeze to death in the treacherous cold. She and Digger checked and re-checked each harness and rigging, more for something to do than from actual necessity, her jittery hands betraying her nerves. They were killing time and her anxiety was rising.

She slapped her arms to generate some warmth. 'What if I fall asleep up there?' she asked. 'It's so cold, I might never wake up!'

'Don't let it come to that, love.' Digger's eyes met hers with a reassuring look. 'The minute you want to come down, you come down. If you are too stiff to climb, your ground crew can belay you down by rope, no problem.'

'But what if they arrest the ground crew before I come down?'

Digger put a comforting arm across her shoulders. 'Well, they might do that, but you can surrender at that point and they'll have to bring you down anyway,' he said. 'The tree protests are mostly symbolic now, don't forget. It's the tunnels that will bring on the most pains for the bailiffs but they don't make for such good telly.'

Sycamore shuddered. The thought of crawling around underground gave her the creeps. She'd rather be up a tree any day. Digger had drawn upon his army experience to design and organise the digging of a complex labyrinth of tunnels, shored up with joists and equipped with air ducting, food and water supplies. It was a fantastic achievement and she was incredibly proud of him, but nothing on earth would induce her to go down there. Digger reckoned that activists in tunnels could hold out underground for weeks to disrupt the bailiffs. She was secretly pleased that his burly physique prevented him from being one of the 'moles', and anyway, there was another tactic, above ground, that was more suitable to his size and immovable temperament: the Sleeping Dragon.

Sycamore stopped in her tracks at a sudden movement overhead. In silent awe, she watched a white barn owl swoop like a ghost soundlessly through the frosty forest canopy above, its immense wingspan almost touching the trees on either side.

'Did you see that?' she whispered. 'Stunning! How could anyone want to destroy the habitat of such a beautiful creature? It's all about money for developers. They make me sick!'

'Me too, my love, me too.' Digger pulled back five layers of sleeve to look at his wristwatch, the only valuable item he possessed. 'It's time.'

They shuffled across the compound and began to clamber up the makeshift watchtower structure. Weighed down by her heavy boots and layers of clothes, Sycamore's laboured breath came in freezing clouds and her fingertips felt icy against the metal scaffolding, even through her gloves. She cursed as her rabbit-skin trapper hat slipped over her eyes, forcing her to feel her way with numb hands.

'Are we glad to see you two!' A frozen-looking sentry handed over the night-sight binoculars to Digger and wasted no time in leaving. Sycamore blew into her gloved hands as Digger scanned the horizon with the night sight. 'Do you think they will come tonight?' she whispered.

'Pretty sure of it,' Digger replied. 'We've got someone on the inside leaking information to us.'

Sycamore was impressed. She hadn't realised they had spies in the opposite camp. 'I wonder if they have someone on our inside leaking information to them?'

Digger snorted. 'Not possible,' he said. 'Everyone here is ready to go to prison to stand up for the environment, for the rights of the land. Why would any of them leak to the police?'

Sycamore shrugged. 'It was just a thought.'

They fell silent as cloud cover blocked the bright moon. In the blanketing darkness, Digger was lost in thought.

They were fighting a losing battle and he knew it.

His network of tunnels would slow down the bailiffs, but would it be enough? There were so many variables. What if a new government came to power? What if it didn't? What if the bailiffs brought thermal imaging? The game would be up, then. He and his protesters had a bunch of new tactics up their sleeves, but the bailiffs were just as smart. Both sides had been doing their homework in a race to get one step ahead of their opponent.

Digger's determination to soldier on was fuelled by the narrow-minded destruction of the irreplaceable habitat, despite the odds being stacked in the bailiff's favour. The soil around these trees had lain undisturbed for millennia, creating an environmental microbiome, supporting fungi and insects that fed horseshoe bats, pied flycatchers, redstarts and wood warblers. In late spring, the ground was a fragrant carpet of protected native bluebells, stretching as far as the eye could see. It was a mystical and magical place, Cwm Coedwig, a place of legend, where traces of the lives of his Celtic forefathers could be found in the woodland barrows. Those ancient people respected the land, just as the original residents of the commune had. In the darkness, the woodlanders of yore sprang up before his mind's eye, urging him to protect their spiritual home. His skin tingled as he swore a silent oath to fight for every last tree in the valley, for the sake of the generations yet to be born.

Sycamore and Digger handed over to the next pair of lookouts as the first traces of morning streaked the night sky. The relief on Sycamore's face was clear to see. Digger hugged his grey-faced girlfriend against the bitter cold as they scurried across the frozen compound, looking forward to the warmth of their bed. With any luck, they'd get some decent sleep before the djembe drums started up again.

Petrol generators hummed resonantly, powering the industrial arc lamps that illuminated the Forestry Commission car park that was serving as the form-up point for the police and bailiff resources. Huw stood on a raised embankment, flanked by his runner, and inspected the assembly with barely concealed awe. He'd never seen so many cops in one place in his entire police service. Was this how Xerxes had felt before the battle of Thermopylae when he surveyed his troops?

The police public order serials wore dark-blue NATO-style helmets, black body armour, flameproof overalls and steel toecap boots. They carried round polycarbonate short shields and were flanked by public order carriers with their windscreen grilles lowered into place. The rearguard comprised three cherry-picker cranes, a bulldozer and an armoured wagon that contained plasma cutting equipment. Bringing up the rear of the massive police convoy was a lorry loaded with metal interlocking Heras fencing.

It was an impressive and intimidating sight, but Huw knew his Ancient Greek history. Despite superiority in numbers, the Persians were ultimately defeated by the Greeks, ferociously defending their home territory. It was a sobering thought. Huw's regular public order runner, Sergeant Stuart Wilson, must have noted the grim expression on his boss's face.

'Everything okay, Guv'nor?' he asked. His job was to manage the comms, transport and written decision logs for his boss, as well as troubleshoot minor issues. 'Anything you need?'

'No, I'm good, thanks, Stu,' said Huw resolutely. The moment of truth had come. His months of planning were about to be put to the test, followed inevitably by public, media and possibly even judicial scrutiny. Now was the last chance to review his decision to deploy his resources in full public order kit with NATO helmets – a measure intended to defend against activist tactics of pouring urine and liquid faeces over their ramparts onto unprotected officers. The optics were not good from a public relations point of view, often leading to accusations of unnecessary heavy-handedness. Should he stand down the riot helmets to less aggressive-looking flat caps? *Sod the optics*, he thought. Safety was his priority.

'It looks like we're ready to move out,' he said briskly. 'Tell the control room to call up the bronzes to check they're all set, then transmit the order.'

As the personal radios crackled into life, Huw recalled a pearl of wisdom handed down on his public order commander training course. *No plan survives first contact with the enemy.* Who was it that said that? Churchill, maybe? Whoever it was, he suspected they knew what they were talking about.

The klaxon everyone had been dreading sounded with an ear-splitting shriek just after seven-thirty, shattering the peaceful midwinter dawn into a million frozen shards.

Sycamore's pulse raced as she and Digger leapt fully clothed from their bed and scrabbled around in the dark roundhouse for their hats and gloves. Before they went out the door, Digger grabbed her arm and pulled her to him. Her heart thumped in her ears as he wrapped her in a bear-like embrace and kissed her hotly. A surge of adrenaline raced through her veins.

'Remember,' he said, his voice urgent and tight, 'do not fight or use any violence because then they can hurt you. Our strongest weapon is passive resistance. Never forget that. Don't do anything to give them an excuse to put you in danger.'

She nodded, too pumped up for words.

The unlit compound was filled with shadowy figures rushing to their designated battle stations when Digger and Sycamore parted ways in the darkness. Her strength and courage were about to be tested like never before, and she was determined to make Digger proud.

A camo-clad teenager named TreeFrog was waiting for her at the base of an ancient oak inside the compound to help her into her roped-up harness.

'Good luck,' said TreeFrog, giving her a warm hug. 'We'll be here for you as long as we can.'

Sycamore took a few deep breaths to help her focus on the climb. The moment she'd been dreading had finally arrived. A comforting oaky warmth emanated from the enormous trunk as she reached for handholds among the gnarled branches. It was almost as if the tree was willing her on. By the time she reached the tree-top platform and padlocked herself to it, her spirits were soaring. She released her climbing rope and watched it drop to the ground like a dead snake. She'd done it!

The frosty dawn view across the treetops and down into the wooded valley was impossibly beautiful. For a moment, she was breathless with exhilaration – until her gaze lit on the police convoy crawling up the gravel valley track like a poisonous glowing serpent. She recoiled in shock. There were so many of them! She hadn't known what to expect, but she hadn't expected this. She watched with horror as the first riot vans reached the top of the track and began to fan out around the commune. They were being surrounded and cut off from outside help. A shudder ran through her and her spirits plummeted. They were done for but at least they could put up enough resistance to make it difficult for the bastards.

A dozen bulky figures were waiting for Digger at the foot of an ancient sweet chestnut tree, where eleven forty-gallon oil drums filled with concrete formed a wide circle around its trunk. The five-metre girth of the ancient tree was virtually hollow with age and decay, supporting an entire ecosystem of bugs and fungi. This tree stood for everything Digger was fighting to save. He'd put weeks of preparation into protecting this symbolic tree – assembling the components for one of the most fiendish disruption tactics ever developed by protesters: the Sleeping Dragon.

'Okay, folks,' he began. 'We all know what we are doing but I just want to give everybody one last chance to back out before it's too late. Nobody will judge you. I promise.' He scanned the faces around him for signs of uncertainty and found none.

'Now, hopefully, we will be here a very long time and things may get pretty uncomfortable. So, before we get started, one final check: you've all visited the outhouse?

You've all eaten plenty? You all have a ton of layers on?' Digger checked for nods as he spoke. 'Any questions?'

'What do we do when we get arrested?' piped up a voice in the group.

'Just give your name and address and a "no comment" interview,' he replied. 'We've got a lawyer who'll get you released in the morning.'

'What about if they attack us? We'll be sitting ducks.'

'Don't worry about that,' said an unfamiliar voice in the shadows.

Every face turned towards the direction of the voice. A figure stepped forward wearing a luminous green hi-vis tabard over an expensive-looking padded North Face jacket and a thermal full-face Russian ushanka hat. He was holding a video camera.

'Hi guys, I'm Rhys. I'm here from Greenpeace,' he announced through his thermal facemask. 'I'll be recording everything. They won't dare to hurt you if it's all on tape.'

'Great!' Digger's wide grin was almost entirely hidden by his thick beard. He hadn't met the Greenpeace guy yet but it was fantastic to know he was there. Taped evidence of bailiffs or police officers exceeding or misusing their powers could help the protesters hold things up even further through the courts. 'Let's go and wake the Sleeping Dragon, folks!' he cried.

After exchanging high-fives and muffled cheers, the group split up and headed to their assigned oil drum stations, where they rapidly formed an unbreakable human chain around the beautiful old tree by inserting their arms into horizontal pipes set in concrete in each barrel and then connecting their wrists to a central bolt using carabiners.

Their thick clothing made it difficult for cutting tools to be slipped down the pipes alongside their arms.

It was a brilliant tactic and Digger knew he had to use it as soon as he learned of it. The beauty of it was that the protester could simply unclip any time they wanted, whereas a bailiff or cop would need heavy-duty industrial equipment to cut through both the steel of the barrel and a massive lump of concrete to release the carabiner. With their legally bound duty of care, Digger knew this would be a huge headache for the authorities, who would have to use high-powered angle grinders and intense blowtorch plasma cutters near human flesh. It would slow down the eviction considerably.

With everyone clipped securely into place, a sombre mood settled over the small group. A clear melancholy voice broke into song, joined by another, then another.

Time is a one-way street,
No chance of turning back.
How many people did I meet
Along life's twisting track?
Was I your son, your brother or your friend?
Did I break your heart, or leave you cold?
Now I've reached my bitter end,
Will the truth finally be told?
I thought I could choose my life,
But my life chose me.
I tried fighting back,
Imagined I was free.
But the damage was done before I knew it.
The lies I told myself helped me through it.
I had great chances but I really blew it.

If I had my time again, would I really do it?
Who will I be when I am dead,
Just a name on a stone above my head?
My time's behind me, no more ahead.
Is there anything else left to be said?

As the final notes faded away, Digger's face was streaked with the tears he'd been unable to wipe away with his arms encased in concrete.

'Hey, man, you okay?' asked Willow, the lead singer.

Digger sniffed hard in an attempt to reabsorb his tears. 'Yeah,' he croaked. 'That tune always gets me. It could be the story of my life.'

THIRTY-EIGHT

Huw was spellbound by the frozen forest that stretched across the valley before him, every tree delicately picked out in a filigree of frost. The ethereally beautiful scene almost belonged to another world. The commune dwellers had chosen an idyllic spot to live and who could blame them? They'd gone about their business peacefully, without damaging the environment or bothering anyone for decades, and now 'the state' wanted them gone. The rail link was a tragedy for these harmless people and their captivating forest home. With a heavy heart, Huw gestured for his runner to pass him the loudhailer from his van.

'Good morning, everyone,' he began, his amplified voice echoing across the valley. 'My name is Huw Evans, from South Wales police. I'm here with colleagues from the bailiff's office on behalf of the High Court. Will anyone come out and meet us so we can explain our intentions for today?' He paused for a long moment, his eyes scanning the ramparts for signs of response. 'I'm not planning on keeping surprises from you. It may help you to know what to expect.'

He left another long pause, the silence stretching out in the freezing air.

The head bailiff rolled his eyes. 'Come on, Huw, you're wasting everyone's time. Let's just put the main gate in and get on with it.'

Huw turned to the bailiff with a steely glare. 'If there's one thing we've learned from years of bitter experience of policing environmental protests, it's that a little bit of communication goes a long way.'

As he spoke, the fortress gate opened slightly and a heavily wrapped diminutive figure emerged, carrying what looked like a bunch of tree foliage tied with straw, followed by a tall figure in a smart padded ski jacket, full-face thermal hat and luminous green hi-vis, carrying a digital camera.

Huw stood waiting for them to approach, mindful not to make any sudden moves that might make them take flight. A smug smile crept across his face. It looked like his communication strategy might bear fruit after all.

As they drew near, the taller figure spoke first. 'Hello, Huw, long time no see.'

It was the last voice in the world he was expecting but he'd recognise his twin brother's dulcet tones anywhere. Huw stepped towards his brother with his hand outstretched, unable to conceal his surprise. 'Rhys!' he exclaimed. 'How have you been?'

Rhys took his hand and shook it, surprisingly warmly. 'Good, thanks,' he replied with a half-laugh. 'I suppose it was inevitable that we would meet eventually, on opposite sides of a dispute.'

'Was it?' Huw's mind grappled with the unexpected situation. 'I thought you would always be away in some far-flung ocean and the chances of us crossing paths were nil.'

Rhys's face flushed. 'Oh… well, yes… I was. But I've moved a bit closer to home lately.'

The head bailiff cleared his throat loudly. 'Sorry to spoil the big reunion, fellas, but haven't we got business to get on with here?'

'Yes, we have,' snapped Huw, irritated by the bailiff's constant hassle. The man could do nothing without Huw's support. 'But my resources are not going anywhere until I say so, and I'm going to take five minutes to try to spare us all a whole lot of trouble. So, you may as well go and wait in your truck rather than stand out here in the cold.'

The bailiff gave him a stiff glare, thrust his hands deeply into the pockets of his quilted Barbour, and stalked off without a word.

Huw stooped towards the little girl and accepted the proffered woodland bouquet with what he hoped was a friendly smile. 'Thank you for the gift, Miss,' he said, handing it to his runner. 'Could you tell your friends I'd like to talk?'

She nodded solemnly and hurried back to the gates of the fortress.

Huw turned to Rhys and slapped his brother companionably on the back. 'So, how about a five-minute chat in my van?'

Rhys raised a jocular eyebrow. 'How do I know I can trust you? You might lock me up in a cell and throw away the key!'

'Only in my dreams.' said Huw, with a belly laugh.

'But seriously, I guarantee your freedom to return to the commune any moment you want, on Mam-gu's life.'

Rhys grinned at the mention of Mam-gu. 'In that case, how could I possibly refuse?'

Rhys swept his long curly black fringe from his pale-blue eyes with his fingers. 'So let me just recap what I think you are telling me.' He glanced nervously around at the long shields stacked behind him and public order bergens on luggage racks overhead. 'You want me to go back into the camp and tell them you are on their side and will slow things down as much as you can, to give them long enough to appeal the High Court eviction order?'

Huw lowered his voice and looked about, as if checking for spies. 'No, not exactly like that,' he said. 'I could get sacked for that because I'd be wasting valuable police resources. I'd lose my pension and everything I've ever worked for. Nobody else apart from you and I must ever know that's what I'd be doing.'

Rhys nodded. He might not see eye to eye with his brother but he didn't want him to lose his job. 'So, what do you want me to do then, Huw?'

Huw shifted his giant frame uncomfortably on the narrow padded bench seat, looking decidedly hot and bothered in his black public-order overalls and body armour. Rhys's gaze took in his utility belt hung with an entire armoury of police issue protective equipment – including a fire extinguisher! It was obviously not designed for sitting around in. 'Well, surely the commune folk must know that there are still two levels of appeal available above the High Court?' Huw asked. 'If not, you need to tell them that the Court of Appeal can issue an injunction to halt this eviction pending another hearing and, if that fails, there's still the Supreme Court.'

Rhys rolled his eyes. *What planet was Darth Vadar on these days?* 'That will take time and money, Huw, neither of which they have. Even you must know that.'

Huw sat back heavily, his kit rattling with every movement. 'Come on, Rhys,' he said. 'With your Greenpeace connections, you must be able to find a good solicitor willing to do the work pro bono and, if you get Mam involved, things will happen quickly. She is the local member of parliament, for goodness' sake.'

Rhys pulled a face. The last thing he wanted was to get his mother involved. 'Surely she's on the side of the developers? This is a government national infrastructure project, after all.'

Huw glared at Rhys, his eyes blazing. 'Is that what you honestly think, Rhys? That Mam just goes along with everything the government wants? Do you honestly not know her at all?'

Rhys chewed his bottom lip. Huw had hit a nerve. 'I don't know what to think about Mam, or you either, Huw, if I'm honest. None of you has ever shown the slightest bit of concern about the planet up to now. In fact, you've all treated me as a bit of a joke for years.'

Huw sighed deeply and fixed his brother with a steady gaze. 'Look, Rhys. I'm sorry you feel that way, but I'm trusting you with information that could finish my police career,' he said. 'This would be a massive breach of my professional integrity. But I'm willing to do this to give the commune people a chance to get their act together and you need to make that happen with Mam's help. Now get back in there, tell them whatever you need to tell them without mentioning me, and I'll put my foot on the brake out here while you and Mam get the case in front of the Court of Appeal.'

Rhys studied his hands as he weighed up Huw's words. Everything he said made complete sense. If he wanted to save the ancient woodland, now would be a good time to put aside family differences. 'What will you tell that arsehole bailiff?'

Huw ran an exasperated hand across his face. 'He's not an arsehole, Rhys; he's just a bloke doing his job.' He grabbed a handrail and hauled himself to his feet. 'I'll start on the easy stuff that'll look good to the bailiff, such as reading out the eviction order and getting the Heras fencing up around the fortress. My officers may have to nick a few people for obstruction, for appearances' sake, but we'll go easy on them. I'll oversee any arrests myself. It's the best I can offer, Rhys. It's up to you to make this happen. Agreed?'

'All right,' said Rhys. 'I'll see what I can do.'

'I suggest you speak to Mam first. She may be able to offer some useful advice.'

Rhys fell silent. He hadn't spoken to his mother for months. 'What's the problem *now*?'

'You don't happen to have her telephone number, do you?'

Digger gathered the commune's elders around a small fire in the centre of the compound, perched on low benches hand-carved from fallen wood. A watery noonday sun filtered through the branches of the bare canopy. He'd stood down the Sleeping Dragon and tree sit-ins when it became clear that the police were not about to simply drive a bulldozer at the gate, and showed a willingness to talk. It had been a good rehearsal but the commune throbbed with nervous tension. All around the campsite, folks were keeping themselves occupied painting new protest banners to hang off the fortress hoardings.

'Has anyone seen the Greenpeace guy since this morning?' Digger asked. 'Does anyone know what he discussed with the police chief? Any ideas, anyone?'

'Yeah, I spoke to 'im,' said TreeFrog's mum, Tamarind, pulling her Aztec poncho tightly about herself. ''E said 'e was going off to make some phone calls, summat about getting free legal aid for an injunction to stop the eviction – pray bonny or summat, and getting hold of the local MP, too, to speed things up.'

Digger raised his eyebrows. Free legal aid sounded promising. Dragging their case through the courts could take years, maybe even long enough for a change of government, but he wasn't so sure about the rest of it. 'Bit late for bringing the MP into all this,' he said grimly. 'Where was he when this thing was going through the planning stages?'

'I'm not sure,' said Tamarind, 'but I think it's a different MP now. The old one was voted out several years ago for supporting the rail link. I think 'e took a few backhanders along the way, though, and the damage was done.'

That sounded about right. They were all rotten and corrupt – the lot of 'em. 'I've got no time for politicians,' said Digger. 'They're all the same, all in it for themselves.'

Tamarind wrapped herself defensively in her cloak. 'Well, 'e seemed to think this one would 'elp.'

'What about his talk with the police chief? Did he say anything about that?'

'Not really… but if you ask my opinion, it looks like they are going to seal us in with their metal fencing and starve us out, like a siege or summat.'

'Is that legal?' asked a wiry guy, his grey-streaked dreadlocks reaching down to his waist. 'I've got six children to feed.'

'Dunno,' she replied, 'but that pray bonny lawyer will know when 'e gets 'ere.'

The wiry guy shrugged his shoulders. 'So what should we do while we're waiting?'

'Let's get those banners out and 'ope Mr Greenpeace comes back with his free lawyer and some telly cameras, is what I'd suggest,' said Tamarind.

Digger looked around at the grave faces. It wasn't much of a plan but it would do for now. 'Okay,' he said. 'Let's meet back here this afternoon at four and see where we are then – unless we get an alert from the watchtower before that.'

Sycamore was crouching over a grey sheet on the ground outside their roundhouse, wielding a paintbrush and tin of red paint, when she heard footsteps approaching. She looked up to see Digger coming her way.

'What do you think?' She stepped back to survey her handiwork.

PLANIT OR PROFIT? read the banner in bold red capitals.

Digger wrapped his arms around her and kissed the end of her nose. 'It's a great slogan, love,' he said. 'Eye-catching and says it all.' He took the paintbrush gingerly from her sticky red hand and added three horizontal lines to the first 'I'. 'Well done, love. Let's go and hang it from a watchtower.'

Digger grabbed a hammer and a handful of nails from the roundhouse while she carefully gathered up the banner. He never criticised her or made her feel stupid, even when she misspelt things; his kind heart was one of the many things she loved about him. Together, they headed to the south watchtower closest to the front gate of the fortress, where her banner would be easily seen from the gravel road.

Digger unfurled the banner across the front of the wooden platform and began to hammer it in place, with Sycamore passing him the nails. She looked up on hearing the crunch of tyres on icy gravel to see a dark-green Land Rover pulling up outside the front gate. The driver, a stout woman in her early sixties, stepped out of the car, followed by her front-seat passenger, a tall guy in his forties with black curly hair. Sycamore recognised him by his North Face jacket. It was the Greenpeace guy with someone she'd never seen before. She hadn't seen him in daylight without his ushanka hat. He was a lot dishier than she'd imagined, but also vaguely familiar. She couldn't take her eyes off him as she tried to work out where she knew him from. With a rush of embarrassment, she noticed the hammering had stopped and held out a nail, hoping Digger hadn't noticed her eyeing up the Greenpeace guy.

But Digger didn't take the proffered nail.

She turned to face him, expecting to see him packing away, but instead he was frozen in mid-action, the hammer in his hand suspended in mid-air, his face as white as a sheet – as if he'd seen Medusa and been turned to stone.

His stunned expression unnerved her. 'What's the matter, Digger?'

His unresponsiveness rattled her even more.

'Digger! What is it? What's the matter? You look like you've seen a ghost!'

Huw was sitting at the desk in the police command lorry, drinking coffee and writing up his decision log, when his mam's green Land Rover pulled up in front of the commune. He grunted with approval. Rhys had clearly got his act together.

His gaze lingered for a moment as his mam and Rhys stepped out of the vehicle, and was about to return to his decision log when a sudden flash of movement caught his eye. He watched from a distance of about fifty metres with a clear and unobstructed view as an IC1 male, mid-thirties, about six-three, athletic build, with jet black hair in a ponytail, heavy black beard, wearing khaki-green and brown camouflage trousers, a khaki green army surplus style parka and black combat boots, carrying an orange-handled claw-hammer in his left hand jumped down from the watchtower, a drop of about 12 feet. He observed the man land using a somersault manoeuvre before leaping to his feet and sprinting in the direction of his mam and brother.

With his heart pounding, Huw grabbed his police radio to call for urgent backup but, before he could say a word, four cordon officers the size of prop forwards tackled the man to the ground. Huw winced in appreciation, knowing from experience on the rugby pitch how much pain the assailant was feeling under the pile of nineteen-stone bodies. Huw leapt from the van and sprinted across to the scene, where the four constables had the would-be attacker comprehensively pinned to the ground, face down in the dirt. They hauled his arms behind his back, clamping him firmly in quick-cuffs as he bellowed and roared.

Within seconds, the fortress gates opened and a wave of protesters flooded out. A woman with red dreadlocks, screaming like a banshee, jumped on the back of one of the arresting officers, tearing at his arms before being forcibly held back by more cordon officers in full public order kit.

'Get him out of here!' Huw yelled above the chaos. His heart raced as he herded his wide-eyed mother and brother into his arms, and steered them towards the command lorry.

'What the hell just happened?' Rhys's face was as white as a sheet.

'I've no bloody idea,' said Huw, 'but those boys deserve a medal for bringing him down so quickly.' He dreaded to think what would have happened if that lunatic had got to Mam and Rhys with that hammer.

'And these people want my help?' Shirley's voice trembled with shock.

'But I don't understand.' Rhys frowned as they reached the lorry and climbed aboard. 'That was Digger. He's one of the good guys and as non-violent as they come. He's the one reminding everyone to stick to passive resistance. It makes no sense.'

Huw harrumphed cynically. He'd seen more than his fair share of 'good guys' lose their heads and behave out of character when caught up in a noble cause. 'Well, we'll find out what he has to say for himself at the magistrates' court in the morning,' he said, filling the kettle and setting out three cups. 'He's been arrested to prevent a breach of the peace. I'll go along myself. I may be required to give evidence anyway, as I witnessed everything.'

'I'll go with you,' said Rhys. 'Maybe I'll be able to get some sense out of him, in the cold light of day.'

Huw frowned. 'I'm not so sure that's a great idea, Rhys, seeing as you seem to have been his target.'

Rhys glared at his brother. 'Let me be the judge of that, Huw.'

THIRTY-NINE

SWANSEA, SOUTH WALES

The dry still air in the magistrates' court chamber was redolent with wood polish and old leather. It was a smell that Dai Bevan loved – the smell of justice. Seated on the burnished mahogany justices' bench alongside two colleagues, he surveyed the packed courtroom. It was standing-room only at the back of the chamber, where the public gallery overflowed with a motley crew with long densely matted hair, wearing colourful home-spun clothes. They looked like a troupe of medieval minstrels.

Dai scanned the benches filled with journalists, court officials, and representatives from community support services. Burly Huw, looking smart and authoritative in his police uniform, was easy to spot. Beside him sat Rhys, who was slenderer and casually dressed in an open-necked shirt. With their identical thick raven hair, ice-blue eyes and chiselled features, it was easy to see why they were attracting curious glances and whispered comments. Dai couldn't remember the last time he'd seen his two stepsons seated side by side. They seemed to have come to an understanding despite their political differences – at least for the day. Shirley *would* be pleased.

Dai checked the court schedule on the top of his stack of papers. It was a full list that morning and the first matter was a bind over for a breach of the peace. He'd already agreed to recuse himself from this case, as his wife was connected to the bizarre incident the previous afternoon, but he was keen to sit in as an observer to find out what on earth had possessed the defendant to run at her with a hammer. He'd spotted a slight problem with the court papers already, though. It seemed the police had been unable to verify the name and address of the detained man overnight, who was listed under the alias of *Digger*. That would make it tricky to issue a bind over and complicate matters considerably. A frown flickered across his features. Luckily, the clerk of the court that day was highly experienced at extracting information from uncooperative folk. He settled himself comfortably for an entertaining morning.

A hush fell over the courtroom as the presiding judge signalled to the court usher, who opened the passage door to the holding cells and called for the first defendant to be brought up. As the door swung open and the jailer led the defendant to the dock, Dai was struck by a remarkable sense of déjà vu.

The man resembled a black bear, primarily due to his powerful build and thick, dark hair and beard. Although his features were almost invisible behind his abundant facial hair, there was something unsettlingly familiar about him. Dai couldn't pinpoint what it was. It might have been his confident walk or even the way his broad shoulders were set. Perhaps he would recognise the defendant's voice.

The clerk adjusted the glasses on the end of her nose. 'Please state your full name to the court.'

In the raised dock, the defendant leaned casually against the handrail. 'You can call me Digger.'

The clerk gave him a withering look over the top of her spectacles. 'You have been brought before the court following detention to prevent a breach of the peace,' she declared, projecting her voice to the public gallery like a Shakespearian player. 'This is a common law matter, with a civil disposal available to Their Worships, to bind you over to keep the peace, thereby avoiding a criminal outcome for you.' She paused, letting her words sink in. 'However, this disposal option is only available if the defendant's identity is known and verified to the court.'

The clerk paused again, casting a sweeping glance around the courtroom. Dai sat back, enjoying the performance. The formal language and dramatic posturing were all very theatrical.

'Regrettably, the court is unable to accept an alias and will have to treat any refusal to provide your full identity as a refusal to accept or comply with a bind over'—she shuffled her papers briskly—'for which Their Worships have the power under the Magistrates' Court Act to *commit you to custody* for a period not exceeding six months.'

A loud gasp rose from the public gallery and Dai chuckled to himself. The clerk had landed her speech perfectly. The defendant grabbed the edge of the dock and faced the bench with blazing eyes. Two court constables stepped closer to the dock.

'Six months?' he cried, accompanied by loud jeers and shouting from the gallery. 'You can't give me six months in prison! I didn't do anything!'

'Order! Order!' called the presiding judge.

As the commotion subsided, the clerk continued. 'So, I ask you once again, please state your full name to the court.'

A long silence filled the courtroom as all eyes were fixed on the defendant standing in the dock, his head bowed in contemplation. Dai watched him intently as the courtroom air crackled with anticipation. Seconds ticked by before the defendant lifted his gaze and fixed the bench with a steady unwavering stare from his piercing pale-blue eyes. When he spoke, his voice was heavy with resignation.

'My full name is Chase Emlyn Garland and I'm a US citizen – although my father was Welsh.'

His chin dropped to his chest as soon as the words were out, his face a picture of naked anguish. A ripple of surprise ran through the courtroom, with distinct gasps from the public gallery.

'Do you have any documentary identification in that name?' asked the clerk, above the hubbub, a note of triumph in her voice. 'Is there anybody who could bring it to the court on your behalf?'

'I still have my US passport.' Chase turned to face the centre of the courtroom for the first time. 'My girlfriend could... could...' His voice trailed off and, for a moment, Dai thought he was having some sort of seizure. His body stiffened, his mouth gaped and his gaze locked on a figure in the crowded courtroom.

'Mr Garland?' The clerk's voice cut through the tense silence. 'Mr Garland, are you all right?'

Chase looked like a man bewitched. 'Travis? Is it really you?'

'Mr Garland, I have to warn you—'

Chase snapped out of his daze in a heartbeat, 'That's my brother! Right there!' He pointed an accusing finger at Rhys. 'He was at the commune yesterday with my ma! Tell them, Travis! That's why I was running – to see them. Tell them, Travis, tell them!'

The gallery erupted in chaos and the presiding judge called for order as Huw and Rhys exchanged astonished looks. The fellow was clearly deranged.

Drugs, probably, thought Dai. They were everywhere lately.

'Order! Order!' bellowed the judge to no avail, as the accused leapt down from the dock. A woman with red dreadlocks in the public gallery let out a piercing scream as the two court officers seized hold of him and bundled him expertly to the floor, pinning his shoulders with their knees and pulling his arms behind him into their handcuffs.

'Travis!' he roared, writhing on the ground. 'Tell them everything!'

'Take him back to the cells,' the judge thundered. 'And clear the chamber!'

Chase's feet stumbled beneath him as the two tight-lipped jailers hauled him along the windowless passage back to the holding cells. Seeing Travis right there in the courtroom had thrown him completely. What the hell was going on?

'You've done yourself no favours, mate,' said one of the jailers as he released the cuffs inside the cell and backed out quickly, slamming the heavy door behind him. Flipping open the metal wicket, he added, 'You might want to think about being a bit more cooperative for your own good if you want to get out of here this side of Christmas.' The wicket slammed with a heavy metallic clunk.

'You don't understand,' Chase called back through the wicket to the sound of receding footsteps. 'That's my brother back there in the courtroom. I haven't seen him in ten years!' His words reverberated in the empty cell passage as the passage door swung closed.

Chase collapsed onto the blue plastic cell mattress, trembling and confused. The hearing had been a disaster but that was nothing compared to the shock of seeing his brother in the same courtroom! Had Ma been there, too? He hadn't noticed her but the thought of his mother witnessing him being dragged away in handcuffs was excruciating.

He lay on the thin mattress and stared at the ceiling, his eyes glazing over the anti-suicide messages spray-painted there. Overnight in the police cell, he'd managed to persuade himself that he'd been mistaken when he'd seen Ma and Travis yesterday at the commune, but now it was beyond doubt they had come looking for him. But how had they found him after all this time? And why? He stood up and went to the wicket, straining to hear whether anything was happening outside the cellblock. What were they telling the authorities? Was he going to be extradited to the States? Was that why they'd hunted him down – to take him home to face justice after all this time? He banged his fists on the door with frustration.

Alone in his cell, with nothing but his thoughts to keep him company, the unanswered questions in his head circled like horses on a merry-go-round. He flung his arm over his eyes, trying to block out the penetratingly bright cell light, which made it nearly impossible to think straight. He lost track of time as he lay uncomfortably on the miserably thin pad. It might have been ten minutes, or it might have been two hours before he heard the scrape of the wicket opening and saw a pair of ice-blue eyes regarding him coldly. He leapt to his feet as a resonant voice boomed, 'Stand back from the door.'

His pulse raced as a jangle of keys scraped against the door and the lock clicked open. He'd recognise those pale blue eyes anywhere. Travis was here and he'd come for revenge. He squared his shoulders, bracing himself to face the brother he'd betrayed a lifetime ago.

As the door swung open, the bulky frame of a police officer in full uniform filled the door. He was the image of Travis – but on anabolic steroids. Chase gasped and stumbled backwards. His legs gave way beneath him and he collapsed onto the bench, trembling. He must be losing his mind. Everyone he saw looked like Travis. His guilt had driven him insane – it was the only explanation. His shoulders slumped as the fight went out of him.

'Take it easy, mate.' The officer's tone was conciliatory as he stepped into the cell. 'You're not looking too good. Do you need me to call a doctor for you?'

Chase shook his head slowly. 'Honestly, Officer, I really don't know. I don't know what to think any more. I mean, look at you... you're the image of Travis but twice his size. You look more like me, especially when I left the army.'

The officer looked him up and down disdainfully. 'I'm not seeing that, myself,' he said. But as their ice-blue eyes locked, something in the officer's expression changed. 'So you were in the army, were you?' He lowered his brawny figure onto the mattress beside Chase.

He was far less intimidating when seated and the tension evaporated from the cell.

Chase nodded, grateful for the gesture. 'Look, Officer, I mean you no disrespect, but I'm having a hard time figuring out what's going on. Can you please explain why my twin brother, Travis, is sitting in that courtroom? I'll take whatever punishment is coming to me, as God is my witness, I will. But I just need some help understanding what's happening… please?'

'Well, that's interesting.' The officer's eyes narrowed for a second. 'You think he's your twin, do you? You've got a twin called Travis?'

'Yes, I do.' Chase searched the officer's face for clues. He was clearly holding something back. 'And he's sitting in that courtroom and I need to know why.'

A look of pity flitted across the officer's face. 'Sorry to disappoint you, fellow,' he said gently, 'but that's *my* twin brother, Rhys, who you were yelling at in court earlier *and* who you ran at with a hammer yesterday. In fact, that was also my mam you had a go at yesterday and, I've got to admit, we are all at a complete loss as to why. Perhaps you need to explain yourself to me, not the other way round!'

'*Your* mam?' cried Chase. '*Your* twin brother?' He clasped his face with both hands and groaned. 'What did you just say his name was? Reese?'

'Yep, Rhys. Why is that so important?'

'Reese… as in "Hugh and Reese"?' A seed of recollection began to germinate in Chase's mind. 'Have you got a brother in the army named Gareth, by any chance?'

'Maybe…' The officer gave Chase a wary look. 'How do you know Gareth?'

Chase hesitated, the memories slowly gathering in his head. 'I met Gareth about twelve years ago, peacekeeping in Sarajevo.' He closed his eyes as he recalled the encounter. 'He told me he had half-brothers in Wales who were twins and looked exactly like me. I had a buzz cut and no beard back then. He said their names were Hugh and Reese.'

'Okay,' said the officer slowly. 'That all sounds about right. Carry on.'

Chase got to his feet and began to pace the cell as the memories gathered momentum. 'I have to admit, I was a bit sceptical, but he insisted and said he'd bring a photo to the dining mess the following night, but he never turned up. His unit moved out the next morning. I never saw him again. Are you "Hugh" by any chance?' He looked at the officer quizzically. 'Of course you're "Hugh"… who else could you be?'

Huw rubbed his chin pensively. 'I've got to say, that is a remarkable story. What are the chances of crossing paths with you after all these years?'

Chase gave a bitter laugh. 'Oh, this is no coincidence, buddy,' he said. 'I came looking for you and Reese about ten years ago. I had a few problems at home. I'm originally from Kentucky, although my pa was Welsh. I thought maybe we were distant cousins or something, but looking at you and your brother, I don't think we're that distant. I can't explain why I didn't think of it sooner.' He slapped himself on the forehead. 'Maybe it's because I saw Ma, too. That's what threw me – seeing them both together. I didn't know she was your ma at the time and, I've got to admit, I can't get my head around that at all.'

'So why did you want to attack them with the hammer?'

Chase's mouth fell open. 'What?' *Attack them with the hammer?* 'No!' he cried. 'You've got that all wrong! I was nailing up a banner. The hammer was just in my hand – though I can see how it mustn't have looked too good.'

'You can say that again!' said Huw. 'We all thought you were going to kill them!'

A burst of astonished laughter escaped Chase's lips. The situation would be almost comical if it weren't so surreal. 'Oh, my word, I'm so sorry to have freaked you out, Hugh,' he said. 'Honestly, I'm not a bad guy. I was raised as a good Baptist by my ma and pa. Can you arrange to get me back into the courtroom to apologise to everyone? I'll accept whatever the fine is, though it may take some time to pay off, as I'm about to become homeless…' His voice trailed off as his mind added two and two.

'Hey! Ain't you the guy in charge of the eviction?' he demanded. 'The guy with the loudhailer? "My name is Chief Inspector Hugh Evans" and all that?' He was furious with himself. He'd been about to trust the man who wanted to destroy the woodland!

Huw's eyes darted to the cell door wicket. 'Whoa, slow down a minute, chum. Everything is not quite as it seems,' he said in a hushed voice. 'Rhys works for Greenpeace, and my mam is the local MP. She's on your side. That's why she went to the commune yesterday. Everyone around here wants to save that ancient woodland,' he muttered. 'Take my word, I am not a bad guy either. I can't say too much in this cell, but I suggest you meet up with them once you are out of here.' He slapped Chase lightly on the back. 'I can get you back in the chamber this afternoon, but the magistrates will want to see your ID first so you can be bound over and released immediately after your appearance.'

Chase pursed his lips as he mulled over the officer's words. He wanted to believe him but it was a big risk. 'Okay, I can go along with all of that,' he said eventually. 'Go and speak to my girlfriend, Sycamore – Teagan Jones – she's the one with the red dreadlocks.' He slipped a thin leather strap from around his neck. 'Give her this key and tell her to look in my US Army footlocker in the back of my old truck. It's where I keep my passport.'

'Consider it done, *cousin*,' said Huw, with a sardonic laugh.

Huw sat alone in the dingy police office on the second floor of the magistrates' court with Chase's passport in his trembling hands. As he stared at the photograph before him, every fibre of his physical being shivered. He'd found the picture tucked into the back of the passport the defendant's girlfriend brought to the court. The four-inch-square black-and-white glossy photograph, with creased corners and a white border, showed two boys of about fourteen, their thick black curly hair tumbling forward over their eyes, standing beside a tractor. The man behind them rested a hand paternally across each of their shoulders. It was as if he were looking at a picture of himself and Rhys, except the man in the middle was not Dai.

Although he had never set eyes on his father in person, Huw knew with absolute certainty it was him. He'd looked through Mam-gu's old family albums often enough as a child to have absolutely no doubt in his mind. The discovery of this photograph exploded every story he'd ever been told about his father's death and his head pounded as he wrestled with the implications. Had Mam and Mam-gu lied to him all these years, or did they not know themselves? It was a horrible mess and, to make matters worse, it meant that the Wild Man of Borneo downstairs in the cells was his *brother*. Worrying questions piled up in Huw's mind. He needed more time to think before he opened this particular can of worms.

He slipped the photograph into his pocket with a stab of guilt and headed downstairs to the clerk of the court's office to confirm Chase's identification with the passport and expedite his release.

'Could you do me a favour, please, Ma'am?' Huw asked the clerk. 'Could you return the defendant's passport after his appearance this afternoon? I've got another appointment elsewhere, so I can't stay.'

'No problem, Chief Inspector,' the clerk replied. 'And thanks for your help in sorting this out. I don't know what you said to him but he's certainly bucked his act up since the amateur dramatics in court this morning.'

'No problem,' said Huw, the words sticking in his throat. 'It was no big deal.'

FORTY

B en and Jerry almost knocked Dai off his feet as he unlocked his Victorian stained-glass front door and let himself into the lofty entrance hall, with its elegantly sweeping staircase and imposing grandfather clock. A Norwegian spruce tree smothered in gaudy tinsel and brightly coloured baubles towered up through the open stairwell, filling the air with the festive aroma of pine. His spirits soared. *Nobody in the world is ever quite so pleased to see you as your dogs*, he thought happily, vigorously rubbing their joyful wriggling bodies.

'Shirley, bach, are you in?' he called out loudly, his voice echoing in the enormous hallway. He broke into a broad smile as she appeared from the direction of the kitchen, wearing a floury apron, and gave him a warm kiss.

'What a rumpus in court today, my love!' he said, eager to share his news. 'That fellow from the commune? He really kicked off!'

'Oh no!' cried Shirley. 'Nobody hurt, I hope?'

Dai took off his wet mackintosh and hung it on the coat stand. 'Oh no, nothing like that,' he said. 'Pretty damned strange, though – he was ranting about Rhys being his brother! Can you imagine? And then – wait for this – he reckoned you were his mam! Had to be hauled back to the cells, kicking and screaming!'

'Oh, my word! The poor fellow must be unwell – or an addict?'

'That's what I thought,' said Dai. 'Huw certainly sorted him out quickly, though. You'd have been dead proud of him, love. A five-minute chat in the cellblock was all it took for the chap to come back, full of remorse and apology, explaining it was all a case of mistaken identity. It seems you and Rhys look just like some relatives back home in Kentucky he hasn't seen in years. He was pretty shocked when he saw you both and lost it a bit, so he said.'

'Really?' Shirley said dubiously as they entered the kitchen where she was baking fruit scones. 'That all sounds a bit woo-woo to me. What about the hammer?'

Dai helped himself hungrily to a handful of sultanas from the open packet on the worktop. 'He was nailing up a protest banner when he saw you – nothing more sinister than that,' he explained. 'But here's the weird thing. I reckon that if you gave that chap a good haircut and a thorough shave, he would be the image of Huw. I couldn't work it out at first but then it came to me. The same build, the same walk, the same ice-blue eyes, thick black wavy hair – the lot!'

he exclaimed. 'If he wasn't a Yank, I'd have said he was their triplet, separated at birth. Oh, except he's about ten years younger than your boys. His real name is Chase Garland, believe it or not. Chase *Emlyn* Garland, actually. How weird is that?'

A shadow passed over her face at the mention of Emlyn's name. 'So, he's American, is he? Did you say Kentucky? Now that is weird.'

'Hmm, yes, I did. What's weird about that?'

'Oh, it's probably nothing,' said Shirley vaguely. 'Let's forget about these boring scones and go down the pub for dinner instead.'

'Great idea!' Dai headed back to the hallway to grab his coat.

'You're paying!' she said with a wicked laugh.

***

Shirley's constituency office was a small shopfront in Aberavon, just across the road from the Methodist church cemetery where her tad Alwyn was laid to rest, along with Lowri's husband, Evan, and son Emlyn. It was one of her favourite places, a peaceful haven where she often met Lowri and sat on the bench under the ancient yew tree, chatting for hours. Lowri always said they were keeping company with their menfolk, who may have gone but were not forgotten, and Shirley couldn't agree more.

The snow fell gently on Sunday morning after Communion as Shirley fumbled with the key in the office door lock, her fingers wet and cold. In the narrow poky hallway, she punched one combination after another into the alarm box to the tune of an increasingly frantic bleep, cursing her senior moment. How could she possibly forget her twins' birthday?

Sunday morning after church was usually precious family time to catch up with her granddaughter Alys for a walk with Ben and Jerry. But Alys had a cold and Dai had already walked the dogs, so Shirley had an hour to spare to check out something bothering her since the court case last week. She could easily have logged on to her desktop at home but, inexplicably, she felt the need to be secretive about this enquiry. She didn't want Dai checking out her search history and getting anxious if it all turned out to be nothing.

Taking the *Swansea Gazette* from her handbag, she spread it open on her desk and turned to the court reports page, where a photograph captioned *Eco-warrior Digger, also known as Chase Emlyn Garland, 36, of Cwm Coedwig commune, leaving court with his girlfriend, Sycamore,* accompanied a half-page article about the rail link protest.

As Dai had said, he was a hairy beast, but she wasn't so sure about him being Huw's double – at least not in this black-and-white headshot with a newspaper covering half his face. She read the article twice, looking for clues, while waiting for her ancient desktop computer to warm up. Eventually, the spinning wheel of death disappeared and her search engine opened.

Astonishingly, the top hit on her enquiry *Chase Garland 1972 Kentucky* was a link to *The World* magazine. She was intrigued. Wasn't *The World* just for global movers and shakers? People like that dishy Barack Obama, the thinking woman's pin-up, who might just be the first black US president one day – with any luck? She couldn't imagine that a minor-league eco-warrior like this Garland fellow would ever grace the pages of such an illustrious publication. With mounting anticipation, she clicked on the link, which took her to a ten-year-old glossy celebrity profile of Greer Garland, the world-famous country and western singer. The wind went out of Shirley's sails and she sat back in her office chair feeling deflated. It must have been a partial hit on the surname and county. Maybe Garland was a common name in Kentucky? It was clear the article had nothing to do with her hairy attacker.

The tune of *Who Will I Be?* popped into Shirley's head and she found herself humming it as she scanned the first few lines of the article out of interest. She was a fan of Greer Garland and had a couple of her albums – such a beautiful voice. The article was accompanied by several photos of her stunning house, with fantastic views over a sparkling lake in the background. *She must be worth a few quid to have a place like that*, Shirley thought, her eye alighting on a lovely picture of Greer with her mam.

The hairs on Shirley's arms sprang up and her mouth fell open. She could hardly believe her eyes – for she was looking at a picture of herself seated next to Greer Garland in her Kentucky mansion. Except it wasn't her but a woman who looked so much like her that they could be each other's double! Just like the woman at the theatre in London all those years ago. That woman had been the playwright's sister – was she also Greer Garland's mother? It was all rather extraordinary.

Scrolling back to the top of the article, Shirley read the glossy profile as thoroughly as if studying a House of

Commons committee report. An hour later, having read the article three times and absorbed every detail about the hunt for missing twin Chase *Emlyn* Garland and the tragic backstory of his Welsh father 'Gryff Morgan', Shirley sat at her desk in stunned silence. It didn't take a Scotland Yard detective to piece together the clues that pointed towards an inescapable conclusion.

The shocking realisation that Bryn had faked his death left her numb with disbelief. Why would he have done such a thing? It was inconceivable. As the numbness started to wear off, she began to tremble uncontrollably. She couldn't tell if it was shock or rage, but the thought that her two sons had been deprived of their father, who was alive all along, filled her with an overwhelming sense of injustice. Tears stung her eyes as she grappled with the betrayal and a physical pain burned in her chest. Rushing to the tiny kitchen, she grabbed a glass of water and gulped it down.

She returned to her office after several minutes spent leaning on the kitchen sink feeling like she was about to throw up and picked up the telephone receiver to dial the international telephone number in the article. She hesitated, on the verge of a decision that would change their lives forever. Was it for the best or was she about to open Pandora's box? And then what? The betrayal could destroy Lowri or it might delight her to know she had an entire family on the other side of the Atlantic, but one thing was for sure: there'd be no going back.

What was it they said about sleeping dogs?

***

Chase spent the best part of the morning searching his footlocker for the photograph of him and Travis with Pa, standing beside a tractor, but it was nowhere to be found. He'd planned to show it to Rhys and his mother when he met them at Swansea police station later that day to discuss the rail link High Court appeal, in what had been deemed by Huw to be a safe neutral space. He was hoping they might recognise his pa. After all, if Huw and Rhys were twins who looked just like him and Travis, was it not possible that his pa, Gryff, may have been a twin himself? Maybe their pa was his pa's twin brother! But without the photo, exploring that possibility was lost. He had to find another way to convince them of the possibility of a genetic link. So instead, he'd taken a trip to the barbershop to reveal his true appearance.

Chase glanced at his father's watch as he hurried along Grove Place on his way to the meeting, leaning into the icy wind, feeling oddly conspicuous with his face clean-shaven for the first time in a decade and his ponytail consigned to the bin. The barber had given him a trendy chop, which restored the bounce to his thick black curls. Even his eyes looked more dazzlingly blue without the carpet of shaggy beard concealing his face. Instead of his customary shapeless camo gear, he wore a clean fitted polo shirt, snug jeans and a puffer jacket that he had picked up in a charity shop for a few pounds. He was finally closing in on a branch of the family tree that might help him trace his Welsh ancestors and learn more about his father – he could feel it in his bones. He might even discover the town where he was born and grew up, which would be incredible. It was an exciting prospect, yet he felt jittery and nervous.

Chase was shown into a public interview room in the front office of the newly built police station, where Rhys was waiting for him. The look on Rhys's face at the transformation of 'Digger' was priceless.

'Bloody hell!' Rhys' eyes widened with surprise. 'I can't believe it! You look amazing – I would never have recognised you as the same bloke from the commune in a million years!' He threw himself onto a plastic chair, looking completely bemused. 'I wish Mam could have made it today to see you for herself. She'll never believe me when I tell her! I can totally see how you must have thought I was your twin brother.'

Chase grinned with relief. At least Rhys was getting it now. 'Where is your ma today?' he asked. 'I was hoping to apologise to her in person.'

'Oh, I don't know,' replied Rhys, sullenly. 'She dropped out suddenly and didn't give a reason. She's been doing that to me all her life because of her work, so I'm not surprised. She'd better not let me down with the High Court appeal or there'll be hell to pay.'

'Sorry to hear that, Rhys,' said Chase. *The poor guy! It must be awful having an uncaring mother.* 'I'm also real sorry I scared you and your ma the other day. I was so focused on you both, thinking you were Travis and Ma, that I didn't even realise I was still holding the hammer.' He stuck out a hand. 'Friends?'

Rhys's smile was warm and sincere, and Chase was relieved to see it. 'Sure! Friends – and comrades, as it happens, since we are both on the same side of the eviction. There's a lot of work to do but I've got to admit I'm just too dumbfounded to think about that right now. There's no way that we're not related. Wait a minute – would you mind if I took your photo on my new smartphone? I can show it to Mam, so she'll have to believe me.'

'What's a smartphone?' Chase looked on with interest as Rhys produced the slimline gadget from his trouser pocket and brought it to life with a press of his thumb and a swipe of his finger. In the ten years he had been in the commune, technology had progressed unimaginably and he found himself fascinated by it. Although he knew about the internet, he had no idea of its power, so it was mind-boggling that this tiny device in Rhys's pocket could make phone calls *and* take photographs – and probably a lot more besides.

'Here, take a look, Chase.' Rhys tapped the device. 'I'll show you some family photos.'

Chase looked over Rhys's shoulder eagerly. 'Do you have any of your pa?' he asked. 'I've got a theory that our fathers could've been twins, themselves. It would explain a lot.'

Rhys scowled. 'Not to me, it wouldn't. My tad went off to sea before I was born. Mam got a letter from America a few years later saying he'd died and been buried at sea.'

Chase ran his finger ruminatively along the edge of the desk. 'I'm sorry to hear that, Rhys,' he said. *A letter from America, though. A potential link, maybe?* 'But did he have a twin, as far as you know?'

'No, he definitely didn't. In fact, he had a younger brother, who he accidentally killed with their tad's military revolver. It's why he ran away.'

Chase was horrified by the heart-wrenching story. How did Rhys's pa manage to live with himself after that? His own guilt for what he did to Shelby was terrible enough but to kill your own brother? It was unimaginable. 'Oh, my word,' he said. 'I'm real sorry to bring all this up.'

'Emlyn, his name was,' Rhys continued sadly. 'He was just ten years old.'

Chase's heart skipped a beat. 'What?' he cried, trembling with disbelief. 'That's my middle name! That cannot be a coincidence, Rhys, Goddammit! If only we had some pictures of them.'

'I'm telling you, Chase, he didn't have a twin.' Rhys' voice was emphatic. 'I'll text my grandmother. She'll send me a picture of him.'

Chase collected his thoughts as Rhys fiddled with his phone. Ten years, he'd been trying to track down his pa's Welsh roots. And finally, here they were, so close to finding their family connection, but something didn't add up and he couldn't put his finger on it. It was driving him crazy.

The smartphone pinged. 'Here, have a look at this,' said Rhys. 'Bryn – that was my father's name – all dressed up in his best suit for his twenty-first birthday, I think.'

The head-and-shoulders professional studio shot of a young man leaning on a Greek pedestal was so crisp that it was possible to tell the time on his wristwatch.

Chase's blood ran cold. A shiver ran down his spine and goosebumps sprang up on his arms as he stared at the image that finally explained everything.

'That's my pa,' he heard himself saying calmly, with a weird sense of detachment – like he was behind glass, or underwater. The whole situation was so surreal he wasn't sure he wasn't dreaming.

Rhys looked at him with bafflement. 'That's impossible. They're probably cousins, lookalikes somehow.'

'I'm telling you,' said Chase, beginning to pull himself together. '*That's, my, pa.*'

Rhys flicked a dismissive hand at Chase. 'How can you possibly be so certain?'

'Look at the watch.' Chase displayed his wrist for Rhys's inspection. 'I inherited it from my pa. He always gave it to me for safekeeping before he went stock-car racing. It was a bit of a superstition thing for him.'

Rhys's gaze went from the distinctive antique watch on Chase's wrist to the photo and back.

The upturned desk struck Chase on the temple as Rhys exploded with a furious cry, sending chairs flying and papers scattering about the room. An alarm blared as the desk knocked against the panic strip fixed to the walls around the room.

'The bastard!' he yelled as the door flew open and three police officers piled in. 'The lying bastard!'

'Leave him!' Chase dabbed his bloody eye with a corner of his new shirt. 'He's just had some bad news.'

Open-mouthed and wide-eyed, the officers stopped in their tracks, only backing out reluctantly when dismissed by Rhys's wave. Chase figured they must have known he was their chief's brother.

Rhys's rage ebbed as quickly as it arose as he stood in the middle of the room, his shoulders shaking. 'So, it was all a lie,' he sobbed. 'He could have come home anytime. He just didn't want to. He never wanted any of us.'

Rhys's naked anguish tore a hole in Chase's heart despite his own shock and he felt compelled to console him. 'Look, Rhys, I'm sure there was much more to it than that, but we may never know.' His voice trembled. 'I'm just as stunned as you are, finding out my pa wasn't really Gryff Morgan. I can't believe his real name was Bryn… Bryn Evans, I assume? And he killed his own brother? I just can't believe it!' Chase stared at the floor, barely comprehending what he'd just learned. His wonderful pa had carried all that guilt for all those years and nobody had ever known. He was devastated.

'I actually feel sorry for my mam, now,' Rhys said, deaf to Chase's words. 'She must never find out about this. It would be too awful for her, all those years wasted grieving when he wasn't even dead.' He rounded on Chase with a wild glint in his eye. 'Promise me you will never speak of this to anyone, Chase, not even your own family.'

'Now hold on a minute,' Chase's temper rose as he took in Rhys's words. 'I need some time to process this before I go making promises I may not be able to keep. Think about it, Rhys – my family is your family. My brother is your brother, my sister is your sister—'

'You've got a sister too?' Rhys paced towards the door and spun back, his hands raised in exasperation. 'Christ, it gets worse!'

Chase's earlier sympathy for Rhys began to evaporate quickly. He didn't care very much for Rhys's dismissive tone. 'That's not exactly fair, *brother*. You don't even know who my sister is!'

'And I honestly don't care!'

'Not even if I tell you my sister is Greer Garland?'

Rhys gave a derisive laugh. 'Greer Garland? *The* Greer Garland? World-famous country-and-western singer Greer Garland? What a load of bullshit.' He sat heavily in the chair opposite Chase and glared at him scornfully. 'You can't seriously expect me to believe that a penniless hippy living in a shack in the woods in South Wales is the brother of a global superstar?'

The atmosphere in the room crackled with tension. 'Well, that's up to you.' Chase was beginning to feel heartily sick and tired of Rhys's condescension.

'Okay, Chase,' said Rhys scathingly. 'Let's assume I play along with your little story. If you really are the brother of one of the richest and most recognisable women in the world, what are you doing living in a mud hut four-thousand miles from home? What exactly are you hiding from?'

His new brother's words had him skewered. Chase examined his grimy fingernails, the suppressed guilt of molesting Shelby forcing its way to the surface. What could he say? He'd just discovered his own father had a devastating secret past and look at the damage that had caused. Was now the time to come clean and end the secrets that had plagued their family for decades? The stakes were high; he might be jailed for molesting Shelby and he would have to face his family's outrage. It was an unbearable thought. Indecision weighed on him as he contemplated his future in prison. His fate, and that of their whole family, might well rest on what he said next.

He ran his hands through his newly shorn hair. 'It's complicated,' he said. 'How long have you got?'

FORTY-ONE

CHASE – 1998

WHITESVILLE, KENTUCKY

Chase lay sprawled on the northern shore, his cheek pressed against the cold wet gravel, his chest heaving as he fought for breath. His body shivered with shock, as much from the cold water that had revived him as he sank to the bottom of the lake as the headwound that radiated blinding pain down the left side of his face. His survival instinct had kicked in and he'd somehow swum up from the depths, but now he felt barely alive. Screwing up his face against the pain in his skull, he glimpsed a beam of light approaching the lake from the southside. As the light reached the water's edge, he heard Travis's voice cursing aloud, along with the splash of the rowboat being hauled back into the water.

'Goddamn you to hell, Chase!' Travis raged. 'May you rot in damnation for what you did to Shelby. If I find you, I might kill you myself. Drowning ain't enough for you. You should suffer in jail for the rest of your goddamned life, you monster!'

The agony of hearing Travis's hate-filled words was almost worse than his physical pain. He crawled into the thick undergrowth like a hunted animal, out of reach of Travis's searchlight, lacerated with shame. He lay on his belly among the decomposing vegetation, breathing in the smell of the damp soil, and wished the earth would open and swallow him. He drifted in and out of consciousness for a time, occasionally roused by the bark of a fox or screech of a hunting owl, and waited for death to claim him.

When he came to, shivering in his wet clothes and feeling like a spike had been driven through his skull into the ground, the vegetation beneath his face stank of vomit, and he had a poisonous taste in his mouth. He curled his knees in front of his chest and rolled into a kneeling position, clutching his thumping head with both hands. His stomach clenched, forcing acid into his throat. He gagged and was swamped with bitter self-loathing as Shelby's terrified screams returned to him. He doubled over, groaning in shame, his forehead touching the damp earth. He remained like that for a while, the cool soil soothing the pounding in his skull until he was finally able to open his eyes. It was still dark. He forced his hand into the pocket of his wet denims, found the tramadol, and crunched a couple between his teeth. He needed to think but the pain pushed all thought from his head. He rolled onto his back and waited for the heavy-duty opioid narcotic to kick in.

After a while, when all that was left of the night sounds was the clicking of beetles in the dirt, he pushed himself back to kneeling and found that he was no longer poleaxed with nausea. He crawled out from the undergrowth, grabbing branches to pull himself to his feet. Travis's searchlight had disappeared and the lynch mob he'd expected hadn't arrived. He needed to get away from there and go someplace where he could work out what to do next. He checked the chain around his neck – thankfully the lock-up key was still there. Under the cover of darkness, it would take him less than an hour by foot to get into Evansville, collect his Harley and put some distance between himself and this God-forsaken place. He took one last look around. He would never return to this place of happy childhood memories and could never see the faces of his family again. He was dead to them and that was how it needed to stay. He was a monster and they were better off without him.

**

It was almost dawn when Chase pulled into the parking lot at the Best Value Inn motel in Chattanooga after over four hours in the saddle of his Harley Sportster. He'd had to fill the small gas tank twice, ignoring the wary looks of the pump attendants checking out the bloodstains on his shirt and the rudimentary dressing he'd fashioned from the contents of Zak's medicine cabinet. He'd hated breaking into the auto shop, knowing the anguish it would cause his good buddy, but he couldn't think where else he could lay hands on medical supplies at that time of night without attracting attention. He'd made it look like the work of vandals to cover his trail but he'd ensured nothing was damaged beyond repair. He'd find some way to make it up to Zak later.

As he rode east along the I-24 through the heartlands of the Bible Belt, the cool breeze in his hair kept him conscious and eased the pain. The giant billboards along the roadside were hard to miss, commanding him to *Go to Church or the Devil Will Get You!* Maybe they had a point. When he was a kid, every Sunday morning was spent at church with Trav and Greer, listening to their parents singing in the choir. Pa was a Methodist and Ma was a Baptist, but they seemed to get along just fine. They were good Christian folk, but he'd not given it much thought back then and hadn't bothered to keep up his faith when he'd joined the army. Maybe that was where it all went wrong for him – when he stopped believing in God.

He covered two-hundred-and-fifty miles before he finally accepted that he'd put enough distance between himself and his shameful behaviour for one night. The gash on his head throbbed painfully and his eyes burned with fatigue. The sallow-faced night porter on the reception desk eyed him with unconcealed distaste. 'Gonna have to charge you an extra twenty bucks, fer gettin' blood on the sheets,' he drawled, openly pocketing the notes that Chase peeled off and handed over. 'And there's a surcharge fer not mentionin' you're here if anyone comes askin'.' His tongue flicked in and out of his mouth as he eyed Chase's roll of bills.

Chase tossed another twenty across the counter and grabbed his room key before the urge to punch the loathsome reptile got the better of him.

His room was poky, and stank of piss and stale cigarette smoke. His boots crunched on the carpet as he went to the window, where a vivid yellow flashing glare penetrated the thin curtains, sending lightning strikes of pain into his optic nerves. He screwed his eyes half-closed and peered outside, expecting to find a liquor store, but the culprit was yet another Bible Belt billboard. This one exhorted him to honour his father and his mother.

Exodus 20, Fifth Commandment. He marvelled at how quickly his brain could retrieve such useless trivia, even in a state of crisis. He swallowed a couple of tramadol and lay down on the single bed, covering his eyes with a pillow, hoping to block out the glare and ease the pain that seemed to be intensifying as the adrenaline of his flight wore off.

Honour your father and your mother.

The neon words were burned into his retinas and hovered in the blackness behind his eyelids. His mind reached way back to when he was a kid to recall the rest of it and it came to him easily. *That your days may be long in the land that the Lord your God is giving you.*

A feeling of calm washed over him, almost as if the words had healing powers. The darkness quickly engulfed him and he was claimed by pain-free sleep.

Chase woke with a jolt, his chest heaving and his heart pounding. The putrid smell of other people's stale sweat filled his nostrils and he gagged. The cheap polyester pillow was suffocating him and he threw it to the floor in disgust, realising too late that it had become stuck to his head wound. He groaned and touched his face, feeling the renewed trickle run down his cheek. The metallic taste of blood filled his mouth and he wiped his encrusted lips with the back of his hand, noticing the rusty streak left behind on his skin. He shuddered at the thought of how bad his wound must be, although nothing would ever compare to the Gulf War, where he'd almost lost his leg.

He tried to sit up, but his head felt like lead and his eyelashes had crusted together. Peering about through half-open eyes, he found he was in a dingy motel room with flickering lights and paper peeling from walls that seemed to be closing in on him. Nausea washed over him. He had to get to the bathroom quick, but as he tried to stand up, his legs buckled and he fell back onto the mattress. He rolled onto his side and hung over the edge of the bed, vomiting onto the filthy carpet. He lay there panting, humiliation chewing at his insides like a hungry rat, grateful there was nobody there to see how low he had sunk.

When Chase came around again, the intensity of light penetrating his congealed eyelids had changed. He rubbed his fists into his gritty eye sockets until he'd cleared enough gunk to open his eyes. It was daytime. Incredibly, he'd survived the night. Tinny music came from a nearby room, and the air was thick with the toxic combination of exhaust fumes and burgers. His stomach churned but he had nothing left to eject. He rolled off the bed and slowly crawled to the bathroom, using the wash basin to pull himself to his feet.

Leaning on the sink in the tiny cubicle, Chase inspected his reflection in the dimly lit mirror. He looked like he'd spent the night in an abattoir. Dried blood caked his face and ears, and his hair was matted in gory clumps. The gouge on his skull gaped whenever he turned his head and the rudimentary dressing, saturated with blood, had slipped and was stuck to his chest. He didn't recognise himself.

'Be grateful Pa ain't here to see what has become of you,' he growled at his mirror image. There was a time when all he wanted was to make Pa proud but his father would have been ashamed of the man looking back at him from the mirror.

Chase glared at himself wretchedly. How could he have let this happen? The words of Exodus 20 played on a loop in his mind. *Honour your father and your mother, that your days may be long in the land that the Lord your God is giving you.*

He couldn't shake off the feeling that he should be listening to the voice in his head, but he hadn't honoured his father *or* his mother, so was God telling him that his life was over? Now that he had burned his bridges with the folks he loved most dearly, what would he do with his life anyway? The future stretched ahead of him, a lonely road to nowhere.

The reality, as far as he could see, was that he had two choices. One: he could neck the rest of the bottle of tramadol and let someone else clear up the sorry mess of his life in a week's time when the stench and the blowflies in the window made them kick in the door; or two: he could pick himself up from rock bottom, get a grip on himself and find a way to honour the man who gave him life, whom he idolised.

Images of his life before Pa died flashed through his mind's eye: the glorious sunny weekends at the stock car circuit; going out with Pa to fix Shelby's horsebox; sitting next to Greer and Travis in the pews at the Whitesville Baptist Church where Pa sang baritone in the choir. All halcyon days when the love of his pa made him believe anything was possible. Pa still loved him – he was sure of that – and wouldn't want his beloved son to end his days alone in a shabby motel in the middle of nowhere.

In that instant, out of respect for his father, Chase chose life.

He looked his haunted reflection in the eye and made a pact with himself. He would become a good man again, do

413

good things, love and respect the land the Lord was giving him, and follow the Fifth Commandment.

The first step was to clean himself up. He stumbled back to the bedroom and tipped his backpack onto the bed. Among his personal papers and the fat rolls of bills that Greer had given him, he found a bunch of dressings and some antibiotic cream, which he'd looted from Zak's medicine cabinet. It wasn't much but it was better than nothing. Using the tiny scissors on his pocket multi-tool, he painstakingly snipped off his matted black curls till his hair was short enough to take a razor to.

The shower cubicle was barely big enough for a child, and reeked of mildew and urine. Still, the pressure was surprisingly good and the water was reassuringly hot as he ran the spray over himself, filling the clogged shower tray with a bloody consommé. The restorative power of the hot clean water was remarkable and he emerged with renewed spirit, but by the time he'd dressed his head wound, he was flagging again. Torn between the need for food and the compulsion to rest, he clambered onto the bed and quickly fell into a deep slumber.

His father was waiting for him in a field of long grass and wildflowers, standing between the indistinct figures of a man and a woman in olden-times clothes, backlit with streaming golden light. As hard as he tried, Chase could only just make out his father's face.

'Chase, *fy mab*,' His father walked towards him, hands outstretched in welcome. 'Will you help me honour my father and my mother?' His voice resonated richly with the timbre of his Welsh ancestors. 'May your days be long in the land of our fathers, my son. The land of our fathers.'

414

Chase reached out joyfully for his father's hand. 'Will you be there?'

His father pulled him into a firm embrace. 'Always.'

Tears of happiness sprang to Chase's eyes as the familiar aroma of his beloved pa enveloped him. The warmth of his father's body against his was so close and so real. He prayed it would never end.

***

Rhys shook his head with disbelief. 'So, you travelled four-thousand miles just because you saw your dead father in a dream?' He gave Chase a look of pure scorn.

'It was a message, Rhys,' Chase said firmly. 'My pa – *our pa* – was a wonderful man. He came to me in my darkest hour and gave me a reason to live. He told me to come to Wales and find his roots, to honour his ma and pa, as the Fifth Commandment says.'

Rhys folded his arms across his chest. 'Go on.'

Chase sighed as the frustration of his early days in Wales came back to him. 'Once I got here, I had nothing to go on, other than a chance conversation in the army from years back with some British soldier called Gareth Bevan, who had twin brothers called "Hugh and Reese" who were my "doppelgangers" – so he said.'

Chase rubbed his face with both hands as he recalled that meeting and how close he'd come to the truth without knowing it. If only Gareth's unit hadn't pulled out the next day before they'd had a chance to compare family photos.

'That was all I had and it got me nowhere. Partly because I wrongly assumed you were all called 'Bevan' and partly because I thought my pa was called Gryff Morgan until five minutes ago, don't forget.'

'That's true,' Rhys conceded. 'You must feel pretty shitty about that, surely?'

Chase picked up one of the chairs Rhys had thrown and sat gingerly on it. It held. He hadn't had time to process any of the shocking information he'd discovered about his pa, so he didn't know how he felt about it yet. Probably about as bad as Rhys felt, finding his dead father had been alive all along.

The two brothers regarded each other guardedly for a moment.

'What about the girl?' asked Rhys. 'The one you—'

'Her name was Shelby,' Chase interrupted. 'I despised myself for years about what I did to her.' His chin sank to his chest as the painful memories flooded back. 'It was only after I met Sycamore that she helped me understand what was going on. I was paying the price of my service in four war zones. The things I saw, the things I did... stuff I will never repeat to anyone'. He raised his head and looked Rhys squarely in the eye. 'I realise now that I had post-traumatic stress disorder and a dependency on opiates for my war wounds.'

Rhys grunted. 'What about now? You still a junkie?'

Chase arched an eyebrow and glared at Rhys. He certainly didn't mince his words but this was not the moment to put him straight. 'Nope, I'm as clean as a whistle. Don't drink alcohol either.' He hesitated and studied his boots intently. 'It accounts for my irrational behaviour back then. I've come to terms with it now, but I know I can never go back and face my folks. It would be too damaging for them if I returned from the dead after ten years. It's better for them this way.'

'How do you know that?' Rhys's face contorted with rage. 'I would have been ecstatic if my tad had returned from the grave.' Chase flinched as Rhys slammed his hands on the desk. 'Honestly, Chase, you're a cowardly, selfish bastard – just like our father. The apple hasn't fallen far from the tree, has it?'

Chase's shoulders slumped as he took in Rhys's hate-filled words.

Could it be true that his wonderful father was nothing more than a coward? And was he a coward, too? Had they really both fled their families in shame, leaving behind a legacy of pain and abandonment? He could see now that he had even more in common with his father than he'd ever realised and it was in his gift to put an end to decades of mental anguish for both families. But the question was: could he handle the recriminations and the consequences of his own actions?

Perhaps his new brother Rhys was right. Maybe he was a coward after all.

FORTY-TWO

A pair of wild roosters scratched about on the sandy sidewalk outside the café on Duval Street, alongside the bleached driftwood terrace artfully draped with old fishing net and conch shells where Justine sat soaking up the early morning sun. Palm trees whispered as the gentle sea breeze passed through their fronds, keeping the temperature balmy and bringing with it a tempting aroma of griddled shrimp. As she waited for Rosa to arrive with the excellent freshly ground coffee, Justine wished the idyllic moment would last forever.

It was her last day in Key West and she wanted to make the most of it, especially since it was her birthday. She was fifty-two but passed for younger, thanks to being boyishly lean. Off-duty, with her hair long and loose, she was often mistaken for a teenager, which did wonders for her ego. The plan was to hop on a charter out to the Dry Tortugas to swim with sea turtles and dive on the coral reefs, not returning till long after sunset. She figured taking the charter was the best way to enjoy the spectacular Caribbean sunset in peace and tranquillity, far from the crowds at the southernmost point clapping and whooping as the sun went down. It was her birthday treat to herself.

She was already wearing her skimpiest swimsuit underneath her strappy vest and Bermuda shorts. Her feet were casually stuffed into Havaianas emblazoned with parakeets, and her kitbag of snorkelling gear was stashed under the table, ready to head straight off after breakfast without returning to her room above Scaff's Caff. She'd ordered a breakfast of stuffed crab omelette with crab cake, red peppers and cheddar cheese, topped with lobster sauce, served with a generous helping of potato bites and wheat toast, to set herself up for the whole day.

'So, how have you enjoyed your break, Justine?' Rosa asked with a friendly smile as she arrived with the coffee and food.

The mouthwatering aromas were almost too good to be true. 'I feel like I've died and gone to heaven!' Justine returned Rosa's smile with warmth. 'I just love it here. I can see why you and Scaff have been here for over forty years. Why would anyone want to live anywhere else?'

'But of course!' said Rosa. 'You look so well now, with your hair loose and your lovely golden tan. You look so much healthier than when you arrived. You've lost that tired and overworked look. I'm telling you,' she wagged her finger light-heartedly at Justine, 'the beach life – it suits you!'

It was true what Rosa said; she'd been there a week already and felt so much better for it. Her last few cases had been soul-sapping stakeouts on cheating husbands and wives, and she was ready for a break. But that hadn't stopped her detective radar from picking up the intriguing couple who ran the diner-cum-guest rooms where she was staying. They were an odd mismatch of a slightly faded South American beauty, who in her heyday must have looked a lot like Salma Hayek, and a deeply tanned sinewy cockney with long straw-coloured hair, who was the spitting image of Iggy Pop. How on earth had this unlikely pair washed up in the southernmost key, just ninety miles from Cuba? She would lay money that they had a great backstory. But when she'd asked, neither Scaff nor Rosa had been especially forthcoming, beyond the fact they'd been there since the late sixties. Theirs was a great life, far from the smog and crime of the city, and she envied them for it.

Justine polished off the last of her toast and rummaged in her kitbag, unable to shake off the nagging feeling she'd left her cell phone on her dresser. She tipped the contents onto the table but it was nowhere to be found. She rolled her eyes, irritated with herself. Missing an important call – even on vacation, would do her professional reputation no good at all.

She passed Scaff in the sandy side passage, on her way back to her room. He was bare-chested and barefoot, carrying a fishing rod and a couple of spiny iridescent fish. Despite being in his seventies, he was in great shape.

'Mornin', Justine,' said Scaff. 'You're up early. Got any plans for your last day with us?'

'Going snorkelling at Dry Tortuga,' she replied. 'Birthday treat to myself.'

"Appy birthday! Twenty-one again?' Scaff asked with a mischievous twinkle in his eye. 'You'll 'ave a brilliant time.' He held up his catch. 'I've got hogfish on the menu tonight – if you're back in time?'

Justine tucked a strand of her tousled coppery-blonde hair behind one ear. 'Thanks,' she said. 'Sounds delicious. I'll probably be famished by then, too.'

'Have a nice day, now,' he called out in a southern States accent as she hurried on her way.

A flight of rickety wooden steps, barely more than a ladder, climbed the outside of the pastel-yellow clapboard conch house to Justine's room, where large windows and high ceilings made the most of the cooling breezes. Her cell phone was vibrating on the dresser as she fumbled with the door lock but the noise stopped as she raced across the room to snatch it up. She stared at the screen in dismay. She'd missed a call from Greer Garland! She hadn't spoken to Greer in years! Her stomach churned as she waited for the voicemail to arrive, praying it wasn't bad news. She ran her fingers through her hair. *What was taking so long?* When the message finally arrived, her hands shook as she pressed play. The tense voice was instantly recognisable. Greer needed her help urgently… she knew where Chase was… could she come immediately?

Her heart skipped a beat. Of all the calls to miss, she had to miss that one! Justine replayed the message twice, trying to read between the lines.

Greer knew where Chase was.

What did that mean? Was he dead or alive? Where was he? Why didn't she say? And what help did she need from Justine, if she already knew where her brother was?

Her pulse raced with excitement. It was a dramatic

development in a dormant case that was still close to her heart, even after ten years – but today was her birthday and her last chance to swim with the sea turtles of the Tortugas. She didn't want to miss that for the world but, at the same time, she couldn't ignore the message.

With no bars on the cellphone screen, no matter how much she waved it around, returning Greer's call was impossible. It was a miracle the voicemail had even come through. She flipped open her laptop, drumming her fingers on the dresser as the Cape Air webpage took forever to load. With two days to go until Christmas, she'd be amazed if there was any flight availability that day – and she was booked on a flight out tomorrow anyway!

She glanced at her dive watch – the charter would be leaving shortly! 'Come on!' she urged the machine as the familiar seagull logo flashed on the screen.

When the page finally opened, it was as she thought. Every seat was taken on every flight. Dilemma solved – she could go on her birthday trip with a clean conscience. She snapped the lid closed with satisfaction, but not before tapping out a quick email to Greer.

No flights today from Key West. Be with you tomorrow.
Love Justine XXX

She realised what she'd done, no sooner than she'd hit send. '"Love Justine, kiss, kiss, kiss,"' she groaned aloud to herself, feeling her face flush hot with embarrassment. It was a professional faux pas that would be hard to explain to any other client but, with any luck, Greer would see the funny side of it.

She caught sight of herself in the dresser mirror and grinned from ear to ear. 'Happy birthday, Justine,' she said to her lightly tanned, youthful reflection. Swimming with turtles *and* a new lead in her most important cold case. She couldn't have asked for a better birthday.

***

Justine drew up at the security gates that stood like giant sentries at the entrance to Greer's estate, overwhelmed with nostalgia for the happy months she'd spent here ten years earlier. It was Christmas Eve and she'd driven straight from the airport with sand in her hair, still smelling of coconut sun lotion and shivering in the thin jacket she'd taken for her winter sunshine break. As she pressed the intercom and showed her ID to the screen, a frisson of pride ran through her.

A spectacular wreath of evergreen foliage tied with a giant silver bow adorned the familiar double front doors of the hacienda as Justine climbed the steps, butterflies fluttering inexplicably in her stomach. She hesitated on the top step. In her hurry to get there, she'd come empty-handed on Christmas Eve, looking like a sack of garbage. What was she thinking? She groaned and smoothed her hair back from her face with her hands. It was better than nothing – just!

She hadn't even knocked when the door flew open. Before she knew it, she'd been dragged inside the house and wrapped in a fragrant embrace. 'Thank God you're here, Jussy.' Greer buried her face in Justine's shoulder. 'I don't know what I would have done if you hadn't come.'

Justine's anxieties melted away as she returned Greer's warm hug and her eyes prickled as she fought to reabsorb her tears. Nobody had held her like that for as long as she could remember and she had nobody but herself to blame for that. The ache inside her caught her completely by surprise. It was a bittersweet moment – wonderful and yet somehow depressing. The realisation hit her hard – she couldn't go on living solely for her work. Something had to change.

'Oh, my word.' Greer was breathless when she finally released Justine from her arms. 'It is so wonderful to see you, Justine. You have no idea.'

Justine was overwhelmed by the warmth of Greer's embrace and the generosity of being welcomed into her gorgeous home for Christmas. Greer's emergency summons was saving her from a lonely Christmas Day in her small Washington Heights apartment, where she'd planned a solitary celebration with a turkey TV dinner and a potted poinsettia. The contrast with Greer's home, festively fragranced with orange and cinnamon candles, mingling with the scent of pine from the most enormous Fraser fir she'd ever seen, laden with oversized frosted baubles and giant candy canes, couldn't be starker. It was the perfect setting for the perfect Christmas. How had Greer ever imagined that she wouldn't come?

Justine and Greer retired to Greer's study after a delicious supper of homemade burgoo, eaten with hunks of soft cornbread at Greer's rustic kitchen table, catching up on the past ten years. They studiously avoided business talk until Greer's mother could join them. The warm glow of the crackling log fire in the grate welcomed them as Justine settled herself into a deep armchair, gratefully accepting the crystal tumbler filled with glowing amber bourbon that her host handed her. Gwenna sat across from her, nursing a bourbon of her own and holding what appeared to be an old photograph – and a British passport! Goosebumps sprang up on Justine's arms as she realised that the family secrets were finally about to be laid bare.

It was good to see Gwenna again after so many years but the flickering flames cast deep shadows on her face, emphasising the hollowness of her cheeks and the sockets of her eyes. She had an air of anxiety and withdrawal about her that Justine hadn't expected. By contrast, Greer was pacing restlessly and seemed barely able to contain herself. Their body language told her that both women were concealing a world of anxiety.

Justine flipped open her notebook and looked from mother to daughter. 'Who wants to begin?' She was surprised when Gwenna spoke first, a tremor in her voice.

'Yesterday afternoon, I received a phone call.' She swirled the ice in her glass, her eyes fixed on the crystal tumbler, her hands shaking with what Justine took to be suppressed emotion. 'It was Chase calling, from South Wales. He's alive and well—'

Justine gasped. That was fantastic news. So why did Gwenna look so strained?

Gwenna took a deep breath and let it out slowly, her eyes glistening. 'He's... he's found his Welsh brothers, my husband's other twin sons.' Her voice quivered. 'I swear to God, Justine, Gryff never knew they existed...' Her face crumpled as the words tumbled out. 'Chase wants to come home but doesn't know how he can – after everything that happened with Shelby! You've got to help me bring my son home, Justine. Whatever it takes.'

Justine's pen hovered over her notebook, her mouth hanging open in astonishment as her brain raced to process

Gwenna's mind-blowing revelations. It was almost too much to take in, in one hit. Chase's disappearance, the hobo's story and Travis's evasiveness were all connected somehow after all! A shiver of anticipation ran down her spine at the prospect of discovering the answers to so many unanswered questions.

She looked round to where Greer was standing by the fireplace, leaning on the thick stone mantel with her head in her hands. Unravelling this story was going to be an emotional rollercoaster. She took a sip of bourbon, debating where to start.

'"*After everything that happened with Shelby*",' she read from her notes. 'What did he mean by that?'

Justine's head throbbed as she crawled into the California King-sized bed in Greer's guestroom in the early hours of Christmas morning. The bed was bigger than her entire New York apartment but she was too emotionally exhausted by Gwenna's astonishing revelations to enjoy it at that moment.

The parallels between father and son were inescapable, and it was almost uncanny how history had repeated itself. Bryn and Chase were both decent men who'd distanced themselves from their families out of guilt after a crisis, both establishing new lives with twenty-thousand dollars in a rucksack, far from home across the Atlantic. It was a tale of terrible secrets kept for good reasons, and tragic failures in communication – leading to years of avoidable family breakdown. Justine couldn't help but admire the strength of the women left behind, who'd kept faith in their sons and brothers for so long, holding broken families together and carrying on for the sake of the next generation.

The haunting photograph of Lowri, Gwenna's husband's mother, especially moved Justine when Gwenna revealed that Lowri was still alive, having not given up on her son for *forty-five years*.

So, when Greer offered Justine the chance to be her permanent chief of staff – to unravel the secrets and lies of the past, and broker a reconciliation between Travis and Chase – she accepted it without hesitation. It would be a huge challenge to help the American side of the family reclaim their father's identity as Bryn Evans and build bridges with their new family in Wales, but she was determined to succeed – to give the incredible woman in the photograph the big happy family she so richly deserved.

It was almost as if her entire career in the NYPD had been preparing her for this moment.

Although Justine's eyes were itching with fatigue, she reviewed her notes of Gwenna's account until she found what she was looking for. *Scaff's Cash* – the words Gwenna used to describe Bryn's sack of money when he fled Argentina back in the 1960s. Justine had more than a hunch to follow now. How many people called 'Scaff' could there possibly be?

As Justine reached across to turn out her bedside light, it dawned on her that an entirely new life awaited her. Lonely Christmases were about to become a thing of the past. Something had, indeed, changed.

***

The spectacular view of Seven Mile Bridge and the pristine azure seas and white coral beaches of the Florida Keys from Greer's Cessna took Justine's breath away as they approached the runway at Key West, with Greer at the flight controls. Door-to-door from the airstrip at The Hacienda to Key West had taken them less than three hours. Justine still felt like pinching herself as she and Greer walked across the airstrip tarmac bathed in warm January sunshine to the chauffeur-driven limo waiting to take them straight to Duval Street.

Greer was uncharacteristically quiet for the twenty-minute drive to Scaff's Caff. Perhaps she was having second thoughts about meeting the people who knew her pa back when he was still Bryn Evans? According to Gwenna's story, it was Scaff and Rosa who got Bryn mixed up in the guerrilla plot, which led to him spending the rest of his life on the run under an assumed identity. You could almost say it was all their fault. Could Greer have only just realised that or was the significance of the meeting only just sinking in?

Scaff and Rosa were sitting on the open terrace when the limo pulled up outside. They got to their feet as Justine climbed from the sleek sedan and greeted her with warm smiles and raised eyebrows. She'd rung them that morning to tell them to expect her.

'What's all this then, Justine?' Scaff gestured towards the luxury vehicle. 'Won the lottery, 'ave we?'

Justine shrugged. 'Kind of,' she replied with a wide grin as Greer stepped from the vehicle behind her, dressed casually in faded denim and a loose cotton shirt but still instantly recognisable as one of the most successful female country and western singers of all time.

'Scaff, Rosa,' said Justine, gesturing towards Greer. 'Meet Greer Garland – Bryn Evans' daughter.'

Time seemed to stand still for a moment as they took in her words, but then Scaff's legs buckled and he dropped back into his seat, his mouth hanging open and his expression dazed. Rosa burst into tears and ran inside, sobbing loudly. It wasn't quite the reaction that Justine had hoped for. Undeterred, Greer stepped confidently onto the terrace and approached Scaff, her hand outstretched. 'I always have that effect on people,' she joked as Scaff reached out to take her hand, the corners of his mouth slowly turning upwards into a bemused smile.

'I don't believe it!' A rumble of laughter formed in his chest. 'I don't flippin' believe it!'

Rosa's footsteps on the wooden terrace signalled her return, clutching a tea cloth and smiling through her tears. 'I'm so sorry!' She dabbed at her eyes with the cloth. 'It's wonderful to meet you, Greer. It was just such a shock! I haven't heard Bryn's name in over forty years. I've thought about him constantly, worrying about what became of him. And now here you are! His daughter – a superstar! I can't wait to hear how that happened. It's unbelievable!'

They sat on the open terrace, palm fronds rustling in the warm Caribbean breeze, with cool frosty beers on the table before them, and exchanged adventure stories until late into the evening. Greer's account of Bryn's death brought gasps from Scaff and tears from Rosa, while Scaff's tale of how Bryn saved his life at sea left Greer at a loss for words.

Glancing across at Greer as she expertly piloted the small aircraft back to Kentucky that night, her face glowing from the reflection of the illuminated dials, Justine couldn't help but wonder how differently things might have turned out if Bryn had never met Scaff and Rosa. In many ways, Greer might never have had the chances she'd had in life if it were not for the sack of 'Scaff's cash'. You could almost say she owed it all to Scaff.

The terrible irony of the whole story was that there never was any extradition warrant for Bryn Evans – she'd checked with the Argentine authorities before going to meet Scaff and Rosa. It was true that he was still a wanted man in Argentina, but the authorities of the time had never bothered to launch an international manhunt for him. He'd lived out his life under an assumed identity for no reason.

Thinking about everything she'd learned over the past few weeks made her wonder – if there really was a God, why did bad things happen to good people?

It was a question to which she had no answer.

EPILOGUE

2012

ABERAVON, SOUTH WALES

L owri sat in the front row of the grandstand that had appeared overnight in the Aberavon Junior School playground, enjoying the warmth of the beautiful handwoven carthen across her knees, a gift from her grandson Chase and his partner Teagan from their heritage craft shop in Y Mynydd Du.

She wore her ninety-two years lightly, her once raven locks now white as snow but still tumbling in a cascade around her slender shoulders, her dove-grey eyes alert and youthful. Shirley sat on one side of her in a smart cashmere coat, holding Lowri's gloved hand affectionately on her lap and Gwenna sat on the other side, glamorous in a faux-fur hat and oversized sunglasses, tapping her toe in time to the music of the Aberavon Brass band. The polished instruments glistened in the bright sunlight as a whipping wind brought a salty tang from the nearby Bristol Channel. Brightly coloured bunting fluttered and snapped overhead, adding to the air of festivity as children buzzed around the playground like over-excited bees. Groups of parents gathered gossiping, awaiting the arrival of the VIP guest for the opening of the spectacular new music annexe.

Gwenna's cell phone bleeped in her purse on her lap. 'That was a text from Greer,' she whispered to Lowri and Shirley. 'ETA three minutes!'

Lowri squeezed Shirley's hand and patted Gwenna's knee with mounting excitement. Today was the culmination of four years of reconciliation and she couldn't have been prouder of the two women by her side, who, by their example, had brought the two halves of her family together. By rights, Gwenna and Shirley had every reason to resent each other and yet here they were, firm friends with so much more in common than their uncanny likeness; connected forever by their love of the same man – and their four virtually identical sons. She was incredibly lucky to have them both.

'So the Lord blessed the latter end of Job more than his beginning,' Lowri murmured under her breath. God had rewarded her faith, just as he had with Job. She'd always known that the terrible losses she'd suffered since childhood were a part of life to be endured. But where she'd lost one family, she'd gained another – and what a marvellous family it was.

Over by the bandstand, Huw and Rhys were posing with Travis and Chase, immaculate in Savile Row tailoring, their arms draped across each other's shoulders as Huw's wife, Cheryl, took a photograph, with Shelby and Sam looking on. Somebody clearly said something funny, as they all fell about laughing. Even with the eight-year age difference, Lowri found it hard to tell the four strapping brothers apart, with their brooding Celtic looks – so like their father. Their pleasure in each other's company was a miracle – they had Justine Cornelius and her exceptional negotiating skills to thank for that. She caught Justine's eye across the playground, exchanging knowing smiles. Such a talented woman and perfect for Greer in every way.

Alys, home from Bangor University for the special occasion, was doing a grand job entertaining her young American cousins – Beau, Hunter, Ryker, Jackson and four-year-old Willa – with the help of red-dreadlocked Sycamore – or Aunty Teagan, as she now wanted to be known. The joy of seeing all her great-grandchildren together was indescribable. Travis's boys were all such cheeky scamps. They reminded her so much of Emlyn – particularly Beau, who was about Emlyn's age. The sight of that child's sunny smile on this day, of all days, brought tears to her eyes.

As they waited for Greer to arrive, Lowri looked around for Dai before remembering he was playing host with Carol and Gareth inside the sensational glass and steel annexe, which commanded fabulous views across the lush green valley once dominated by the old colliery gantry. Vaughan and Wendell were also inside, getting a head start on the champagne reception awaiting Lowri and her guests. When Lowri last looked, the two nonagenarians were hitting it off like long-lost university chums, befriending each other on social media and exchanging email addresses.

At that moment, a long wheelbase Jaguar pulled up outside the school gate. Lowri's heart swelled with pride. She still had to pinch herself to believe Bryn's daughter was country and western superstar Greer Garland. Photographers pressed around the luxury saloon in a scrum of clicking shutters and camera flashes. Excited screams went up from the crowd as the chauffeur opened the rear door and Greer emerged onto the plush red carpet, a radiant smile illuminating her face. She wore a white satin trouser suit, white Stetson and white tooled-leather cowboy boots set with garnets. Her dark-blonde hair tumbled around her shoulders in glossy curls. A warm glow suffused Lowri. Her granddaughter had certainly amped up the star quality for the folks of Aberavon and they were loving it.

The low winter sun behind Greer formed a halo around her as she stood on a low podium. When she spoke, her melodious Kentucky accent rang out in the crisp fresh air and the crowd fell silent.

'As we approach the fiftieth anniversary of the tragic death of a thirteen-year-old boy right here in Aberavon,' she swept her gaze across the gathering, 'I'd like us all to take a moment to remember Emlyn Evans and his brother Bryn, who blamed himself for Emlyn's death for the rest of his life. Some of you will remember that terrible time for yourselves.'

She paused as voices in the crowd murmured and heads nodded sombrely.

'Emlyn's death set in motion a journey that crossed three continents, spanned five decades and brought two new families into existence. Emlyn Evans was my uncle,' her voice faltered with emotion, 'and his brother was my father, Bryn Evans.'

A gasp rose from the audience. Greer paused for a few moments as the commotion subsided.

'My father was never able to speak of the tragedy,' she said, 'and I grew up in Kentucky with my twin brothers, Travis and Chase, unaware, just as my father was himself, of his other twin sons, my brothers, Huw and Rhys, back here in Wales.' She turned to the two men with a luminous smile. Rhys pinched the bridge of his nose while Huw studied his hands intently. 'Thankfully, we've found each other now,' her eyes crinkled with pleasure, 'and we have all come together here today in Emlyn's honour to dedicate this wonderful music annexe for the schoolchildren of Aberavon in his memory.' She paused and took a stuttering breath. 'Emlyn Evans, you will be forever in our hearts.'

Smiling through her tears, she reached her hand towards Lowri and said, 'It is a great pleasure for me to invite Emlyn's mother, my amazing grandma, to open the new building.'

The crowd erupted into thunderous applause as Lowri stepped forward. She'd planned to say a few words to thank her incredible granddaughter for her astonishing benevolence but the lump in her throat made words impossible. The moment was too overwhelming – a testament to the power of forgiveness that had mended her broken family.

Plastering on a delighted smile, Lowri grasped the large pair of ceremonial scissors and sheared smoothly through the wide satin ribbon in one graceful slice.

'I now declare the Emlyn Evans Music Annexe – *open*!' Greer announced. 'Great job, Grandma!'

The brass band struck up with brio as Lowri linked arms with her granddaughter, crossing the threshold of the stunning new music facility together. Her slight figure was dwarfed by her four towering grandsons following behind. Greer's two beaming grandfathers were waiting for them, proffering glasses of champagne.

'Well done, darlin'.' Wendell kissed Greer warmly as the hordes swarmed into the new building for the first time. 'You've done a wonderful thing here for these folks. I cain't begin to tell you how proud that makes me today.'

'Why, thank you, Grandpa.' Greer slipped her arm around Travis's waist as he and Chase joined them. 'It means the world to me that Emlyn will be remembered through music for all time, and that our family has come together in love and forgiveness in his name.'

'And to think,' Lowri clinked her champagne glass jauntily against Chase's soda bottle, 'all it took to make all this happen was one courageous phone call.' She rested her pale slender hand on Chase's burly forearm and smiled into his sparkling ice-blue eyes, so like Bryn's. 'Your father would be proud of you, Chase.'

Chase leaned forward and softly kissed her translucent cheek. 'You have no idea how much that means to me, Grandma,' he said. 'I just wish he was with us today.'

'I wouldn't worry about that, my love.' Lowri swept her eyes across the handsome faces of her four virtually identical grandsons. 'He's here.'